UNDENIABLY INFATUATED

J. SAMAN

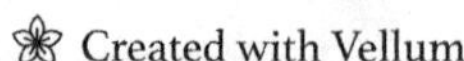
Created with Vellum

***This book can be read as a complete standalone. This family tree is simply a reference if needed.**

Boston World Family Tree

*This Does Not Contain Spoilers And Will Be Updated As The Series Progresses

Fritz Family

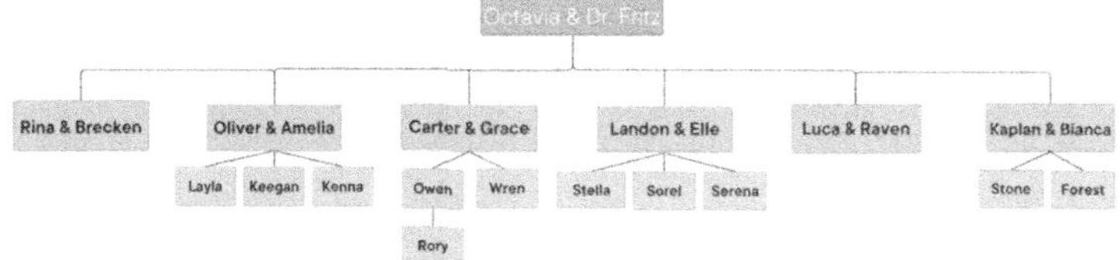

Central Square

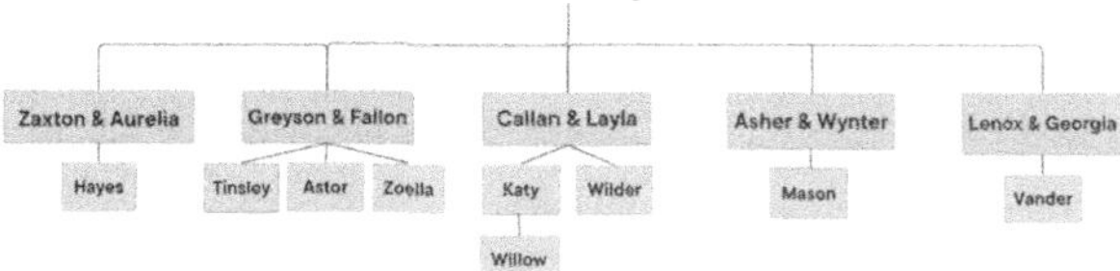

The Edge

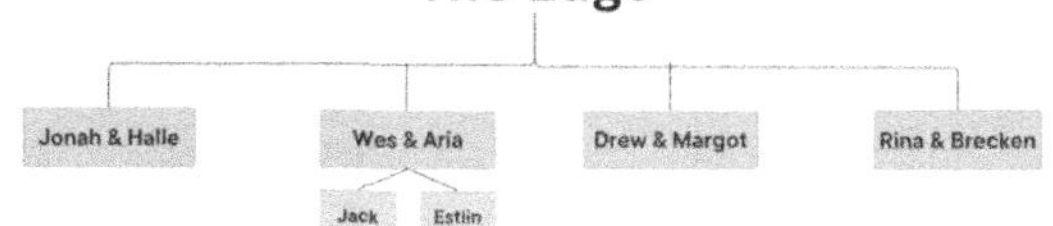

1

STONE

"Motherfucker, I hope this helps," I murmur under my breath as humid air blasts across my face, and the salty brine of the ocean hits my tongue. I climb out of the car with my duffel bag in my hand and watch the taillights pull away, leaving me alone in the ink black of a moonless midnight. Not even the stars are out to greet me, hidden just beneath the thin layer of clouds. The darkness of the night matches my mood so perfectly, I can hardly stand the irony.

Staring out toward the marina, relief to be here and dread for the reason why slam into my chest and quicken my heart for about the thousandth time today. I squint, my eyes following the muted path along the dock until I find my girl. All the way down on the end, Benthesicyme, the largest boat here, the daughter of Poseidon and goddess of the waves, rocks gently in the rustling water, eerily illuminated with blue mood lighting my staff must have turned on along the bow and up the mast. It's the only light out here, and it's barely enough to see by.

I head in her direction, praying she's the start of my salvation.

There was a time when I thought I was God. Invincible. So badass nothing could touch me. I'd jump out of airplanes and get tattoos and piercings. I'd drink my friends under the table and sleep with any woman who was willing. I was that asshole. The billionaire playboy who threw lavish yacht parties and bought out clubs for his birthday.

Somehow, I made it through college and medical school—though barely for both. My last name got me a residency I didn't deserve, and I didn't care enough to feel anything but entitled about it. I skated through on looks, charm, money, and a family name that could get me through any door Boston—and most of the world—had to offer.

Then last week happened.

Now here I am.

Needing a serious come to Jesus moment and a week of soul-searching.

The dock creaks beneath my feet, the air still and eerily quiet with the exception of the water lapping gently against the stone pillars. I pull out my phone and use the flashlight so I can see. It's something out of a thriller, and I feel like any second I'm going to get jacked from behind.

Grabbing the bow pulpit, I haul myself up and onto the front of the ship and land with a dull thud on the deck. I turn off the flashlight on my phone and breathe out a sigh. Everything should be set for me to sail out tomorrow morning as I had her fully stocked and gassed up earlier today.

I pull back the hood of my sweatshirt to roll and crack my neck as exhaustion seeps into my bones. If I want to set out around dawn tomorrow, I need to get some sleep. Just as I head toward the companionway that will lead me down to my cabin, something heavy and hard smashes me in the middle of my back. The wind whooshes from my lungs in a rush, and I stumble forward, my bag slipping from my hand, and my phone clattering to the deck as my chest slams against the railing.

"What the fuck?" I turn in time to catch a shadowy figure swing a lifebuoy and nail me straight in the chest. Before I can stop it, I tip back over the railing and do a messy backflip over the side of the boat. I fall fast and land face down in the water with a hard and painful splash. Frigid, salty water surrounds me, the shock of it all momentarily eclipsing the burning in my chest.

Who the fuck is on my boat?

Breaking the surface, I cough and sputter for air, spitting out slimy marina water. I squint high above me toward the deck of the ship as I wipe the burning salt from my eyes. The shadowy figure is leaning against the railing I just went over, staring down at me. I can just barely make out her long braid whipping beside her dark form.

A woman? What in the hell?

"How did you get out here?" she snaps down at me as I tread water. "Were you following me? How'd you know I'd be here?"

"Huh? What? Following you?" I bluster, nonplussed, wiping more water from my face in an attempt to see her better, only it's futile. It's too damn dark out here and the blue hue coming off the mast is throwing shadows and distorting everything.

An annoyed, shrill noise escapes her throat, and she brushes at her face as she leans further over the side. "Uh-huh. Where's your phone?"

"My phone?"

"Yes, jerk. The phone you've been videoing me with."

"Videoing you?"

"Do you have more than two brain cells you can rub together to actually answer my questions instead of simply repeating them back to me?"

That snaps me out of my shocked stupor. "How could I know you'd be here when I don't even know who you are? You're trespassing on my boat. If anything, you're the one who should have gone over the side. Not me."

She stumbles back a step only to recalibrate and hang halfway over the railing as if she's trying to get a better look at me. "Oh my god. Stone? Is that you?"

"Uh. Yeah. It is. Who the hell are you?"

"It's Tinsley."

"Tinsley?! What the absolute fuck are you doing here?" Tinsley is one of the last people on earth I thought it would be. Last I heard, she was still in LA doing her pop star thing. I haven't seen her in a while. A couple of years at least. She was my little brother's longtime girlfriend. And by longtime, I mean they dated from seventh grade into his junior year of college. Their breakup last year devastated him and shocked the world. Everyone thought they were it. That magical, fairy tale happily ever after couple.

"Hiding. What are you doing here?"

"Trying to finally get my shit together. You attacked me."

She sags against the railing, reaching down for me as if she can somehow pull me back up when she's a solid twenty-five feet above me. "I'm sorry. I didn't know it was you. I didn't expect you to be out here. You scared me. I thought maybe you were press. Here. Catch."

She bends and then tosses the lifebuoy over the side and nearly hits me in the head with it. As it is, it smashes into my shoulder and dunks me a second time before it careens off me and starts to float away. I'm in too much shock—and pain, let's be honest, that's the third time that buoy has hit me and it freaking hurts like a bastard—right now to chase it.

Tinsley Monroe, my brother's ex and America's Hollywood princess, snuck onto my boat and is hiding here. Why?

"Ah! I'm sorry," she bemoans. "Crap. I'm doing everything wrong. Hold on. I'm coming."

"What? No—"

Before I can finish, she climbs over the side of the boat and jumps. Plummeting gracefully through the air in a straight line, she lands beside me with a splash that smacks me right in the face. I clear my eyes and search around the dark water for her, my heart stopping when she doesn't immediately come up. People have drowned swimming to what they thought was the surface when it's actually the sea floor.

"Tinsley?" I call out in a panic, spinning around in a frantic circle and ready to dive under when I feel her body slide up along mine. She emerges like a mermaid, flipping her head back and making her long braid swing in an arc behind her, spraying water as it flies.

Only this girl. I swear.

Drama and mayhem follow her wherever she goes.

"Are you okay?" she asks, grabbing on to me as she swims away to grab the buoy.

"Am *I* okay? Why on earth would you jump over the side of the ship?! Do you know how insanely stupid that is? You could have drowned!" I'm shouting. It's loud and abrasive and I don't give a fuck. It's not exactly a short drop from a ship like this.

"I was rescuing you, you ungrateful ass!" she exclaims, splashing me.

"Who said I needed rescuing?" I splash her back.

"I don't know!" she cries, her hands flailing about. "I didn't think it through all that well. You were just floating here and not moving."

"That's because I was trying to figure out who the fuck was on my ship and knocked me overboard!"

"I said I was sorry about that!" she snaps, shoving another splash in my direction only to deflate slightly. "I was scared. You scared me! I had a couple of glasses of wine, took a sleep gummy, and then a noise woke me up, only to find a strange man on the boat. I'm a woman out here alone, Stone. I wasn't taking chances." She shudders. "Christ, the water's cold. You're going to turn into Jack if you stay out here any longer." She wraps an arm around herself, the other looped through the buoy.

"What are you even talking about? Who's Jack?" I sputter, totally thrown off by the random topic change.

She gives me a *duh* look I can just barely make out in the darkness. "From *Titanic*. Leo DiCaprio. He froze in the water because Rose wouldn't make room for him on her door or whatever she was on. Clearly, I'm Rose in this scenario because I should just let you drown and save myself since you're not being very nice to me."

"Uh-huh. Maybe you shouldn't have mixed wine with a sleep gummy."

"Maybe not, Doctor. Thanks for your unsolicited medical advice. Now how do we get back on the boat?"

I roll my eyes and wrap myself around her, dragging her back against my chest. "This way, little Rose. I wouldn't want either of us to freeze in these icy Florida waters." I push her along toward the stern of the boat.

"You're being sarcastic, but hypothermia is no joke. I can barely feel my toes and fingers."

The transom is up, but there's a ladder we can use. I push her up it in front of me and then climb one-handed, carrying the freaking buoy with my other. She hops up onto the deck, shivering and shaking in her barely-there tank top and shorts, and I don't hesitate before I tear off my sodden hoodie and T-shirt and pick her up bride-style into my arms. She needs to get undressed, but I'm not going anywhere near her clothes. Water drips and drains off us, splattering everywhere, and how did this become my night?

"What are you doing?" she asks, her voice thick and wobbly

reminding me how cold she is. Her arms wrap around my neck, and she clings to me, snuggling in closer—likely for warmth—but the unexpected press of her body feels a lot better than it should.

I clear that away. "You said you could barely feel your toes and fingers. I'm not letting you walk when you're soaking wet, half-frozen, and probably a little inebriated. I'm taking you downstairs. You need a hot shower, and so do I."

"I'm not showering with you," she barks indignantly, her teeth chattering.

"Excellent, since I don't think we can both fit in any of the ones on board, and you're not at all my type," I sneer, even as an unwelcome part of my brain suggests that might be a lie.

"I thought every woman was your type."

I roll my eyes at her snark.

She cups my face in her hand, worry etched across her face as our eyes lock. "Did I hurt you? I feel really bad about hitting you and knocking you overboard."

"Nothing I won't recover from."

She searches my face. "Why are you here? Did Forest send you? Does he know I'm here? Is that why you came?"

I tilt my head, my tone growing harsh even if it shouldn't. "Why would Forest send me? You broke up with him last year. Did you tell him you were coming here, or did he suggest my boat as a place to hide out?"

She loved Forest but was no longer in love with him. At least that's what she told him. They still talk and are friends—as much as exes can be friends. Forest still keeps close tabs on her. A little too close for an ex, so her question isn't out of left field. But it would seriously piss me off if he told her to come here without giving me a heads-up first.

"No. I didn't tell him. I don't know why I asked you that. It just made sense in my head. Why else would you be here?"

"I already told you. I'm here for me. Not you. It's pure coincidence."

"Okay." She licks her lips nervously. "I believe you, and I'm sorry for all of this. I didn't think anyone would be here," she says earnestly, her hand still on my face, and I can't bring myself to brush it off. "I thought I'd be alone. The last time I saw you was on this boat, right before the start of your fourth year of medical school. Remember? You brought a bunch of us out for a weekend trip."

I swallow and nod, suddenly realizing I've stopped walking and have been staring at her as she speaks. She's so much prettier than I ever allowed myself to take note of. Fucking gorgeous with the way her lavender eyes, framed by dark, wet lashes, sparkle. Pinpoint freckles dot her petite nose and cheeks, with a broken heart-shaped one beneath her left eye. Her sumptuous lips are full and soft-looking, and... I snap my gaze away and start walking again, feeling a strange and uncomfortable heat climbing up the back of my neck.

"You told me you didn't know when you'd be able to come back since you were going to have no time going forward between the end of medical school and the start of your residency. You even mentioned you were possibly thinking of selling the boat because of it."

"This is my first time back since then, so you weren't wrong in thinking that." I walk us into the companionway, flipping on a couple of lights as I go so I don't bump into something and drop her. "I came here to be alone too, so I get it." And even though I did come here to be alone, oddly, I'm not disappointed she's here. At the very least, she's distracting me from my thoughts.

"Oh." Her cold hand drops from my face, the lights bringing some clarity back to her eyes. "Stone, I can walk. I don't need to be pressed against you when you're, well, shirtless like this."

I chuckle. "Why? Because you like it?" Shit. Why the hell did I say that? I quickly redirect. "I'm shirtless to try to warm you up with my skin since you did the crazy girl thing and jumped off the side of a boat into cold water. Speaking of, why *are* you here? This seems like a strange place for you to come considering I haven't seen you or spoken to you in a couple of years and you don't exactly sail."

She twists away from me, but I catch a faint hint of a blush, even with her pale skin and slightly blue-tinted lips. "You first. Why are you here? What does getting your shit back together mean?"

For some reason, I don't want to tell her the truth. I don't want her to look at me the way I know she will. With pity or disgust. "It just means I needed a break from everything. I'm planning to sail out of here tomorrow at dawn and get lost in the Bahamas for ten days or so. It's also my boat so the better question is, *again*, why are you here?"

I walk through the galley and living room, then down another flight to where the bedrooms are.

"You're not going to tell me?" I ask when she's still not sharing.

She wiggles in my arms as we reach my cabin, and I set her down, doing everything I can not to take in her body in her now see-through tank top and shorts. She's visibly not wearing a bra and immediately she wraps her arms around her chest to hide her perky tits and hard nipples from my view. I drop my gaze and go to grab towels.

I don't know what's wrong with me. I've never reacted to Tinsley like this before. Yes, I noticed her. She was impossible not to notice. But she belonged to Forest and that's how I've had her categorized in my head. She is the absolute last woman in the world I should be reacting to.

I enter the bathroom, only to pause when I find her things everywhere. Her makeup and hair stuff are all over my counter and her shampoo and conditioner are in my shower. It's like she's moved in, not just planning a short stint.

"Tinsley, what the hell is going on?"

She edges in, hovering around the doorway, her big, pretty purple eyes, the color of rare amethysts staring up at me. "Are you mad? I wouldn't blame you if you are."

I hand her a towel, wrap one around my waist, and lean against the wall. "How long have you been here?"

"Just since this evening," she swears solemnly, averting her gaze, and I can't tell if it's because she's lying to me, embarrassed about being caught here, or if it's something else I can't figure out. Regardless, I don't like any of it. "I couldn't come during the day. Someone could have recognized me, and I don't want anyone to know where I am."

"Why?" I press through gritted teeth, losing my patience.

She looks down at the floor, but she's covered in goose bumps and still shaking from the cold, and something squeezes in my chest.

I sigh. "Go shower. You're shivering and I can't stand to see you freezing." I shove past her. "But after you're done, we're going to talk, and you're going to tell me everything."

She flips around and grabs my arm, stopping me. "I'll tell you everything. But only if you take me with you."

2

TINSLEY

"No," Stone says, simple as that, his green eyes hard and determined.

My stomach plummets into my feet, and I can already feel stupid tears prickling my eyes. "Why not?"

"Go shower, Tinsley. I'm freezing and soaking wet and in no mood for games. I want to get in there after you so I can go to bed."

He's angry and annoyed. He wanted to be here alone and I'm intruding on that. I get it. I'm not sure I was ever his favorite person anyway. He was always a little cautious and distant with me. Plus, something is clearly going on with him if he's here and talking about how he's trying to get his shit together.

"How's this?" I offer. "You go shower since this is your room, and I'll gather my things and move down the hall to one of the other bedrooms." I give him my sweetest smile. The one I wear at award shows. Only I must look like a drowned rat, and after that dip in the marina, I probably don't smell much better.

He grumbles something under his breath that sounds like "Just go fucking shower already," and then he leaves me here, storming out of the room and back upstairs, probably to grab the stuff he dropped when I knocked him overboard.

I gnaw on my lip and shake out my tingling hands. I don't know what to do. I don't want to leave. The thought of going back to California or even to Boston sends a rush of panic through me. This is the most freedom I've ever had. It's exhilarating and liberating. It's the happiest I've been in so long and it only took a couple of hours like this to get me here. That's telling, and I don't want it to end. Not yet.

I'm tired, so incredibly tired. I just need some time to sleep and think until I find a little clarity and a lot of courage, and I can make the changes I know I have to make with my life. So I can't leave. I can't go back. Not yet. I need more time. Just a little more time without it feeling like a crushing weight is bearing down on me every time I take a breath.

Truth be told? I know I had no right to break into his boat and camp myself out without at least asking. It was stupid and wrong and definitely insane, but I didn't exactly think it all through when I did it. I was in desperation mode. I needed a break before I had a breakdown. It felt like I couldn't move or breathe as the walls of my life closed in around me.

I had no freedom. No space. Nothing for myself. A team of people surrounding me at all times telling me what to do and when and how to do it. Much of that started when the letters started—I was a minor then, so it was understandable—but it's been two years since my stalker went to prison, and nothing has relented. If anything, it's gotten worse.

Since I broke up with Forest last year and then briefly tried dating a few other guys, the press has been relentless. They stalk my every move, even following me to the gynecologist for my annual and then reporting I was pregnant from the guy I had just ended things with. That was a fun one. They throw out false claims about a hundred different men I'm dating and make it so that I can't leave my house to do anything, let alone live my freaking life.

Last week, the press got ahold of a leaked photo of me kissing my co-star in a scene from a movie we just finished filming. It spread like wildfire—something I believe the studio had a hand in to ruckus up free PR—to the point where Forest called me upset that I'm so public with my new relationship that I'm not even in.

It was my breaking point.

My label is pushing back on me, and my agent and manager are shoving me in a million different directions I'm not sure I want to go in. My manager, Apollo, is especially driving this train to the max, and it's turned into a wreck. He's the one I need to get rid of first. I can't write music. I can't leave my house. My cell is blowing up nonstop. I haven't been sleeping with the stress of everything.

I get it. Poor celebrity Tinsley. If you don't want the heat, you shouldn't have started cooking in the kitchen. But the truth is, I love what I do. Most days, the ends are worth the means, and I can handle it. I grew up in the spotlight. Being the daughter of Greyson Monroe, a famous rock star, leads to that.

But it was never like this for us growing up. There was never this level of frenzy before.

My dad suggested I come home and hide out in Boston for a bit, but the press would find me there without even breaking a sweat. No, I needed to go somewhere no one would ever think to look for me, and Stone's sailboat immediately popped into my head. It felt perfect. Genius in a way, since I knew he didn't use it.

I flew across the country and had the plane drop me in the middle of nowhere in Georgia. My assistant rented a car for me under her name, and I made my way to and through Florida, driving mostly at night, and now here I am.

My staff put out a story that I'm at an undisclosed yoga

retreat for the next few weeks. The kind that doesn't allow you to bring your cell phone in because it messes with their vibe and aesthetic. I gave my family the same bullshit story so they wouldn't worry, not to mention I didn't want any of them to know I'm on the lam like a cut-rate thief and committed a felony by breaking into Stone's boat.

I have no clue how to sail, but frankly, that wasn't part of my plan. I figured I'd hole up, get some sun, write some music, and live off Diet Coke, prosecco, and charcuterie for a week. Heaven, right?

Something else not on my bingo card for this week? Seeing Stone.

But the idea of floating around the Bahamas for ten days sounds too good to be true, and no one will know because no one would ever think I'm with him. It's brilliant. Other than the sailing around with Stone part, but I can work with that. It's a big boat, and there are three other bedrooms for me to choose from.

Only, he doesn't think my idea is as brilliant as I do.

Quickly, I gather all my things and head down the hall to the room I shared with Forest the last time I was here. I didn't want to sleep in here because Forest and I didn't have the happiest time together that weekend. It was the beginning of the end for us, but it's the second-largest room, so here I am.

I toss my things on the bed and scoot into the bathroom. I'm freezing and oh my nipples and tits! They are on full display through my paper-thin white tank top. I look like I just stepped out of a wet T-shirt contest. I face-plant into my hands, wondering how much Stone saw. Then again, I got more than an eyeful of him half-naked.

Hello sexy muscles and tattoos.

I snicker to myself as I start the shower and strip down. I always tried not to look at Forest's older brother, but Stone Fritz is one of those guys who is impossible not to look at. Especially when he's shirtless. He has that gorgeous, bad boy, untouchable thing going for him.

Not that it matters.

All I want from Stone is for him to allow me to stay and tag along.

The shower feels like heaven, and I scrub myself twice from head to toe, singing to keep my nerves at bay and my mind quiet. I wrap a towel around my chest and enter the bedroom just as the bedroom door bursts open and I start. A hiccup of a screech jumps out of my lungs and my hands reflexively jerk, dropping my towel in the process.

Oh. My. Hell. Oh my hell!

My face heats to volcanic proportions, and I dive down, snatching the towel off the ground and pulling it up in front of me.

"What are you doing?!" I shriek while doing my best to covertly tuck my towel back around myself without flashing him again. "Do you normally burst into bedrooms where women are showering and naked?"

His green eyes are wide with shock as they do a slow, raking sweep of me, his tongue gliding along his bottom lip as he goes. The moment his eyes meet mine again, they grow hard and accusing. "Why did you tell me to come in if you're naked?"

His dark hair is wet and all over the place as if he didn't bother brushing it after he showered. He's wearing a tight-fitting green T-shirt that makes the green in his eyes look darker, a bit more sinister, and gym shorts that hang low on his hips. So low that—wait. Did he ask me a question?

I snap myself away from his gym shorts, feeling my face heating once again, and clear my throat, reforming my embarrassment into ire. "I didn't tell you to come in."

He folds his arms over his chest, his temperament hot and angry. "Yes, you did. I heard you say to come in."

I shake my head. "I did not."

"Yes, you fucking did, Tinsley!" He's out of patience now. "I wouldn't have come in otherwise. You think I want to see you like this?" His hand pans out toward me. "See you drop your goddamn towel?"

"God, you're such a dick. It wasn't meant to be a striptease."

"Now is not the time to talk about my dick or stripteases."

My brows furrow and I tilt my head "Huh?" I wave that away. "Whatever. I was *singing*. The lyrics were 'come in, come on in, baby, and be part of my heart.'"

He pauses, his eyes doing a slow, blinking thing. "Oh. All I heard was 'come in.'"

"Well, I wasn't saying it to you." I tuck my towel tighter. "I didn't even hear you knock."

Stone saw me naked. A giggle rises up my throat at how awkward that is, and I smash my lips together to try to stifle it.

He sighs. It's not a happy sigh. Large hands scrub up and down his face, the motion bunching his biceps and the fabric of his shirt that's barely holding onto them. Hot damn, Stone Fritz is cut. I mean, I knew he played Division 1 hockey in college, but I don't remember him being like this. Too bad he can be such a jerk. And is my ex's brother.

I nearly giggle again and redirect my thoughts. "So, um, can I get dressed, or did you want to stay and be part of the audience for my next show?"

It's not a real offer, it was pure sarcasm, but by the look on his face, you'd think I just asked him if I could shove a cattle prod up his ass and turn the electricity to full blast.

Without a word, he turns and leaves, slamming the door behind him. "Your loss," I tease, and I don't know why I'm teasing him, other than poking the bear he's turned into since I asked him if I could tag along is fun. I might officially be losing it. Or maybe he was right about not mixing wine and the sleep gummy.

"Tinsley, just hurry up and get dressed," he growls through

the door. "It's late, I'm fucking tired, and we need to figure this shit out."

"Go to bed then," I call back to him as I slip on clean underwear, a new tank top, and a fresh pair of sleep shorts. I'm going to need to do some laundry. I didn't bring a lot with me. "I'm not keeping you from your beauty rest, Prince Charming. I'd love to get some myself."

"Are you decent?"

"Depends on your definition."

Another growl, and this time, there is no stopping my giggle.

"Cut the shit."

"Fine. I'm decent. You may enter, Your Majesty."

He opens the door but doesn't fully enter. He lingers, halfway in and halfway out. His stormy eyes do another sweep, likely checking to see if I was lying about being decent, but that dark look is back, and it makes my belly drop and my nipples once again perk up. Well, that's not the best reaction to have with him staring this intently.

I fold my arms over my chest to hide them and raise a *well* eyebrow at him.

He clears his throat, his gaze locking on my face before it drops to the floor. His hands dive into the pockets of his track shorts, tugging them down a bit, his shoulder hunching forward.

"Talk. Tell me why you're here."

"Do you have your phone on you?"

He nods. That's it.

"Google my name and see how many hits you get from just the last few days alone."

He doesn't pull out his phone. Instead, he leans against the frame and lifts his chin until his eyes catch mine. "So you're running from the press and you thought you'd do it here where no one would ever think to find you."

Damn, he came to that conclusion fast, and when he puts it like that, it all sounds so simple and shallow, which makes me frown. "More or less."

"And if I called your handlers to come and get you?"

That pisses me off, and I march over to him, getting right up in his face. "I'm not being a diva. I'm not being a spoiled brat princess. I appreciate that you're mad, and I know I shouldn't have just come here without speaking to you about it first, but I was starting to lose it and don't want to lose it, Stone. I don't want to be that pop star who has a nervous breakdown and ends up cutting off all her hair and dancing naked through the streets of LA."

"Huh?"

"I'm a caged lion at the zoo!" I exclaim, staring up at him because he's freaking tall, begging him to understand me. "Do you know what happens to those lions after a while? They either go postal and eat a tourist or they're so hopeless and beaten down they're merely shadows of their former selves. These past few years have dumped a lot of shit on me, both good and bad, but I haven't processed any of it. I keep moving, keep going forward, keep doing what I'm told. I don't even know who I am anymore other than what I am to everyone else."

My voice cracks, and I do my best to clear it. I will *not* cry in front of him.

"I won't be in your way. I'll keep to myself. But I feel like I'm drowning. Like I'm losing pieces of myself, and I'm scared of what will happen to me if I don't recover them. I just need a breather. A week off and away from the world. Please, Stone. *Please* let me come with you."

"Forest would have a lot to say about it."

I squint at him because that's not at all what I thought he was going to say after I unloaded all of that on him. "Why would he care if I'm here?"

"Because you'll be alone with me on this boat?"

"Are you planning to get down and dirty with me?"

He looks disgusted, his eyes studying me as if to remind himself of what I look like naked and all the ways I don't even remotely turn him on. And wow, isn't that a shot to my ego? Not that I was planning to do that with him, but still. A girl likes to be desired regardless. Probably better though. It's been way too long since I've been good and kissed—or laid for that matter—and Stone gives off the vibe that he's good at both.

That would be a colossal mess in the making.

"Didn't think so," I continue, brushing all that off. "And since I'm not planning to do that with you either, there isn't much he could have to say. So I guess it's tough shit for Forest if he doesn't like it." I shrug. "He's not my boyfriend anymore. He hasn't been for a long time, and while I still care very much about him, he doesn't get to dictate my life. That's part of my problem right there and one of the things I'm aiming to fix. That said, I don't exactly want people to know I'm here, so if you don't tell him, or anyone else for that matter, I won't either. It'll be our secret."

"This is a bad idea."

I grin, some of the pressure in my chest easing because it sounds like he's caving and there is resignation starting to flicker in his eyes. "Probably, but don't all the best things in life start off as the worst of ideas? Come on. Say yes. You don't want my mental health on your conscience, and let me tell you, she's holding on by a thin thread."

"I can see that," he deadpans, and I laugh and shrug. "Who knows you're here?"

"No one," I promise.

"Why not?"

"Because I didn't want them to tell me not to do it or try to talk me out of it, which they would have since this isn't my boat."

His eyes narrow. "Where does your family think you are if they don't know you're here?"

"At a yoga retreat."

"Such a celebrity thing to do."

My eyebrows bounce at the sardonic edge to his tone, but I ignore it because he's not wrong. "Now you're catching on. My ruse worked. Well, until you showed up and foiled my plans. But I'm not above begging. I'll even drop to my knees."

"And let your mouth do all the work for you, Little Rose? You think I'm that easily swayed?"

"What?" I tilt my head and then blanch when I realize what I said. "Oh. No! Totally not what I meant. I wasn't talking about... you know... *that*." A laugh bursts out, and then I do the stupid thing and glance down at this dick. Again.

He cups my chin and lifts it, his eyes cool and controlled, but with something else lingering there that I can't quite make out. "I know that's not what you meant. Or what you want from me." He pauses and stares a little harder as if he can see through me straight into my soul. Finally, he gives a tight nod, sighs again, and says, "You'll keep your distance from me."

It's an agreement, an order, and I salute him. "Yes, sir."

His eyes grow blacker than the night outside the windows, and he leans in, his chest practically touching mine now, the heat and spicy scent of him bearing down on me. My heart starts to race, and my inhales are short and choppy like I can't catch my breath, but I don't dare move. Not with the look he's giving me.

His mouth dips to my ear and he whispers against me, "Don't call me sir again and don't beg me with those big, pretty eyes of yours. I promise you'll regret the outcome."

My teeth sink deep into my lip so I don't... I don't know. Implode. Spontaneously combust. As it is, I'm dying to reach up and touch his pulse point to see if his heart is thrashing the way mine is. Somehow, I doubt it. I think this reaction is all mine, and it's not one I want to have or even fully understand.

I will keep my distance from him. That's for sure.

He pulls away and immediately takes a step back but hasn't quite managed to break the spell he just put me under. Another step, and he clears his throat. "We leave tomorrow at dawn."

I do a slow blink and snap myself out of my trance. "Wait," I call to him as he turns his back on me to go to his room. He stops but doesn't turn around. "You never told me why you're here. What does getting your shit together mean?"

"You've got five hours to get some sleep, Little Rose. Hopefully, you come to your senses and change your mind about this before I cast off."

Then he's gone. His door shuts behind him, and I'm left standing here going through the events of the last half hour. I have no idea what just happened but whatever that was, it made me restless in a way I've never been before. Little rose. He's called me that a few times now. My hands fist at my sides, and I bounce in place, staring down the hall at his door.

Maybe he's right.

Maybe I should come to my senses, get off the boat, and return home.

But I already know I won't.

3

STONE

Dawn cracks through the partially drawn curtains, and I cover my face to hide from it. I haven't slept for a second, but that's not even the issue plaguing my mind. I'm an intern in the pediatric emergency room. We're used to not sleeping. It's not even the kid that I nearly killed that kept me up—first time all fucking week for that.

I shouldn't have said yes to Tinsley.

But there was also no way I could say no.

That's what I battled with. The secret I'm about to keep and the reasons for it. Her reasons but also mine. My brother—despite what she says—would take a big fucking exception to me spending ten days sailing around the Bahamas with the woman he's loved his entire life. I wouldn't blame him for that. Hell, if it were reversed no way would I let that go down.

So not telling my brother, not kicking her ass off this boat, it all feels wrong. Like a lie because it might as well be. But again, there was no way I could say no to her. I could see it in her eyes, all over her face and body, and hell, she's *here*, isn't she? A certain level of desperation is required to do what she did. Running out on your life in the darkness of night and hiding out on a boat you have no business being on while keeping it a secret from everyone you know is not a normal reaction to life getting a little tough or being a little too much.

She's a woman about to break—whether that's break free or break down remains to be seen.

How can I turn her away and send her back to what got her here in the first place?

I can't.

I'd immediately regret it and never stop worrying or thinking about her. I feel infuriatingly responsible for her now. It takes a bit of being unhinged to recognize it in another, and she's teetering right on the edge. Perhaps more so than I am. I won't let her fall over without a safety net. Not when she says this is what she needs, and I can give her that.

I may inherently be a selfish, self-serving prick, but even I have my limit.

I'll call it my karmic restitution. I won't look or touch or think—shit, I shouldn't have been doing that in the fucking first place—about what she looks like naked or her on her knees or the way she'd beg or how she called me sir. *Christ*. I groan into my hands and stir a little under my sheets.

What is wrong with me?! This is Tinsley. Forest's girl. She is not a woman I can think of like this. It makes me feel like the worst sort of man. She's falling apart, literally begging me to help her, and I'm thinking about that bullshit.

No. This all stops now. It's ten days. Ten days both of us need for our own reasons.

And that's all it'll be.

I'm helping out someone I've known my entire life. My brother's ex. My friends' and cousins' friend. When this time is over, she'll return to her life, and I'll return to mine, hopefully with both of us on the upswing. I'm here to get myself together, not tear myself further apart.

My eyes snap open, and my hands fall to my sides as I hear something. I strain, and there it is again.

Fucking hell, the woman is awake, singing and chirping away like a Disney princess. How will I ever survive this with her? My next stop is Freeport. From where we are, if we sail most of the way instead of using the engine, it's a solid two-to-three-days-at-sea journey. From there it's short stints to other islands, but those days at sea...

"Stop singing. It's six in the morning," I shout, and my forearm covers my eyes.

"Oh, sorry. Did I wake you?"

This girl. A ghost of a grin flitters across my face, and I growl to hide it.

"No."

"Oh, good. I was worried there for a beat. I'm going up to the top of the boat—I'm not sure what you call it—to do a little sunrise yoga before we get underway."

"Yoga?"

"I figured if I do yoga, then it's not a total lie that I'm at a yoga retreat. Smart, right? Do you want to join me?"

"No."

"Do you say anything other than no?"

I scowl. "No."

She laughs. Why is she laughing? "Come on. I saw you shirtless last night, so I know you work out. Yoga is good for your mind and body, and I haven't done outdoor yoga in *so* long. Please join me. We can start fresh with each other and put last night behind us."

The thought of seeing her do yoga, bending and twisting in those positions is a definite no. "I have stuff to do before we get going."

"I get that. If you change your mind, I'm going to do like twenty minutes or so. After that, I'll make breakfast. Do you like eggs and turkey bacon? I noticed the kitchen was stocked last night and didn't even put it together how that's probably not normal for when it's not in use. Anyway, I'll make breakfast for you since you'll be busy with your boat stuff. I don't eat toast because my nutrition team tells me carbs are the devil, but I can do almost anything like a master chef if you'd rather have something else."

I sigh. It's loud. A bit frustrated. A lot resigned. There might also be a touch of humor at the end because she's damn fucking cute, and I don't know how to handle that side of things. I've hung around Tinsley plenty of times but I'm not sure I've ever talked to her this much one-on-one before.

"I eat carbs. I eat all the fucking carbs."

She moans. "If I make you carbs, can I steal a bite or two? I miss bread like I'd miss a lost toe. It's phantom but so real to me."

A laugh bursts out of my lungs. Shit. I scrub my hands up and down my face and sit up, my sheet slipping to my waist as I stare at the door she's on the other side of.

"I'm not sharing my breakfast with you, Tinsley."

"You're very growly. Is this a morning thing, a Stone thing, or a Stone with Tinsley thing?"

"A Stone thing." I blow out a silent breath, feeling a little bad for being so growly with her. Other than breaking into my boat, she hasn't earned it, and she really hasn't done anything wrong.

"Noted. I'll give you space then while I go do my yoga."

"Are you decent?" I don't know why I ask. Why the fuck am I asking her that?

"Define decent?"

I'm smiling. Stupidly smiling. That's why I asked her. To discern what level of trouble I'm already in and how to avoid digging myself in deeper.

"You said yoga. People don't wear a lot to do yoga. I've seen them." And Tinsley strikes me as the type who doesn't either.

"I'm um. Well. I'm—"

"Do you want me to come out there in only my gym shorts or boxer briefs with no shirt?"

"Ah! No!"

"Excellent. Go put on a fucking bra and an outfit that won't make me hard and we'll survive this trip."

A pause. It's heavy. "I'm not sure I like your level of honesty. For the record, I'm wearing a sports bra and cropped yoga pants. And I didn't know my braless state made you hard."

Me either. No joke, me either. The last time she was on this boat, she wore a bikini like ninety percent of the time, and I intentionally didn't look. Not once. But after seeing her naked last night, with all her smooth skin and sweet, perfect curves, I can't have her traipsing around in anything less than a winter parka. Definitely not in only a sports bra and tight-as-all-sin yoga pants.

I just can't.

Honesty is how we'll get through this unscathed, and I plan to start now. "I'm a straight guy. Boobs are our thing, especially my thing. Any boobs. Your braless state makes me hard. I don't like it. I fucking hate it. So let's not encourage it. In fact, how about both of us wear clothes this week? Then neither of us will be tempted to look at things we shouldn't. Now that we've established that, if you're planning on staying, can you be a good girl for me and get dressed?"

The air is so silent. So unstirred.

"You just asked if I would be a good girl for you," she replies in a low voice.

I freeze, my hand on my forehead, my eyes staring straight at the door. Did I ask her to be that? A good girl? For me? My head whips down, and sure enough, my dick is jerking in my briefs as if to say, *yeah, bro, you sure as hell did, and we hope she says yes, sir*.

Fuck.

Are you my good girl? Are you even capable of being one for me?

Things I will never ask her.

"*That's* what you focus on? Not the fact that I admitted that your braless state makes me hard?"

Shouldn't that be worse?

A huff. "Fine. You're right. Just don't call me that again, and I won't call you sir again, and I'll wear clothes, keep my distance, eat carbs, and live my worst, best life in the best and worst of ways." She giggles. It's a little manic. "I'm so excited for this. Thank you again. I'm going to throw on a shirt, and then head to the top of the boat. At some point, you'll have to teach me all the names for things. I'm ready for whatever you've planned for us. And don't worry. I know it's not *me* making you hard."

If I hadn't felt like a total creeper, asshole, piece of shit before, I certainly do now.

Like I need her to throw me slack for my dirty, inappropriate, wayward thoughts about her. Not good.

Whatever. If she's willing to dole it out, I'll take it.

I'm here to get myself together. To put the man I've been aside and become someone new, someone better. What happened with the boy was my wake-up call. I want to be the doctor I know I can be. I want to be a man who isn't afraid of his own reflection or stepping foot in a trauma room.

I want to be a man I can be proud of, and I haven't been him.

Not ever.

So this is my time. When I return to Boston Children's Hospital, I will be the doctor I should have always been. The one who knows. The one who learns. The one who puts his patients and nothing else above him.

And Tinsley Monroe won't get in the way or distract me from that goal. She won't. Which is why I want her to wear a bra and a shirt and why I want her to understand what this is and what it isn't.

Her door closes down the hall, and I peel myself up and out of bed. I take a brief shower. I dress in shorts and a T-shirt and head to the engine room, all business.

Everything looks good in here, and I turn her on, getting Benthesicyme ready to sail. When she's all set to go, and I think I've killed enough time to miss Tinsley's yoga, I head to the upper deck. The morning is so beautiful with how the sun rises from the ocean, spraying everything it touches with shades of pink and gold. I start the engine, listening to the gentle hum—her engines are powerful but quiet—and feel the pulse thrum beneath my feet rising through me.

I go through my checks, keeping the sails locked down.

"Last chance!" I yell out when everything is set, and then I wait. And wait. I give it about ten solid minutes and even yell it two more times "This is it. You're about to be stuck with me."

Another pause.

"Do you hear me?"

"Yes!" she cries. "I hear you. I'm staying! I'll wear a goddamn bra and a shirt over it. Now sail us out of here. Your breakfast is almost ready."

Your wish is my command.

And it is because I back out of the marina and steer us east toward the sunrise. Ten minutes later, Miami is directly behind us, and I'm taking a northeast course toward Grand Bahama Island.

This sort of yacht is all automatic. I simply punch in coordinates or even a location and it tracks us that way. I don't have to pull lines or angle myself over the side of the hull to get her to tack how I want. That's what comes with a ninety-foot luxury sailing vessel, but she is powerful, her sails are no joke, and her pitch can be mighty if you're not used to it or ready for it.

The moment we hit the open ocean, I call down to her. "I hope you're ready and holding on to something."

"Wait! I'm coming up."

I roll my eyes but give her the grace she requested as she carries a large tray filled with food and coffee up the stairs and sets everything down on the built-in table by the sun deck.

"Ready?"

Wind and ocean spray whip across her, rustling a few flyaways from her tight bun as she makes her way over to stand beside me. There is no hiding the smile lighting her face, and I remember this about Tinsley from our last time sailing. She loved it. Even as Forest stayed downstairs or under the sunshade the entire time. Sailing is definitely not his thing.

"Ready."

I raise the sails with a push of a few buttons and then cut off the engine.

A high swells in my gut, and a weightlessness tracks through my limbs.

The boat tilts, and the pull of the wind carries us, all guided by me. It used to be lines and pulls and jibs and booms, but even though it's not, it can still be fun. It can still be wild. It can still be up to the ocean for how this goes. Automation means I don't need a crew to sail a ship this size—even if she can accommodate up to four permanent crewmembers—and that's what I had been counting on for this trip.

Just me, Benthesicyme, and the ocean. And now Tinsley.

I stand behind the wheel, my girl half tilted into the white swell, the sunny, salty air wrapping around me in her endless embrace.

"Holy shit!" Tinsley cries, her hands flying high above her head as if she too is trying to catch the wind. "This is incredible!"

"Just wait. It's about to get better." With the navigation screen before me and the wheel at my command, I take my lady out to sea, pushing her to her max, tightening her sails, and savoring her wind as it propels us forward at nearly forty knots.

This is what I needed. This is what I was after.

Nothing humbles you the way the ocean can. You are nothing in comparison to its strength and might. I never did right by the opportunities presented to me. I never cared enough to give them the respect they deserved. I was cavalier, and it cost me. It nearly cost a family everything.

I rushed with that boy. It's why I almost didn't catch his meningitis.

I blew off his symptoms and half-assed the exam because I was anxious to get in on an incoming trauma, but his mother was persistent. The nurse was persistent, too. She told me I needed to take his symptoms more seriously, and I didn't because I thought it was just a cold or the flu, even though his rapid flu came back negative. Still, I was positive about it.

So much so that I brushed off his stiff neck and sensitivity to light and fever that didn't want to come down. I wrote all those off, and truth be told, I didn't consider meningitis on my differential until his diagnosis all but smacked me in the face, and he started decompensating. Until the nurse not so artfully told me she suspected it was meningitis and that I was killing him by waiting and blowing it off.

If I hadn't finally listened to her, I never would have done the blood cultures and lumbar puncture. And that... I have no words for that. I was arrogant. I was cocky. I was fucking stupid. And I nearly killed that boy.

My error would have. Bacterial meningitis is extremely deadly. And contagious. The boy survived but ended up in the ICU and needed to be intubated. If I had caught it earlier, even started antibiotics a few hours earlier, he might not have gotten as sick as he did. His organs might not have started to fail him.

I should have caught it sooner. It should have been in my differential from the start. I should have spent the time and thought it through. I haven't been able to see a patient since. I haven't slept much, and I've barely eaten. I've been sick with all of it.

So yeah, I'm here to get my shit together.

I just hope it's not too late, or worse, that this week ends up costing me more.

4

STONE

"Stone?!" Tinsley yells from below deck where she disappeared to about an hour ago. I think she's making dinner, though she didn't say. It's been her way of earning her keep. After she cooked breakfast yesterday, she also made dinner and seemed put out when I made breakfast this morning, though all that talk about no carbs went out the window when I set croissants with raspberry jam before her. She devoured them and moaned her way through so loudly and with so much pleasure on her face that I had to leave before I made her come just to prove I could do a better job of getting those noises out of her than the croissants could.

It was a problem.

"Yes?" I call back, locking the sails down and getting ready to drop anchor for a bit. I have to figure out the weather and what I want to do next if Grand Bahama Island isn't an option anymore, and I wouldn't mind a little dinner and maybe a swim.

"Did we stop or am I hallucinating?"

I chuckle. "You're hallucinating."

"Such a dick," I hear her grumble before her voice climbs again. "I was going to tell you dinner is ready, but now you don't deserve my awesome food."

My stomach growls reflexively. I missed lunch because I was busy navigating us and going over weather charts, so now I'm starving.

"Yes, we stopped."

"Oh, gee, wow, thanks for the real-time update there, *sir*. Or wait, that's a no-no word, right? How about I call you captain?"

God, she's such a brat. I fucking love it and can't stand it. I've ignored her for about thirty-six hours now. Not so easily done when we're the only two people on this boat and there are only so many places you can be on it. She's given me space, and I've given her space all the while I've covertly watched her. Just trying to figure her out a bit is the excuse I've given myself, but it's like she's a magnet for my brain and eyes.

And my stupid dick.

She plays guitar and sings along and writes stuff down in a notebook, and she's taken to the ocean so well with not even a hint of seasickness despite how much the boat is moving. I need to cut her some slack. These issues are my own, not hers, and I need to get over them. It's a simple attraction and nothing more.

"Do you want to eat dinner up here tonight?"

I don't know why I ask. We haven't sat down and had a meal together yet. We've been totally separate, in adjacent spaces, or even in the same room but doing other things and not talking. This is fire I'm playing with, but it's as if with all this water surrounding me, I feel as though I can't get burned. Or more like I know what that fire is, and I can look at it and even admire it, but I won't get too close and I sure as hell won't touch it.

"Umm. Like together?"

I smile and rub my jaw as I stare out at the endless ocean and the sun that's just starting to go down. We'll have another hour and a half at least of light, even after the sun descends, and I can already tell tonight's sunset is going to be incredible. It's my favorite time of day out here, other than dawn. Everything gets slow and quiet, and the stars start to peek out.

"Only if you want to. You went to all that trouble to make..." I trail off, letting her fill in the blank.

Her head pops up through the opening leading from the companionway and she looks around until she spots me. She had been hiding just inside, though I could see her from this angle.

She gives me a smile, her lavender eyes catching the sun just right, and I swear, she's a fucking siren, angelic voice and all, only I have no interest in jumping to my death for her.

"I made burrito bowls with ground chicken, black beans, veggies, and cauliflower rice. It's one of my favorite meals."

"Cauliflower rice?" I question, scrunching my nose. "Sounds awful."

"It's good. Trust me. You won't notice the difference. I promise, you'll love it. I'm trying to get you to keep me on board, not throw me off, remember?"

"You mean the way you did to me?"

She laughs and points her finger at me. "Right. Exactly like that. Only the opposite. If that makes sense."

"I won't throw you off, Little Rose. At least not out here in the middle of nowhere with no land in sight." I hold in my smirk, but I can feel it starting to slip when her jaw goes slack at my last comment, and her gaze flashes wildly to the ocean. "Why do you seem nervous?"

She bites her lip and throws her hands up. "I don't know." She laughs in a self-deprecating way. "I'm jumpy, and I want you to like my dinner. I honestly contemplated making more croissants because I could eat those all day and orgasm over them accordingly, but I figured since you missed lunch, you needed protein."

I choke on nothing. Jesus hell, this woman is going to be the death of me. She's talking about orgasms, and I definitely got a glimpse of that this morning with the croissants, and the fact that I can easily close my eyes and picture her naked—

Shit, don't close your eyes!

My jaw clenches and I throw her a dangerous look. "Comments about orgasms go into the previous articles of this ship along with shirts and bras."

She tilts her head in a placating way. "Aw, poor Stone. So easily riled up. Fine. No more orgasms, food, or otherwise. But will you eat the burrito bowl, or should I make you something else?"

Damn, she is jumpy and seriously anxious for me not to throw her off or hate her or whatever this is that has her willing to make me something else. I may be an asshole, but I'd never be that much of an asshole.

"The burrito bowl sounds great. Do you want a margarita to go with it?" I sure as hell could use a drink.

Her eyes light up like that's the best idea I've ever had. "Absolutely! I'll get the food. You get the drinks." She spins around, her dark hair flying behind her, and excitedly scurries below deck. For someone whose life is at a bit of a crossroads, and she was admittedly a hot minute from a breakdown, she rebounds fast. Or maybe it's this freedom making her this buoyant, though it's clear she doesn't have her bearings around me yet.

That makes two of us.

Other than my guilt at keeping this from Forest, and everyone else for that matter, it shouldn't be this difficult. I shouldn't be reacting to her the way I have been. I shouldn't need to keep my distance, and I shouldn't be watching her regardless of that. I can't explain it. It's more than simply being stuck on a boat with her or getting a flash of her tits and pussy when her towel dropped.

I don't know where it came from—this weird sort of infatuation I have with her—but fuck me, I need it to stop.

I follow her down into the galley, mix up a pitcher of margaritas, and bring it along with some glasses and ice up top. The air is warm, and the wind is gentle, at least for now. The boat is anchored tight, giving us a slight rocking, but it's otherwise steady. It's a perfect evening to eat topside and watch the sun sink into the ocean.

Tinsley carries two good-sized bowls of food, and I have to admit, it smells and looks good. She's a better chef than I thought she'd be for a Hollywood princess, but then again, I'm discovering there are a lot of things about her that surprise me.

She sits down, and I pour each of us a drink, and for a moment, we're silent, both staring west toward the giant fireball in the sky as it makes its descent to greet the dark blue ocean.

"Boston or LA?" I ask as I take my first bite. It's seriously fucking fantastic. She wasn't kidding, and though I can tell that the cauliflower isn't actual rice, it's pretty decent too.

"Boston," she answers quickly and then her head snaps back to me as if that answer surprised her. She takes a sip of her drink, licks her lips, and then digs into her food. "Yeah, I guess Boston," she says after a contemplative moment. "I like fall. I like seasons. I like that my family is there, and I miss them and wish I saw them more often, even if they're a bit overbearing at times. LA is tough."

"Because of what's going on with you right now?" I press when she leaves it at that.

She shrugs as she continues to eat. "I guess. I don't know anymore. Not much feels right at the moment, but I suppose that's what I'm working on. What about you? You're a Fritz. Boston is your bloodline. Do you ever think about going somewhere else?"

I shake my head automatically. "No. Not ever. I mean, maybe because of the whole Fritz thing, but like you said, it's my bloodline." I take another bite and point to the bowl with my fork as I chew. "This is really good."

"Ha!" She does a little victory dance in her seat, complete with jazz hands. I make a show of rolling my eyes at her, but she plows right past that. "I knew you'd like it. I won't even gloat about it."

"You mean more than you're doing now?"

She's still dancing, and I dip my fingers into my water glass and flick the cold drops at her.

"Ah! Okay, stop. No more gloating." She wipes her face where I got her. "How long can you stay on this boat without needing to stop?"

"Depends," I answer as I chew. "If it's fully stocked the way it is now and I don't need a lot of engine time, a couple of weeks. I've never gone that long or even attempted it though. This will be my longest stay on her."

"Are we going to talk about that yet? Why you're out here."

My glass meets my lips and I take a few hearty gulps. "After dinner did you want to go for a swim?"

She makes a noise in the back of her throat, annoyed that I won't give her my sad tale of woe when she's given me hers, but I don't care. My mess is my own to figure out, and frankly, I don't want to see it in her eyes when I tell her about the boy. The pity or the *you get out what you put in* expression that I'll find there. It'll make me sick, and right now, I'm barely getting by. I'm trying to work on this. Both of those will throw me over the edge.

"Can we swim out here? It's not dangerous?"

"Nah. We'll stay close to the boat but it's pretty safe, and we'll do it when it's still light out."

"Okay. Let's finish up. No bikini, right?"

I chuckle and shake my head. "Do you own anything else?"

She grins. "Nope. But I'll pick the one that covers the most."

IF THAT'S the one that covers the most, I'd hate to see the one that covers the least. I'm forcing myself not to look. I truly am. And for the most part, I'm succeeding. Even as she finishes the rest of her margarita and I finish mine, only to realize we finished the pitcher.

"I'm the queen of the world!" she yells from the bow pulpit, her arms stretched out wide though we're not sailing into the wind.

"I thought I was Jack, and you were Rose," I quip.

She turns her head and shoots me a raised eyebrow. "I thought you never saw the movie."

"I never said that. I just didn't get the immediate reference in the water."

"Oh? Who did you see it with?" Her eyebrows bounce suggestively.

I move in behind her the way Jack did with Rose in the movie. I don't touch her. I don't dare do that, but I stand behind her, and her arms launch wide again while mine do the same behind hers.

"I saw it with Katy, Keegan, Kenna, Wren, Mason, and Vander. Katy was obsessed with that movie for a solid month, and she made us all watch it. Owen somehow got out of it, lucky bastard that he was. Is it weird that your people are my people, and my people are your people, and yet no one else on the planet knows we're out here but us?"

"Weird? Maybe. Does it bother me? A bit, yeah."

She falls quiet for a moment before her hands meet the railing. "They can't know, Stone."

I sigh. "I know they can't." Without another word about it, I swing myself over the side and dive straight into the ocean. And fuck is it cold out here. She thought the marina was cold, that has nothing on the open Atlantic, even in the Bahamas.

I burst up through and push salty water and wet hair away from my face so I can look up and see her. I squint against the remains of the sun as it reflects off the hull of the boat.

Her jaw is slack, and her eyes are wide with terror. "Oh my god! That was terrifying! Don't do that again."

"What? It's the same drop as in the marina. The water's just deeper, and I dove instead of doing a half-assed backflip. I've done it dozens of times."

She shakes her head. "I don't remember you doing that last time we were on this boat."

"You mean when Mason and I got drunk together and we both did it?"

"I never saw that."

No. She was too busy fighting with Forest below deck.

"Are you coming in?" I ask instead of mentioning that. I can't say his name to her. I don't know why. If anything, I should. His name is a reminder of just how off-limits this girl is to me. But I think that's why I can't do it either.

What I'm doing here with her is wrong. The way I can't stop looking at her is wrong. Thinking about Forest only makes me feel more like shit for that, and since feeling like shit is all I've been doing lately, I don't want more of it.

I'm helping her. She needs this. That's all this is, and all there is to it.

Forest doesn't have to enter into that. Neither does anyone else.

"I'm not jumping again. I may be a little tipsy from the margaritas, but I'm lacking the sleep gummy, so my inhibitions are still intact. I'll meet you in the back."

She jogs aft, and I swim that way to meet her. The transom is down, and she easily slips into the water from it. We don't talk much. We simply swim and watch the sunset, and when it's fully down, we climb back onboard and go our separate ways. Her to the front of the boat with her guitar, and me lying on the sundeck, staring up at the stars and listening to her sing and play.

And part of me can't help but wonder, could anything be more perfect than this?

5

TINSLEY

"I didn't know you get service out here." And by out here I mean the middle of the freaking ocean. As in, there is nothing around. Nothing visible but blue water and blue sky and the sun.

"That's because you haven't bothered to turn on your phone," he quips without bothering to look up. "But we don't have regular service out here. This is a satellite phone."

"Then what difference would it make if I turned on my phone if we don't have service?"

It's also not true. I turned on my phone shortly after we left Miami and texted my parents to let them know everything was good, that I was safe, and that I'd be out of touch for about ten days or so. Since the stalker, they're jumpy when it comes to me. Understandably so since I was a minor when all of that started, but I'm not a child anymore. I'm not a little girl. And I'm tired of feeling like I have to ask permission for everything I do.

He ignores me. He's absurdly good at that.

This is our third full day on the boat, and I've held to my word. I've kept my distance from him. We take turns cooking and cleaning up, but other than that, we don't talk or interact much, last night's dinner and swim notwithstanding. At home, there are always people around or someone calling and texting me. Even when I'm alone, I'm not truly alone.

So all this quiet and solitude was fabulous when I drove down to Miami from Georgia, and even the last two days as we sailed. It was the mental recharge I needed to start things off. I wrote almost a full song, the words and notes flowing through my head like the boat cutting through water, and after that, I relaxed in the sun, and read a smutty rom-com.

Stone's been quiet and introspective, and I haven't wanted to interrupt that even if I still don't know what brought him out here.

Today, I'm starting to get a little antsy. It doesn't help that Stone won't let me do much with the ship and spends all his time sailing us in a very serious and concentrated way. Plus, the boat's really been moving, choppy water that makes us rock from side to side and high winds so loud it's difficult to hear myself think, let alone sing. I can't read because, with the way the boat is moving, it makes me a little nauseated. I've been strumming my guitar, sitting in the center of the boat since I've found it's the most stable part, rocks the littlest, and has shade with the hard top hanging over me, but even here I can hardly hear what I'm playing.

So yeah, I'm antsy. Possibly a bit bored. I need a change. Something to do to occupy me. At least until we stop somewhere or the boat settles.

"Who are you texting?" I ask when I can't take his silent dismissal for another second.

"My parents," he says without any inflection to his voice or even bothering to look up from his screen "I'm letting them know we're sailing to Nassau."

"I thought you said we were—" My fingers freeze mid-strum and I lift my chin in his direction as I snag on one word. "We?"

He glances up quickly before returning to his phone, typing in rapid fire with two thumbs. "I told them you're with me."

"What?!" I shriek, shooting to my feet as he continues to text.

"I didn't think it was right that you didn't tell anyone where you are. What if someone needs to get in touch with you? You told me your phone is off and in the bottom of your suitcase. That's not safe. They said they'd let your parents know. I'm sure they're worried about you."

"Are you kidding me?" I set my guitar down and fly at him. He jumps back from the wheel—the ship evidently on autopilot—and I just miss him. "You better not have, Stone. I mean it. My parents would be supersonically pissed that I not only lied to them but snuck onto your boat the way I did."

"Why? You're an adult. What can they do?"

True. I am an adult, but as an adult, I don't want to answer questions that I know my parents will ask. Not to mention answering to others and doing as they tell me has been one of my toxic traits for, well, my entire life.

"Stone, please tell me you didn't tell your parents I'm with you."

"It's just my parents." He shrugs indifferently. "They won't mention anything to Forest." He tilts his head. "Why don't you want them to know that you're with me?"

My eyebrows shoot up and my palms tingle, ready to strangle that cocky, surefire smirk from his handsome face. "You better not be serious."

"And what if I am? What will you do? My parents and I are close. I tell them everything."

I narrow my eyes skeptically, studying him. Unfortunately, he has a hell of a poker face. "I don't believe you. You wouldn't do that. You don't want anyone to know I'm with you any more than I do."

He holds his phone out in front of him and wiggles it back and forth. "Come see for yourself."

I charge, and he shoots to his right, putting the leather captain's chair between us, and fuck him for being so fast. "You missed, Little Rose." His phone pings with an incoming text, and his smirk grows into a Cheshire grin. "I wonder what they have to say. Should I read it out loud?"

"Really? You want to taunt me like that?"

His head bobs toward his shoulder, and he makes a passive noise.

"You broke our pact."

Another shrug, and he returns to his phone, typing something in. Hmm. Okay. If he wants to play dirty, I'll play even dirtier. I rip off my shirt and then shimmy out of my shorts, then toss both in his face. I'm wearing a hot pink bikini. The kind that's a lot of string and not a lot of fabric. I planned to be on this boat alone, after all.

"If you get to break our pact, so do I. Should I bend over to give you the full boob and ass effect?"

His eyes flash, growing molten as a stream of emotions passes over his face, tightening his lips in displeasure. I fold my arms under my chest, making my girls lift. Now it's my turn to smirk.

"Put your clothes back on," he grits out, and a muscle in his jaw tics.

"Let me see your text." I hold out my hand, palm side up.

Neither of us moves, other than for me to flip some of the wind-tangled strands that escaped my braid out of my face.

"I mean it, Tinsley."

"You know, I didn't do my sunrise yoga this morning. The boat was moving too much. But maybe I should do it now." I turn and hear him curse when I start to bend into a downward-facing dog, and he gets a view of my ass since these are more than a little cheeky.

"Cut the shit and put your damn clothes back on."

"Just let me see your phone so I know you're lying. How *hard* can that be?" My gaze drops to his swim trunks, but with the angle of the sun shining directly on him, I can't actually see anything or tell if he's hard. Shame.

"You're being a brat."

"And you're being a dick," I throw back at him, righting myself and glaring at him. "Speaking of. Let's see how excited we can make the little guy. I've always wanted to sunbathe topless." I reach behind my neck and start to undo the knot there. I don't actually intend to show him my tits again, but he doesn't know that. The threat is there and he's reading it loud and clear.

He growls in pissed off defeat and tosses his phone at me, making me catch it.

"Wow. You must really want me to put my clothes back on. And here I thought I looked pretty good in this bikini."

He's not amused, but I sure as hell am.

"For the record, you didn't make me hard."

I pout mockingly, staring down at his shorts again. "Aw, poor little guy. Do you have performance issues?" My eyes flash back up to his. "Is that why you came out here alone instead of with one of your usual companions?"

He moves around the chair and sidles up to me. His hand wraps around my waist to hold me steady as the boat rocks, towering over me and forcing my neck to crane to meet his eyes. "Oh, Little Rose, I think we both know I have no issues with that, and you can call my guy little all you like, but there is nothing little about me, soft or not. You're cute when you think you can tempt me to prove it to you."

I smile. It's not a kind smile. "Except this isn't a challenge I'm trying to win. The last thing I want to see is your *tiny, limp* guy, even if we both know you want to see my girls."

His gaze shifts, dropping down between us just as a text comes in, and he immediately draws back, his expression showing me all the ways he's sworn to hate me for eternity.

"Unlock it," I demand, and shockingly, he complies.

He does it with his face for me to find his text is already pulled up on his screen, and I see it's a group chat he has with Mason, Vander, and Owen, his friends and cousin. Mason and Vander are my friends too since their dads are best friends with my dad and long before they had us, they were in a very successful rock band called Central Square. My father was the lead singer and is where I get my own vocal talent from. Owen I don't know as well, but he's my best friend Wren's older brother.

I quickly read through his texts, making sure there's nothing about me in them, but something catches my eyes, and I freeze before slowly looking back up at him, my eyes wide and my mouth gaping open as a shiver runs up my spine. "We're getting a storm? A hurricane?"

I hand him back his phone and go for my clothes, slipping back on my tank top and shorts because now the game isn't so fun.

"Possibly. When I checked the other day, it was tracking in a different direction as all the models had it curving east and blowing out to the open ocean by now. It swung more west than they were anticipating and stalled. Right now, I have us heading south instead of north where we were originally going, so hopefully if we do catch any of it, it's just the tail."

"Stone." I pause for a beat and audibly swallow.

I don't like storms. Not any kind of storm. When I was nine, my parents thought it would be fun to take me and my younger siblings camping, and we got stuck in a horrific thunder and lightning storm complete with hail and monsoon-caliber rain that flash-flooded our tent. I nearly drowned trying to get my siblings who were little above the water in our tent. I had nightmares about it for years. I am not okay with this. Not to mention, a hurricane is an entirely different level of beast.

"Why didn't you tell me?" I bite into my lip, and I can feel myself shaking. I'll be honest, this all sounded like a great idea and a fun adventure, but the no-visible land thing with a hurricane nearby is disquieting and frankly freaking me the fuck out. Stone is obviously very experienced with sailing—he's been doing it his whole life with his father—but the idea of a hurricane out here...

My heart starts to pound as panic sets in.

"Hey." He steps forward, putting his hand on my arm, only to immediately pull away and then think better of it and bring me into his chest and hold me. "It's okay. She's a big ship and meant to handle rough seas. We'll be nowhere near the heavy stuff, and it's only a category one at its center. We'll be fine. This is why I didn't tell you. I didn't want you to worry. It might blow right past us and not be a thing."

"When is it supposed to hit?"

"According to my radar and the reports the guys are telling me, maybe sometime overnight. If at all," he tacks on. "All that said, I do think you should tell your parents where you are."

"Because we could die tonight?"

He pulls back and makes a show of rolling his eyes. "We're not dying tonight, Little Rose." He releases me and goes back to the wheel. "I'm going to lower the sails and keep the engine on autopilot, and we'll go slow. As it is right now, we're getting great tailwinds, and they're pushing us along at a good clip."

"How far are we from land?"

He keeps his back to me as he answers, and I don't like that.

It feels like he's trying to hide something from me. "The storm will make landfall over Great Abaco, which is closer to Grand Bahama than I want to be, so I had to change our course and head south. We're about ninety nautical miles from Nassau." He throws his head over his shoulders and briefly meets my eyes. "But like I said, it won't be a big deal."

6

TIN[illegible]

"Not a big deal!" I cry, losing my mind as the boat rocks wildly from side to side. "It's a good thing I don't get motion sick!"

"That's what makes you the perfect sailor."

He's so deadpan I want to strangle him. Again. It's a running theme with us.

Rain falls in buckets from the sky, the wind is howling like a freight train, and just to add a bit of fun to our nightmare, it's thundering and lightning. Lightning. As in shots of electricity that strike the ocean. The actual ocean we're in. We're on a freaking ship with a tall-ass mast, and there's nothing else around. We're a goddamn floating target.

The rain started about two hours ago and it wasn't bad at first. Now it's bad.

"Try to get some sleep," Stone suggests. He's been doing—I don't even know what—from what I've not-so-affectionally termed the cockpit that's off the family room, though I don't think that's what they call it on a ship. He's in front of three screens with a control panel that has a million buttons he's been pushing. He's also been in touch with the US Coast Guard as well as local Bahamian authorities.

"I can't sleep, Stone." I'm pacing so I don't topple over, mimicking the motion of the ship. "I'm sorry. I know you don't need my drama or hysteria right now, but I'm seriously panicking and woman enough to admit it."

A crack of thunder rumbles so loudly it not only shakes the boat, the fucking dishes in the cabinets rattle and makes my goddamn teeth chatter. I am not okay. There is no amount of wine and gummies that would be sufficient to see me through this. I go into the galley and pour myself a double shot of tequila. At least Stone was smart enough to have his boat fully stocked with the essentials.

"Do you have a bucket list?"

"Huh? A bucket list?" he parrots only half listening to me.

It doesn't deter me. "Yes. A bucket list. A list of things you want to do before you die. I've never made one, but even though I've led this extraordinary life, I don't feel like I've done much with it or taken advantage of the opportunities I've had. Like, I've never been kissed under the Eiffel Tower in Paris. I've never jumped out of an airplane or gotten a tattoo. Or a piercing, for that matter. I've never gotten lost in Tuscany the way my parents did or walked the Great Wall of China. I've been to all fifty states, but I don't think I've been to a single national park. I've never had a one-night stand or a hot fling."

I swallow down the double shot just as a bolt of lightning flashes out the starboard window. I watch in horror as it electrocutes the ocean about a hundred yards from us.

Holy shit, I'm going to die tonight.

I pour a second shot and then bring one to Stone.

He takes the glass from my shaking hand and tosses the alcohol down his throat. "Thanks."

That's it. How is he so calm?

I start to pace again, fighting against the fierce dip and

sway of the boat, feeling so helpless, my fingers knot and unknot in useless spindles. "So yeah, I haven't done any of those things. I've never explored. I've had no real adventures. I've been a good girl who did all the good girl things she was told to do. And what did that get me? A stalker. A boyfriend I clung to a little too tightly because I was afraid of life and said stalker. I've never lived or done anything for myself. And right now, that feels immensely tragic. Like a world filled with regrets."

I pause as lyrics about worlds of regrets and lives yet to live fill my head. My guitar is down in my bedroom, but that's too far away at the moment.

"I know I told you not to call me a good girl because it low-level turned me on since that's what the hero calls the heroine in the dirty books I like to read, but I don't think it does anymore. Being a good girl has been the regret of my life." I suck in a breath and let it out along with the words. "It's caged me into the status quo. It's trapped me into saying yes when I should have said no. It's made me complacent when I should have been impatient. Unfulfilled and outlived, I might have killed the girl I saw the potential to become."

"Those sound like song lyrics."

I nod. They are. It's forming in my head.

"They might be. But how sad are they? I want to be a bad girl, Stone. Only what if it's too late and I missed my chance?"

Jesus, I'm losing it. I'm totally rambling, and I don't even know if I'm making sense.

I hiccup a shaky breath and a quiet gasp as the boat gives a particularly hard lurch when a huge wave crashes into the side of us.

"Hey. It's okay." He stands, taking me by the shoulders and holding on when I'm anything but steady. I whimper, and a tear tracks down my cheek. "No, Tinsley. None of that. Where's the tenacious pain in my ass who broke onto my boat and then kicked me over it? The Rose who jumped into the black water without a life raft?"

"I did that, didn't I?"

"Yeah, you did. It was pretty great. Definitely sexy."

He wipes my tear with his thumb, pulls me in, and holds me tight, tucking the side of my head against his chest. I can hear the steady rhythm of his heart and feel the strong wall of muscle that cocoons me. It settles me, but only just.

"We can do some of those things, you know. We can bucket list the fuck out of this trip. Bad girls are tough and brave. You've been caged a little too long, but it's in you."

I sniffle. "I'm trying to be her, but it's not going well. Please tell me the truth about how bad this is for us."

He pulls back and cups my face in his large, warm hands and stares straight into my eyes. "We're fine. I promise I'm not just saying that. I know it looks and feels bad out there, but we're perfectly safe in here. The top of the mast is capped in rubber and the ship is fiberglass, not metal. It's also built to handle anything the ocean can throw at her."

Another tear tracks down my cheek. "I'm sorry. I'm trying to be tough because I know you're already dealing with a lot, but I'm failing miserably. I'm a city mouse. I've always been a city mouse. The most time I spent at sea was when I went sailing with you, and even then, we just went to the Keys and were never far from land. The idea of capsizing or the boat falling apart and us drowning in the ocean is about the most terrifying thing I can think of, and right now, it feels like that's not that far from reality."

"We're not going to capsize, and this ship won't fall apart. You're not going to drown." His thumbs drag across my cheekbones. "I won't let anything bad happen to you. Ever. Okay?" His green eyes search mine. "I swear."

Comfort seeps into my bones like a warm blanket in front of a blazing fire on a snowy night. I've held on to comfort like this before. A little too hard. I had a stalker, Terrance Howard, who, at first, wrote words of love and poetry, but they quickly morphed into anger and violence. I clung to Forest, and I clung hard. For much longer than I should have. It's a mistake I vowed never to repeat and yet here I am with his brother, begging him to tell me everything is going to be okay. It's not how I want to be anymore.

My spine straightens. "I'm okay."

He smiles, searching my eyes. "See, there's my brave girl. I knew you were in there."

"You're the only one who's ever seen her, let alone believed in her existence."

"Then they never saw you, did they?" He kisses my forehead, and my heart changes its trajectory, my feet losing purchase as the ground beneath me shifts, and much like the ship, I start to tilt, unable to get my bearings. "Let's go try to get some sleep, and by the time we wake up, the storm will be over."

He wipes more of my tears away and takes my hand, walking us down a flight to where the bedrooms are. He's being sweet, sort of how he was that first night when he carried me dripping wet and freezing cold to the bedroom for a shower, only infinitely more tender. It's almost making this worse. Gruff Stone I can handle. Sweet Stone is poking holes in my skin and allowing my ooey, gooey center that's a lot softer than my tough shell to seep out.

Still, I allow him to lead me, and I force myself to trust what he's telling me. He's not freaked out. He's calm, composed, and in control. I like that. It's comforting, and I cling to that like a baby koala clinging to a tree.

It's also late. It's like one in the morning. "There's no way I'll be able to fall asleep tonight."

He sighs. It's a resigned sigh. Almost like he was afraid I was going to say that but knew it was coming anyway.

"No, I suppose you won't be able to. And truth be told, I don't want to be thinking about you alone in your bed with those tears." He hisses out a curse. "You'll sleep in my bed tonight." Without another word, he leads me into his room, and I don't object. I'm wearing the same tank top and shorts I've been wearing all day, and I can easily sleep in them, but he hands me one of his T-shirts that he pulls out of a drawer. The ship is swaying so aggressively that I have to stand with my feet shoulder-width apart and brace my hands on the wall.

Thank God I'm not seasick, but there is no way in hell sleep is happening tonight.

"You can use the bathroom first," he offers, and I don't argue with him. I go into the bathroom, do my thing, wash my hands, steal his toothbrush to brush my teeth, and get out of there. I can't look at my reflection. I'll lose it if I do. It's bad outside. I can hear it and I can feel it. I get that this is a crazy fancy ship and not a small dingy, but weather like this could take down a cruise ship. Weather like this blows houses over.

I come out, and the room is dark. Stone is shirtless, only wearing his low-slung track shorts. Wordlessly, he goes into the bathroom and shuts the door, and I climb into his bed. It smells like him and that's the most comforting thing I have right now. It surrounds me, and I take it. The storm sounds like an airplane is barreling down at top speed right outside the window.

Another crash of thunder. This one makes me gasp.

Maybe Stone was right. I should have told my parents where I am.

A moment later, he exits the bathroom, staggering over to the bed as he fights the momentum of the boat.

"Are you sure it's safe for you to go to sleep? Should we take watches or something?" Not that I have any clue what I'd be looking at on those screens.

He climbs in beside me, slides his hand beneath my body,

and drags me over, holding me against his chest. He smells good. Like his sheets but in a more potent form. Like the sun and the ocean and something spicy that's all him. He's soft skin over a wall of muscle, and even though I'm scared out of my mind, I can't help but be aware of him and how it feels to be in his arms. Despite the raging storm, he makes me feel safe and protected, which isn't something I get a ton of in my day-to-day life. I have my parents, and I have my family and lifelong friends that I'm very close with, but they're mostly on the East Coast and I'm in LA.

There is nothing safe about LA or the music and film business.

Nothing safe about being stalked by a violent man when you're still only a teenager.

"I'm not going to sleep," he whispers, shifting me in closer so that my chest is flush with his, my head tucked beneath his chin. He's rigid and tense, but it's a battle for him to stay that way as his hand runs down the back of my hair, twirling a lock around his finger only to release and start all over again. "I'm going to get you to sleep and go back. But she's fine for a couple of hours heading in this direction, and the storm is going in the other. It won't last much longer like this."

"No. Shit. Stone, just go. I'm fine." I suck in a shaky breath, feeling awful and selfish for keeping him here. "I am."

He runs a soothing hand down the back of my head. "Shh. It's okay. Just relax and go to sleep."

"Why are you being nice to me?"

He chuckles lightly, the sound vibrating through his chest and into my body. "Because I can't stand to see you like this, and I'd do anything—even be nice—to take that fear away. I also knew about the storm and didn't tell you. I should have. You probably would have changed your mind about coming, and that would have been the right thing to do. I didn't think it'd hit us. Yet another thing I was heedless with."

I peer up at him, able to make out his face in the darkness now that my eyes have adjusted. "What does that mean? Another thing you were heedless with?"

He looks down at me, and our eyes lock before his momentarily drift down to my lips before climbing back up. He doesn't answer, but I didn't expect him to. That's Stone. His cards held tight, and his heart locked away.

"Close your eyes, baby girl. I've got you."

I place my hand on his chest, his skin hot beneath my palm. I don't know what I'm doing or why I'm doing it, but I don't care, and I don't want to stop either. "What if I can't go to sleep? What if I need something to help take my mind off everything?"

He licks his lips, that dark look he had the first night crawling back over his features but there's something else there too. Hunger. His gaze dips to my mouth once more, and his grip on me tightens.

"You said you'd do anything," I tack on when he doesn't move or respond.

"You really want to test that?"

Do I? "Yes. So will you help me or not?"

7

STONE

Frustration and desire slam into me with the same force the waves are slamming into the boat. I'm as riled and torn up with chaos as the ocean. She has no idea what she's asking of me. I don't think she gets it at all. Since the moment she jumped into that marina to "rescue" me, my every waking thought has been about her.

I watch her. I listen as she moves around and plays guitar and sings. Especially when she sings because she sounds like a fucking angel. And when all that's done, I fall asleep thinking about her. *Dreaming* about her. It's torture. A punishment I can't escape. One I don't understand either. I had zero fucks to give where Tinsley Monroe was concerned for years and years, decades and decades. A few days on my boat, a couple of back and forths, a few flashes of skin, a couple of songs, and I've become infatuated like a schoolboy.

I hate it.

I can't fucking stand it.

Tinsley Monroe is a plague occupying my every breath, and I don't know how to stop it.

She's been holding to her word since we set sail. Clothes have been on, and distance has been maintained.

It doesn't matter.

I'm here to get myself together and my head on straight, and touching her feels like falling off a cliff. But hell, do I want to take that freefall? Still...

"You're not mine to touch."

She huffs. "I'm not his either." She pulls away from me, and I already miss the feel of her hair and the warmth of her body against my skin. "You know what? You're probably right. It was a bad idea. Honestly, I'm good. Go back to making sure we survive the night and I'll rub my little nub and put myself to sleep."

And that's it. I don't know why, and I don't even know how it happens, but suddenly I'm throwing the blankets off the bed and crawling between her goddamn legs. She gasps, propping herself up with her elbows until she's half sitting up. Wide eyes stare down at me as if she too doesn't know what to make of me in my new position.

"Show me," I grit through clenched teeth.

"Show you?" Her eyebrows hit her hairline, her hair all over the goddamn place, and I want to do so many unholy things to her it's ridiculous.

"I won't touch you. I *can't* fucking touch you. So show me how you like to be touched. Show me all that I'm missing by keeping my hands, mouth, and cock to myself. Show me how you touch yourself until you come."

She barks out an *are you crazy* laugh, and I might be, I seriously might be. Because she's wearing my shirt, and I can smell her, and she smells so fucking good I can hardly stand to be here and not touch her or rip her panties off and shove my tongue and nose in her cunt. And she's so goddamn pretty, even more so when she fucks with me the way she is now, and heaven help me, I *like* her fucking with me.

She's frozen, doing long, slow blinks at me, still unsure what to make of my demand. Lightning flashes, illuminating her for a split second, and then thunder booms like an explosion, but the boom comes a few seconds later than the last one did. We're sailing away from the storm.

"I get it," I toy. "You're all bark and no bite. Are you afraid of the challenge or do you not know how to make yourself come?"

That snaps her out of her stunned stupor, and she laughs. "Do I know how to make myself come? Honey, I'm a master at personal orgasms. I just get a little bored of them after a while. It's why I was hoping for a hand—literally—in helping me out. But if you're not man enough or don't know how it's done"—her head tilts, her expression growing mocking—"then take my underwear off, and I'll show you how to pleasure a woman."

This fucking girl. I could make her come in under two minutes. She'd be ripping at my hair with her back arched, and her head thrown back and my name screamed as a battle cry against the storm.

I like this Tinsley. This fierce, confident, sexually alive woman. It's fucking hot. It's goddamn sexy as hell. And right now, I want nothing more than to watch her touch herself with my face right between her legs as she does.

"If that's what you think I need." I let that end there and hook my fingers into the sides of her thong and slide it down her long, creamy thighs. She lifts her legs in the air and takes over for me so the underwear can make its escape, and holy *fuck* this view. This motherfucking view. I'm dead. Gone. Will never be the same.

I'm salivating, desperate to put my mouth straight on her pretty pussy and eat her all night long. *Holy hell.* This was supposed to be calling her bluff, but clearly the joke's on me. I've never been this hard in my life. Certainly never wanted a woman as badly as I want her.

"Oh." She smirks tauntingly down at me from between her spread thighs. "Did you think I'd falter?"

It's so funny. I've been with a lot of women. All different kinds of women. And I always felt like the one in charge. The man who ran the show and drew all the lines. Tinsley is running the show and drawing all the lines.

And yet...

"Shut up, Tinsley and touch your clit. Rub it hard and fast and show me you can make yourself come faster than I could. If you go past two minutes, you'll get my fingers. If you go past four, you'll get my tongue, but I'm not promising pleasure from either source. And now would be a fantastic time to call me sir."

I smack her pussy when she doesn't move, but fucking hell do I feel it quiver against my fingers, its wetness coating them.

"You've got one minute and forty seconds."

She licks her lips and her hand slips between her spread thighs that my face is all but inches from. Soft fingers circle her wet opening and then drag up to her clit. I scoot forward.

"That's it, my Little Rose. Does it feel good?"

"Pretty good. How does it taste? *Sir*. Or are you simply there for the front-row show?"

I smile. It's like the sunrise after the shitshow outside our windows.

"The show is already more than I should be indulging in."

"What are you afraid will happen? You'll like how I feel more than you should?" Her words mimic mine from when I first carried her soaking wet body down to the shower.

My answer is simple. "Yes. I shouldn't like the view, and I shouldn't want to touch you as much as I do."

She huffs. "Sucks to be you and your hardline stance then."

Her fingers ring and rub her clit, swirling around and around while they increase their pace. Her hips roll up into her hand, grinding, undulating, setting a rhythm as she fucks herself that is nothing short of hypnotic. Every second she draws closer, her pussy gets that much wetter, and I grow closer to losing my absolute mind.

"Still afraid to put your money where your mouth is?" she pants, and my hands ball up the sheets, gripping them so tightly my knuckles crack. I lick my lips, and my willpower is shot. Nonexistent. A haze of lust and a burning desire for the woman who isn't mine cloud my thoughts and better sense, but I want her. I want her so badly.

"You want me to take a taste?"

Her head is back, and her neck is arched as I imagined it would be as she continues to work her clit. No one has ever touched themselves the way she's touching herself in front of me. Not ever. They're shy. They're self-conscious. They're scared. Tinsley is all fucking in and wanting more. Including me.

"Yes." Her hand snakes through the back of my hair and she tugs me. "I want you to take a taste. Even if it's not for either of our pleasure, even though I think that threat was bullshit. I don't think you could handle tasting me and not wanting me to moan and writhe for you. All for you. *Sir*."

My hands are somehow on her inner thighs, and I'm spreading her wider until she's fully open and fucking gorgeous for me. Because she's right. I can't handle not making her moan for me. I can't handle not giving her all the pleasure I'm dying to give.

She also said she doesn't want to be a good girl anymore. I can help with that.

"Little rose, you are so messy and so very, very wet. My bad girl, you're dripping on my bed. Now I have to clean it up, but I will punish you for that."

I dip in and start to lick it up, the drip of her pussy gliding along the inner angle of her ass cheek. She squeals and hikes up her hips to try to push me away, but I hold her down and lick and taste and fucking devour.

God. Hell.

I bite her inner thigh in warning. "You wanted me to taste you. That's what I'm doing. If you pull away from me again, I won't let you come. I'll tie your wrists so your fingers can't reach and keep your legs spread so they can't rub together, and I'll edge you all fucking night long."

Her eyes flash open and her chin shoots down but here is something she doesn't know about me. I'm not kidding about this. I'd love nothing more than to tie her up and bring her to the brink over and over again until she can't take another second. I'd own her. Have her begging me.

"Time's up. You didn't come. I guess that puts me in charge now."

Her bottom lip catches between her teeth. "Stone."

I grin like the devil as I use the pad of my tongue to lick up her pussy without giving any pressure to her clit. "Yes, baby girl? Is there something you need?"

She's panting. Watching. Nervous. "I... um..."

"Yes?" I ring her opening with my finger but stay away from her clit and I don't slip inside her either. I'm toying with her. Angry that she got me here. Furious that I'm touching her because I can't help myself. Hateful for what kind of man and brother this makes me that I can't stay away from the one girl who is eternally off-limits to me.

I should punish her for all those things.

If she hadn't made me want her so badly, this never would have happened.

I take her clit into my mouth and suck it hard, two fingers plunging straight in and immediately finding her front wall.

"Oh, god." She throws her head back, and her hips buck up against my mouth. "Yes. That. God, just like that."

I release her clit with a wet pop and pull my fingers back,

toying with her once more. I blow cool air on her. Lick up her pussy. And repeat the motion. Lick. Suck. Pump. Then draw back the moment she gets close.

"Christ, you're a sadist."

I smirk. "Not usually. But right now, I'm having a lot of fun making you desperate."

She tries to drag me in again with her hand in my hair, but I hold firm. "I swear, I will kill you if you don't make me come. Seriously, I'll toss you overboard into the storm."

I chuckle against her, the vibrations making her moan. "Beg me."

"What?"

"You heard me. Beg me to make you come, and I'll give you the best orgasm of your life. But you have to mean it. And I want you to call me sir. Because when I have you like this, I own every inch of your body. It's mine. Mine to do with as I please because you belong to me."

"Oh." She writhes but doesn't immediately respond. She's thinking that through, weighing her pride versus her desire. I'm not a big one for humiliation, but the thought of her sweet voice begging me makes my cock throb. "Please make me come, sir."

When she calls me sir, she gets so wet. Her body twists as if she's about to come from saying those words alone. And when I plunge two fingers back inside her, her pussy convulses and squeezes me like a fist.

I start a slow pump. Nowhere near what she needs, and I still stay away from her pulsing clit.

"Stone. *Sir.* I begged you. Now hold up your end of the bargain. *Please,*" she tacks on, panting. Her hips bounce. Her body convulses. "Actually, fuck this. I don't need you to make me come." Her hand comes back, and she starts to rub her clit again. I smile. So impatient, she has no idea what I was about to give her. "If you want to know what I taste like when I come, put your tongue inside me now because… I… oh! Yes! That."

I lick her clit, helping her fingers along while fucking her with my own until she starts come all over me. In the past, before I ever touched a woman, they knew all my rules. One night. No strings. Just fun. They could say yes or no. That was their choice, and I was fine either way, but the rules were finite, and rarely did I make exceptions for a repeat.

All this felt so important before. Like the boundary between me and the woman. Not just physically, but emotionally.

But I want Tinsley to cross all my lines. I want her to deconstruct my boundaries.

I want Tinsley. Plain. Simple. Wholly.

I'm in awe of her. The fact that she did what she did to get here. That she's taking her life and her mental health into her own hands. I like her defiance, her strong, willful spirit, and her impudent mouth. I like her voice and laugh and the way she looks at me like she wants me—and not because I'm Stone Fritz the way ninety-nine percent of every other woman I've been with does.

Simply put, I like every fucking thing about her.

It's not even that she's easily the most beautiful woman I've ever seen. It's not even that she's strong yet vulnerable in the same breath. It's that she's unafraid to be who she is whereas that's the thing I'm most afraid of being.

Being myself is what's failed me the most.

I hate the man I am.

I want to be better than him.

But how is that possible? How can I rise above that when I crumble at the first brush of temptation? I am undeniably infatuated with Tinsley Monroe and I'm not sure there's a way to stop it.

I slip my tongue inside her along with my fingers while she

continues to rub her clit. I taste her cum. I lick every drop of it. I want more of it. More of her. Over and over again, I want that. And not just for tonight. I have seven days left on this boat.

Seven days before we have to part ways and return to reality.

She sags into the bed, a sated smile on her lips and her arm over her eyes as she gives a small, incredulous laugh.

"I should keep you and your wicked mouth and talented fingers between my thighs, even if you get off on torturing me. I don't think I've come like that in... oh... yeah—" Her head pops up and her eyes meet mine, crinkling at the edges and looking contrite. "Is it awful to say I can't remember the last time I came that hard?"

Pride puffs my chest while simultaneously making me feel like shit. I shake my head, at a loss with that one.

"Do you still want me to call you sir?" She smirks. She thinks she's being taunting and sassy.

I give her cunt a dirty lick from her ass all the way up to her clit. "You know I was only half serious about all that sir stuff, right?"

"What?" she screeches and then gasps as I swirl my tongue.

I laugh. "I won't lie, it gets me hard as hell, so if you want to call me that, I certainly won't mind. I like to dominate, and I like control in the bedroom, but I'm not a Dom, and you sure as hell aren't submissive."

"Oh my god! You're such a jerk!"

She smacks my head, and I suck her sensitive clit into my mouth until she bucks and yanks at my hair, trying to pull me back. "We both know you liked it. Lie to yourself and me, but it's true. If you didn't like what I just did with you, you wouldn't have come so hard."

"Maybe it's because the name Stone sounds stupid. Like calling you a rock. Any name, including sir, is better than Stone."

I bite her inner thigh, making her yelp and rip some more at my hair. "Maybe. But likely not. Now that you look calm, you should get some sleep. I'm going back to check the navigation station to make sure we're still on course."

Before she can say anything, I get up and leave the room. Because if I don't, I'll fuck her. And then she'll really be mine when being mine isn't in the cards for us.

8

TINSLEY

For the longest time I stare up at the ceiling feeling the boat list and violently sway beneath me, and listen to the storm outside. Stone left to go make sure we don't hit a rock or an island or get swallowed by the storm and the sea. Speaking of, it's getting lighter, less intense. That's all good, but I'm no longer thinking about the storm. It's ironic. I wanted him to make me come to take my mind off the storm, but now that he did that, I can't stop thinking about him instead.

For one, I can't believe we did that.

That was *so* not part of our plan or pact.

For another, I can't believe *I* did that.

I've never been sexually shy, but I've never been sexually aggressive either. Probably because I've only slept with two guys, and one of those is his brother. I trusted Forest with my life, with my body, and with my heart. He's one of the best men on the planet, and I hated breaking his heart. I loved him. I just wasn't *in love* with him anymore.

We were kids in love, but I started to feel it. That drift. That lacking. That need for more. Then the stalker came, and I clung to Forest because he was safe and comforting and made it easy for me to do so. Hell, he encouraged it. I clung to him for far longer than I should have. Part of me knew it, I think, but everyone pushed us together, with Forest pushing the hardest. It wasn't until Terrance Howard was in prison and I could take a deep breath that was my own that I came to the horrifying conclusion that I was no longer in love with him.

It took me a year of feeling like that, hoping and praying that type of love would return. And when it didn't, I had to end it. It wasn't fair to either of us to keep it going. He was my childhood sweetheart, but we outgrew each other. He just refused to see it or accept it.

Some days, he still refuses to see it and accept it.

So maybe that makes what I just did with Stone even worse. Forest would flip his shit if he knew I was here—Stone wasn't wrong about that—and he'd absolutely lose his fucking mind if he found out his brother just went down on me and gave me a better orgasm than he ever did. That thought makes me cringe and feel like the worst sort of woman for thinking it.

But I'm not with Forest anymore.

And I'm tired of everyone telling me what I can and cannot do. Who I should and should not want. How I should and should not live my life. Where do I fit into that? Where is my say? Maybe I should care that it's my ex's brother, but right now, I don't. I want to take what I want for the first time in my life. I want what we just did. I want to spend the next week with Stone inside me.

It won't go beyond that. I know it won't.

Everything we're already doing is a secret, so what's one more?

Maybe that makes me a bad person, but it's not easy finding a partner you can trust in my world. The entertainment industry is dog-eat-dog. Everyone wants something from you, but Stone doesn't care about any of that. I've known him my entire life. Our families are very strongly connected. He's a billionaire. A doctor in Boston. Our lives are a million miles apart. It'll be this week and nothing more.

I glance down at my body. I'm wearing his T-shirt and nothing else.

A deranged laugh rips from my lungs. I can't believe I had him like that between my legs. Not even my gynecologist has seen that much of me. I begged him to make me come and I called him sir. The bastard was pulling a move on me with that, but he was right. I did like it. I liked everything he was doing and saying because it was so different from anything I've had before.

Maybe I'm not as innocent as I thought I was. Or maybe I just don't want to be.

Maybe that version of me is dead or dying, and the woman I want to be is finally coming out of her shell. The woman who takes charge and goes after what she wants. Who doesn't let anyone else dictate her life.

I don't want to be a bad person and I'd never want to hurt Forest more than I already have, but... this is the first time I've ever gone rogue, seeking freedom and adventure. I like it. This feeling welling up inside me, it's a strange sort of confidence.

I cover my face with my hands, and my legs kick up and down as I let out a shrill, girlish giggle. Am I really considering this? Am I actually going to do it?

I shoot out of bed, nearly tripping over the blanket Stone tossed on the floor. I throw it back on the bed and head for the door. "Fuck it. What happens on the boat, stays on the boat." It's like Vegas. And when the week is over, our fling will fade into a memory—hopefully a happy, wild one—and nothing more.

With my heart hammering in my chest and my fingers tingling with nerves, I make my way out of the bedroom and up the short flight of stairs to the main living area. I can still hear the rain pounding the deck on the ceiling above me, but the wind has all but died down, making it easier to walk without constantly feeling like I'm about to topple over.

The galley is cool and quiet but there is no escaping the humidity and electricity in the air. I hear a noise from the control area and head in that direction, following the trail of lights that illuminates the wood floors.

Stone is sitting in his chair, using the mouse to click something on the screen. He's still shirtless, only wearing his shorts, and I take a minute to admire the muscular lines of his body and the colorful ink adorning his skin. He must hear me because his head whips in my direction, and when he sees me standing here, he sits back and stares at me. His eyes are volcanic as they drag up along my bare legs to the hem of his shirt that hits me about mid-thigh, before he continues his perusal, taking in my braless state.

I smirk when he snags on my breasts, bouncing and swaying as I walk toward him. Good. I hope he's hard. It's exactly how I want him. Without waiting for an invitation, I walk right in and straddle him. He makes a pained noise, his palms landing on my hips to hold me in place.

"You're supposed to be sleeping," he admonishes, but the way he's looking at me, sleep is the last thing he wants me to do.

"The storm is letting up."

He nods, his palms skimming down until they reach my bare thighs only to drag back up to safe territory as if he's struggling to maintain his control with me sitting on him like this. The shirt is just barely covering my pussy, but he refuses to look down.

"It's headed north, and we're headed south. We'll reach Nassau by morning."

"Good. Do you need to stay out here?"

"Are you planning on sleeping in my bed tonight?"

I grin. "Depends."

"On?"

"You."

He licks his lips and leans in ever so slightly, and I loop my hands around his neck to draw closer to him. "What about me, baby girl? You got what you wanted from me."

I roll my hips forward, finding the hard ridge in his shorts. My lips part as it hits me in just the right place. "Not everything," I whisper breathlessly.

"Jesus, Tinsley," he grunts, his hands back on my inner thighs, trailing up and making me shiver with anticipation. "You make it impossible to do the right thing."

His thumb brushes my spread-open pussy, and he growls when he realizes I never put my underwear back on and I'm completely naked under his shirt.

"All I've ever done is the right thing. I'm tired of it."

"And all I'll I've ever done is the wrong thing. I'm trying to change that."

"Those two don't dance together in the dark all that well. So what do one wrong and one right equal?"

"A fucking mess?"

I lean in and nip his chin. "Good. I've been dying to get dirty."

He holds me still. "Fucking you is crossing a line I swore I wouldn't."

I roll my hips again and his pupils blow out, black and dangerous and sexy as hell. "Do you want me, Stone?" It's a rhetorical question. I know he does. His thumb is still rubbing my clit almost like he can't help himself, and his other hand is gripping my thigh so tight I wouldn't be shocked if he left marks. He's a man reaching the limit of his self-control.

Still, I want him to answer me. Because if he truly doesn't want to do this, then I won't push it. I'll go back to being distant and give him his space. But if he wants me, if he's willing to cross this line with me, I want to dive headfirst into the deep end of the ocean and see how far beneath the surface he can take me.

"You know I do. Wanting you isn't the issue."

He's right and I'm being selfish. I tickle my fingers across his smooth jaw and through his dark hair. "I don't want to be a regret or a mistake to you, and I don't want to cause you more hassle or trouble than I already have. You're working on something. It's why you're here, and I'd never want to derail that." I kiss his neck. "We'll blame tonight on the storm and tomorrow it'll be like it never happened."

I move to stand, but he catches the back of my neck before I can get far. "It's already tomorrow. And it's already too late to stop." With that, he pulls me in and slams my mouth to his. "I don't *want* to stop," he growls against me. "Even when I should." His lips take over, his hold forceful as his tongue immediately enters my mouth and clashes with mine. It's manic and rough and deliciously untamed.

I drop back down on his lap, straight onto the hard length of him, my hands up in his hair and across his shoulders. His free hand snakes up my shirt, squeezing my ass and pressing me against him as he devours me, both of us grinding, moaning, and groaning like two teenagers trying to beat the clock before their parents get home.

I run my hands all over him, wanting to feel the hard planes and firm ridges of his shoulders, chest, and abs. This isn't gentle and it's far from polite. He starts to lift my shirt and I help him yank it over my head, our mouths only breaking for that half second. It's barely enough time for us to catch our breath.

He cups my tits and groans only to break our kiss and push me back until I'm leaning against the desk in front of the navigation equipment, fully splayed out for him. His heated gaze rakes over every inch of my body, and I have to fight the chills that sweep over me. He's unapologetically fucking me with his eyes, and I try to keep my breathing steady, but that look he's giving me makes it nearly impossible.

He shakes his head, his full bottom lip tight with tension. "Fuck, you are one beautiful woman." Reaching up, he squeezes my tits together in his large hands as he dips to nibble and kiss along my jaw and down my neck then to my cleavage. "One week, Tinsley. That's all it is and all it'll ever be."

"What? I don't understand. You called me yours."

"Tinsley," he rasps, uncertainty warring with lust.

I sniffle, my voice distraught. "I thought you loved me. I thought that's what calling me yours means."

His head shoots up, and I can't fight my giggle at his stricken expression.

"Fucking brat." He punishes me by pinching my nipple until I squirm on his lap.

"That's for the sir bullshit you pulled on me." I pat his cheek. "Don't worry, baby cakes, there's no love here. How's this?" My fingers glide through his hair, holding the sides of his head as his lips meet the crook of my neck and slide back down, his teeth grazing along the swell of each breast until I gasp. "I'm yours for this week, and you're mine. Only because I'm a jealous and possessive girl who doesn't like to share, and you're a Fritz man with a bit of a reputation as a ladies' man."

"Ladies' man?"

I sigh in feigned resignation. "Fine. You're right. That term is old-fashioned. You're a player."

He chokes on a strangled laugh and comes up to meet my gaze. Smartly, he doesn't bother denying it.

I cup his strong jaw and stare into his green eyes. "Seriously, though, I'd like to have some fun with you this week. But the moment we dock back in Miami, it all ends. No messiness. No ugliness. No one knows but us. We go our separate ways and it never happened. Our secret stays here."

Simply put, we both have too much to lose, and it's not like there's the option or potential for anything real to bloom between us.

"I don't have any condoms here. Sex wasn't part of my plan for this week."

"I'm on the pill and I've been tested."

"You're good with no condom?" he checks.

"I am if you are."

"I've never fucked a woman without one." He stares quietly at me for a moment, his eyes glazed. In one smooth motion, he takes my hips and lifts me until I'm standing. I stare down at him, confused and worried he's somehow taking exception to my rules when he leans forward and starts to run his pointer finger back and forth along my slit while his mouth eats at my breasts.

I suck in a sharp breath, my eyes closing, unable to fight it as pleasure spikes through me. His hot breath falls across my nipples and I shiver, my legs suddenly shaky and ready to give out as he picks up his pace without applying any pressure. It's making me unbearably wet and needy, my skin hot and prickling. My hands fall to the table behind me to hold me up and I angle my hips toward him.

Maybe it's all this newfound and uncharted freedom at my fingertips, but I've never been so brazen. I like it. I like this version of me. The one Stone can't seem to help himself with as his hands drag up and down the curve of my waist and along my ribs. A swell of nerves takes hold of me.

I'm about to fuck my ex's brother. A man who is infinitely more experienced than I am

He starts to slide his shorts off his hips and what if I can't handle all that he comes with? What if it's too much for—

"Holy shit! You're pierced."

He pauses and looks up at me through hooded eyes, a devilish smirk twisting his lips. "Only this one. You should see Vander if you think this is a lot."

I shake my head, gnawing on my bottom lip, unable to drag my gaze away. "I'd rather not." I swirl my finger in the general vicinity of his dick. "Um. What do you call that and what does it do?" Because not only is his dick big—I mean, all of him is tall and muscular without being the overly bulky sort of big—but yeah, he's not only huge but he has that.

"It's a penis and it does many things."

I glare at him.

He can't keep the amusement from his expression or voice. "Fine. No jokes. It's called a deep shaft reverse Prince Albert. You'll love it. It'll make you come. That's what it does."

Interesting. "Can I touch it?"

He groans, his head falling back. "Baby girl, you're killing me right now. All sweet and doe-eyed and innocent about to be corrupted. Yes, you can fucking touch it. Touch away. Play with it. Lick it. Whatever you want. But then you're going to get fucked by it."

Jesus. I'm sweating.

I slip to my knees between his spread thighs and his cock jerks, practically hitting his abs. "He's jumpy."

Stone chuckles lightly. "Despite your assessment of me, it's not every day I have a beautiful and eager woman kneeling for me."

Reaching out I grip him in my hand, firm yet soft, like velvet over, well, stone if you'll forgive the pun. It pulses in my hand, and my empty core clenches. Tentatively, I drag my hand up his shaft until I reach the barbell just beneath his head. It's a hard little ball but easily moves from side to side.

"Fuck," he hisses. I do it again, only this time I bring my tongue in on the action, rolling the other end of the barbell that comes out of his slit. It's an odd feeling, but very cool at the same time.

"Good?" I check.

"Too good."

I preen a little from the praise and continue to lick and play with him, watching his reaction the entire time. I love this power over him. The ability to give him pleasure and watch him lose it a little. Once I'm feeling more confident and comfortable, I stand and place my hands on his shoulders. With our eyes locked, I straddle him again, hovering in the air.

He plays with my pussy, but I'm already more than ready for him. With one hand on his dick and his other on my hip, he lines himself up at my entrance, and slowly, I start to sink down. It's insanely intimate like this, more so than I was prepared for. Our eyes are locked, and our bodies are close, and he's sliding inside me. Stretching me. Making me feel every inch of him including his piercing.

Once he gets halfway in, he thrusts up, shooting all the way inside me, straight to the hilt. "Holy, god, Stone." My head flies back and my hands rip at his shoulders.

"That's it. *Fuuuck.*" He blows out a heavy breath, his forehead tight and tense, his face flushed. "Shit, Little Rose. I wasn't expecting it to be..." Another breath. "You good?" he questions, his voice ragged and rough.

"Too good," I say, throwing his words back at him. I'm panting. And *full.*

He glances down between us, and something crosses his face. Something I can't quite read. "All fucking mine," he murmurs so low I'm not even sure I heard him correctly.

His hands grasp my hips and then he raises me up before he slams me back down, his eyes glued to the spot where we're connected. I gasp and whimper, digging my nails in.

"Come on, baby girl. Take me. Start bouncing on my cock. Have some fun before I really start to fuck you."

Oh my god, what have I gotten myself into? I'll never survive him, and we've just started. With my feet on the floor, I push up and then drop back down, feeling him slide in and out of me without resistance. Then there's his cock ring. It glides along my front wall and when he's seated all the way inside of me? There are no words. Only tingles and deep, deep pleasure.

The kind of pleasure that crackles at your vision and flares like fire through your limbs.

He rolls my hips while he pulls me forward and my clit rubs against the base of his pelvis. I cry out, already lost. I'm all sensation. Especially when he starts sucking on my tits that are right up in his face.

Sweat gleams on his shoulders and chest as his lips part with an exhale before his mouth captures mine, moving urgently. I suck in a breath as he plunges into me, shooting his hips up and using his grip on my hips to pull me down onto him. His tongue fucks my mouth at the same pace and I moan into him, feeling the thick ridge of his cock with every grinding thrust.

His hands slide back, groping and squeezing my ass and using it as leverage to push me forward. That's how he fucks me. Alternating between deep, hard jabs and slower, rutting undulations. It's mind-bending and soul-twisting, and I'm so drunk on it, I can't do anything other than hold on and try to fuck him back.

Tearing his mouth from mine he kisses down my throat to my chest where he catches my nipple in his mouth, quick and rough, and I yelp when he bites me, using his teeth and making sure I feel it. My hands wrap around his neck, and I draw him closer.

"Stone..." A single word. It's all I can manage. I squeeze my eyes shut, getting so close I can hardly stand it. All that foreplay, the way he continues to work my clit even as he fucks me, the way his cock and piercing rub my front wall as he does that. Nothing has ever felt better than this.

I roll my hips, rubbing myself against him, taking him in as deep as I can.

It's not enough. Not for him.

Suddenly he's standing, taking me with him, and pulling out of me as my ass lands on the desk. He shoves the keyboard and mouse out of the way, and then he's bending me all the way back. My thighs wrap around his hips, and I whimper as he slams back into me with a powerful fucking thrust that I swear tickles my belly.

"Now you're feeling me. And fuck am I feeling you. Your cunt is like heaven."

He bends me in half, his chest grazing mine, and I open my eyes to find him right there, watching me, his face above mine, our lips barely an inch apart. My pussy clenches around his cock and he opens his mouth with a primal groan. His cock thickens, and his pace picks up. My hands shoot above my head, plastered to the wall on either side of the screen so my head doesn't smash back into it.

Other than that, I'm helpless. At his mercy. Loving every inch he's giving me and the way he rubs my G-spot every time. I moan, holding his eyes and pushing into every thrust. I don't want him to stop. Not ever. It's too good. And I'm close. So very close.

And the way he's taking me...

Eyes all over me, hands on my tits and hips, and pressing down on my lower belly. His mouth is everywhere, kissing and nipping and tasting. Warmth spreads through me making my legs shake and my eyes roll back in my head.

"Please," I beg, the words tumbling out of me. "Please. Oh god, please. Yes."

"Baby girl, whatever you want, I'm going to give it to you. All week, I'm going to give it to you. Every fucking chance I get, I'm going to be inside you, hearing and feeling you come for me. There is no way it can only be this once. No fucking way."

He dips in until there's no space between us, our sweaty chests one, our mouths sharing moans and grunts as his thrusts grow harder and faster. And then I detonate. Explode.

My pussy tightens around his cock, and his barbell rubs my sweet spot, and I scream, my eyes pinching shut and my mind splintering.

His ragged breaths pant against my cheek, his hands squeezing my tits and driving me higher.

"Oh, fuck. Tinsley. Fuck." He growls, his teeth sinking into my shoulder as he shudders and then stills. My body continues to jerk, milking everything he's got from him, his cock in so deep as he comes.

He collapses against me, pressing me down into the table, his cock giving me one last spasm that has me trembling.

Holy shit.

I don't know what I was expecting, but that...

He stays inside me, making no move to pull out. I just fucked my ex-boyfriend's brother. And maybe I should care. In fact, I know I should. But all I can think about is doing it again.

Shit.

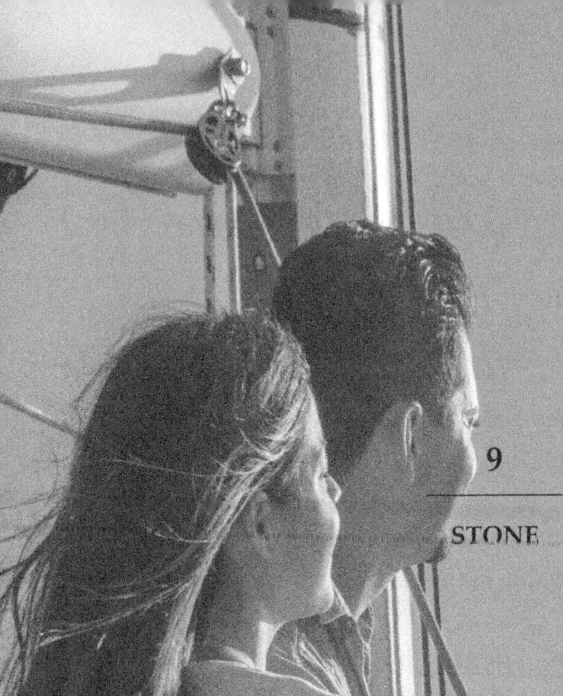

9

STONE

What the hell am I doing? And why is she so goddamn addictive?

Rain continues splattering against the deck and windows. What was a steady pummeling is now more of an intermittent tropical shower. Tinsley is fast asleep, her nude body curled into mine, and if I didn't feel like a total and complete asshole before, I do when I realize Tinsley is the first woman to sleep in my bed since my second year of medical school, and that night there was no cuddling or holding the way there is now. There certainly wasn't any pleasure at the sight of her the way I feel right now when I glance down at Tinsley beside me.

So again, what the hell am I doing?

But more importantly, what the hell is she doing to me?

I'm already thinking about the next time I can be inside of her. And the time after that. I'm chasing the end—the moment where I've had enough and she's out of my system—only there's a small voice in the back of my head laughing at that ridiculous notion.

I have a haunting premonition there will be no end to wanting her.

I suppose that's karmic justice. I've been a player, just as she said. Sleeping with women and moving on to the next without a second's thought or backward glance. I was always honest. Always upfront. I had no time or desire to try for more, and no one held my interest in a way that challenged me to change that.

Until now.

I didn't see her and Forest together a lot. They were kids, and then they were in LA. The last time I saw them together was here on the boat, and they spent most of the weekend fighting about one thing or another. I know how Forest felt about her. I know how he still feels, how he's been distant with all of us over the last year since their break.

But Tinsley is done with him and has been for a while.

It shouldn't make this easier for me, but somehow it does.

I run a possessive hand down her spine and curl it around her hip, dragging her closer. She doesn't stir. She's either an incredibly heavy sleeper or I wore her out. In addition to the fun tongue fucking I gave her and the pounding against the navigation desk, I fucked her two more times in this bed.

The sex wasn't what I'm used to, but that might be what made it better than anything I've ever had before. The fact that I took her bare only heightened that. There's something about her, and with how quickly I reacted to her that first night, I can't help but wonder now if she's somehow been there all along, but I ignored it or pretended it away because she was Forest's. It wasn't just the flash of her naked body that stirred this up. There was a reason I had her keep her distance from me.

Part of me knew I wasn't safe around her, but moreover, she wasn't safe around me.

Now it's too late, and the man in me hates what I've done to

Forest. The *I'm a dirtbag* part who is staring at the naked and dreamy girl beside him says it's only for a week, so no harm, no foul. I slip down the sheet covering her and take in the soft lines of her body. Her full, perfect tits and peach nipples beg for my mouth, and I slide lower until I'm able to capture one between my teeth.

She squirms and hisses, her eyes still closed. "That hurts."

"But I bet it feels good too."

I get a sleepy smile for that.

My finger slides between her legs and... "Christ, how are you already this wet?"

She giggles lightly, and the sound makes my chest inflate, and a smile of my own springs to my lips. "Because I was having a dirty dream about you."

I open my mouth wide, taking as much of her breast in as I can. She moans, her hands in my hair, pressing me deeper. "So I did this to you? What was your dream about, Little Rose?"

"You know Rose is the character who arguably let her guy die, right?"

"True, but I like the name for you. Roses are pretty and smell good but have annoying thorns that like to poke. Just like you. Now answer my question."

"You were going down on me."

Immediately I flip her onto her back and trail kisses down her belly. "Go on. How did I eat you? Was it soft and gentle, or did I eat you like your pussy is the last meal I'm ever going to have because I'm on death row?"

"Death row. You hiked my legs up and made me scream."

Fuck. Like holy fuck. My heart gives a thump as if to say, *dude, you sure we can only have one week of her*?

I've never wanted to keep any woman, and it's not because I'm anti-relationship. I'm not. My parents are the happiest fucking couple on the planet, as are all my uncles and aunts. The notion of love and forever doesn't scare me. I simply liked being single and wasn't ready for that yet. Being single fit me. It was easy with zero drama. I figured that'd come later when I met the right someone. That now was the time for fun and not serious.

But Tinsley Monroe is fucking with my head and my head cannot be fucked with on this. She doesn't belong to me. She never will. I cannot want, I cannot imagine, I cannot pretend. Not where she's concerned.

That doesn't mean I won't fulfill her dirty dreams about me. I hike her up and spread her legs until she's gorgeously open and exposed to me, and ring her clit with my tongue. Her hips jolt, and she moans—her sounds make me hard like nothing else—while her fingers find my hair.

"Is that what you dreamed about?"

"Yes. Oh, yes. Christ, your tongue. Do it again. Do it all. Make me come. And whatever you do, don't stop until we have to."

It's as if she's echoing my thoughts.

"Your wish is my command."

I eat her until she comes. Until she's screaming and writhing and unable to take another second of the pleasure and pressure I'm giving her. Then, in one smooth motion, because I can't wait another second, I slide inside her. And her eyes—those pretty violet eyes—they hold mine. All sweet and innocent and drunk on lust.

This girl affects me like nothing else.

I thrust into her, my hips smacking against hers as I continuously slide inside her tight body until we're both weak in the knees and our minds are quiet.

Mason: I shouldn't have to ask Vander to check your ship's navigation to let us know that you're still alive.

I smirk through my yawn as I rub a hand up and down my

face. I fell back to sleep only to wake to the loud ping of my phone. I had the volume up in case the Coast Guard or my parents were trying to reach me. Blinking, I shift in the bed, looking to my left and finding the space Tinsley occupied empty. After I took Tinsley again, I sailed us into port and then came back to bed and crashed.

Me: But you did, so you know we not only survived but made it into Nassau.

Vander is a cybersecurity company owner and CEO by day, and by night, he's one of the world's best hackers. I had no illusions that he was tracking me, and I know better than to argue about it.

Owen: And you see, all I caught from that was we and something tells me you're not talking about Benthesicyme.

I stare at his text, reading it over a few times as the words don't quite make sense. And then it dawns on me. Shit.

Mason: The plot thickens. Spill. Who's the honey you're shacking up with?

Double shit.

Me: No one. I was talking about Benthesicyme.

Vander: You wouldn't lie to your best friends and family, would you?

Triple shit.

That's not something we do. It's a pact, more or less. Mason comes from a family of football royalty and it's his first year playing in the NFL. Vander's mother owned and ran Monroe Securities, and Vander dropped out of MIT after being arrested for hacking—though the arrest has magically disappeared—to take over the company. Owen is Owen Fucking Fritz, the eldest grandson in our Fritz family, and with that, especially in Boston, famous simply for being a billionaire Fritz. I'm also a Fritz, son of the eldest Fritz son and heir to the Abbot-Fritz foundation.

So yeah, trust in our world isn't all that easy to come by and I won't be the one to break it. Even if I won't give details.

Me: Fine. Yes, I'm here with someone.

Owen: And who is someone? Do we know her?

Yes, of course they know her. Mason and Vander's dads are best friends with her father. They were in Central Square together, a famous rock band together for fuck's sake. Plus, Owen's little sister, Wren, is best friends with Tinsley.

Me: She's just a girl.

Mason: Except aren't you there to get your mental game back?

Me: She needed a bit of rescuing, and I was in the right place at the right time. That's all it is. For real. I'm still here getting my mental shit back together.

I hope. Part of me feels like being with Tinsley derailed some of that, but it's too late now.

Owen: Best wishes.

Confetti crackles across my screen, and I groan even as I reluctantly smile.

Owen: On not focusing on the woman you're rescuing. I'm sure that'll work out well for you. But more importantly, if you're saving her, then you're already headed in the right direction for coming back to work.

Owen works with me at Boston Children's Hospital where he's a general surgeon.

Me: Thanks. Here's hoping. I'll catch up with you later.

Mason: Enjoy your rescue mission.

Vander: And remember, if you do want to tell us about her or anything else, it's us. And this is where it stays. But I promise not to dig either if you want it to stay between you and your dick.

Me: I appreciate that. I'll be in touch.

I climb out of bed and take a quick shower, enjoying the few minutes of quiet. Hot water cascades over me, energizing my limbs and relaxing my muscles.

Immediately, images of last night flicker through my head, and my tired dick jerks. Jesus. How is that even possible right now? My forehead plants onto the marble wall. A week of Tinsley. It'll be a week of wanting her constantly. Of not being able to get enough because I know our time will come to a fast end. All she has to do is look at me or smile or simply breathe, and I'm harder than steel.

Better still, she seems to be as insatiable as I feel.

I've crossed the Rubicon. My die is cast.

Time to go find my girl and figure out what's next.

10

STONE

We don't stay in Nassau longer than it takes to refuel and restock food and drinks. Nassau has too many ships. Too many tourists. Too many eyes. Tinsley is hellbent that she'll be spotted, and I believe her because it wouldn't be tough. It's one of the largest ports in the Bahamas.

Instead, we head east toward Eleuthera and Lighthouse Beach. Nothing is as clear and beautifully wondrous as the water and beaches of the Bahamas. It only took us four hours to sail here, especially now that the water is calm and the sun burned off all the remaining clouds.

I drop anchor about a hundred yards out, unable to get closer because of the sand belt and reefs that surround the island, not to mention, we don't want to be too visible if anyone else comes. Right now, the beach is empty, the storm more than likely having kept people away, and the fact that there's not a lot on this part of the island because of the sharp craters of rock that line the beach.

We eat lunch on the ship, enjoying the stillness and quiet, though Tinsley doesn't know how to stay still or quiet for long.

She's always humming or singing something, whether she's aware of it or not. You'd think something like that would be annoying, but with her, it isn't. The way she sings is sweet and warm like honey sliding down your throat, and when she puts some emotion into it, her voice gives me chills.

"Do you want to swim to the island?" I ask after we're done, and everything is cleaned up.

She peers out at the pretty, deserted beach. "We're by the reef, right? Are there sharks?"

I smirk and take her hand, leading her down to the transom. No jumping off the side of the boat today. "There are sharks and a lot of fish, but none of them will bother you. I have flippers and snorkels we can put on to help us swim, and a bag that will keep our stuff dry. What do you say?"

"I say let's do it, but if I get eaten by a shark, you'll have to be the one to explain it to my parents."

"Deal. Or you could call them."

She rolls her eyes at me. "And tell them I'm here with you?"

I shrug. "What are you afraid will happen?"

She sighs. "My parents aren't the problem. Not really. They love me and worry, and after the way my stalker terrorized me for years, I don't blame them for that."

Darkness creeps over me. I remember her stalker. I remember Forest talking about him. Some dude named Terrance or something. He told me about the threatening letters the guy would send her. I think she was only seventeen when they started, and I remember she moved in with Forest when he started at UCLA so she wouldn't be living alone. He liked that. He liked that she leaned on him, and he felt like her hero and protector. Then they caught the guy and there was a brief trial, but I believe in the end, he made a plea deal and is in prison.

"It's everyone else. It's my agent, my manager, and even my label. My career and my life have become theirs and not mine.

Especially with my manager, Apollo. He's forceful with the things he wants me to do and has trouble hearing the word no. Not to mention he gives me the creeps. I feel like he's always there watching me and not giving me any room to breathe."

I stare at the side of her face, and I see it. The exhaustion. The hopelessness. The fear. I've seen that in my own reflection a lot lately.

"Part of why I came out here was to try to figure everything out. To give myself space and time and build up the strength and courage to do what I need to do."

"Which is?"

She gnaws on her lip, her eyes still on the sandy beach in the distance. "Fire everyone. Not my parents. I love my parents. But I likely need to set some boundaries there too. Remind them I'm an adult and a woman now since I haven't shown it. I've been weak and timid, but it's not who or what I want to be anymore. I want to take control, and I want to be in charge, and I want them to answer to me and not the other way around."

"So do it. I think what you did is pretty brave. You came down here, found your way to my boat, snuck on it, and hid it from everyone. You took the steps you needed to take, and now you can take the rest."

She turns to me, glancing up into my eyes. Hers are so vivid and beautiful against the sun and the water they're almost too much. "You think so?" she asks, her expression serious.

I lean in and kiss her. It's not a kiss for sex. It's not a kiss based on lust. It's a kiss because I have to kiss her right now.

I cup her face in my hand and press our foreheads together. "Yes, I think so. I think Tinsley Monroe can do anything she sets her pretty little heart and head on. It's your life, Little Rose. Be the thorns when you need to be and the petals when you don't."

Her lips touch mine, her hands on the back of my neck, and for a few minutes, we kiss and kiss and kiss. Then I gear us both up as we laugh at how goofy we each look in our snorkel masks and flippers. Tinsley snaps a picture, only to shake her head and immediately delete it. I don't have to ask why she deleted it. Pictures are dangerous in our world. In our situation.

We dive into the cool, clear water and swim all the way to shore, removing our gear and dropping it off to the side while I pull things out of my backpack and set up a few towels for us to lie on.

For a while, we're both quiet. Lost to our thoughts. Me thinking about the boy, about medicine, about who I've been and who I want to be, and how I can make that happen when she interrupts my thoughts.

"You know, I've traveled all around the world. I've been to hundreds of countries on five different continents, and I can't remember the last time I saw anything as beautiful as this."

My head rolls and I squint at her through the lenses of my sunglasses. Tinsley is wearing nothing but a black bikini and sunglasses, her long hair up in a high ponytail splayed across her towel. She looks unbelievably hot like this and yet quietly adorable as she scrunches her nose.

"How is that possible?"

She shrugs. "Because I go from city to city, country to country. I don't have time to sightsee or explore. I can't remember the last time I had this much downtime. It's all write, record, tour, and repeat. And throw in a movie or two in there as well."

"You're taking the time now," I point out.

"Because I was literally losing it. I've been writing songs while I'm here, and it's the first time that it's felt natural and not forced in so long."

"Do you not enjoy it anymore?"

She releases an exhausted and sad sigh. Her head rests on my shoulder, and I wrap a hand around her waist, pulling her in close. "I love it," she voices after a quiet moment of listening to the waves and seagulls. "I love the music, I should say. I love performing on stage. I love my fans. I'm starting to love making movies because it's challenging and different for me. I don't love the stuff that comes with it. The way I'm handled and how my life is run for me. I don't love feeling like I'm missing out on things because I always have to be somewhere else. I don't love being followed by the press, photographed, and lied about as they trash me simply because it's easy to do and makes for good clickbait."

My thumb drags up and down her hip, lightly playing with the string of her bottoms. "But now you're going to change the things you can. The rest, I guess, you have to live with if you love what you do."

"True. What about you?" she asks. "Did you become a doctor because that's what most of the people in your family do? You also haven't told me what brought you out here. I haven't pushed it, but you know all my dark and ugly, and I'd like to know yours."

"I nearly killed a kid," I admit, staring out at the shoreline because I can't look at her as I say this. "I was reckless and lazy and made stupid assumptions I had no business making because I thought I was above it all. I was arrogant—so fucking arrogant—and it nearly cost the kid his life. It would have if his mother and the nurse on his case hadn't pushed me the way they did. After that, I lost confidence. I was second-guessing everything, afraid to get my hands dirty in a trauma, and when you work in the emergency department, that's a dangerous thing. We run at a sprint and use our medical knowledge and intuition to guide us. But I was an asshole. I had always been an asshole. I thought I was better than and above everything, and when I learned I wasn't, it shook me to my core."

I can feel her eyes boring into the side of my face.

"The hospital stepped in and told me to take a couple of weeks off to get my shit together or I shouldn't bother coming back." I swallow and turn to look at her. "But here's the thing.

Despite the fact that I'm a world-class asshole, I want to be a doctor. Not simply because it's the Fritz way, but because I remember being a kid and watching my father, uncles, aunts, and grandfather save lives. I remember thinking they were superheroes. I remember thinking being a doctor was the coolest thing ever. And truth be told, it is. I love being a doctor. I love the high and adrenaline rush that comes from being in a trauma and saving a life. I love telling the parents of a child that their kid is going to be okay and watching the fear and nerves turn to pure elation. It was the only thing about myself I considered to be selfless and good."

She thinks about this for a moment, and thankfully there isn't a drop of pity in her eyes as she slides her sunglasses up her head. "So how do you get your shit together and your confidence back?"

I give her a *fuck if I know* shrug. "I spent a few days studying. Going over disease processes and symptoms and everything else I could. I didn't study much in med school because I didn't think I'd have to. My arrogance knew no bounds. But all that studying I finally did wasn't enough. I was hoping I'd come out here and take this time to be alone with my thoughts and rearrange my outlook on myself and life, and something would click for me. Being alone on the seas, you have to rely on the same things we rely on in the emergency room."

She twists until she's on top of me, her arms wrap around my neck, and her eyes pierce into mine. "You let me stay on the boat even when you didn't want me to. You got us through the storm. We survived it because of you. You were calm and collected and knew exactly what you were doing. But more than that, you went out of your way to reassure me that you wouldn't let anything bad happen to us, and I'm not even talking about the fooling around. Selfish assholes wouldn't have done all that you've done for me. I was scared, but never at any point did I not have total faith and trust in you. You made a mistake, and it knocked you down a necessary peg. You're trying to do better and be better. Not everyone would take that path. Some would give up or not care enough to change. I think you're amazing for doing that. From where I'm looking, you already have your shit together, and I can see the man you want to be there inside you. You just have to see it and believe it for yourself."

My heart thrashes painfully in my chest, her words pinching a nerve I've been reluctant to feel. Her faith in me does something to me I can't explain. It makes me want to be that man she sees because the idea of proving her wrong or disappointing her isn't an option I'm willing to allow. I want to be a good guy for her. A hero. A savior. Someone she can rely on when she needs it.

What we're doing is stupid and reckless and probably cruel and selfish. But I'm here with her, and it feels good. It feels right. Like the best thing I've felt in so long, I can't remember anything ever feeling better. I already know I won't regret a second of being with her. My only regret will be that it's not long enough.

I have no response other than to lift my head and kiss her. Because kissing her feels like salvation. Like she's somehow able to restore the broken and not-so-pretty parts of me. So I keep kissing her, and the more I kiss her, the deeper I get, the more in trouble I am, and I know when this is done, she won't only be my salvation but likely my first real heartache.

She's my brother's ex, and there's a chance I might be falling in love with her.

11

TINSLEY

At this point, I feel like nothing Stone does should surprise me. And yet here we are riding south in a Jeep he rented—the windows and doors gone and the warm Bahamian air whipping around us—with his hand resting across my thigh while listening to Wild Minds, who are friends with my dad, and singing along. We went from distance and avoidance to this. Some weird version of not quite friends with some very fun, dirty benefits.

Stone is different. He's smiling. He seems lighter. Happier. Just more at peace and calm with himself. I've known him my whole life, and we've spent time together before because of our family connection and my relationship with Forest, but I've never seen him this way. Historically, Stone is a vault. You never truly know what he's thinking, and that's exactly how he designs it. Stone has always been untouchable, with a mysterious and cocky way about him.

But not this version of him. Not right now. I've seen him cocky. I've seen him as a playboy. I've seen him look like he was missing something.

Since we spent most of that day lounging on the beach after

we dove off the back of the boat and swam a hundred yards to shore, he's been more like this and less like that. Yesterday, we sailed up to the north part of Harbor Island and spent the day walking around and keeping our heads down. My hair was shoved through one of Stone's baseball hats, and I had on glasses, a T-shirt, and shorts. It was a risk walking out and about, but the local Bahamians didn't pay me much attention, and it was worth it because the island was so beautiful and fun.

We got conch fritters, margaritas, and ice cream, and it was perfect. After that, he took me to a beach with pink sand and we set up on a secluded part of it where we relaxed. We didn't talk a lot, but it wasn't awkward. If anything, it was comfortable. We both had a lot on our minds and simply got lost in the peace of being there. We lay there, his hand playing with mine, our bodies close like we couldn't handle any distance between us even if we didn't fill the void with chatter.

I've thought a lot about what Stone said to me. About being the thorn when I need to be. This time away has brought me the clarity I was seeking about the schedule I've been allowing myself to maintain and the people I've been allowing to run it. It's come at the expense of my health, and when I return to LA, I'm going to make some changes and prioritize myself more than I have.

After that decision, things just felt... better. My soul felt lighter.

Whatever Stone was working out for himself seemed to have the same effect on him because today he's been easygoing and relaxed. Smiling and playful even. He's been teasing me and touching me whenever he can—not just sexually—and I've even gotten him to sing along with me.

When I asked him what we were doing today, he smiled and said, "I want to show you the island."

I have zero complaints. This island might just be the most gorgeous thing I've seen. Eleuthera is a long but very narrow island of sprawling stretches of wild beauty, a rocky shoreline, and thick foliage on either side of the windy two-lane road.

"Are you going to sing along to every song?"

I throw him a side-eye and then shoot across the center console to lick his ear because he both loves and hates it when I do that. He swats me away, and I continue to belt out the lyrics, harmonizing with Jasper Diamond, who is the lead singer of Wild Minds, until the song ends.

Once that's done, I answer him. "Yes. I'm going to sing along to every song. You put it on, I'll sing it. If I don't know the words, I'll make them up as I go. You should invest in noise-canceling headphones if you don't like my voice."

His hand travels up my thigh to my hand, where he starts to toy with my fingers. "I love your voice. I'm not into pop music, but every time one of your songs comes on the radio or I hear someone play one, I always stop to listen."

And just like that, a fleet of butterflies takes flight in my stomach, and my face heats hotter than the sun blazing down on us.

"You do?" It comes out as a squeak.

He rolls his eyes as if I shouldn't be as floored as I am. "Don't look so shocked. You're Tinsley Monroe. You're the world's biggest pop star for a reason. Everyone is obsessed with you."

Now my heart hiccups, but I can't let that happen. No, my heart is on official lockdown. Even if it sort of loves the idea of him being even a little obsessed with me—or my voice.

"Including you?" I play, trying to douse those hiccups with ice water. I lift my sunglasses to the top of my head and bat my eyelashes at him.

He shakes his head, but there is no hiding the smile. It's been glued to his lips all day, and it's a hot look on him. I like this Stone. I mean, I liked the broody, gruff Stone too. Speaking of hot, that Stone is nuclear. But there is something about him like this that not only warms my heart but also lights up my insides.

A girl could easily fall in love with this Stone. Not that I have any plans to.

"How do you know where we're going?" I ask, needing to change the subject.

He throws me an *are you seriously asking me that* look. "It's a two-lane road heading north and south up the island."

I give him an unamused look. "I'm aware, but you seem as though you know exactly where you're going. Like you have a specific destination in mind."

"Because I do. I spent a lot of my childhood on this island and sailing around it. It's one of my mother's favorites."

"I don't remember Forest doing that."

It slips out, and his lips form a thin line at the mention of his brother, and once again I'm reminded of the exact nature of what we're doing.

"That's because he'd stay with one of our family members whenever we'd go. Sailing wasn't his passion like it was ours."

I don't know what to say in return, so I let it die there and return my gaze to the ocean on my right.

"Okay, look left and then right."

"Huh? Why?"

He slows the Jeep down. "Don't argue with me, woman. Just do it."

And when I do, I freaking gasp. The island is a tiny, narrow rock with hardly any land on either side of the road. On the left is deep, dark, rowdy blue water, and on the right is calm turquoise water. "Holy hell. Stone, what is this?"

"It's called the Glass Window Bridge. It's where the Atlantic and the Bright of Eleuthera meet."

I'm in complete awe, my head swiveling like it's on a spit, back and forth.

We continue on, and a few minutes later, we're pulling off

the road on the Atlantic side of the island. He stops the Jeep and pulls up the parking brake. "What are we doing?" I ask, searching around but not seeing much other than a sharp embankment of rocks that drop down into the Atlantic. He comes around and helps me down, holding my hand in his as we start to walk toward the edge of the cliffs overlooking the water.

"You need to do something for me."

"Uh. Okay," I hedge because this doesn't sound good, and the look in his eyes isn't quite selling it.

"I'm going to head down, and when I call up to you, you follow and come down too. Not before."

I squint at him. "Are there going to be clowns jumping out of cakes screaming 'Happy Birthday' at me?"

"What?" he barks out with a bemused chuckle. "I thought your birthday was in March."

For a moment, I'm thrown that he remembers when my birthday is, but I quickly press on. "It is, but I'm not so big on surprises now because of it. On my seventh birthday, that happened, and the fact that I still remember it and the subsequent terror should be telling."

He smiles and steps into me, pressing his chest to mine as he flips his sunglasses up his forehead and peers down at me with those hot guy green eyes of his and a look that goes straight to my core and hardens my nipples.

"Do I look like the clown type?" He runs a finger up my neck and along the angles of my jaw.

I shiver and swallow hard. "No. But I'm simply saying my legs would stay closed if you were."

He licks the seam of my lips and whispers against me. "No clowns. Do you trust me?"

Do I trust him? Such a simple question with such a profoundly meaningful answer. "Yes. I trust you."

His fingers slide into my hair and then around so he's

cupping the back of my neck and staring into my eyes from inches away. "Will I always protect you and keep you safe?"

"Yes. You will." My chest tingles with how fast and easily I answer that, and my limbs feel weak.

A smile curls his lips, and he trickles kisses to my neck, almost as if he's trying to hide it from me. "That's my girl. If you want to walk down together, we can. But it's not what I was hoping for."

Hmm. "You want me to come down after you?"

"Yes." A kiss. A soft, lingering, sweet kiss that essentially plies me with dopamine and endorphins and makes me his... something. I have to be his something because I refuse to be his.

Still...

"Okay. You go down first. Just so I know it's safe."

Another kiss, this one making my toes curl and knees buckle, and then he lets me go and follows a path by a sign that says Queen's Bath. I stand here for a couple of minutes, listening to waves crash and birds squawk overhead. Then I start to get antsy. He never told me how long it would take him to get wherever it is he's going. And why am I up here when he's gone ahead of me?

Another minute goes by, and why hasn't he called up to me? "Fuck this. I'm done waiting."

I take the same path he did, curving around rocks and winding my way closer to the ocean when I pause, staring down at several large, cavernous pools of crystal clear, blue-green water cut into the rocks abutting the dark blue Atlantic. The sun glistens, sparkling off the water and the sand-colored earth, warming everything around me.

I've never seen anything like this before.

My breath catches, and for an untold time, I can't drag my gaze away. The splash and crest of waves as they slam into rock. The aquamarine that you see in photographs but aren't sure actually exists. The fucking serenity and wildness and majesty and the cool way it grips you in the pit of your stomach and refuses to let go.

"Wow."

It slips out, but it's so relevant and yet so limiting and lacking in expression for all this is. Eventually, something else catches my attention, and my gaze drifts down until it catches on Stone sitting on the edge of one of the pools—the one right on the ocean side—staring up at me with an unreadable expression.

"What are you doing?" I cry out to him, pissed that he all but left me up there when there was all of this.

"Waiting on you," he calls back with a beaming smile. "It took you five minutes to find me."

"What?" I snap, careful with my footing in my flip-flops as I wind my way down and around the pools and the wet rock. "I was a little distracted." I pan my hands at everything before me. "You didn't call up to me."

His smile turns lopsided. "I did. Several times. I'm guessing you couldn't hear me and that wasn't the best plan."

"Why couldn't we come down here together? I don't get it."

He laughs and stands, meets me halfway and wraps his arms around my neck before he spins me around to face the incredible view before me. His face rests beside mine, cheek-to-cheek.

"I wanted to see your face when you saw this for the first time, and if I was directly in front of you or behind you, I would have missed it."

My lips part and my eyes blink wide behind my sunglasses. "You..." I swallow, my tongue thick, and my voice equally so. "You wanted to see my *face*?"

He kisses my neck, and I feel him shrug against me as if it's not a big thing. "You looked stunningly awed and dazzled. Exactly what I was hoping for. It's beautiful, isn't it?"

"It's incredible."

"It's got nothing on you, Little Rose." His nose brushes up and down my neck until I shiver against him. As it is, I'm biting my lip. Why is he saying these things? What is he trying to do to me? "Let's get you undressed so we can enjoy the water, and I can enjoy you."

"What is this?" I manage, still flabbergasted and overwrought.

"Natural pools carved by centuries of waves pounding the rock. The Atlantic spills over at high tide and then at low tide, like it is now, we're left with these pools. They're heated by the sun and warm like a bath. Hence the name."

"It's not a problem to go in them? I don't want to disturb any natural pools we shouldn't."

"We're not. I'd never do that. But keep your shoes on. The rocks are sharp, and sometimes there are small sea creatures that like to hang out on the bottom."

His hands slip down the front of me and start to undo the button and zipper on my shorts before he slides them down my waist so they pool at my feet. My breath hitches when the dull edges of his thumbnails drag up the outsides of my thighs before they reach my shirt. He grabs it and tugs it up and over my head, leaving me in only my bikini. I step out of my shorts and kick them over to the side so they stay dry.

Behind me, I feel him move as he takes off his shirt. I think I still need a minute—maybe a touch of space after what he said —so I lower myself to the edge of the pool and slip into the water. It's as warm as he said it would be, but not in an unpleasant way. If anything, the heat feels good against my skin, and I close my eyes and sink beneath the surface.

There's a ticking clock in my head. Five more days.

I'm dreading it as much as I'm anxious for it. I've never been a girl who's done anything casually. Nothing in my life is half-assed. I've been forcing myself to see this situation with Stone for exactly what it is and nothing more, but little by little, he's starting to creep into places I can't have him, and it's scaring me.

That ticking clock is becoming a weapon. Something with the potential to hurt or maim when it finally goes off.

Impenetrable arms snake around my waist, and I'm tugged hard and fast into a strong body. He pulls me up and spins me around, but before I can fully catch my breath, his lips fuse with mine, and his hands squeeze my ass beneath the hem of my bikini bottoms.

"Did you think I brought you down here just to show you how pretty it is without seeing how pretty you are in it?" He lifts me up and sets me on the edge of the pool, my feet up to my knees in the water.

"Maybe," I pant, breathless and dizzy. "But I should have known better. You're not expecting to get me naked so you can fuck me out here where anyone can catch us, are you?"

His smirk tickles my neck, which is unfairly sexy and gives him a definite advantage. "Maybe," he says, throwing my word back at me. "But since we got to this island a few days ago, fucking you here is all I've thought about."

"And when our sex tape ends up on *Intertainment*?"

"Then you can tell your fans that I made you come at least twice."

"You're trouble. And you're going to get me in trouble."

His hands tickle my ribs just beneath my breasts, and I can't help but laugh as he slides up higher, taking my top with him without a second's thought or hesitation about us getting caught.

"I'm not your trouble, Tinsley, but you're definitely mine." He pulls back and gives me a grin that, straight up, will have me agreeing to anything he wants me to do. His fingers rake through my hair and drag my face back until it's in line with his. "There will be no sex tape. There will be no us getting caught. I'll always protect you, and with that, the last thing I'd ever do is compromise you. You trust me, remember? Trust me now."

The way his eyes sear into mine has me reaching behind my back and undoing the string that's holding my pushed-up top at my neck. Stone makes it so easy to believe. I'm not sure I've ever felt like this with anyone. Safe and protected yet invincible. Hungered and craved yet worshiped. To the point of madness and frenzy. To the point where I'm not sure I ever want my feet to touch the ground again with how high he makes me fly.

It's the craziest thing. I was with a guy who I loved and trusted above nearly everyone else. But then one day, I realized the way he loved me and the way I loved him weren't enough. It wasn't the right kind of love for what we had. I deserved more, and so did he. Forest didn't mean to be stifling or restricting, but he didn't know how to handle what was happening with my life and my career.

He was a regular guy doing the regular college kid thing, which was the complete opposite of me. I tried. I tried so fucking hard to be the girlfriend he wanted me to be because I loved him. I used to believe that love was the solution to all my problems.

Then I came to comprehend that love can sometimes be a Band-Aid to bigger problems that are not only ready to erupt but destroy. Love can be toxic and ultimately what leads you to ruin. I was a hairsbreadth from it on more than one occasion. Trying to be everything for everyone and having nothing left to give to myself.

Sometimes all you can do is save yourself when that happens, and that's what I did.

I left Forest and have spent the last year feeling like I'm trapped in a snow globe.

I don't know what I'm doing here with Stone or why I'm

doing it. I only know how being with him makes me feel. Like I'm finally free. Like I'm finally seen. Like I can be me, and he wants all of it. I'm jumping in blindly but fully cognizant of the choice to do so.

This level of trust is something I hardly give anyone.

But I'm trusting Stone.

Outwardly, he has as much to lose as I do. Inwardly, I know my heart is at risk, but it's too late to stop what we're doing, and more importantly, I don't want to.

I undo the string on my bottoms and shift until the fabric follows the same path as my top. My legs spread on the rock, and Stone stares down at my pussy like he's drugged.

"Fuck if you're not the most beautiful woman I've ever seen."

He kneels before me and glances up.

"Hands back on the rocks and hold on, my Little Rose. I'm about to make you lose your mind. Or what's left of it." A wink, and then he splits my thighs wider and starts to ring me with his tongue and all I know is him. *This*. The pleasure and the danger.

He promised he'd always keep me safe and never let anything hurt me. He just never considered he could be the thing that hurts me the most.

12

STONE

I'm angry. Burning with a vitriol and animosity so acute and profound, there's no calming myself down and getting it back under control. I thought helping Tinsley would be my karmic restitution. Only now I realize Tinsley was my karma. The bad kind. The punishment side.

For ten perfect days, she was mine.

All of her. Every incredible thought, sound, touch, and inch. Even before I had her.

It was stargazing and talking while wrapped around each other. It was island-hopping while keeping a low profile. It was quiet and working stuff out. It was her playing music and singing to me. It was sleeping with her, and sleeping beside her, and not being able to get enough of her. Not even for a second.

But now those ten days are over, and I have to go back to my life while pretending she didn't flip it upside down and irrevocably change it.

Part of me wonders if I hadn't always been such a selfish, spoiled prick if there would have been another way this could go. That maybe karma would have been in my favor instead of against me. I found everything I could ever want in her, and I have no choice but to let her go.

So yeah, I'm angry, and I have no one to be angry with but myself.

Tinsley is quiet as I sail us back into the marina. I'm quiet too. She's standing in front of me, her hands on the wheel alongside mine and neither of us can think of anything to say. I don't want to be here, and I don't want to do this. I want to turn the boat back around and sail us away, back into our hidden abyss, free of reality.

I step in closer to her, my chest to her back, and everything hurts.

It's ironic. I've been with a lot of women and the only one to ever make me feel is the one I can never have.

My lips find the crook of her neck where it meets her shoulder—it's come to be one of my favorite places to kiss her—and she starts to tremble. If she cries, I'll fall apart. I'm barely hanging on as it is.

"How are you feeling about going home?"

She makes a noise in the back of her throat. "Depends on from which angle you're asking me."

"You came here to escape and get a break so you didn't have a breakdown."

"Right." She sighs and reaches behind her head to wrap her hands around the back of mine to hold me in place. "From that standpoint, I feel good. I wrote some songs that are just for me, that feel like they're mine and not the label's. I found my clarity and made some decisions about my life and how *I* want to run it. I feel good about that, Stone. Like I've finally got this and I'm strong enough to take it on." She sighs and holds me tighter. "I couldn't have done any of that without you. You pushed me when I needed it and brought out the strong, guileless woman I always knew was lying dormant in there." She takes a breath. "What about you? Do you finally believe that you're no longer a selfish asshole and that you can be the doctor and man you want to be?"

My lips curl up into a reluctant smile at the way she says that. At how she always believed I was this guy, even when I didn't. Her faith in me pushed forth my own. "Yes, I feel ready. I know the path I'm now meant to take and the man I will be. But more importantly, I know the man I will never be again."

"I think you're the bravest person I know. Change like that isn't for the faint of heart."

"Back at you, babe. I think you're the strongest, most amazing woman I've ever met."

Maybe I shouldn't have said that, but I don't care. It won't change anything, and I wanted her to know because she is all of that. I'm not sure I'd be standing here feeling this way about what's ahead of me if it weren't for her. If she didn't make me believe it for myself.

We fall silent again, slowly pushing through the water, our bodies connected, tethered, and intertwined.

"I'm trying to come up with a reason to start a fight," she says, her voice shaky.

"A fight?" I parrot, my voice not a whole lot better.

"Yeah. You know." Her fingers drag up the back of my hair. "If we fight and part being mad at each other, then maybe I won't feel like this."

"Like what?"

"Don't make me say it."

Fuck.

"If you don't say it, I won't, but I don't think I can fight with you." I kiss her neck and take a deep inhale of her skin. "It's not how I want us to end."

"It wasn't supposed to be like this."

She's right. It wasn't. Not even close, but here we are. I stopped pretending this wasn't more when I took her to the Queen's Bath. When we spent our nights rocking on the boat talking and staring up at the stars and then wrapped around each other as we slept.

Unequivocally, it's been the best ten days of my life.

"I thought we just agreed not to say it," I murmur.

She sighs and I'm trembling as I wrap my arm around her waist and steer with my other hand. I could pull into this marina blind for the number of times I've done it. Good thing too because she's all I'm focused on.

"It'll be weird when we run into each other," she murmurs after a quiet beat.

"Then maybe we shouldn't do that for a while."

She nods against me. "Probably not. Thank you for letting me stay and come with you."

My eyes pinch shut for a second before I reopen them and blow out a silent breath. "Thank you for sneaking onto my boat." I pause. Swallow. "I think..." *I think I might have fallen in love with you.* "I think you're incredible, and I..." *Don't want to let you go.* "Wish you everything wonderful and special because you deserve it all."

"Same with you, Stone."

We leave it at that, and I cut the engine and steer Benthesicyme into the dock. I release Tinsley and do what I have to do, tying the boat up nice and tight so she doesn't drift. My crew will come and clean her up in about an hour and take care of shutting and locking everything back down.

I don't know if I can ever come back to this boat.

At least not for a very long time.

It'll be haunted by Tinsley's ghost and impregnated with our memories.

When I return, I find Tinsley staring out toward the water, her duffel bag in her hand. I cross the deck, catch her face in my hands, and kiss her. My tongue sweeps into her mouth and I memorize the way it feels, the way she tastes, the sounds she makes, and the scent of her skin. I memorize everything because, in a few moments, that's all I'll have left.

My memories.

Her phone rings and it snaps us apart. She does a slow blink and then fishes through her purse. Her face pinches up in regret, and she slides her finger across the screen.

"Hi, Mom."

I can hear Fallon's sharp voice through the speaker with how loud she's talking.

"I'm fine. I swear. I'm sorry I've been MIA, and I'm sorry I haven't called." She pauses and listens. "Yes, I know you and Dad have been worried about me, but I'm good and about to head back home." Her watery eyes meet and cling to mine. "I'll tell you about it when I get there." Another pause. "That's why I didn't tell you where I was going, and I appreciate you not having Lenox track me down." She laughs, and I mentally cringe. I hadn't thought about them having Lenox, who is Vander's father, track her down. If he had, he'd know she was with me, and likely Vander would too. "Okay. I love you too. Bye." She slips her phone back into her purse and sighs only for it to ring again. She groans and pulls it out, grimaces, hits decline, and then puts it back in her purse but it's too late. I already saw it was Forest calling her.

Reality nails me in the gut like a missile-guided sucker punch.

"When did you turn it back on?"

She skirts my eyes for a moment. "When you were tying up the boat."

"How many missed calls and messages did you have?"

She smirks and then giggles lightly. "Oh, about ten thousand."

"How many from him?" I shake my head after the bitter words slip out. I don't want to know, and I don't want to be jealous or resentful of my brother more than I already am right now.

My parents have been calling too, but unlike her, I never turned my phone off. I've talked to both of them a couple of times this week, along with the guys.

I reach out and take her hand, holding it between us as I play with her fingers. "How are you getting home?" We haven't talked about this. Not a single word. We were living in the moment, but now the moment is over.

"I have that rental car. I'm going to drive up to where my plane dropped me and do the reverse."

I shake my head. "You're not driving through Florida and into Georgia by yourself."

Her lips purse and her eyes narrow in annoyance. "Actually, I am. I did it once already and I can do it again."

"Tinsley—"

"Don't Tinsley me, Stone. This is how it's going to be. If anyone finds out I've been in Miami or anywhere close, they could easily put two and two together and extrapolate that I was with you."

"Fine." Because that's hard to argue, but I'll follow her in my car and then rearrange my flight from there. "So, this is it then." It's not a question. It's a definitive statement and I pull her back to me so I can kiss her one last time. Her tears track against my cheeks, and I wipe them away with my thumbs. Just as I did during the storm. "Don't cry, my Little Rose. I can't handle your tears. It feels sad now, but by next week, you'll be back to taking over the world, and I'll be back to taking care of sick kids, and little by little, what this was will fade."

It's a lie. At least for me, it is. She'll never fade for me.

She reinvented me.

Her hands hold my face, and she gives me one last kiss before she races off the boat. No goodbye. No take care. That's it. She's gone.

For a moment, I stand here. I don't turn to watch her because I might fucking chase after her if I do. How did this happen? How did I become this guy when I've never been this guy before?

Karma. You fucking bitch.

You'll owe me big time when I've earned your favor and not your fury.

There will likely be times when Tinsley and I run into each other in the future. It's inevitable with how our families are aligned. But I vow here and now to avoid her as much as I can, and maybe, if I'm lucky, we'll both find other people and be happy.

I want that for her. I want her to be happy. Settled. Even if it can't be with me.

I give Tinsley a full three minutes, and I head off the boat. I see her taillights pulling out of the parking lot, and where we are, it won't be difficult to find her and follow her. And after I've made sure she gets on her plane and is safely flying home, that'll be that.

It has to be.

13

STONE

Two years later – Present Day

"A TOAST before tonight's festivities begin." Owen holds his crystal tumbler of bourbon up toward me, his blue eyes light yet intense. "To the new chief resident of the emergency department at Boston Children's Hospital. Congrats, brother. I'm so fucking proud of you."

"Cheers," everyone cries, holding their glasses up and we all clink them together before taking a sip. Tonight is my grandmother, Octavia Abbot-Fritz's, ninetieth birthday and she decided to celebrate it with a massive fairy-tale-themed ball. Since she is essentially the reigning queen of Boston, the entire city has turned out for it.

It's like a Disney royal ball threw up in here.

Candles and flowers everywhere. Crystal chandeliers. Blue, purple, gold, and pink up-lighting on every available hard surface. A six-piece orchestra is playing background music for the cocktail hour, and for dancing later, there will be a twelve-piece band. Tables in the main dining room are set as if the King of England were dining at them. There are waiters passing trays of delicate canapés as well as crystal martini glasses filled with different colored drinks.

It's great if balls are your thing. They're not exactly mine.

"Thanks, man," I reply. "I appreciate that. The formal announcement isn't until next week though."

Owen chuckles and half-heartedly rolls his eyes. "And yet everyone in the hospital already knows so I'd say it's been announced."

My supervisor let me know just this morning, but evidently news spreads fast in a hospital. I wasn't expecting it. I thought they'd let it go since we're already four months into our third and final year of residency and the person who was originally named had a family situation that pulled him out of the program. She even laughed at my floored expression and told me I'd earned it and that I'd really proven myself as both a doctor and a leader over the last two years.

It's what I've dedicated myself to becoming, but hearing it validated by someone I like and respect and not just from my family felt good. Like redemption.

"Do you think you'll stay in Boston once your residency is done?" Bennett, Katy's fiancé, asks me. I nearly laugh and the rest of us let out a low chuckle. Boston is our town. We may do medical school or sometimes even residencies—for those of us who are doctors—outside of Boston or even New England, but most of us always seem to find our way back home.

Forest is an exception, and his reasons for staying in LA are obvious, though he's never been like the rest of us. He never wanted to come back to Boston. He likes his space without his family always breathing down his neck the way they do to us.

"Without a doubt," I tell him.

"You saved a life this morning and were named chief resident. Now we just have to find you a woman, and your night will be complete," Mason throws out.

I laugh. No one else does.

My smile slips. "Don't start with that again. The last woman you set me up with I caught taking covert selfies and videos that had me in the background, and she tried so hard to get me in bed, she practically crawled under the table at the restaurant to suck me off. It was not a good look. I ended up paying for her Uber home and leaving before our appetizers came."

"If we don't say anything, it goes unchecked," he presses, sipping his pink cocktail before tilting the rest of it down his throat and setting the empty on a passing tray. "And I'm sorry about that woman. She was a bad call, but in my defense, she used to date one of my teammates, and he said she was fun in bed. Something you clearly need."

"It's not natural that you don't date," my brother agrees, finishing off his drink in a hearty gulp and grabbing another from a passing tray. "There has to be someone you can make it past dinner with."

"Doubtful," I tell him. "All the women in this city seem to only want me for my dick or my money. That's why I used to have rules. One night. No strings."

"And you abandoned that because..." Forest trails off, the inflection in his voice and his eyebrows raised in question making it clear he thinks I'm crazy because I did, and my gut sinks like lead. Forest and I are about as close as he lets any of us be with him, but that's not all that close, and I think part of that is my fault.

I take a sip of my drink and casually stare around the room, pretending that this conversation isn't rubbing my skin raw. "Because I'm no longer the asshole I was." It's my standard answer, and it's not a lie. "When I meet someone I can stand talking to for more than thirty seconds, then maybe things will change."

"Maybe?" Mason sputters. "When was the last time you got any?"

"When was the last time I saw your mother?" I throw back at him because I'm getting salty.

Mason's green eyes narrow into tiny slits. "Really? You're going to be a dick like that? The woman is literally right over there." He points somewhere I don't bother looking.

It was a low blow. Even for me. I love his mother, and I respect her as both a woman and a doctor. But for real? I don't need this shit tonight. Or any other night. I get them poking and prodding at me, and I admit, it's not healthy and likely a little strange that I'm so picky and disinterested, but it can't be helped, and them pushing me about it isn't going to change that.

"Fine. Apologies." I hold up my hand in surrender. "But let it go and I won't have to be a dick to get you to stop."

"We'll let it go when you let *her* go," Vander follows up, and I inwardly cringe, making a concerted effort not to glance over at Forest.

Two years ago, when I finally got back home, I was in rough shape. The guys knew I had been with a woman, but that's all I've ever told them. At the time, Forest was in LA, so he didn't know anything about what was going on with me because I never told him. He still thinks I met my mystery woman after I came home from my trip and had a wild weekend with her before she left with no way for me to contact her.

But since I haven't returned to my pre-Tinsley bachelor ways, they've been on my ass to either find my mystery girl or get me laid to end my long self-induced suffering.

I brush it off with a super mature middle finger since that seems to be the mode I'm operating in at the moment, which immediately earns me a hiss from Katy, who shouts, "I saw that, but worse baby Willow saw it!" from halfway across the ballroom.

I sigh and throw up yet another hand in apology. That makes two in less than five minutes. I'm on a roll. And to think, I was actually in a good mood when this night started. Katy is also a little nutty when it comes to swearing or vulgar gestures in front of her four-month-old. Still...

"I'm sorry! To you and baby Willow." I turn to Bennett. "She needs to cool it with the baby Willow sees and hears us stuff. The baby is four months old."

Bennett simply shrugs because he's too in love with Katy and their daughter to ever try to pick that fight. Even if he knows it's as nutty as we do. "Katy is Katy " is his only reply. "But nice attempt to dodge this."

Christ. This night has hardly started and it's already like this.

"How many women did you sleep with after your ex-wife put you through the wringer?" I ask him.

He rubs at his jaw. "Only Katy."

I lean against an empty cocktail table, rolling my glass around in my hand. "Well, I haven't found my Katy yet."

"You could try to meet someone," Owen suggests mildly, unfortunately keeping the conversation alive. He used to be my safety net as he always kept his mouth shut about it after what he went through with his ex. Now he's with Estlin, happy and in love, so I guess that makes it open season on me for him now too.

"Christ, just stop already," I grit out. "I've tried to meet women."

And that's not a lie either. I've gone on dates. I've met women. But none have made it past that first date into anything else. The truth is, my life has changed in the last two years. *I've* changed. That was the goddamn purpose of that trip. To no longer be the selfish asshole I was.

I dove headfirst into all things pediatric emergency medicine. I started a charity for kids with chronic medical conditions to make sure they get everything they need and help their parents financially when insurance—if they have that—isn't always enough, and I've stopped sleeping around because I've decided I want real and more, but so far, the only person who has been able to tempt me to that is a no-go.

"There are lots of single women here tonight who you're not related to. Let's set you up. I'll be your wingman. Between the two of us, we'll find you the hottest woman in the room. Maybe just get laid. Start with that. It doesn't have to be love. Lust can do for an icebreaker, and sometimes that turns into more. You just have to be open to it and give it a chance." Mason picks up another pretty drink, this one gold, along with a few passing appetizers. He pops a small beef Wellington in his mouth and chews as he stares meaningfully at me.

I hate it when Mason is serious. It's not his standard MO, and it always throws me.

I take a hearty gulp of my bourbon and stare around the room, mulling Mason's offer over. "I'm not trying to be a monk. I'm busy with work and the charity, and most women I've met bore me. Looking around this room, I'm not seeing anything that changes that."

Only just as the words slip past my lips, the sea of gowns and tuxedos part, and there she is. Her dark hair is twisted into something elaborate at the back of her head, showing off her long, graceful neck. The strapless white, beaded gown hugs her perfect tits and then flares out into a sparkling bell shape starting at her waist. Bloodred lips and shimmery violet eyes with a long fan of black lashes make her face stand out among the rest.

Fuck.

Two things immediately stop my heart other than how fucking stunning she looks. One, that she's here when I didn't think she'd be—though I didn't exactly ask. I simply assumed since she makes a point to avoid all the places she knows I'll be.

And two, she brought her movie star boyfriend with her. Tall, blond, and douchey, Loomis Powell dutifully stands by her side. They starred in a movie together last year that was a huge success, and since then, have been photographed together. A lot.

Completely avoiding all things Tinsley as I had planned has been all but impossible given the heights of her movie and musical career. She's all over every magazine cover and social media feed. She's on freaking network news, on the radio, and on every streaming station. She. Is. Everywhere. And if that's not bad enough, I've had to listen to Forest gripe about Loomis.

Case in point...

"I can't believe she fucking brought him. Is she intentionally trying to hurt me?"

I turn my back to her, gulp down the rest of my drink, and flag a waiter for another. If it weren't my grandmother's ball, I'd leave now. Instead, I have to stay through the cutting of the cake and dancing since I promised her one. I've managed for two solid years not to see Tinsley in person, but it seems tonight my luck has run out.

I sigh.

Maybe the guys are right. Maybe she doesn't have to be perfect, just someone to get the ball rolling again. It was ten days, two years ago. At this point, I'm bordering on pathetic. Not quite as bad as Forest but getting there. She walked into my life when I was at a crossroads, and so much of what I walked away with from that time revolved around her.

Yes, she's beautiful. Yes, she's special. She wouldn't be who she is or have gotten as far as she has if she weren't. But she's not mine, she never was, and it's time I get the fuck over it.

Maybe it's good that I'm seeing her tonight with that guy. It'll force me to finally face this. My problem is that every woman I've gone on a date with knows who I am. They know I'm Stone Fritz. They know what I'm financially worth. They know my family name and the connections they hold. They titter and try to overplease. They have no opinions for themselves that they're willing to share and default to what I want or what they think I want.

It's a bore.

Reluctantly, when the pull becomes more than I can bear, I twist back around. Tinsley is laughing and smiling with her friends and my cousins, but her gaze is also drifting. Unsettled. And when she turns just so and catches my eyes, it's as if time slows and the room around us fades.

It's just us. No one else.

Her full, red lips part, and her lavender eyes widen. She visibly swallows as our gazes lock, unable to be dragged apart. I do a sweep of her just as she does a sweep of me. My chest tightens, making taking a deep breath a challenge. I raise a *were you looking for me,* eyebrow, and find myself smirking despite myself.

She's a princess and I'm the villain.

Her in sparkling white and me in all black. If that's not fitting for us, I'm not sure what is.

Her eyes round and her features tighten as she offers a timid smile and a small wave. The worst thing about this? I want to go to her, even after all this time. Looking at her now, it's as if no time has passed at all. It's two years ago, and I'm right back on that boat. I want to touch the soft skin on her back, smell her perfume, see her eyes up close, and feel her smile against my lips.

Until I realize my brother is standing directly beside me and she could be staring at him in resonating shock just as clearly as I believe she could be staring at me.

"Fucking bitch," he snarls, chugging down most of his vodka in one go.

"Don't call her that," I clip out, my tone harsh, my head whipping in his direction.

"What?" he barks incredulously, panning a hand in her direction. "Dude, she brought her *boyfriend* to my grandmother's birthday ball knowing I'd be here. If that's not a bitch move, I don't know what is."

I shake my head. "I don't care."

He's fuming, his cheeks are ruddy, and his eyes are wild. He's already had a few drinks and it's starting to show on him. "Since when do you give a shit what I call my ex-girlfriend?"

My gaze casts over to his, hard and unrelenting. "I care what you call any woman, and Tinsley doesn't deserve that from you or anyone else. Don't call her that."

He slams down the rest of his vodka neat and practically chucks the empty glass on a nearby table. It just barely hangs on, but thankfully doesn't smash to the floor. "I can call her whatever the fuck I want."

"You two broke up more than three years ago. She's allowed to bring a date."

"Fuck this," he grumbles under his breath and storms away, carving a path straight for her. She smiles when she sees him coming, but it doesn't quite reach her eyes. She taps her boyfriend's arm, and he looks, noting the direction of her gaze, and follows it to find Forest headed straight for them.

I turn away. I don't want to watch it. Not any of it.

"What is he doing yelling at her like that?" Vander shoots out, annoyance and dismay coloring his voice and pinching his face.

"He's drunk and he needs to get that hothead temper under control," Owen agrees.

"If he doesn't, I'll make him," Mason asserts.

"What?" I turn back to find Forest visibly enraged as he confronts her, only it looks like her boyfriend is all over it, and so are the other women who seem to be defusing the situation. She doesn't need me to come and fight her battles.

Still...

"I've got him." I march over there, quickly cutting the distance with long strides, and grab my brother forcefully by the arm, pulling him back and away from her. I can feel Tinsley's eyes on my back, but I focus on my brother. "Let's go, Forest."

"Fuck you," he slurs as he tries to push me off, and I get right up in his face.

"You're drunk, you're making a scene at Grandma's party, you're scaring not only Tinsley, but everyone else here, and Katy has baby Willow in her arms. Get your shit together and do it now."

He holds my gaze for a moment and then starts to simmer. He licks his lips, glances around at everyone around us, likely noting that he's created a bit of a scene, and then says to Tinsley, "This conversation isn't over," before he turns and walks away.

Instantly, I catch eyes with my mother and father across the room, and they give me a look that indicates they've got him and follow after him to make sure he's okay. I breathe out a sigh of relief and turn back to everyone, skirting Tinsley. It's not because I don't want to look at her. It's because I do.

"You all okay?"

"We're fine." My cousin Keegan rolls her eyes. "He needs to get over this crap already."

"Yes, well, that was likely all my doing. He's not my biggest fan." Loomis extends his hand to me. "Loomis Powell."

I shake his hand even if I'm not his biggest fan either. "Stone Fritz."

"Nice to finally meet you. Sorry if my being here caused a show. Your grandmother was gracious enough to invite me."

I tilt my head, and my gaze briefly tracks to Tinsley before returning to him. *Finally*? Has she spoken to him about me?

"Don't sweat it. As Keegan said, he needs to get over his crap already."

"Thank you for stepping in with him," Tinsley says to me, her voice soft and hesitant.

"No worries," I tell her and give baby Willow a kiss on the top of her little head since she's cute and small and distracts me. "You all good now?"

I get a round of yeses and thank yous.

"Great. I'm going to go find my drink. Anyone want anything?" I'm trying for unaffected and nonchalant, but I have no clue if I'm selling it. I walk away and no one follows me, perhaps sensing I need a minute after that incident with Forest, or perhaps they have no need. Either way, I find myself alone at the bar, sipping a freshly filled glass and staring out at the room.

Forest has gone off, who knows where, and Tinsley is talking with her parents while her boyfriend chats with Keegan. And touches her hair. And her cheek. What the—

"It's a special night, isn't it?" my grandmother's voice startles me, and I turn to see her, dressed like a queen in red with matching lipstick, her signature blonde bob perfectly coiffed.

"As always, Grandma, everything you do is perfection. You look stunning. Ninety agrees with you." I lean in and place a soft kiss on her cheek.

"Charming me, are you?"

"Tonight, of all nights, you deserve to be charmed. Are you enjoying yourself?"

She pats my hand and leans her weight against me. For ninety, she's in incredibly good shape, but she's still ninety. "It's heaven except your grandfather has gotten into a debate over some kind of cardiothoracic surgical technique with your father, and I had to bow out."

I make a sardonic scoff. "Surgeons."

She laughs lightly, looping her arm through mine and watching the end of the cocktail hour. "I heard you received chief resident. I'm so proud of you and the man you've become."

That earns her another kiss. "Thank you. That means everything to me coming from you."

"I'm so thrilled Tinsley was able to make it."

Christ. Not her too.

"I was not, however, thrilled to see Forest speak that way to her and her guest."

"I'm sorry you saw that, but it's handled, and no feathers are ruffled other than Forest's." I take a sip of my newly refilled drink.

"I invited her specially."

My head whips in her direction. "You did? Why?"

She purses her lips. "Because she's very dear to me, and I didn't want her to feel as though she had to stay away and not attend when I knew she wanted to. All of her friends and family are here. She asked if she could sing a song tonight for me, which is so lovely of her to do."

"Forest isn't happy about it."

"I love Forest with all my heart, but it's time he finally understands that she doesn't belong to him."

"I think he's more upset that she brought her boyfriend."

She draws back, her green eyes sparkling with something in them that I can't quite figure out. "Whoever said he was her boyfriend?"

"The world," I deadpan.

"Well, things aren't always how they appear to be, are they? I wonder if that'll make a difference for you." She gives me a wink and then glides back into the crowd, and I'm left here a little befuddled, trying to discern exactly what she meant.

14

TINSLEY

"He can't take his eyes off you for more than a minute or two," Loomis murmurs under his breath so no one else can hear as we dance to the light notes of Frank Sinatra. "They always drag back. I think I'll offer the poor bloke a smile and a wink to cheer him up. He looks miserable."

"Which one?" I find myself asking before I can stop it, only to follow that up with, "Never mind, don't tell me."

I don't want to know. It doesn't help anything. And likely, Loomis is just trying to get a rise out of me. He knew coming here tonight wasn't going to be easy, but Octavia called me herself and asked if I'd come, and she included Loomis in that. And since I absolutely adore that woman, there's very little I wouldn't do for her. Including seeing Stone and dealing with a drunk and angry Forest. I've never seen Forest that bad, though in the last few years, his mood swings are more noticeable. At least toward me.

I wasn't going to come. Forest and I haven't been on the best of terms lately, and I wasn't sure what seeing Stone would be like. Just knowing he's here makes my heart flutter and my stomach twist in anxious knots. I haven't seen him or spoken to him since he kissed me goodbye and I ran off his boat in dramatic fashion.

I've intentionally avoided him for two years but found myself seeking him out from the moment I stepped through the ballroom doors, just to get it over with. I ripped the Band-Aid off, and it hurt like hell as it tore at the scab it was covering. I smiled at him. He didn't smile back. And then Forest came over to me like a raging beast, making his displeasure at Loomis being here known.

Even when Stone stepped in and took care of it, he still barely acknowledged me, and it's a bit more than I can handle. I didn't expect fireworks or stolen kisses in a dark corner, but a hug and a *hey, how are you*, might have been nice.

"The older one," he tells me, purposefully ignoring my protest because that's how Loomis works. "The one you want watching you."

My eyes close. "I don't want him watching me."

"Liar."

"I don't. Not either of them," I tack on emphatically. "The less I have to do with those particular Fritz brothers, the better, as neither is good for my heart." It's the truth, and he can't argue it.

"Isn't that why you brought me? To keep the lions and the lovers at bay."

"I brought you because Octavia Abbott-Fritz called and told me I had to come and that she'd love for you to attend as well, and you do not turn down Octavia Abbott-Fritz."

"Certainly not with a name that proper."

"You're English. You practically invented proper names, *Loomis*."

He chuckles. "Luv, I'm part posh and part London rubbish. I invented everything, and what I didn't, I stole. But you're dicking me around."

There are very few people in this world who know about

my ten days with Stone, and Loomis is one of them. My parents are another two. Wren is the fourth because she's the sort who holds secrets and doesn't like to splash them about. When I got off the boat, I was an absolute mess—more so than I was when I first got on—and I needed girl talk. She's been my closest friend since we were in diapers, and she didn't disappoint.

"That's what she said."

"So you claim, but did you see those boys fighting over you?"

"Can you stop taunting me with this? I brought you because you're my boyfriend."

He laughs lightly, and I do too. Loomis isn't my boyfriend. He's my best friend and one of the few people in Hollywood I trust. We met during a screen test and had insane chemistry, though none of it is sexual. We've been inseparable since. We're dubbed the next George and Julia—thankfully, not the next Rose and Jack. It's why the media thinks we're together, and our agents, along with the studio of the next film we're about to start working on together here in Boston, have used it to their advantage.

We've come out and said we're just friends on numerous occasions, but no one ever believes that. They believe what they want to believe, and Loomis and I appear to be the perfect Hollywood couple. But the truth is, these last two years everything has changed for me, and though I can't control the media or how they get off on savagely stalking without remorse or consideration, I've learned how to navigate and balance work and life while putting myself first.

Loomis tugs me in a bit tighter. "Sorry, my darling," he drawls in his posh British accent that wins over all the rom-com audiences. "I don't know what to tell you. It's not a taunt if it's true. He hasn't taken his eyes off you. If it helps, the poor bloke isn't happy about it either. Look and see for yourself. The miserable chap is standing in the far corner in the dark."

As if following Loomis's command, my head twists over my shoulder, and I immediately lock onto a pair of dark green eyes. My breath catches. Shit, he's intense. And ridiculously freaking hot in his all-black tuxedo. He's scowling, but there's something else to his eyes and expression. It's not displeasure or anger. It's scrutiny. Like he's not simply staring, he's watching with purpose.

I quickly turn back to Loomis, who smirks and places a chaste kiss on my cheek. "Perhaps he doesn't like that we're dancing. That my hands are on you when his can't be."

"Please stop."

"Shall I kiss you and really drive him mad?"

I stomp on his foot, and he bursts out laughing, taking my hand and twirling me out before spinning me back into him and then dramatically dipping me. We get a round of applause for it and that only drives the devil in him higher.

He rights me and gives me another spin, and as my eyes flash around, I can't help but give one more look only to find the place Stone had occupied empty. He's gone. I do a quick search, but I don't see him anywhere in the sea of people. My gut sinks, but I force myself to believe it's for the best.

It's not as if it matters anyway.

"Boston is bloody cold."

"It's October."

I get a hip bump. "You say that as if it explains why my nipples are freezing to my shirt."

I snicker. "You need to start getting used to it, gumdrop. And wear a coat. You're here over the winter filming a cuddly, spicy holiday movie that's set to come out next year. Guess what? It's cold here this time of year."

"I don't appreciate your negative disposition."

"Me either. So how do we change that?"

"With sunshine and rainbows," Loomis sings at the top of his lungs, and I roll my eyes, even if there is no stopping my smile. He's drunk, and Loomis doesn't do drunk all that often. It's fun to watch when he does, though. So unlike Forest! The way Forest spoke to me still has me shaking.

Loomis had his driver drop us off on the corner since he's staying in a rental flat, as he calls it, five doors down from my parents' warehouse in the North End. Immediately following the party tonight, my parents hopped a flight to Europe, as my dad has a series of tour dates that couldn't be moved. They were in the works long before the movie picked Boston as its filming location.

Plus, he hasn't toured in years. My younger siblings, Astor and Zoella, are now in college and my parents can finally do it. They've sacrificed a lot for us, and I don't want them to sacrifice anymore.

"No. With moondrops and snowflakes," I toss back at him, and he twists to give me a befuddled look.

"What on fucking Earth are moondrops?"

"No clue. How's this? Raindrops and snowflakes," I sing in a light soprano.

"Brilliant. Even if you're horribly off-key."

I smack his arm, and it only makes him laugh harder. I've never been off-key a day in my life, and he knows it.

"You're sure you don't want me to stay with you now that you're all alone?" he asks, his brown eyes growing serious as he takes in the large brick structure before us. I get it. It looks haunted and intimidating.

"Positive," I tell him. "I grew up in this house."

"House?" he scoffs. "Luv, this is a *ware*house. Not quite the same thing. Besides, with everything going on right now between your ex and the media all over you, I don't like it." He turns to me and takes me by the shoulders, staring earnestly into my eyes. "I know you're Miss Independent, and I understand your reasons, but it's a big place to be alone."

"I'll set the alarm and snuggle into my childhood bed. Besides, there's a huge perimeter of cameras set up at all the exits, and the pool side is used for local boys' and girls' clubs, which means the locals protect it. If the press wants to hang around, they will, but they won't break in. No one can."

He twists his lips, trying to hide his displeasure. "If you say so. Still, I'm only a few buildings down and can be back here in under a minute if I run. Promise you'll ring if you need me."

"You're cute when you're overprotective, but I promise I'll call if I need you, though I'm positive I won't." I reach up and wrap my arms around his neck so I can hug him. "Tell me you're going straight home."

"I'm going straight home," he repeats but there is a twinkle in his eyes.

"Alone?"

"Swear on my grandmum's cold, dead heart." He holds his hand over his heart, his cheeks rosy, and along with his smile, there isn't much on him that isn't glowing. He's adorable. Too bad I'm not into him, and he's not into me. Otherwise, we would be perfect.

I punch in the code for the front door and then turn back to him, leaning against the wood. "You're good? Did you want to stay here because you're lonely?"

He rolls his eyes. "No. Absolutely not, and I'm rarely ever lonely. I was simply taking care of one of my two favorite ladies on this planet. I've grown especially fond of my space. I'll wake you tomorrow with breakfast and coffee. Get some sleep." He leans in and places a kiss on my cheek, and then he's gone, keeping his head down and his body naturally twisted toward the buildings as he walks a block up to his place.

I didn't notice any press lingering about, but that could change now that we attended the ball tonight. We had been keeping an insanely low profile over the last two days since we arrived in Boston.

I watch him go for a minute and then head inside, shutting the door behind me and falling against it with a heavy thud. A light on the second floor of the warehouse, which is the main living space, is on, and the dull, yellow glow filters and defuses down, trickling along the stairs as if to beckon me up.

I yawn and start to unzip my gown because this bitch is tight, when there's a pounding at my back.

"Loomis!" I screech, flipping around and unlocking the door in a start. "What did you—" My voice hurdles to a sharp standstill as I fling the door open and find Stone on the other side.

"You're not Loomis."

Stone's tux jacket is gone, leaving him in a black button-down shirt with the sleeves rolled up to his toned forearms, revealing his colorful ink. He's standing a solid three and a half feet away from the door. It's as if he pounded and then stepped back because he changed his mind and was ready to run for it instead. He looks hot and dangerous, and I hate how I notice both, but I do.

"He didn't come inside."

I blink, but a smile finds my lips when I catch his meaning, and I respond with, "Isn't that what you like to do?"

"Only with you."

Before I can think it through or question anything, I step out the door, grab him by the collar, and drag him inside. I tell myself I'm doing it in case there are paparazzi hanging about, but somewhere in the back of my mind, I know that's not why. The door slams behind him, and once again, I lock it up tight and set the alarm.

Then I shove him. Hard.

"You're too cool to say hi, let alone smile at me. Is that it?" I shove him again. I'm angry, but more than that, I'm riled up. He's here. I wish he weren't but the fact that he is makes me high and annoyingly giddy. It's fucked up, and it's so wrong. But I can already feel it. That undercurrent. That vibe thing we do. The we shouldn't but we want to.

It's still there, humming like a tired truck driver trying to stay awake.

It's been two years and I had convinced myself I was over it and over him. That I only clung as hard and fast as I did because of the emotional state I was already in. But considering how I felt when I saw him earlier tonight, especially when he stepped in and handled Forest, and how I want to tear his clothes from his body and climb him like the mast of his ship, I'm starting to question that.

Which I don't want to do. I was much happier in my other place.

So I shove him again. Because he's letting me, and if I don't, all my physical energy will go to something else.

"Hi," he deadpans, but I don't get a smile out of him. He's too busy waging an internal battle that's written all over his face. He shouldn't be here, and he knows it, but more than that, he's locked in the same paradox I am. Wanting to be here and not wanting to be here.

I roll my eyes and flip him off. He reaches out and captures my middle finger, holding it between us.

I squint accusingly. "I didn't give you permission to touch me."

He gives me the cockiest smirk I've ever seen. "Then tell me to go."

"What are you doing here?" I volley back instead, but he knows. I can see it all over him in the triumphant gleam he's now sporting. He knows I don't have it in me to tell him to leave. Not when I want him to stay as badly as I do.

"I had to know. That's what I'm doing here."

I shake my head, hating his half-assed explanation. "Know what?"

"Your boyfriend didn't come inside." He gives my finger a little tug, but I don't budge. I don't pull away either.

"So?"

"So if he were a date, he would have sealed the deal. He would have done whatever he could to get you to invite him in for the night, and if he were your actual boyfriend, he'd be staying with you and nowhere else. If you were mine, that's how it would be. There's no way I'd let you stay here alone without me."

"I'm not following, Stone, so how about you cut to the chase and go."

He takes a small step—hardly much of anything at all—but every move and shift he makes, I'm hyper-aware of.

"Do you often bring fake boyfriends to special events?"

Well, shit. I laugh. Kind of loud. "Honestly? Yes. If that guy is Loomis, I do. He's my award show buddy."

"Right. Your *buddy*. You're not trying to sell him as more?"

"I never said he was my boyfriend, fake or otherwise. It's you assholes who don't know how to read or believe printed statements."

I tear my finger from his grasp and turn off the alarm. I think I finally want him to go. I'm seriously angry for no reason other than he's challenging me when he doesn't have the right to. Loomis and I take it as a joke and run with it at this point. That's on the gossip rags and not us. Only, it felt safer when Stone believed Loomis was my boyfriend. Now I'm in dangerous territory, and I don't like it.

Stone crowds me, pressing my back into the door, and with his eyes locked on mine, he reaches beside me to punch back in the code he just saw me use to disarm it. My heart pounds, quickening my breaths and making my skin zip and zing with tension and feral energy. The speed at which my body betrays me and becomes his wanton creature seriously pisses me off.

"What more do you want? You got what you came for. Mystery solved. Loomis isn't my boyfriend, but I never said he was." I try to push him back so I can think clearly without him surrounding me, but he's not having it.

His hands plant into the door on either side of my head and he dips down, caging me in. "And yet, the world believes he is. I thought so too. For over a fucking year, I thought that." He shifts in closer until his hard body is practically flush with mine. My breath catches and holds in my lungs. "Until my grandmother planted a seed tonight and I stood back and watched it grow before my eyes."

"That's why you were watching me." I huff, feeling foolish for believing he had been watching me because he couldn't take his eyes off me, as Loomis claimed. Now I know the truth, and it stings more than I'd like it to. My hands are on his chest, which is so strong and warm beneath my palms and splayed-out fingers. And somehow, he moves in closer. So close my elbows bend and press into the door, and the toes of my expensive heels tap against his shoes.

"You have no idea, Tinsley. Fucking none." He leans in, our eyes locked in a duel both of us are determined to win. His lips ghost over mine, and I fight the urge to whimper. "Tell me I shouldn't bring you upstairs and spend the night making you scream for me."

"You shouldn't bring me upstairs," I whisper, and his expression shutters closed before I utter, "It's too far away."

We move at the same time, our lips colliding, fiery and furious, and yet the second it happens, we both groan in satisfaction. He lifts me off the floor in my gown, layers of stiff satin and sharp beads adjusted so I can wrap my thighs around his waist. My arms encircle his neck, and I grip his shoulders and the back of his hair while I hold on tight. My back slams back into the door, and we devour each other like we didn't think we'd ever get this again, and it's just as good as we remember.

Impatiently, he works his hand up under the layers of the gown until he finds my thigh, then slides it up to the edge of my panties. A finger slips beneath the thin satin and grazes my clit before he pushes it inside me. I moan, unable to stifle it.

"Fuck," he curses. "You're wet. Goddammit, Tinsley." His forehead mashes into mine, and he breathes harder than he was a moment ago. "What am I doing? I shouldn't fucking be here. I shouldn't fucking care."

I don't have an answer for that, especially as he starts to slide his finger in and out of me. I can't think about anything else when he does that.

"This doesn't mean shit," he snarls against me, nipping at my lips, my chin, and down my neck while he slowly works that finger like he's trying to punish me.

"Thank God for that." My hands drag through his hair, helping to guide his mouth along until he gets pissed and tears away to come back to my mouth. "I'd hate to think about you getting clingy."

His finger slips out, his body shaking against mine, and just when I think he's about to come to his senses and leave, his lips attack mine with renewed vigor. Plastering me against the door, he uses it as leverage to rip and tear at my dress with the hand he was just using on my pussy.

"I mean it, little Rose. It's just tonight. This is all sorts of bad."

"I already told you I was done being good," I pant against him, and that sets him off.

Somehow, I end up on my feet, and he's got two hands on my dress. The zipper is torn apart instead of unzipped. Beads and crystals shoot out in all directions, clanging to the floor. By the time he's done with it, I'm only wearing a strapless bra, a thong, and my heels, with my hair half hanging around my back and shoulders and my gown in tatters at my feet.

Stone steps back, his dark, hungry gaze feasting on me inch by inch. "Take your hair down and remove your bra but don't rush it. We've got all night, and I intend to use it."

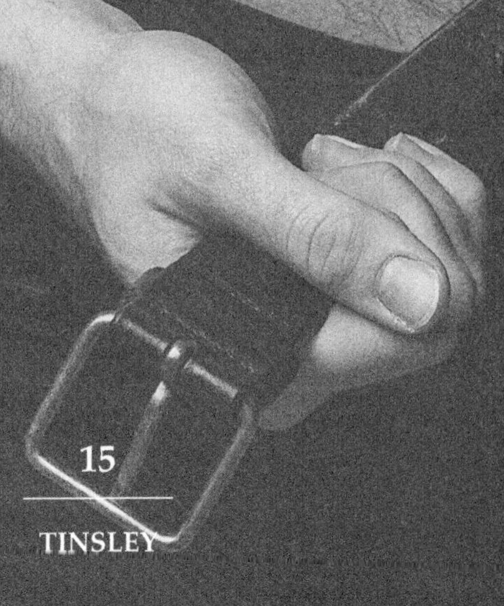

15

TINSLEY

There will come a time—probably tomorrow morning when the light of day flashes across my face in the reflection of my mirror—that I will likely regret this. That I'll look back on what I did tonight and want to smack myself upside the head. The last time we played this particular song, it turned into a hell of a lot more than I bargained for. But as I watch him, the way his chest is rising and falling, each breath deeper than the last, and his dark eyes that are sinful and demanding, I can't find it in me to care about tomorrow morning or any regrets I'll have.

The heavy ache between my legs is running this show, and I suck in a sharp breath as I reach up into my hair to remove the bobby pins holding my long mane up. He watches me, his wild gaze fixed on my fingers as I move deftly and quickly, dropping the pins to the floor. That'll be a moment of reflection too, when I have to clean them up, but it doesn't matter. The way he's looking at me, the way he kisses and touches me, how he knows all the right moves and ways to make me lose my mind...

Yeah, tonight's happening, whether it's stupid or not.

But he's right. It can only be tonight for a lot of reasons, chief among them, I won't start something with him that leaves me hurt and reeling again.

After the last pin is out, I run my hands over my breasts, squeezing them and plumping them up in my bra while my thumbs drag over my nipples just to fuck with him a bit. He always liked my tits, so why not remind him just how much? He makes a low, angry noise deep in his throat, and his fists clench by his sides. I'm disobeying him, and I bet if I called him sir right now, he'd be back on me in a heartbeat, taking over and destroying me for good.

"You fucking tease." His gravelly voice is pure, unadulterated lust. "I'm going to have you begging me to let you come."

"Your threats don't scare, *sir*. Or have you forgotten that I'm pretty good at doing this on my own?"

He blinks once, slowly, as if trying to make sure I said that word to him. A flush rises up his cheeks, and then he's back at me as I knew he'd be. Grabbing me by my thighs, he flips me around and presses the side of my cheek against the door. He takes my earlobe between his teeth, sucking on the diamond there.

"Keep your hands on the door, little rose, or I'll spank you with my belt for being such a dirty tease and playing with your tits before I gave you permission to."

Jesus. I've never been spanked before. Not like that anyway. My insides squirm at the thought, and now I'm not sure what to do.

Sensing my indecision, he chuckles lightly against my ear, making me shiver. "You want to feel my belt, you devious girl?" He moves behind me. The sound of metal jingling and leather whipping through fabric has me biting into my lip and my pussy clenching. What is it about this man that always has me hurtling willingly to the edge and tumbling over it?

His hand rubs along my ass cheek in a soft circle, and then a gasp flees my lungs when I feel the leather of his belt does the same on the other cheek. Oh, my hell in a handbasket. I wiggle and worm, unable to stop it.

"Hold still, baby girl," he whispers huskily against my ear, and I bite my lip harder in order to obey his command. "Do you want pain, pleasure, or both?"

I shake my head, my legs trembling terribly even as I bite back my smile. I'm in the mood to play, and I know he'll oblige. "Whatever would please you, sir."

He growls against me, his forehead pressing into my spine as he takes a breath. "My little rose, you are playing with fire."

I get a thwack on the ass, not hard, but enough to startle and have me gasping again. And then moaning. Because fuck am I keyed up. My skin was already humming, and that smack was like a spark in the dark. He sinks down and licks where he just spanked, and my knees give out.

"I said to hold still." His voice is a deadly purr, and he bands the hand not spanking me across my lower back to hold me up. *Thwack. Thwack.*

My eyes roll back in my head. I never ever considered how getting spanked with a belt of all things could possibly turn me on, but here I am. A writhing, whimpering mess of a woman. It's the heat of it as it raises my flesh. The naughty taboo. The dirty depravity. The strange, alluring humiliation. How controlled he is with the intensity of his strikes. The way he gives me no choice but to take it and want more of it.

"Did you like that, my bad girl? Is that what you were looking for?"

All I can do is nod, my fingers gripping the door that barely provides purchase. "Yes, sir. It is."

"You're such a filthy fucking goddess. Christ, Tinsley. What you do to me." He presses the hard ridge of his cock nestled beneath the silky fabric of his pants into my smarting skin, and my clit pulses and throbs.

Another thwack, and he's kissing it, licking it, turning that sting and heat into a smoldering inferno. His fingers slip under the back of my bra, and then it falls away, drifting to the floor. A tug on either side of my hips and my thong shreds as he rips it from me. My eyes snap wide, and I glance down to see the silky fabric fall.

Oh, my heavens to Betsy. He just ripped my panties off the same as he did my dress.

I've never been this turned on in my life. If he told me to crawl to him, I would. I'd do anything for him right now. Anything for the pleasure I know he'll give me.

Bending to his knees behind me, he nips, bites, licks, and kisses my ass before he splits my cheeks and rings my forbidden hole with his tongue.

Holy shit!

"Stone. I can't... I haven't—"

"Shhh, baby girl. You are mine tonight. I am your sir, and I will take what I want." As if to prove his point, he licks me there again, and I shudder, the sensation foreign but not as unpleasant as I imagined.

His tongue trickles lower, his hand jerking my hips back and spreading me open wider to give him a better angle and access. His tongue dives straight in, swirling around before he does the same motion on my clit. He rains kisses along my upper thighs and then plunges back in and repeats the motion, switching it up. Giving me what I need, what I'm desperate for, only to immediately pull back.

My asshole. My pussy. My clit. My thighs.

On and on he goes. Edging me so exquisitely, I'm a panting, pining, begging mess. To the point where I can't take it another second. It's too much.

"Stone. I'm..."

I don't even know what I am.

"At my mercy, which is exactly where I intend to keep you tonight." Another lick. Another spanking with the belt, this one a bit harder than before. A punishment. "It's been two years, and yet here I am. You drive me to the end of my sanity. I don't know how to turn away. I don't know how to stop. I see you and I crave you and I have to have you. There is no other way for me. How do you do that to me?"

"It's the same with me," I admit, because it's true. I hate him and I want him. I'm crazy about him, and I can't stand him. But no matter what, I'm inexplicably drawn to him. A magnet, helpless and incapable of fighting the pull.

"You taste better than I remember," he murmurs against my soaked flesh. "Two fucking years of jacking off to endless fantasies and memories, and they never could live up to the real thing."

Oh my hell. My eyes pinch shut, and my teeth bite into my bottom lip so hard I'm shocked I'm not tasting blood. I've thought of him too. Pleasured myself to memories of him more times than I can count.

All I know is...

"I want you inside of me. Please. I *need* it, sir."

A low, strangled groan flees his lips. "Soon. I'm not done playing with you yet."

I whimper and grind against him, desperately seeking his mouth where I need it most.

Thwack.

I yelp in surprise, the belt already half-forgotten, and then his teeth dig in straight over the spot on my ass. More playing. More teasing. More driving me crazy. And just as I'm about to lose my mind completely, he sucks my clit into his mouth right as two fingers plunge straight into me, curl just right, and tip me over the edge.

I come. Hard. It's an explosion. A tsunami. A fucking seismic event. I come all over his fingers that are working me hard and lips and tongue that are all over my clit, sucking and flicking it. My hand slams into the door, and I scream out, grinding down into his face and fingers, my toes curling in my heels that I'm somehow still wearing.

He growls against me. "Yes. That's it. All over my face, little Rose."

I collapse against the wood, breathing hard, eyes closed, mind spinning. He rises behind me, his body coasting against mine so I feel every inch of him as he goes. It's a reminder. He's not nearly done with me. That was simply the start. His appetizer. He has yet to make a meal out of me, but I have no doubt he will.

I feel him start to undress, clothes falling to the floor, and how will I recover from this? Fear ripples through me at the thought that I might not. I did the last time. I forced myself to because I was making a lot of changes in my life, and after I ran from him and cried my eyes out to Wren, I pushed him from my thoughts and away from my heart. That's likely what I'll have to do again.

He's dangerous to me. A potent drug I grow to crave the more I taste. I could shove him out the door and save myself. Protect my heart from the man I nearly gave it all to, even when he didn't want it or ask for it. But I don't want to. I want tonight. The same way I wanted that first night with him back then.

It's only tonight. There is no ship. There are no ten days at sea.

It's this and then nothing.

I'm only here for three months. I can avoid him. It's a big enough city, and I'll be careful when I see his people and mine. How difficult can that be?

"You're thinking too much," he murmurs against me, gripping my hair and using it to turn my neck so he can force my gaze. "That's not a luxury we can afford tonight."

He's right. It's not. I either give into this and all the subsequent aftermath, or I call it quits now.

"If you still want this," he tacks on, his voice even and low, though there's something flickering in the back of his eyes. Something that makes my heart ache. I don't even know what it is, and it's gone almost immediately, and he's back to being Stone. Hard. Cold. Impenetrable.

This was him back then, too. Brief flickering moments of softness and vulnerability, and then gone. I can handle that familiarity. It's a certainty, one he won't go back on. He's too resolute for anything else. And the truth is, all I feel right now is pure, undeniable lust. The kind that only has one way of sating it.

"I still want this."

I reach behind and grip his cock, feeling it pulse against my palm, toying with the barbell through his shaft and head. He takes my hand and plants it back on the door, pushing me halfway against it. Before I can so much as utter a sound, he takes hold of my hips, yanks them back, grips his cock, and thrusts deep inside me.

The noise that tumbles past my lips would be embarrassing for how loud it is, but considering how good he feels—better than anything—it can't be helped.

His forehead presses against my spine between my shoulder blades, and he holds himself still, breathing heavily and murmuring something under his breath that I can't make out. With an angry bite to my shoulder, he starts to pound, his thighs slapping against mine, driving himself in as deep as he can go.

I gasp and clench around him, my breathing ragged and uncontained. My palms flatten against the door beneath my cheek, a barrier to protect myself as he moves hard and fast, taking me without mercy.

He fists my hair, turning my face so his lips can attack mine from the side and his tongue can slip inside and kiss me sloppily. I moan into him, tasting him like this and only wanting more. His hands run down my sides, slap my ass, and reach around to cup and squeeze my breasts. Calloused thumbs drag over my hard nipples, running circles across my skin before he grips them and uses them as leverage while he fucks me. For as brutal as he fucks me, his mouth is soft and gentle, worshiping me as he rains kisses down my jaw to the back of my neck and shoulder.

"Fucking perfect," he grunts, pulling on my nipple and licking my skin, tasting me.

The feeling of him slipping in and out of me, the sounds we're making, the smell of sex, and his spicy cologne all around me are so intense that my back arches and my ass grinds back. My eyes blink open, and I find him there, his eyes on me, watching me from inches away.

"There's my girl. I was waiting." He picks up his pace.

"Oh, god." My eyes start to close again as the head of his cock with that goddamn barbell pounds vigorously against my front wall.

"Un-uh. Look at me. *Look* at me," he repeats more forcefully. "I want to watch you. See your eyes. And tomorrow, when you're sore but still so fucking turned on you have to touch yourself just to try to ebb it, I want you to think about who made you that way."

My eyes cling to his, and I know it's a sight I'll never forget. The sheen of sweat on his brow, the fierce, possessive, wild look in his blown-out green eyes, the flush on his cheeks, and the parting of his lips to accommodate his ragged breaths. He makes me come undone, but I do the same to him.

One hand continues to abuse my tits and nipples while the other slides down to my clit.

"Ah!" I cry as he presses in on it with a firm pressure that has me trembling and shaking uncontrollably.

"Your cunt is soaking me, baby girl. No one has fucked you right since me, have they?"

I shake my head, too close to speak. Too close to tell him

that he's the last one who's been inside me and that I'm starting to think he's the only one who ever should be again.

His hips pick up their pace, his hands and fingers are rubbing and rough, and with his eyes on mine, I lose the battle, close mine, and come harder than I've ever come before. He buries his head in my neck and lets out a roar, his body shaking so badly that I force myself to hold still so I can feel him as he comes undone inside me.

He gives my sensitive clit one final tap, and then his arms wrap around me. For a moment, all he does is hold me, breathing hard with his face nestled against my skin. Spinning me around, he captures my face in his hands and kisses me, just the way he did that last night on the boat. Only I'm not running right now. His hands sweep under my legs and around my back, and he lifts me, holding me bride-style, his lips never leaving mine as he heads for the stairs, carrying me up them, ready for round two.

16

TINSLEY

A sharp *bang, bang, bang* pounds like a gong in my head, and I jolt up, the sheet slipping down my naked body. Immediately, the intrusive sun blinds me as it shoots a freaking laser beam of light directly on my face. "Fuck!" I squint and slam my eyes shut, holding up my hand as if to ward it away. My head throbs a little, and my body aches.

I flop back down and shove a pillow over my face, needing to roll back over and sleep for another ten hours when that bang starts again, and I remember what woke me.

Shit. Ugh. The door. I can only imagine what my face and hair look like, and the last thing I want to do is open the door and face Loomis like this.

Twisted in the sheets, I stumble and fall out of bed, landing on the rug on all fours with a heavy, painful thud like a cat, minus the grace just as there's a third round of bangs followed by a ring of the bell.

"Ow. Okay. Christ, Loomis, I'm coming."

Coming.

I shoot up to my feet and find the spot Stone had occupied

all night empty. I expected it, but it still makes me frown, only to quickly sigh in relief. Imagine if he were still here and I had to face a morning after with him? No thanks. It's better that he's gone, and what was I expecting? Him to say goodbye? Again, no thanks.

I throw on the first things my hands touch in my drawer, a pair of black joggers and a pink oversized loose-neck sweatshirt, forgoing the underwear and bra for now. I fly down the stairs, my sweatshirt falling off my shoulder, and I push it back up as I do a quick scan around. The bobby pins and crystals are piled neatly on the entry table, and my ruined dress and undergarments are folded on a chair.

Well then. He cleaned up his mess at least. Almost like it never happened.

I fling open the door, anxious for the coffee and breakfast Loomis promised me, only to feel my smile slip into another frown when I see it's Forest and not Loomis. I really need to start checking the camera before I just fling the door open.

"Hi," I squeak in surprise.

"Hi," he responds, his expression serious and mournful, but with a hint of anger burning beneath as his gaze flickers around my face and hair, likely noting last night's makeup I never washed off and the snarls in my hair from my updo—from having Stone's hands in it. His tight brown eyes are rimmed in red and held up by purple bruises, and I wonder if he slept last night.

And then another thought hits me.

Does he know I was with Stone last night? Is that why he came this morning?

"What are you doing here?" I tuck into myself, shielding my body from the chilly fall air as it slips past the door and inside the warehouse.

"I wanted to talk to you. Is now a bad time?" He takes in my appearance again and then looks past me as if expecting to find someone—likely Loomis, I tell myself—there behind me. I run my fingers through my hair, trying to undo some of the snarls, but my makeup has to be a smeared nightmare, and no amount of Jesus can save it.

"Uh. No, no, of course it's not. Come in."

I step back and he enters, dropping a kiss on my cheek that is more routine than anything else. I like to think Forest and I are friends, or at the very least friendly, but sometimes I'm not sure we are. Like last night. Friends only works when both people are invested in that outcome, and he might still be a work in progress on that. I've also been avoiding him a bit. It makes it easier if we only see and speak to each other in small doses.

"Where's Loomis?" he asks, still searching around the first floor of the warehouse, which is mostly open space. There is a large recording studio on the other side and some furniture and things about, but it's not like the second floor, which is the main living area.

"Getting breakfast." I hope. I don't like lying to Forest, and I've never once told him Loomis is my boyfriend. But I haven't done much to dispel his belief that he is either. I had hoped Forest would have moved on by now, but it's been a struggle for him, and while I don't want to hurt him, he also needs to understand I've moved on and I'm not coming back to him.

He nods, wipes at his nose, and slowly turns back to me. He and Stone look nothing alike, which has always helped me keep them separate in my head. Stone is insanely tall and broad with a square jawline, dark hair, and bright green eyes. Forest is shorter, though still tall by any standards, and leaner with sandy hair and milk chocolate brown eyes. And when he smiles the way he is now, I remember the guy I grew up loving and feel the pang of guilt that always accompanies it.

"I'm sorry," he says and steps forward to envelop me in a hug. "I'm so, so sorry. I was drunk and way out of line last night.

I had no right to speak to you or Loomis that way. It was the first time I've seen you together with him, other than in tabloids, and it got to me. I wasn't expecting it." He pulls back and rests his hand on my cheek, searching my eyes. "Can you forgive me?"

I swallow and nod, relief shaking my limbs that he's behaving like this and that he didn't catch me with his brother. Which again makes me feel like shit because I was. Here comes that regret I was expecting, or maybe it's not regret so much as more guilt.

"Yeah? You sure? You don't look so sure."

I giggle lightly and relax. There he is. "I'm sure. You're forgiven, and I should have told you I was coming and that I was bringing Loomis with me."

"It still didn't give me the right to behave like a belligerent asshole." He sighs, his hand dropping to his side. "Will you tell me the truth then? About the two of you, I mean."

I shift and adjust my sweatshirt back up my shoulder. "Forest, he's not my boyfriend, just my very dear friend."

But when I say that, some of the anger that had dissipated comes flaring back, only it's tinted with suspicion and something else. Before he can respond, there's a knock and a ring. My heart hammers again, but I go to the door, and this time, it's Loomis as expected, his hands full of to-go bags and coffee.

He gives me a quick once-over and then snickers. "Well, my love, this is a pleasant surprise. You look like the cat had his wicked way with you last night, and you enjoyed every second of it."

My eyes pop out of my skull, and a blush takes over my face. Forest clears his throat and Loomis chokes in an *oh shit* way.

"It's Forest," I mouth, silently overpronouncing the words so he can read them.

Loomis's eyes widen, and he tilts his head as his questioning gaze sweeps from me over to where Forest is hidden behind me and then back to me. I give him a little headshake, but it's clear I must look like I was ridden hard and hung out to dry.

He steps inside, and I shut the door.

"Right. Sorry, mate. Ignore all that. I didn't know you were here." He shifts things around in his arms and sticks out his hand. "We didn't get a proper introduction last night. I'm Loomis Powell. It's very nice to finally meet you. I've heard loads about you."

Forest hesitates for a long moment, but eventually, he sticks his hand out, and I watch as he tries to crush poor Loomis's hand. "Forest Fritz." That's all.

Okay then. So much for that apology.

Forest releases Loomis, who tries not to grimace or visibly shake out his hand. "I'll just bring this up to the kitchen then and give you both another minute." Loomis shoots me a quick look that says *if you need me, I'm right here*, and heads upstairs, obviously knowing exactly where to go, and the illusion that he's staying here with me is complete, and now Forest thinks I'm lying to him.

Awesome.

"I'll go," Forest says, starting for the door only to pause when his hand meets the knob and his head twists back to me. "But for what it's worth, you don't have to lie to me. That hurts like hell, Tins."

I shake my head. "I'm not lying about him."

His eyes narrow again as they skitter all over my face and neck. The blatant question is there. *If it's not him you fucked last night, then who was it,* and I should have kept my mouth shut.

Frustration and sadness take over, eclipsing all the anger. "I don't know what else to say to you. You're either lying to me and he's your boyfriend, but you don't want me to know or he's not your boyfriend and is clearly using you, and you can't trust him." He turns and steps into me, standing close but still keeping enough space between us that I don't feel closed in. "I hope you know how much I care about you. You can trust me with anything, and no matter what, I'll always be here for you." He sighs. "You deserve better than some asshole using you. You deserve better than him. You deserve me." Another sigh, and he shakes his head as if he wishes he hadn't said that. "I'm heading back to LA today, but when you're back home, I'd like to meet up and talk some more. Without the interruption."

With that, he leaves, shutting the door with a resounding bang behind him, and I collapse against it.

"I'm not using you," Loomis shouts down from the second floor, and I crack, a much-needed laugh tickling my lips. "But I'm guessing it was big brother and not little brother who gave you that rather impressive hickey on your shoulder."

Oh, shit.

17

STONE

My feet pound in a steady rhythm of left, right, left right as I run and fucking run faster, trying to chase away the images from last night that refuse to leave my brain away. When I left the party, I had no intention of seeking her out, and when I somehow found myself at her parents' warehouse, I told myself I'd watch her and Loomis go inside, and that would be that. I wasn't planning on knocking, let alone confronting her.

But he didn't go inside.

And he kissed her cheek goodnight as if they were only friends.

In that moment, I didn't care about anything else. It had been two years, and I was desperate to touch her. Infatuated by her beauty and presence. And hateful because hating her makes life tolerable. You'd think I'd be better at this by now, but I'm not. She's always there. Eradicating her is like trying to get cockroaches out of a New York City apartment. Impossible. But that doesn't mean you want to live with them either.

I run faster. Harder. The music blasting so loud through my

AirPods I'm likely giving myself permanent hearing damage, but so be it.

Anything not to think for a little while.

That is until my phone pings with a text and I slow down to a walk.

Tinsley: You gave me a freaking hickey!

I laugh, using the hem of my shirt to wipe my sweaty face and neck. For a beat, I debate not responding. Tinsley is my one weakness. I've done everything I could to be a better person and man, and the first brush with her and the temptation she poses, I crumble.

Glancing around, I shift over to the edge of the sidewalk on the corner, angling my body toward the alley. I give another look, make sure no one is paying attention to me, lift my shirt, and snap a picture of my right lower quadrant, capturing the dip between my hip and abs.

The picture shows up on my screen, displaying the large reddish-purple welt, and I tap the blue up arrow to send it to her.

It goes through and I start walking again, nearly home that is only another two blocks away. An unstoppable smile threatens my lips as I wait for her reaction. Luckily, I don't have to wait long. I didn't expect to.

Tinsley: OMG! Wow, that's one hell of a hickey. At least yours isn't visible unless you lift your shirt.

Me: Yours is only visible if you wear something that shows your shoulders.

Tinsley: So you knew you left your mark? Bastard!

Me: Only after I knew you left one on me.

Tinsley: It's not my fault your V thing is sexy.

I stumble over nothing. Shit. This woman is going to be the death of me.

Me: it's not my fault the dip between your shoulders and neck is insanely sexy. I take it you haven't seen your tits yet?

My smile grows to epic proportions, and I practically skip as I head into my building, saying good morning to my doorman who looks at me funny. Yeah, I'm not a big smiler during my daily comings and goings.

Tinsley: I cannot believe you! Three hickeys!

Me: That's only because I couldn't give your pussy one.

Though I did try. And the belt marks on her ass... no welts or broken skin, it was just a little red, but fuck, I'm getting hard just thinking about them.

Tinsley: You're unbelievable!

Me: Funny, that's exactly what you said last night, only you were moaning it.

Tinsley: I'm not amused.

Me: No one has to see them unless you show them off, which you better fucking not.

Those are my tits. My spot where the curve of her neck meets the top of her shoulder.

Tinsley: Your brother already saw the one on my shoulder as did Loomis.

Oh. My gut sinks like she just filled it with lead. I punch in the code for my floor and the elevator whisks me up sixteen stories.

Me: Did you tell Forest who gave it to you?

Tinsley: No! Of course not. He assumed it was from Loomis, but Loomis knows.

It's a relief, but I still feel like shit. I hate that my brother saw a hickey on her shoulder that I put there. The elevator doors open, and I step out into the hallway, looking left instead of immediately heading right, and debate my next move as I linger in between the two apartments on this floor.

Me: You don't have to worry. I won't give you anymore since my mouth won't be on your skin again.

Then again, I didn't shower when I got home at three

because I could still smell her on me and that's where I wanted to keep her. Knowing I wouldn't have it again.

Tinsley: Sucks to be you.

She has no idea.

Me: Sucks to be you. You like my mouth.

Tinsley: I like a lot of things that I shouldn't have but still crave. Like carbs.

I laugh. This fucking girl.

Me: I got you to eat carbs.

Tinsley: You get me to do a lot of things that aren't good for me. But I don't regret them.

Me: Me neither.

I pause.

Me: Bye, my little Rose.

Tinsley: Bye, Stone.

My chest squeezes to the point of sucking the air from my lungs and I no longer hesitate. I go left and pound on his door. And then pound again when he doesn't immediately answer.

"The fuck, Stone?!" Mason growls from inside before his door swings open, revealing all six-foot-six of him in only his boxer briefs with his wild reddish-brown hair all over the place.

"How did you know it was me?"

He steps back to let me in, rubbing at the sleep crusting his eyes. "Because no one else who is awake at this hour would dare bang on my door when it's the Sunday of my bye week."

"At this hour? It's almost ten."

"Your point?"

"I fucked Tinsley Monroe."

His eyes widen and his jaw goes slack. Without warning he reaches out and pinches my arm.

"Ow!" I smack his hand away. "The fuck did you do that for?" I rub at my smarting skin.

"Nope. I'm not dreaming."

"You're supposed to pinch yourself to determine that."

"Only dumbasses do that. It hurts to get pinched."

I roll my eyes and head straight for his kitchen to make myself coffee. Mase doesn't drink caffeine or eat junk during the season, but he keeps his pantry well-stocked for me. It's what best friends and neighbors do for each other. It's why I have his green sludge powder shit at my place.

I pour the beans into the machine and switch it on, and he joins me, taking a seat at the island after having put on a pair of sweatpants. The grinder clicks off and the coffee starts to brew, but now I'm onto omelets, cutting up veggies and ham and pulling out the goat cheese we both like in them but would never order in public.

I also don one of his aprons. It has an arrow pointing up toward my face and says, "*I'll feed all you fuckers, just try me.*"

Mason watches me do all this, and I keep my head down and back to him as I work. It felt good to finally tell someone. Tinsley said Loomis knew, and I felt that meant I got a freebie too. Since Vander and Owen don't live here, Mason is who I have. A guy who goes through women the same way he plays—fast, hard, and unapologetic. I was the same way until Tinsley ruined all other women for me.

Owen is a dad and older than me by several years, and he's generally who I talk to about real shit because he's both of those things. He was the ideal option, but I won't bother his Sunday with his woman and his daughter. Vander doesn't have time or trust for women, so he wouldn't have been much help.

The moment the veggies start to sizzle in the pan is the moment he's done waiting me out. "She's the girl, right? The one from two years ago?"

I nod and roll my head over my shoulder to meet his eyes. "Yeah. She is."

"Thought so. I didn't see you fucking her unless she was the girl."

The girl. Yeah, she's the girl, all right. I sigh.

"Seems a bit like instalove."

"What the fuck is that?"

He shrugs. "You know, where you fall instantly and shit."

I stare at him, utterly perplexed. "That's a thing? How do you even know what that is?"

He looks away, and I know something is up with him. "Katy told me about it. She read it in some book. So is that what this is?"

"No, it wasn't instant, though I suppose it was fast. Or maybe it wasn't. Maybe it was brewing for a while, and I pretended it wasn't because she belonged to Forest. I honestly don't know anymore." My brows crinkle. "How are we having this conversation?"

"Men talk about this stuff."

I move the veggies around in the pan. "Do we though?"

"We do now, motherfucker, so spill it. Are you instalove with Tinsley?"

I turn back to the pan before I burn shit, and add the scrambled eggs, watching them pop and sizzle with the veggies. "No. I'm eternitylove with Tinsley, and I don't even care how ridiculous that sounds since you whipped out instalove first. Are you going to tell me your instalove story?"

"What makes you think I have one?" He's hedging. He can't even meet my gaze.

"Because you do."

He points at me. "This is about you, not me."

"I'll tell you mine if you tell me yours."

He runs his finger along the counter. "I met someone who is with someone else, but I like her. A lot. Now tell me about you and Tinsley."

Fine. I launch into the whole story because I need to tell someone and he's asking. When I'm done, I sit down beside him, take a sip of my coffee, and dig into my omelet. Mason is frozen. He hasn't even touched his green slime smoothie I made him as an apology for waking him up early on his bye week.

Finally, he blinks and sits back on his stool, nods to himself, and then gulps down half of his smoothie. Vomit. The thing is like sludge and tastes like it too.

"This explains the ink on your back." He uses his glass to gesture toward my left shoulder.

I forgot he was with me when I got it up in Lenox's shop in Maine. It's of Benthesicyme but has a twisting of purple roses up the mast. At the time, he just assumed it was because Benthesicyme saved me and or fixed me or whatever you want to call my metamorphosis from asshole to human.

"Dude, all this time it's been Tinsley Monroe you've been in love with. Fuck, brother. That's some rough shit." He digs into his omelet and leaves me stranded with that. "Between you and Forest…" He shakes his head as he chews. "He's never quite been one of us, though, has he?"

"Does that make what I did any better? He's still my brother."

"I get it. Sorta. I mean, Tins is amazing. I've just never thought of her like that. Considering how my family and hers are, to me, she's more like a sister or cousin. Kind of like how Katy is to us. But, I mean, hell…" He looks at me. "What are you going to do?"

"There's nothing for me to do." I continue shoveling eggs into my mouth. "It was one more time. One last night. Now it's back to me pretending she doesn't exist."

"Except that hasn't worked for you. So maybe it's time you try something else?"

"Like what?" I ask him plainly, a bit serious, even as the words roll off my tongue dripping in sarcasm. "You just told me you're into a woman you can't be with. This is no different. You're an older brother. If you were in love with one of Quinn's or Crew's exes…" I leave that hanging between us.

"I know. But still." He's bothered by this. Seriously bothered. Mason likes the people in his life to be happy. But there is no fix for this. "I'm glad you finally told me. It's bothered me how you refused to try to find her, but now I understand why." He pauses and turns to me. "She worth it?"

I keep my eyes trained on my eggs. "It doesn't much matter. She's not mine, and she never will be."

He's quiet, frowning and Mason doesn't do frowns. He's a fucking puppy who frolics in the sunshine. This morning is the most serious I've seen him in a while.

"She's not Forest's either."

I shake my head. "She'll always be his first."

He doesn't like that answer, but he doesn't argue with me either. "She's in Boston for the next few months shooting that film. And clearly it wasn't one-sided if you spent the night with her last night."

I shrug. "If I don't run into her again, it won't happen again. And even if I do run into her, it won't happen again. Whatever Tinsley and I had is over. So maybe you're right, maybe it's time I get myself back out there and try to meet someone new."

18

STONE

Mason vows to find me someone, and I leave it at that. All I know is that it's time to get over my infatuation with Tinsley. And for most of the week, I'm feeling better about it. My hickey starts to fade, and I get lost in the day-to-day of work. That is until my luck runs out on day five.

A buzz brewing like strong coffee zips through the emergency department, perking people up and getting them anxious and excited. My teenage patients are the first to report it to me. I have three sitting in observation for various reasons, all telling me they have to be discharged or at least brought upstairs since now they're all besties after being stuck in here together for the last few hours.

"You're not supposed to be on your phone," I tell one of them. "You have a concussion."

"I don't care. My brain will heal. This is life or death."

"Same for us," one in the next room calls out. The walls here are a little too paper-thin for anyone's good. "If you bring her up, you have to take me too."

"What's upstairs? Other than the cafeteria and patient

rooms." I lean against the door, my arms folded over my scrub top. I'm not discharging them. Two are waiting on beds upstairs and one is under concussion protocol and has another five hours here before I'll let her go.

"Tinsley Monroe is here," the kid across the hall gripes in that teenager, everyone is a drag way. "I heard one of the techs say she's going to put on a concert. Like an actual concert."

"I heard she's going to take pictures with everyone and hand out things to us."

"Tinsley Monroe is here?" I ask dubiously, though I don't know why. Nothing she does surprises me.

"Yes! OMG. Show him the picture, Abby!" That's the girl next door. The one who is about to be admitted for anemia.

Abby flips her phone around and there's a video of Tinsley hiding her face, heading into the hospital with security surrounding her, her guitar on her back. "My mom took that picture and just texted it to me."

Christ.

"Did your mom post that picture or just send it to you?"

"Just sent it to me. She was heading out to get lunch and saw her. Like this very second saw her. You have to help us, or I'll legit die."

"You won't die because it's my job to make sure you don't."

"Um, that's great and all, but can you help us or not?"

I pull out my phone and text Tinsley.

Me: Are you here?

She replies instantly.

Tinsley: Define here.

Me: My hospital. Are you at Children's?

Tinsley: I am, but you can't tell anyone.

I roll my eyes.

Me: Three of my teenagers already know. One's mom saw you walking in and snapped a picture.

Tinsley: Shit. Ask her mom not to post it on social media

for at least four hours. And bring them up! I'm on the fifth floor in the auditorium.

I slide my phone back into my pocket. "If your mom doesn't post that picture for at least four hours, I can take you all upstairs. I have an in with the artist."

"Oh my god. Oh my god."

Her heart rate starts to spike.

"Only people with stable vitals get to go though," I call out to the three of them, raising an eyebrow at Abby.

"I can't help it!" She tries to climb off her gurney. "Tinsley is my absolute favorite. I've been to two of her concerts. She's everything."

Tell me about it.

"Do you actually know her?" Beth, the girl next door, asks.

"Yes. I know her. Very well," I tack on for no reason.

"He's Stone Fritz. He definitely knows her," Kateyln from across the hall yells. "His younger brother is Forest Fritz as in Tinsley's ex. I'm Googling it all now."

Thanks for the reminder.

"So, will you take us?" she continues. "For real?"

I sigh. It's going to be a long afternoon. "Yes. I'll take you up."

I think I'm their new hero with how loudly they scream, and I watch as Abby winces. Yeah, concussions suck.

"Put your phone away, or it's not happening."

She does so immediately and I, along with two nurses, wheel them upstairs, down the hall, and past a fleet of security. I show them my ID badge, and they let us all through. Tinsley has taken over a large auditorium we use for our M&Ms, or morbidity and mortalities. Her face shines like the sun as we enter, and she quickly catches my eye and throws me a playful wink.

She's wearing a green sweater dress that hugs her curves perfectly. Her hair is down in long, thick, silky waves, and her makeup is show-worthy, yet casual with red lips and black-lined eyes.

"Hey!" she calls out through her microphone. She's all the way down the tiered auditorium, sitting on a stool with her guitar in her hands and a microphone cued up in front of her. "I'm so happy to be here with you this afternoon. Boston, as many of you know, is where I'm from, and I still consider it my home. I wanted to come in and hang out with you all for a bit, but I need you to do me a favor, okay?"

She has the entire room wrapped around her finger. Including me.

"You can record and take pictures, and I promise to take selfies with anyone who wants one, but please, please, please do *not* post it on any social media or even text it to your friends until an hour after I leave here. I'm not here for the press, I'm here for you, so if you could help me out with that, I'd be forever grateful."

The room is filled with about two hundred kids, all here for one reason or another. Many are with their nurses or aides. Most have oxygen tanks or IVs attached to them. They're sick kids and Tinsley Monroe is making their year by being here just for them. And fuck if it doesn't make me love her more.

But loving her doesn't change anything, and I have to believe eventually I'll get over it. People do. They do that all the time. They fall in and out of love and they move on. That's my plan. But right now, the woman down front is throwing a serious monkey wrench into that. Especially as she starts to strum on her guitar and sing to her fans.

"Did you know she was coming?" my father, Kaplan, who is a cardiothoracic surgeon here, asks me, clapping me on the shoulder as we watch Tinsley sing and perform. Something we've seen her do dozens and dozens of times over, but it never gets old. On his other side are Owen, who is a general pediatric surgeon, and my uncle Luca, who is a neurosurgeon.

"Nope. One of my teenagers told me."

"Mine too," Owen admits. "Rory is going to kill me."

I snicker, thinking about his six-year-old daughter, who is a huge Tinsley Monroe fan. "Can't you just ask Tinsley to play for her? Isn't that one of the perks of a friends and family discount?"

"Rory has seen Tinsley in concert about five times in her six years, and Tinsley always goes above and beyond for her. Still, I will catch shit if Rory hears about this, and I didn't drag her out of school for it."

The first song ends with a raucous round of applause.

"All right, my loves, who wants to pick the next song? This concert is about you, so tell me what you want me to play."

"Old MacDonald," someone calls out in front, being a total wiseass, and Tinsley cracks up.

"That's not one of mine, but I'm happy to oblige."

She starts to strum the chords, and everyone titters and giggles. She sings the lyrics and points to random children to fill in with which animal they want.

From there, it's one song after another. Some kids stay till the end. Others show up halfway through. Many have to leave for one reason or another. Tinsley makes a point to stop whatever she's doing and take a selfie with anyone who asks, and she plies them with kisses and hugs and signed T-shirts. She's a queen, and we're all here as mere mortal subjects.

"This is a song I wrote a couple of years ago," she says, strumming a song that sounds familiar though I can't quite place it. "It's called 'Into the Storm.'"

"They caged me in the status quo, trapped me into saying yes when I should have said no. I became complacent, staring out at the world with too much impatience. Unfulfilled, it was the start of a deadly prequel, and with no surprise, I began to plot her demise. I'd come undone and chased the storm, sinking like a rock instead of skipping like a stone."

The song continues, but I'm rendered speechless.

"Those sound like song lyrics."

"They might be, but how sad are they?"

They're a little different than what she said that night. More put together and complete. But I have no doubt it's them. I haven't heard this song. I couldn't do it. I couldn't listen to the album she released after that trip, but hearing the lyrics now, I know this song can't be about anything else.

It continues, talking about strength and rebirth. Flipping all those sad lines on their heads. The song ends, and her gaze flickers up to mine for a beat before she immediately goes into the next song. It was so fast that no one other than me would catch it. But I did, and I know she sang that for me.

It was a thank you.

It was a look at where those ten days got us.

My father trickles off, as do Owen and Luca. They have patients they need to get back to, but my shift ended over an hour ago. I haven't been able to force myself out of here.

Tinsley plays without a break for over two hours, and I stand in the back as she takes another hour with the kids, not rushing a single one, answering questions and smiling for pictures.

When it's finally done, when the last child is gone, and all of my patients are brought where they need to be by their nurses, she climbs the steps, her security hot behind her, and greets me with a timid smile that doesn't speak to the wild love she gave everyone else.

"Hi."

I smirk. "Hi."

"You're still here."

"My shift is over."

She likes this.

"I liked your song."

She doesn't have to ask which one I'm talking about. "I played it for you."

I nod. I knew that.

"Walk me out?"

Anything, I nearly reply. And because I'm a fucking fool, I reach out for her hand. She takes it, and we walk across the empty floor to the elevators like this.

"You look happy," she notes as we wait for the elevator to come. One opens, but it's full of people and we decide to wait for the next one.

I laugh. It's an absurd statement, but despite the fact that I haven't had the girl, I've had everything else. "I am. I'm in a good place. The place I wanted to find and be in. What about you?" We haven't caught up. We haven't exchanged stories after the ten days. We fought and we fucked, but we didn't have the quiet after. The one we always had without fail.

"When I got home, I immediately fired my manager, Apollo, who didn't take the news well, but the relief I felt in firing him was immense. I never felt comfortable with him. He gave me sleazebag, creepo vibes, and then as if to prove my point, he went around and trash-talked my name all over town. Thankfully it backfired on him, but still, it wasn't fun. After I got rid of him, my agent and label followed. I had a heart-to-heart with my parents. I had always been reluctant to use the label my dad did. I thought it would feel like I was trading on his name, but the truth is, Eden Dawson is the best, and so is Turn Records. I hired a new agent and manager and signed with Turn, and all three have been the best decisions I've ever made." She pauses. "Other than breaking and entering on a ship that wasn't mine."

My hand holds hers a little tighter. I knew some of this. Sort of. It was all very second and third-hand. But hearing her say it and seeing the gleaming, contented smile on her face is everything. It's what I wanted for her, even if I couldn't share in those triumphs and this happiness with her.

"What made you come here today?" I ask as the elevator doors part, and her team lets us go in one alone. I wish they hadn't. I want to kiss her senseless and wouldn't even consider it if they were in here with us.

"I do this in LA every six months or so. I love kids. I love being with kids. Sick kids break my heart, but they need the most love, and concerts aren't always accessible for them. I do the same thing at women's and children's shelters when I can."

And with that declaration, I bring our joined hands up to her face, spin toward her, and take her lips with mine. It's not even intentional. It's just a have-to sort of gig. Immediately, I part her lips with mine, understanding how we're on stolen seconds. She kisses me back, and it fuels me. I press her into the side of the elevator, my free hand on her hip, squeezing and pulling her into mine.

She feels me—all of me, every hard inch she's turned me into—and I revel when she gasps, only to tear myself away the moment the car slows and before it dings to sound our arrival.

Still, I don't let go of her hand. I should. I need to. But I don't. I walk her out the front of the building, her security back by our side, likely having taken the stairs, and we head outside into the cool Boston afternoon.

"Next time, pick a day I'm not working," I tell her. "Seeing you only makes me want you, and I'm trying very hard not to want you."

She looks down at the ground between us, and I play with her hands, holding her close only to freeze. The fuck?

"Are you engaged?"

"What?" Her head snaps up, and I raise her left hand between us, the one sporting a huge rock on it. "Oh." She laughs. "We filmed the engagement scene today. I must have forgotten to take it off before I raced over here. I'm still wearing my set outfit too." She reaches up with that hand and smooths out the crease between my brows. "Did that bother you?"

I clench my jaw and snatch her hand away, holding it firmly and rolling the fake diamond on her finger in vicious circles. "Considering I fucked you less than a week ago and just kissed you? Yeah, you being engaged would have bothered the hell out of me."

"Good thing I'm not then." She shrugs, with a mischievous glint in her eyes and a smile curving up her lips. "Since it matters so much to you."

"You're being a tease again."

"Maybe. It's a beautiful fall afternoon, and I'm riding a post-performance high. Plus, I made out with a hot guy in the elevator today."

"Did you now? I hear he's a good kisser. And amazing in bed."

She snorts. "Is that so? And how do you know who I'm talking about? I could have kissed a dozen people in the elevator today."

"True." I lean in and whisper by her ear. "But I bet I'm the only one who made your panties wet."

"You're flirting," she accuses, and I laugh.

"I'm definitely flirting. It's harmless though when we both know it won't go anywhere and I won't see you again."

"I hate that we do that. I wouldn't mind being your friend, though I suppose we were never that before."

"No. We weren't."

And I can't be her friend now.

We pause. Stare. And finally, I utter, "Bye, Tinsley."

"Bye, Stone." She leans in and kisses my cheek. "For the record, I checked with the emergency department. I knew you were working today." I get a wink and she steps back, releases me, and walks away with her security detail.

It isn't until I get home an hour later that the news breaks.

Tinsley Monroe Engaged to Ex's Brother.

19

TINSLEY

The moment I get home from the hospital, my world falls apart once again, and that high I had been rocking from the performance and Stone's kiss crashes at my feet. It's on the doorstep. I see it before we even reach the stone steps. We're maybe a hundred yards out, and I'm staring at it, trying to pretend it's something else when my heart starts to race in a pattern that tells me it already knows better. It's the same red envelope. The same block handwriting.

What. The. Fuck?!

My breath comes out in a torrential rush, and Loomis is beside me, all fun and smiles since we're supposed to have dinner together, until he notes my expression and follows my gaze.

I hear him swallow.

"Should I pick it up?"

"How?" I ask, my voice hoarse. Neither of us is able to tear ourselves away from the envelope sitting innocuously on the step when it's anything but innocuous. "How is that even possible unless..."

Loomis's head whips frantically around while he moves

protectively closer to me. I love my friend. I love him so much and am so grateful every day he's in my life, but more than that, I'm grateful he's standing here beside me right now.

"We should call the police," he murmurs urgently.

"The Boston police aren't involved in this, and if I do that, it'll get out to the public, and I don't want that. It'll start all over again, Loomis. The media, not just the paparazzi, but the media frenzy."

"Fine. The bloody FBI then, Tinsley," he barks out, only to soften his voice and wrap his arms around me. "I'm sorry. I've had obsessed fans. Fans who try to scale my fence or break into my home or see me on the street and chase after me for a picture or a cheek kiss. I've never had this, and it scares me for you. Especially after what you told me you went through last time with it. Tell me if you want me to pick it up and dispose of it. I will. You'll never have to see it or open it."

It's tempting So very tempting.

"It needs to go to the FBI. But first, it needs to go to…" I trail off.

"Your men," he finishes for me.

I haven't told him what Lenox and Vander can do, but he knows the family I come from. The family I'm affiliated with. And he knows I have extra reach even if he doesn't fully understand its magnitude.

I glance around. There is no crowd, but we're far from alone on the street and people most definitely recognize us. We get a wider berth in Boston, but we still get watched. "Do you think he's here?"

"Don't know. All I know is you're not staying in this warehouse another night. You have cameras, yes?"

"Yes."

"Brilliant. Let's have a look at those, shall we? And this letter…"

"I'll pick it up. Not you."

He nods. I hate that's the precaution we have to take, but it's a real one. I trust Loomis with my life, and when this originally started, I hadn't even met him yet, but I can't have his prints on this red envelope either. I won't do that to him.

"Wait!" he calls out. "Let's snap a picture of it first."

"Smart."

I pull out my phone and take a picture of it just how it was left and then pluck the five-by-eight envelope up. I need to call Lenox. And my father. He's not going to be happy, and I know exactly what he's going to say. This is his first world tour in years, and the last thing I want is to ruin or disrupt that for him by having him come home just so he can play papa bear.

But I don't need a papa bear watching over my every move. I carry a knife on me. Pepper spray too. I know self-defense and have a security team, but more than that, I won't go back into hibernation and allow everyone else to take over and call the shots for me.

"Fucking asshole. It's been years. Why now?"

"I wish I could tell you, but what I can tell you is that you're not going in there without your security checking the building first," Loomis tells me, just as I hear my name called.

Both of us spin in place to find Wren jogging toward us, letting out an annoyed and relieved huff when she finds us. "I've tried to call you like a dozen times," she bursts out. "Stop being so cool and ignoring me."

I check my phone and sigh. "I'm sorry, I had it off since I was at Children's."

She waves me away, pulls me in for a hug, and then smacks my arm, making my brows pinch. I'm close with Katy, Keena, and Kenna. But Wren has always been my best friend in the group. She and I kept in touch the most when I left as a teenager.

"Are you fucking my cousin again?!"

"Jesus, Wren." My head swivels like it's on a spit. "How about a little care with that mouth of yours?"

"Fine, but what the hell is going on with the two of you?"

"Which cousin?"

She scoffs, not enjoying my humor, only I'm not fully kidding. The question is valid. "Oh, that's a good one. Stone. I'm talking about Stone."

My heart starts to boom. "What about him?"

"Dude, it's all over the internet. All over social freaking media. *Boston's Landing* and *Interntainment* are reporting it, but it's catching everywhere."

I'm out of patience. "Wren, reporting what?"

"That you're engaged to Stone."

"What?!" I scream, and every head within a two-mile radius turns my way. It's five in the evening on a Friday, and people are starting to get out of work and crowd the streets. At least it's almost dark out. We had a half day of shooting, and then I went to the hospital. But... "How? How on earth could anyone think I'm engaged..." I trail off and then stare down at my left hand. Fuck. Fuckity fuck fuck. The stupid prop engagement ring and someone caught us standing outside the hospital together. I kissed his cheek. I smiled and flirted with him. He smiled and flirted back. We were us.

Crap!

Just then, something flashes out of the corner of my eye. "Tinsley! Loomis! Over here."

Double crap!

In our next breath, we're surrounded by the press, mostly local because Boston isn't New York or LA, but there are still plenty of them.

"Loomis?! How do you feel about Tinsley being engaged to another man?"

"Has she been cheating on you with Stone Fritz?"

"Tinsley, how long have you and Stone Fritz secretly been dating?"

"Does Forest know you're in love with his brother?"

"Come on!" Wren cries, waving us on, her blonde hair whipping about as she starts to run in the opposite direction. And stupid me, I called off my security detail when I met up with Loomis and knew we were hanging out at my place tonight. "Dude, move!" she calls again, snapping my attention away from the hordes of people surrounding us. "I've got my brother's Rover waiting!"

"Hard to argue that." Loomis shifts closer to me, and we flee, walking briskly through the press who follow us, keeping our heads down and refusing to answer questions. Loomis opens the front passenger door for me, and I climb in, slamming it quickly closed behind me. The moment Loomis is in the back seat of Owen's large SUV, Wren starts driving us slowly out of here, making the paparazzi part like the Red Sea out of the way.

Speaking of red, the red letter is burning against my hand, and I drop it to my lap along with my face. What a fucking afternoon this turned out to be.

"Where are we headed?" I ask in a low voice as I slide out my phone and pull up *Interntainment*. The first thing that comes up are pictures of me and Stone outside the hospital. Us holding hands. Us smiling at each other. Us standing close as we talk. Me touching his face. Him touching mine. Me kissing his cheek.

"Stone's," she answers as if that should be obvious, but there is a catch in her voice. "Everyone is already there."

He has to be furious.

He didn't ask for any of this. I kissed his cheek on the street. I touched his face. I told him I knew he was working in the ER because I did. It was one of the reasons I picked today. I hadn't planned on going to see him, but I liked the idea of it happening by chance or him knowing I was there and coming to see me. It was stupid and reckless. A girl who wanted a boy to notice her move.

And it's costing us. Both of us.

My eyes close, and I resist the urge to cry. Everything feels like it's pressing back down on me the way it did back then, and I can barely catch my breath. Still, I can't let it consume me. Not again.

As if echoing my thoughts, a text comes in.

Apollo: I just saw the video of the media swarm. Congrats on your engagement. Let me know if you ever need anything. I'm always here.

I snort out a sardonic laugh. For one, I can't believe how fast what just happened made it to the internet that Apollo already saw it. What was that? Seconds. For another, what an asshole he is texting me after everything he did to me. He bad-mouthed me all over

LA after I fired him. He called me a diva and told anyone who would listen that I was impossible to work for and with. He tried to ruin my career, but it backfired on him to the point where a few other artists he was working with left him.

Whatever. I don't care about him. he's trying to rub in what just happened because he knows I hate it.

Ugh.

"I didn't mean to cause a mess," I murmur, my voice thick. When everyone thought Loomis and I were together, they'd take pictures and follow us a bit.

But I haven't been surrounded that way since Terrance Howard went to jail and then later, when I broke up with Forest. It's part of what had me running. That and a shoddy team I'd hired surrounding me. In the last two years, I've rebuilt everything from the ground up to be my own. And the paps didn't bother me so much after that.

This is different. This is a scandal. And they're going to chase it because it's a juicy one.

"I don't see how this is a bad thing," Loomis pipes up from the back, scooting forward and ducking down until he's positioned as close as he can be between the two front seats. "For the moment, the world thinks you're engaged to Stone. If you have the press all over you, it makes it tougher for those letters or the person behind them to find you. Regardless of that benefit, if you want this story gone, it's easy enough to explain you're wearing a prop ring and were just playing at the hospital for the children and ran into a family friend. There. Done."

I nod slowly. He's right. It's why I have a PR team. They're the ones who made the statement that Loomis and I are just friends, and though no one believed it, it's what you do, and then the press moves on to the next thing.

"Letter thing?" Wren questions, and I hold up the envelope.

"My stalker boyfriend is back."

Wren hisses out a slew of curses. "Shit. God, Tins, I'm so sorry. I thought he was in jail."

"He got out a few months ago. I hadn't heard from him, but apparently he thought today was the day to change that."

I knew Terrance was released from prison a few months back, but he hasn't tried to reach out, and I've had Lenox keep an eye on him. Terrance is on parole and not allowed to leave California or get within a hundred yards of me or any of his other victims.

But there is no postage on this envelope. It wasn't in the mailbox.

It was hand-delivered to the front step.

"Something isn't adding up," Loomis muses, and I turn, catching his contemplatively creased brow, his hand on his jaw as if he's trying to unravel something incredibly elusive. "You were brought out the back entrance of the hospital after a surprise visit. You've done those dozens of times before, and not once have those videos or photographs leaked early. Not to mention, the person who photographed you wasn't close enough for you to see or notice. Paparazzi are anything but subtle and would have come as close as possible. Same with fans. Then, on the same day, less than an hour apart, you receive an envelope."

He has a point about the horrible timing of it. "We don't know what time the envelope was left yet. But are you suggesting the person who leaked the photos is my stalker?"

"I honestly don't know. But it just feels off. That's all I'm saying. It just feels off."

"Whatever it is or hopefully isn't, you have a safety net now." Wren changes lanes and brings us closer to Boston Common. "Stone is used to press." She shrugs, her eyes on the road. "We all are. Being a Fritz in this town comes with them, so he knows what he's doing. It'll get sorted, but it's good to figure it out, and we do that in person."

"I know." Because I do. She grew up being a Fritz, but I grew up being a Monroe, and we're equally as famous in Boston, and definitely more famous throughout the country and the world. I know how these things operate and I wasn't surprised she was taking us to Stone's. Doesn't mean I want to deal with this with an audience attached, but it's not necessarily a bad thing either.

I have about a thousand missed calls and texts, but I leave it on Do Not Disturb. I can see them, but they don't know they're reaching me yet. I should turn it back on, but I have no desire to right now. Not until I talk to Stone. And Vander, if he's there, and if not him, then definitely Lenox. Vander wasn't involved much the first time with Terrance, but Lenox certainly was.

I can't talk to my PR team or even my parents until I know what's happening and as many details as I can.

"Can I ask about you and Stone?"

I sigh. "I have no idea what you're talking about."

She laughs and reaches over to poke my shoulder. "Such a slut for those Fritz boys."

Loomis chokes on his laugh.

I scrub my hands over my face. "Only one, it seems, though not really since that's all done and over with. I'm sure I'm going to hear it from his brother." I wince. That's a call I'm not looking forward to.

"I don't know why you care," Loomis throws out, and I fold in half, my forehead to my knees as we get closer to Stone's building.

"I don't know why I do either," I admit. "Guilt, I guess."

"You need to be more like Elsa and let it go."

"Easy for you to say, Wren. You haven't hit your Fritz-world scandal yet."

Wren shudders. "And may I never. I remember what Owen and Rory went through with his cunt ex. That was enough for me. Oh, look, the press is here. Good thing we're going through the back door, and no one expects the hot blonde with the big sunglasses to be aiding and abetting."

"You mean the one who likes it in the back door."

She throws me a sideways glance and a smirk. "Don't make me stop and roll down your window to tell those assholes of the press that I've got their leading lady right here."

"You do and I'll tell Owen his best friend took your virginity."

She gasps. "You do and I'll tell Forest you slept with his brother. Several times."

"Ladies, while this back and forth is amusing and endearing, can you please just get us somewhere I don't have to lie awkwardly along the back seat. My back is starting to spasm like I'm ninety."

"Done. We're here." Wren pulls into the garage, the metal gate closing behind her, and I breathe a sigh of relief only that relief doesn't last long as she parks in one of Stone's spots and we all climb out of the car. I'm already dreading this.

I like being strong. I like the Tinsley who did what she had to do for herself, her life, and her safety. I like the woman who stopped taking others' bullshit as gospel and wrote her own story instead. It's gotten me where I am now, which is mentally healthy and feeling good.

I fired my last agent and manager and hired ones who listened to me and believed in my vision for myself and my career. My last album—the one I wrote all for myself and not for what the label wanted—tripled my previous ones in sales. My last movie had a more emotional complexity to the character and really pushed me to be more with my acting.

I've found my stride. My rhythm. My fucking happy place.

And now this.

It's like a magnet, going straight for all that hard-won strength and trying to force it out of me. I could fall on those around me—I've done it before—but I refuse to. It's part of what kept me attached to Forest for longer than I should have been. The problem is, I might not have a choice with some of it. I turn back my phone off Do Not Disturb.

Time to go figure out what's up with my stalker and how to get unengaged from Stone.

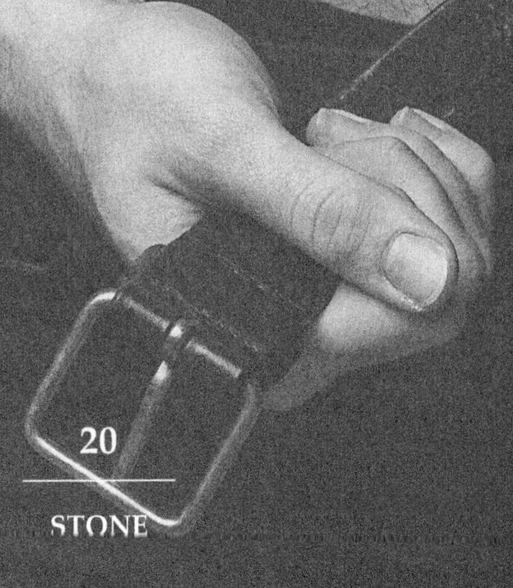

20

STONE

"How'd he take it?" Katy asks when I get off the phone with Forest.

"He's seriously not happy, and he's very confused. He also sounded drunk, so that didn't help."

Actually, he was fucking pissed and wasn't shy about letting me know it. Forest's call made, oh, I don't know, the tenth I've had to field in the last hour. It doesn't help that Tinsley's had her damn phone on Do Not Disturb. That threw Forest into a bit of a tizzy. My parents simply laughed. Once upon a time, my father's face was splashed across the news for a bullshit engagement and not to my mother. They assured me there were ways to get it cleared up and cleared up fast.

Honestly, I'm not all that worried about it.

I wasn't smart and I wasn't cautious, and neither was Tinsley, and it cost us. It's nothing that can't be fixed. It's the bullshit hype that's annoying.

But with the phone calls, my friends and cousins came over. Now my house is filled with my people and resembles a frat party with all the booze, takeout containers, and pizza boxes littered about.

This is what we do when a scandal hits. We circle the wagons, but no one asked me before they all came over for this giant powwow. They more or less showed up. At least they brought food and distraction. Happy Friday to me.

I flip open one of the containers and grab a random taco.

Katy is sipping a margarita and eating her taco with a pensive look on her face. Katy is no bullshit, and I've always loved and admired that about her. She's one of my favorite cousins even though she's not related to me by blood. But right now, given the circumstances of the day and my inability to fully explain away the pictures, I have a bad feeling about what's to come next.

"I think we're all a bit confused. I had no idea about you and Tinsley. You're like Superman and Clark Kent. You're never together in the same room at the same time."

See what I mean?

"There is no me and Tinsley."

"Uh-huh. You might want to work on your sales pitch before you try to sell that story."

I shrug. That's been my go-to response. I don't know what else to say. I told Forest and my parents an abbreviated, glossed-over version of the truth. That I was walking her out of the building, and we were talking. I noticed the ring on her hand, and she explained it was a prop. We talked for another few minutes, she kissed my cheek goodbye, and that was that.

Except the problem is, there's a reason the press concluded we're engaged, and it's not simply because she had a rock on her hand. If you look at those pictures, it's all right there in color. The crime of my life is that I'm undeniably infatuated with Tinsley, and there is nothing that can change it. Not time or distance or guilt.

Only now, it's splashed across the tabloids for all to see.

I take a bite of my taco and pour myself a healthy glass of

tequila—no ice and no mixer—because it's turning into that kind of a night.

Katy is the only one with me in the kitchen, but I can hear everyone else chattering away. Owen, Estlin, Bennett, Vander, Mason, Kenna, and Keegan are all here doing who knows what out in my great room and dining room. Wren left about half an hour ago to pick up fucking Tinsley since no one could reach her, and they'll likely return with Tinsley's British boy toy since they're pretty much inseparable.

Why couldn't the press have seen her with him while wearing that ring?

Only the moment I think that, something ugly and unwanted slithers over me. The funny thing is, I'm not mad. I'm not upset other than having to handle my family and friends and dodge questions I refuse to answer. I don't even give a shit about the media being all up my ass. I'm a Fritz. We do this every now and then. It's just how we roll in Boston. Ask my parents and Owen. The media catches something from us that sparks their attention and bam. Being a family of famous billionaires comes with that.

But this is different. More than that, it's her.

The thought of everyone thinking she's mine when she's never been mine feels like my deepest, dirtiest secrets and desires are on full display.

"Just so you know, the way you were looking at her…" She trails off, fanning her face. "Hot. So hot."

"Katy, ease up. It's already been a fucker of a day."

She smirks, her eyebrows bouncing. "I can tell since you're eating a tofu taco."

I glare balefully down at the taco in my hand. "You could have warned me."

Now it's her turn to shrug. "You could have told me."

Touché.

"I was wondering why the chicken tasted like squishy toes."

"Ew! Gross." She smacks my shoulder and then laughs. "Fine. It sort of does. Unfried tofu has the worst consistency. What the hell was Mason thinking ordering that? I realize he's trying to eat healthy, but this isn't healthy, it's simply cruel." She drops her half-eaten taco down on her plate and washes down her last bite with another sip of her drink.

"Asshole needs to stop with that. He's not vegan or even a vegetarian. He could have ordered chicken instead of torturing all of us."

"I heard that!" Mason calls out from the other room. "Tofu is a good source of protein."

"It sucks!" I shout back. "It's full of isoflavones."

"What the fuck are those?"

Katy snickers, and I wink at her. "They're chemicals that look like estrogen in the body."

"Fuck," he hisses.

Katy cracks up. "You're such a dick. You should tell him they have no effect on testosterone or estrogen in men."

"No way. Next time, he'll get me chicken and not tofu."

"You're a dick!" Mason shouts like a pouting child.

"Katy already called me that!" I yell back. "And if I see one of your stupid peanut butter protein bombs instead of real cookies, I'm going to kick your ass out."

"I got you chocolate chip, princess. You're being a moody bitch. And a dick. You're engaged. You're supposed to be happy."

Katy bobs her head and hitches her shoulders up. "He's not wrong."

"I'm not actually engaged," I exclaim to everyone and anyone who's listening.

"Uh-huh. Tell that to the line of press surrounding our building. Now buck up, buttercup. I get to plan an epic bachelor party for us."

I roll my eyes but find myself chuckling. Fucking Mason.

"I'm sorry I'm being a dick, but can you blame me?" I ask Katy as I chuck the taco in the trash and go for the pizza, trusting there's no hidden tofu on that. And sure enough, because Vander loves me, he ordered my favorite margherita pizza with bacon. I grab a slice for myself and keep digging until I find the one with cauliflower crust for Katy, who is a diabetic and shies away from carbs when she can. "Here. Eat this."

"Awesome. Thank you." She takes a bite and talks around her mouthful as she chews. "I'd be a moody bitch too if it were me. It must suck to be fake engaged to the woman you're secretly in love with."

"You're such a bitch, but I fucking love you."

She stands and drops a kiss on my cheek. "Just keeping it real. And I love you too."

Katy heads back out toward the great room, and I follow her, grabbing another slice as I go and taking my hard-earned drink with me.

Just as I scarf down my second piece and take a seat in the great room, the door swings open without a knock, and Wren, Loomis, and my little rose walk in. Tinsley looks beautiful and sexy, but her lavender eyes are heavy and troubled, and she seems edgy. It's not the reaction I thought she'd have. I figured she'd be annoyed and come in here all business with a battle plan her formidable PR team had already cooked up.

Her expression has me frowning and glued to my chair as she waltzes straight up to me. "I'm sorry about all of this."

I shake my head. "I don't give a shit."

Now it's her turn to frown and I quickly correct myself.

"No, I mean, I don't care about that bullshit outside. It's noise and a headline, and it'll die the moment we tell them it's bogus. But why do you look like there's more going on than just a little press bomb? Was it Forest? Did he say something?"

Brother or not, I'll kick his ass all the way in LA if he said something that hurt her.

She collapses to the floor, sprawling out like a starfish, and I get a series of what the fuck looks from everyone except Loomis and Wren, who obviously know what this is all about. "I thought you were going to be mad. I wouldn't blame you for being mad."

"I'm not. It was my fault too. I should have been more cautious. Is that look only about me? You've never given two shits in the past if I was mad at you."

"My stalker is back," she declares and it's as if the wind is swept from the room. Somehow, I'm on my feet, ready to tear the world apart. Vander stands too, his eyes on her.

"Does my dad know?" he asks, and my pretty little rose shakes her head, her eyes closed.

"I just got the letter tonight." Her hand extends in the air with the red envelope clutched in her fist. "But I'd be beyond grateful if you'd call him and the two of you could figure this out. As far as I knew, Terrance Howard was in California and incapable of coming to Boston."

My heart stops dead and becomes a lifeless lump in my chest.

"What does that mean?" Mason questions. "Did you see him?"

"No. But it wasn't mailed."

"It was hand delivered?" Owen challenges. "As in, to the warehouse?"

"Yes."

Mason drags a hand across his face and starts to pace over to the window. "Jesus, Tins. The fuck?"

"Yep. Good times." Tinsley sighs. "And bad timing, though I'm not sure if there's ever a good time for a stalker."

"What does it say?" Keegan pushes.

"Don't know. We can revel in the fun of opening it together."

"Where's your security?" Katy asks, tucking into Bennett. Both Rory and Willow aren't here tonight. They're with Owen's parents and Katy's adoptive parents respectively. I'm glad there are no kids here right now, and from the look on Katy's face, she's thinking the same thing.

"I released them for the night when I met up with Loomis."

"Why?" Kenna tilts her head, chewing on the corner of her lip.

Tinsley twirls her arm in the air. "I hadn't heard from him since he went to prison other than his apology letter. That was four years ago, and since then, I've been stalker-free. Now I use them mostly for crowd and press control because there haven't been any threats in so long. Loomis and I were going to hang out tonight and watch a movie. No security needed."

"I'm sorry," Estlin cuts in gently, held tightly by Owen. "I don't know the details of this the way everyone else does, but was this person violent with you?"

"No," Tinsley answers, and she sits up, brushing some of her long hair back from her face. "He liked to send letters, and his letters were increasingly threatening. I think things would have progressed to violence, or at least he would have attempted it. But thanks to Lenox, we figured out who my stalker was, and made sure the police and FBI knew it too. When they raided his home, they discovered things on his computer as well as in his home that spoke to his threats turning physical. He was doing this with two other women and was sentenced to ten years in prison, with parole after four. He sent me an apology letter after he had been there for a few months. That was the last I'd heard from him."

"Hmm. Okay." Vander crosses the room, grabs his computer bag, and sets himself up at my dining room table. "Tinsley, come here." We all stand and walk toward the table, taking seats or leaning against the wall or buffet. Loomis makes himself and Tinsley a drink at the bar, and I like that he didn't ask. I like that he's telling me he's here to stay because Tinsley is important to him.

"There's food in the kitchen," I tell him, and catch a hint of a crooked smile.

"Cheers. Thanks for that." He disappears and returns a minute later with a couple of plates. One he sets down in front of Tinsley, who doesn't seem the least bit interested in eating.

"What are you looking for?" Kenna wonders, her elbows digging into the wood table, her chin resting in her hands.

"Terrance Howard," Vander explains simply, and for a few minutes, we don't do much other than watch him work, his fingers furiously flying across the keyboard of his custom-built laptop. "Interesting."

"What?" nearly all of us ask in unison.

Vander holds up his hand as if asking for a minute, then slips out his phone. He rests it face up on the table, the screen lit up though it doesn't look like any screen of a smartphone I've ever seen. Then again, that doesn't surprise me. This is Vander after all. He punches in a series of numbers, and then it rings twice before a gravelly voice echoes through the speaker.

"Vander?"

"Yeah, hey, Dad. I have you on a secure line. Tinsley is with me, as are my regular others plus an extra." He glances over at Tinsley and then back behind her, indicating Loomis. Tinsley nods, and that's good enough for Vander. "You can talk freely."

"What's going on?" he inquires.

Tinsley shifts beside Vander and speaks into the phone. "The press thinks I'm engaged to Stone because they snapped pictures of us talking outside Children's with my prop ring from my film set on. That's why we're here. But we're calling you because my stalker is back." She proceeds to tell Lenox the rest of the story, and we can hear him moving in the background and telling his wife, Georgia, he's going into his office.

"What's the timeline?" he demands, but I miss some of their back and forth when Loomis comes over and drags my attention away.

"What is your stance on this fake engagement business?"

I shake my head. "Is now really the time to talk about that?"

"Yes," he insists, his gray eyes intent. "I need to know how desperate you are to get rid of the tag Mr. Tinsley Monroe."

I give him a dubious look. "I think you of all people know I can't be Mr. Tinsley Monroe. You know her history with my brother."

"Right. I understand you on that. But if your brother weren't part of the equation, then how would you feel about it?"

I search his face, my eyebrows drawing together. "Loomis, what is this all about?"

He licks his lips and glances over in her direction. She's still talking to Lenox as Vander works, and everyone else murmurs in low voices. He turns back to me. "She can't sleep at the warehouse tonight. I would stay there with her along with an army of security, but the truth is, it's an accessible building. I know they have security, but it's not the same as say... a high-rise, for instance." He tilts his head meaningfully in my direction. "I'd have her stay with me, but it's a one-bedroom flat in a building of apartments."

That surprises me given his celebrity status. "Really? Why?"

He smirks slightly at my perplexed expression. "I grew up poor in a tiny studio in London with my mum and two brothers. I save nearly every penny I earn so I can give all of them a better life than what we had."

My respect factor for him just jumped exponentially.

"Are you suggesting she stay here with me?" I nearly choke at the idea.

He folds his arms as if he's getting ready to do battle with me. "Where else would you feel comfortable with her staying?"

"Who said I feel comfortable with her staying here?"

He rolls his eyes over my bullshit. "Don't play me for a fool. I know you're in love with her. I suspect you've been in love with her for the last two years. A man doesn't stare at a woman the way you stare at her unless he's mad for her, and I happen to know you showed up and paid her a visit after the ball."

He waits me out for a beat, and when I don't deny it, he continues.

"She could impose on her friends and uncles, but right now the media thinks she's your Hollywood princess, and that gives her another round of protection. If they think she's engaged to you, they'll be all over you both. As much as I know she hates that, and I hate that for her, cameras have a certain element of security to them, don't you think?"

Fuck if he isn't right. But that doesn't mean I can have Tinsley live here or continue to pretend to be engaged to her. I'm just not sure if I'll have a choice.

21

STONE

"Do your parents know yet?" Lenox questions and that catches my attention, drawing me back to the phone conversation.

I walk toward them, ending the conversation with Loomis. I have no answer I can give him. If she moves in here, I'll fuck her. I don't know how he hasn't realized that yet or maybe he doesn't care about that side of it. But I do. I care about that a lot. I was serious when I said the other night was the last time.

I may have kissed her in the elevator earlier, but I knew that was all it was going to be.

"Not yet. It's the middle of the night in Greece.

"I'm calling them."

Lenox isn't a big talker. He's the definition of the strong, silent type, but he's also the insanely loyal type. I had no illusions that he wasn't going to call her parents, and I'm sure Tinsley didn't either. A point she proves when she simply sighs and sags.

"I've got him," Vander exclaims and turns to Tinsley. "Terrance is in California. He met with his parole officer this afternoon, and it seems he is home since he used his credit card to order a pizza and is currently streaming a movie on his home television using a streaming service he pays for."

Tinsley starts to visibly shake, and I don't think twice about it. I don't question what the fuck I'm doing or who the fuck I'm doing it in front of. I walk over to her, lift her out of her seat, drop her back on my lap, and start rubbing her back. I get a quick, questioning look from her, and I know I'm getting something similar from everyone else in here, but so be it.

These are my trusted people, and if Katy already put it together, I have no doubt everyone else already had their suspicions.

Her look quickly fades when Greyson's voice comes through the phone, immediately filled with worry. "Lenox? What's up, man?"

Tinsley leans over the phone. "Hey, Dad. I'm sorry we're waking you and Mom, but something's come up." She relays the story yet again, from the engagement to the stalker, though this time, she informs him that this particular letter does not appear to be from this Terrance Howard guy.

"Hold on. You're telling me the press thinks you're *engaged* to Stone, and not only do you have a stalker again, but it's not the same guy as before?" I think Greyson is about to have a stroke, and I hear Fallon in the background, equally as upset.

"No, it's a copycat," Lenox jumps in. "I suppose there's the option that he had someone place a letter for him, but I don't see anything in his financials to indicate that he paid someone, and nothing on his phone or computer that speaks any communication about Boston, Tinsley, or letters. Vander, do you have the footage I just sent you?"

"Yes," he replies. "I'm pulling it up now."

"What is it?" Greyson asks.

"It's the warehouse cameras," Lenox clarifies. "Watch him. He knows what he's doing."

All of us hover around Vander's chair, leaning over his

shoulder to watch the video of the cameras on the side of the building. There's only a small streak of black that comes and goes quickly, and then the front camera picks up where a guy—or, hell, it could be a woman for all we can tell—wearing all black, baggy, nondescript clothes drops the envelope on the porch and is immediately gone. It happens in under three seconds, and then poof. Evaporated."

"Where is he?" Tinsley asks, searching the other cameras.

"That's the thing," Lenox inserts. "He knew exactly where they were and the perfect points to evade them. After that, there are no other cameras in the area of the warehouse for five houses, and that camera shows no one resembling her person."

"So this person has either been staking out the warehouse or had insider information?" Owen questions.

"Seems that way," Vander agrees. "Could be either."

A tear hits her cheek, and then she laughs mirthlessly as she wipes it away. She climbs off my lap and goes back into the great room to retrieve the envelope. She slides it open and lays it flat on the table.

"Roses are red, violets are blue, you thought I was gone, but I always see you." She reads each word aloud slowly as if she's trying to absorb and seek the meaning and purpose of every syllable. "Huh," she muses after a beat. "A poem."

"Yeah? So?" Mason queries.

"Is that not his normal way of writing to you?" Keegan tacks on.

Tinsley looks up and shakes her head, only to speak aloud for those on the phone. "No. It's not. At least it wasn't for a while. When they first started, he did poems like this, but those stopped about six months in, and then it was only threats. Angry, violent threats. And those lasted over a year until he went to prison."

"It's a copycat of someone who knew what the early letters

looked like," Vander surmises. "But why? Why pretend to be him?"

"Perhaps someone is just trying to scare you and thinks that's the easiest way." Kenna rolls her glass back and forth between her hands, her head tilted in contemplation. "It's not a violent letter, but they certainly want your attention."

"When did the news of the engagement break?" Mason asks.

"Around the same time the envelope was dropped," I answer. "I got the notification on my phone maybe five or ten minutes after the timestamp of that video."

"Yes, and we arrived about half an hour after that," Loomis supplies.

"Who had access to the original letters to know what they looked like and how they were worded?" Vander comes back with.

"The letters went public," Tinsley explains "They were evidence, and a lot of it became public disclosures or leaked. I don't know how many of his letters are online, but I'm sure there are at least of few of those."

Katy stands and starts to pace around the table. "So all of this could be found with a simple Google search. Okay. Easy enough. But who wants to scare you while making you think it's Terrance Howard? Right now, only we know it's a copycat, but that information wouldn't be difficult for law enforcement to figure out quickly considering he's across the country."

"You're suggesting the person who did this wants us to know it's not him though he's copying him?" Tinsley is at her wits' end, her hands running through her hair before she picks up her drink and downs half of it.

"Looks that way," I agree. "But who and why?"

"Simply put, it could be anyone for any number of reasons," Bennett says grimly, and we all grow silent. Are they only trying to scare her? Or is this the starting point to something more sinister?

"We're on our way home," Greyson states emphatically, and Tinsley immediately shoots to her feet.

"Dad, no. That's crazy."

"The hell it is! My little girl is being threatened by a new psycho."

"Stop. I love you, and I know you're scared, but I'm not a little girl. You have tour dates, and you're not canceling those. Besides, there isn't much you can do here."

"I don't care," he argues. "I don't like being so far from you with this. Especially when it's literally happening on my front doorstep."

"I don't need you to fly home. I mean it. It's a copycat and likely just some douche trying to rile me up. We'll send it to the FBI. For all we know, the loser was dumb enough to put his prints on it, and all this will be settled in a matter of days."

"Let's hope. Regardless, until they're behind bars, you're not staying at the warehouse," Loomis inserts.

"It has—"

"Cameras. Yes, luv, I know." He cups her jaw and holds her gaze. "Yet we just proved this person knows where they are and how to hide from them. As far as I'm concerned, you've got three options. Stay there with me and an army of family and security by your side, and that will include sweeps of the building before you're allowed to enter, stay at my flat that has one bed, one bathroom, and a bloke who snores and hogs the blankets, or…" He trails off, but his eyes flash over to mine.

And fuck. *Fuck!*

"You'll stay here," I state loud enough for everyone, including the people on the phone to hear.

"What?!" she shrieks, and I lift my chin to meet her eyes, only to stand and peer down at her. Loomis steps away, and now it's just me and her.

"You're going to move in here until this gets resolved."

As much as I don't want her living here, she has to. I'll go out of my mind otherwise.

"No. Absolutely not."

"We'll be engaged," I continue, ignoring her protest. "The world already believes that, and we won't dispel it. Hell, we'll perpetuate it in public. People will become obsessed with it. Especially in Boston. That will keep you safe. My building has security including metal gates, a doorman, and cameras at every entry point, not to mention you require either a fob or a code to get to any floor, and we're on the top. Mason lives next door as an extra buffer, and ours are the only two apartments on this floor. Being engaged means you have a man on your arm, and you're not easily accessible. It means I'm your go-between in addition to Loomis or the security you will have with you at all times."

"I don't need a man on my arm," she grits out, furious with me. "I'm perfectly able to take care of myself."

I put my hand on her arm and squeeze it so she listens. She's defensive, and I get it. We're talking about limiting her freedom and telling her what she can and can't do. That's part of what drove her to come to the boat the first time. She needs freedom and a sense of autonomy and control. But now isn't the time for that.

"I know you're strong. We all do. None of us are saying you aren't. But this is bigger than one person can handle, and I know you know that. Copycat or not, someone is trying to, at the very least, scare you. Face it, you're going to be my fake fiancée whether you or I like it or not."

And I don't hear anyone arguing. Not her father or mother, not Lenox, not any of her friends. They know this is the right call and the way she stays safe.

"I'm not living here with you, Stone!" she snaps in frustration. "It's not happening. It *can't* happen."

I take a step until I'm standing above her, staring straight into her eyes. "Tell me you're not scared."

Her head slides to the right, and her gaze goes with it. Un-uh. Not happening.

I clasp her chin and tilt her face back up to mine.

"Tell me," I demand.

"Fuck you."

"I'm not offering that. Will you be able to sleep in that warehouse tonight?"

"She's not sleeping in the warehouse," Greyson grits out. "Not tonight or any other night until this asshole is taken care of." He exhales a harsh sound. "Stone." My name is heavy, like a thud. Like he doesn't like this one bit but doesn't know what else to do. He doesn't want Tinsley staying here, and my guess is he already knows about our past. Tinsley is very close with her parents, and I have a feeling they wormed it out of her.

"She'll have her own wing," I tell both her and Greyson. "The guest bedrooms are on the other end of the condo from my room."

She's shaking her head, but I can tell she knows she's already lost the fight.

"Agree to this," I clip out. Doesn't matter if she does or not, I'll be her fucking shadow anyway. She tries to draw away, but I won't let her. I hold her arm tighter and force her to stay.

"Stop it," she screeches, trying to shove my chest the way she did the other night, but I'm not budging. "Give me space."

"Answer me, little rose."

"Little rose?" Owen repeats and then pauses, and I reluctantly lift my chin to him. It slipped out. I certainly never meant to call her that with an audience that includes all of our best friends and her parents. He stares at me before his gaze drops to my chest, but it's not my chest he's picturing. It's my back. "You have—"

"Yes," I cut him off, because at this point, why deny it? But that doesn't mean I want Tinsley or her father to know about the tattoo I have there. Lenox never told Grey about what he tattooed on me, and why would he? He had no clue I was with Tinsley those ten days, nor did he know what the roses on the mast signified.

Tinsley didn't see it the other night because I took her mostly from behind or with her on top of me, and that was entirely by design. Plus, it was dark. She likely wouldn't have noticed it anyway.

"Fuck," he hisses under his breath and drags his hands through his hair.

"What?" Tinsley, followed by Wren, questions.

"Nothing," Vander and Mason bark, and yeah, this is going from bad to worse.

I drag her chin to me, getting us back to the issue at hand. "You're staying here. Tomorrow, we will have your security bring us to the warehouse to collect your things. Vander and Lenox will work on the copycat, and Greyson will continue doing his shows, so no one thinks anything is off. That's the plan. Now we both have to live with it."

22

TINSLEY

It's moments like this, I wish I could breathe fire and incinerate everything. Fucking asswipes who think it's funny or cute or get off on scaring and hurting others—primarily women. People who terrorize and remove freedom and choices from others. I know I'm being petulant. I know everyone is worried about me, and with good reason. I know Stone is trying to keep me safe, even going so far as to disrupt his own life and infuriate his brother in the process.

I know Loomis and my father, and honestly, everyone else agrees with the plan because it makes the most sense. I know all of this.

But it doesn't mean I'm happy about it.

It doesn't mean I want it.

I barely survived ten days at sea with Stone, and the thought of living with him for the next three months...

Is he high? Does he not realize the severity and potential impact of entering into this?

A fake engagement. One that will be monstrously public. I'll have to smile and touch him and act like I'm in love with him. All of that is a nightmare, but then there's the flip side of this. The private side.

He can say whatever he wants about separate bedrooms and wings and space. It all sounds good, neat, and tidy, even when it's anything but. It's a recipe for disaster. We don't know how to be around each other without it getting physical. I think at this point, we've proven that.

My relationship with him is complicated enough, but being his fake fiancée and living with him will take this to the next level. I don't know what I'm more afraid of—this copycat stalker or getting my heart seriously and irrevocably broken.

Without another word, I storm off down the hall in the direction of the wing he mentioned would be mine. I need a minute. It's clearly been a day, and my head is not on straight. I plow into the first open bedroom door, slam it shut behind me, and lean against the wood. It's a big bedroom. All clean lines, white linens, and... a nautical theme complete with a strange tower-like thing that has multiple tiers of fabric beds and a body out of white rope. I don't even know what that is, but nope. Not this room.

Spinning around, I open the door only to practically plow straight into Stone. Ugh.

"Move!" I push him aside as best I can and squeeze past him, heading for the other bedroom I know is here. "What kind of single man has all this space?" I gripe, passing room after room and finally opening the door for the next bedroom. I like this one. It has a big bed, more white linens, and nothing nautical to be found.

I go to shut the door behind me, but he's there, pushing it open and crowding me inside before he takes the liberty of shutting the door for me.

"You're being a brat."

I roll my eyes, proving his point, but the brat in me doesn't care. "Are you going to spank me to get me back in line?"

His eyes darken. "Is that what you need to stop acting this way and let us help you?"

Is it? Argh. This is the problem. I want him to freaking spank the brat out of me.

"You know what? Men suck. You're all exes and stalkers and former lovers and fathers and studio execs and agents and people who generally believe they have dominion over my life. I'm going to buy an island and fill it with champagne, charcuterie, vibrators, dirty romance books, and fucking peace."

Honestly, that sounds amazing, and I might have my assistant start looking into that.

He picks me up by my hips and sits me on the bed so he can stand over me. This is not a smart move. I can already feel the heat we can never seem to escape crackling between us.

"I get it," he barks, angry and frustrated and hella annoyed with me. "This sucks. I won't pretend otherwise. I don't want you living here because that means you're fucking here when avoiding you and keeping my distance were the only things keeping me sane. Having you here is a pain in my ass, and pretending to be your fucking fiancé will be nothing but a headache and a constant strain."

I scowl. "You're doing that honesty thing I hate again."

He leans forward, his hands planting into the bed on either side of my hips, forcing the upper half of him into me. I angle back, not wanting him this close. "Let Vander and Lenox work their magic. Let the FBI do their job. Amp up your security. And with any luck, you'll be out of my hair and back in that warehouse with your new stalker buddy in jail. But the one thing I can't have is you out there putting yourself at risk simply because you like the way I fuck you a little too much and it scares you enough that you don't want to live here."

I snort. It's unladylike and weird-sounding, but again, I don't care. "Oh, and you don't like fucking me a little too much for me to live here with you?"

"I never said I didn't. But I'm willing to put all that aside if it means no one can get to you." He searches my face, serious yet earnest. His forehead meets mine, and he breathes out a harsh breath, his eyes closing. "I can't let anything happen to you. Not when I can do something to stop it. If you were anywhere else, I wouldn't sleep, little rose. I'd be sick with how much I'd be worrying about you. Don't you get it? This isn't a joke."

My heart shudders and quakes, but I push it back. Force the bitch away. And focus on his nickname for me. Little rose.

"What was Owen talking about?"

His eyes flash open and he draws back, and I take a deep breath because the air smells a little less like him.

"Nothing important to you."

Hmm. Okay. Maybe it's better if I don't know.

"I don't want to get my heart broken."

"I don't want to break your heart," he quickly replies.

"I have to run all of this by my PR people."

He folds his arms across his chest. "Go for it, but the wheels are already in motion, so I'm not sure what else they're going to have to say about it."

"I'm sleeping in this bed and not with you. No sex this time. I mean it."

He smirks. "Excellent. All the bullshit of a fiancée and none of the benefits."

I laugh and fall back onto the bed, shoving my fists in my eyes. "I hate this, Stone. I know I'm being a brat and I should be more grateful for all you're doing for me, and I am. But I'm tired of this. The walls feel like they're closing around me, and I'm getting claustrophobic again."

The bed dips beside me, and then he's gathering me in his arms and pulling me into him, my head over his heart. For a moment, I listen to its steady rhythm, and it soothes some of my brat into submission.

"Why are you being nice to me? If anything, you're the one who should be mad."

He chuckles, the sound vibrating against my ear. "I don't know, but I'm not. I'm partly to blame for the engagement stuff."

"I don't want to live here."

"I don't want you to live here."

"Can we ignore each other while I do?"

I can practically hear the smile in his voice when he says, "That was my plan."

His fingers drag through my hair, playing with random locks, and I get lulled into it. Into him. It's the dance we do. The one that feels as natural and right as breathing. The one I can't seem to stop no matter how many times I try to change the song.

"I haven't told you this, but I've been meaning to. Actually, I've wanted to tell you for a while." I lick my lips and swallow. "I'm really proud of you, Stone. You became the man and doctor you wanted to be."

His hand in my hair stills for a beat before it starts to move again. "You were part of that, you know. You saw something in me I didn't, and that made me start to believe in it too."

"Part of me wishes I could go back. Just escape to the boat, but that's not reality, and I can't run from this again."

He pushes me down until I'm staring up at him as he hovers over me. "No, we can't go back, and you can't run from this. No matter how much I also wish we could." His eyes flicker around my face and then drop to my lips before he slowly forces them back up. He takes my left hand and brings it up between us. I still have the stupid prop ring on, and he starts to play with it. "I'm going to get you a different ring."

"What?" It comes out as a bark and a laugh.

"This is your prop ring, not a ring I would put on your

finger. If you're engaged to me, Tinsley Monroe, that makes you mine, and you'll wear a ring that I would buy you."

I squint at him. "I'm not letting you buy me a diamond, Stone."

He presses some of his weight on me. "Lucky for me, I don't have to ask for your permission. But you will wear it."

"Ah, there's the Stone I know and love. You don't get to tell me what to do, lover. Fiancé or not."

In a flash, he's on top of me and has my arms pinned above my head. "And there's the Tinsley I love and can't get enough of. Stop fighting me on everything just because you can."

"And to think, I was once so infatuated with you."

He growls and presses all his weight down on me. "Little rose, I'll always be infatuated with you. But that doesn't mean I plan to let you call shots in this fake engagement." He bites my bottom lip, kisses my forehead, and then climbs off me, leaving me reeling from that admission. I start to replay his words in my head—all the things he just said to me—when he grabs my hand and wrenches me up, snapping the thoughts sharply off when he smacks my ass. "Now move it. You have phone calls to make and so do I."

We exit the room, and I nearly trip over something as it goes scampering by me. A scream hikes its way up my throat, only to have Stone slap his hand over my mouth to stifle it.

"Relax. It's my cat, Doe."

My eyes pop out of my head, and I watch as the beautiful gray and white cat with bright blue eyes nuzzles against his legs. I speak against his hand. "You have a cat? You? A cat?"

He bends down and picks it up and it stares at me with a territorial look that says *you better not steal my man*. So it's like that, huh? I reach out and settle the argument for both of us, letting her know she can keep him as I scratch the top of her head around her ears. It does the trick, and immediately she starts to purr and nuzzle against my hand.

"I found her loitering outside the emergency department. A tiny, scrappy thing that liked to hiss and swat at me. She reminded me of you like that, and I knew I was rescuing yet another feral stray."

I laugh and smack his arm, obviously proving his point. "In my wildest dreams, I never pictured you as a cat owner. I don't think I could be more surprised than if I woke up and my hair was neon green like the Joker's. Why did you name her Doe?"

He shrugs. "I didn't know if it was a John or a Jane until I brought it to the vet, but any patient who comes through our doors without a name is a Doe, and Jane didn't seem right for a cat's name."

Stone has a cat. A cat he rescued. A cat he clearly adores since he's holding it close and petting it gently. It's insanely sexy and endearing in the worst of ways. I hate it when he does stuff like this. When he surprises me and makes me want him.

"That explains the weird, tiered thing in the other bedroom that looked like it was made out of rope and fluffy white fabric."

"She likes the light that comes in through that window, so I put her climbing tower in there."

"Stop talking," I demand, covering my ears like a small child would. "You're easier to tolerate when you're mute and unlikable."

His lips bounce up into a crooked grin, and dammit, these are going to be a long three months. I need Lenox and Vander to work a miracle and find this asshole and do it fast so I can get out of here. I scoot around him and march back out into the great room. I'll have to look around this place more. It's big, and I only caught glimpses of other rooms through the open doors.

Katy, Kenna, Keegan, Estlin, and Wren are all sitting on the floor around the coffee table, laughing with a half-eaten pizza, a bottle of tequila, and a bowl of limes between them. I join them, scooping the bottle up off the table and pouring myself a glass since there are extras. Wren takes the opportunity to drop a slice of pizza on my plate with a look that says *don't get bitchy about the carbs,* and I don't.

Tonight, I'm eating all the carbs.

"You two get it all worked out?" Keegan asks, snatching the bottle from me and refilling hers.

"Uh, yeah, sort of." Stone takes in the scene before him with furrowed brows. "What are you doing, and where is everyone else?"

"We're drinking. Obviously." Wren holds up her glass and swirls it in the air.

"And we suggest you do the same," Katy agrees.

"All the guys went to get Tinsley's stuff from the warehouse," Estlin supplies. "Loomis said he'd pack up your stuff and bring it back, and the guys went with him to take a look and see if they could find anything helpful. And to adjust some of the cameras."

"We were told not to leave until they got back," Kenna explains.

"Oh, and Forest called both of your phones twice." Wren scrunches her nose. "We didn't pick up, but he probably called because Grandma made a statement about your engagement."

"She what?!" both Stone and I yell at the same time, only mine comes out as a screech, and his is more of an incredulous bark.

Wren shrugs. "Take a look for yourself. It's all over *Intertainment.*"

"Fuck," Stone hisses and snatches his phone off the table. He unlocks it with his face and does a little search, and I stand, taking my glass with me, so I can see what Octavia said.

A video comes up of Octavia and Dr. Fritz Senior walking into some sort of event dressed up in gowns and tuxedos. All the Fritz children are there. Rina, Oliver, Carter, Landon, Luca, and Kaplan. And all refuse to acknowledge the press, let alone answer any of the questions being thrown at them. Especially Kaplan, since he's Stone's father.

"Octavia! Dr. Fritz! How do you feel about your grandson Stone being engaged to Tinsley Monroe?"

Octavia's face lights up. "I think it's wonderful, and we couldn't be happier about it. Tinsley is a very special person to our family, and she's been a very special someone to Stone for a long time. It fills my heart with joy to see them happy and engaged."

"Jesus, Grandma. Really?" Stone runs an incredulous hand across his face and through his hair. "What is she doing, and what the hell was she thinking doing it?"

"What about your other grandson, Stone's brother, Forest? How did he take the news?"

"Forest and Tinsley will always remain close friends, but that's all they've been for quite some time now." Octavia smiles, waves, and keeps walking even as questions continued to be hurled at her in rapid fire.

"Well, there goes my PR people putting a fast end to this." I glance up into his eyes. "It looks like we really are engaged now." No wonder Forest called each of us twice. This is getting out of hand quickly. "How will we ever undo this?"

23

TINSLEY

I spent all day yesterday with the FBI and dealing with the business of being fake engaged to Stone. My dad's attorneys surrounded me—since mine are in LA—and Loomis was with me since he was there when I discovered the envelope. They promised to get a run on the prints and assured me that the LA office was going to question Terrance Howard.

I already know it's not him. I already know it's a copycat.

But since the FBI is in the dark about what Lenox or Vander have been doing, I simply nodded and thanked them.

After that, the rest of the afternoon was spent on the phone with my agent, manager, and PR company, devising a plan for being in this mess and then one for how to get me out of it.

Stone wasn't concerned. He said people in my industry get engaged and unengaged all the time. Married and divorced. The world hardly bats an eyelash when a celebrity does that. It's not a big thing.

He wasn't wrong, and I went to sleep alone in my bed with Stone across the apartment and very limited contact between us, feeling comforted by that.

That is, until I wake up this morning to a black box sitting on my bedside table.

For the longest time, I don't move. I don't even get up to pee or brush my teeth though Lord knows I need to do both. I simply lie in bed in the silence of the room, wrapped in heavy white blankets, and stare at the box like it's Snow White's shiny red poison apple. Beautiful and alluring, but ultimately deadly and fucking stupid to trust.

I tell myself it's fake, and I should just open it and get it over with. What kind of crazy asshole would spend real money on a rock for a fake engagement?

But then the voice in the back of my head pipes up, arguing that Stone never does anything the conventional way, and if it is fake, why undertake the cloak and dagger of leaving it on my bedside table when I'm asleep? It sure as hell wasn't there when I went to bed last night, so that means he snuck in here at some point to leave it for me. Why wouldn't he simply give it to me and make sure I know it's fake just like we are?

Fake rock for a fake engagement.

On and on the vicious cycle goes until I can't take it another second, so annoyed and frustrated that I let it—and him—have any sort of power over me. It's a ring, real or not, but it doesn't mean anything. That's what I tell myself as I sit up, draw my knees and blankets to my chest, and lift the small, black square box from its resting place.

Balancing it on my knees, I hold my breath and open the box only to wish I hadn't. My lungs empty of that breath I was holding, only to immediately refill with a sharp gust of air. A sob sticks in the back of my throat, and I snap the lid shut, wanting to chuck the box across the room. Out the damn window.

"Goddamn him!"

I clench it in my first, feeling the sharp edges dig into my palm, and flip the lid back open. The ring gleams at me, beckoning me with its beauty and softening me to it. Not to the man, but to the ring. It's not something I would have ever picked out for myself, but I absolutely love it to the point where tears pour down my cheeks, and I want it to be real. For me.

"Fucking bastard."

He got me a giant round diamond sitting in a nest of diamond and platinum petals held together by a band of diamonds twisted to look like the stem complete with thorns. A rose. He bought me an engagement ring made to look like a rose.

How dare he?

How dare he mess with me like that?

I point blank told him I didn't want to get my heart broken and that I didn't want him to buy me a ring, and then he goes and does this? I'm furious. Absolutely enraged.

Rose was smart to let Jack die in the freezing water. Think of the heartache and emotional warfare she saved herself from.

Snapping the box shut, I slam it down on the nightstand, only to see a slip of paper I hadn't noticed before floating to the ground. Clamoring out of bed, I pick it up and read it.

Be the thorns when you need to be and be the petals when you don't.

I hiccup a strangled noise and crumple the paper in my fist. That's what he said to me on the boat, and it's been my mantra since. What emboldened me and gave me confidence, he's now using as a weapon against me. Even if it's unintentional.

I toss the paper in the direction of the box and storm down the hall, only to remember he's working a twenty-four-hour shift and isn't home. I could text him a tirade, waxing poetic about all the ways he's a total son of a bitch and that I officially hate him, but my thoughts are too scattered and chaotic. I need to work them out first, and the best way I know how to do that is by writing them out. My mind works best when I'm writing music, and more often than not, I do that the old-fashioned way with a pen and paper.

Only I don't have any on hand since most of my stuff is still shoved into the various suitcases and boxes Loomis brought over the other night. Stone has to have something in his kitchen. Everyone has a pen and paper in there. I locate his junk drawer full of batteries and flashlights and stop dead when I come across a six-pack of condoms.

Bitterness clogs my throat, and I swallow, feeling it go down like a jagged pill. Of course he has condoms in his kitchen. He brings women home. He probably cooks for them the way he's cooked for me and then fucks them on the counter before he even does the dishes.

"Argh!"

I'm a boiling hot mess of lava. Slamming the drawer shut, I tear down the hall to his office. His office is big considering he's a doctor and not a lawyer or something businesslike. I start with his desk, going for the top center drawer, and finding... more condoms.

In his office?

It makes me wonder, and I give up my search for paper, as once again my curiosity wins out. I don't bother with his bedroom. For one, that's too invasive, even for me and my monster of wrath and destruction, and second, because it's his bedroom and he sure as hell has condoms in there. Probably a Costco-sized box along with lube, nipple clamps, and a vault of sex toys he's used on women who call him sir.

Despite my rage, the Tootsie Roll center of me couldn't handle seeing that.

Instead, I go room by room, opening drawers and searching furniture I know I shouldn't be searching. If he ever did this in my house, I'd kill him, no questions asked. But my search isn't in vain. I find condoms everywhere. Even in the front entry table like he's too impatient to get his dates past the door before he fucks them.

Like he was with me last week.

Stupidly, I'm hurt. And feel foolish. My anger slips into heartache and humiliation.

I haven't been with anyone other than him in the last two years, and he's only one of three lovers I've ever had. It wasn't that I was saving myself for him because I knew the score between us. It's just not so easy for me to find a lover when I was so emotionally invested in two out of the three. Not to mention, I didn't want a Hollywood fling or affair. I didn't want to be used by someone looking to increase their celebrity status. I did that once after Forest and it was awful.

Still the fucking good girl.

But I was simply another fuck to him. One of many by the looks of it. And we didn't use condoms because I naively trusted him.

My elbows plant on the entry table, and my face drops into my hands. I don't cry. The tears from the ring are all dried up. I simply give myself a minute, and when that minute is over, I go back to my room, strip down, and climb into the shower. Mason has a four o'clock home game, and I told him I'd be there for it. Thankfully, Stone will not be.

As the hot water cascades down on me, all my anger and bitterness turn mournful. I don't even know why.

Not fully anyway.

I was never supposed to give him pieces of my heart. That was the promise I made, not only to him, but to myself, and for the last two years, I believed I had kept that promise. Yes, I had feelings for him, and yes, those feelings were strong. But this feels different, and I hate it.

That ring has me all twisted up. It's confusing me. And it stops now.

As I get ready to go, I contemplate leaving the ring here and not wearing it. Or leaving it on his nightstand the way he did to me in a silent protest. But in the end, I slide it on my finger without looking at it or appreciating it in any way, vowing to treat it with total indifference.

He didn't get down on one knee and ask, and I never said yes.

This ring has no power. It's yet another prop.

I make it to the stadium, riding celebrity style in the back of a large black SUV with two burly security guards in tow. Immediately I'm whisked through security and up a private elevator to the suite floor, except before I can reach the suite, a tall, thin man with wiry hair and equally as wiry glasses intercepts me.

"Miss Monroe." He pants, his brow dotted with sweat, and my security guys step forward. One hand goes up, the other over his heaving chest, where he rattles his badge that says Albert Pussé, Event Coordinator for them to see. "I'm so glad I caught you," he continues once he's caught his breath. "I was just alerted of your arrival and rushed right up. We have a situation I'm hoping you can help us with."

Oh boy. I don't like where this is going.

"What can I do for you, Mr. Pus-sé?" I stutter over his name, nearly calling the poor man pussy instead of noting the accent on the e. Still, what an unfortunate last name.

"Amber Woods's people just called and informed us she's ill with pneumonia and can no longer be here today to sing the national anthem."

I have no clue who Amber Woods is, but that's not the point, or why he's telling me she has pneumonia.

Oh no. Please don't do it. Please don't ask.

"Since you're here, would you be willing to sing the national anthem for us? It would be such an honor for us and mean so much to the organization and the fans."

Fuck. Fuckety fuck fuckers. I can practically hear my agent and manager screaming *NO!* in my head.

I smile sweetly and say, "I'd love to help, but I'm not prepared for that. I haven't practiced the song."

"We have thirty minutes until the anthem. I'm sure that's enough time to run through it a few times. I remember you sang it at the Super Bowl two years ago and brought the house down. With your talent, I have no doubt you'll be able to do it again with a standing ovation."

I don't mention how the fans will already be standing since it's the national freaking anthem, but is he kidding me? That's one of the most difficult songs for an artist to sing. The vocal changes alone are a nightmare, and most people who do these gigs practice for weeks leading up to it.

"It's a nationally televised game," he exalts with a hopeful smile as if that'll sweeten the deal for me. Only I'm not looking for extra airtime right now, so it makes it worse.

"I have nothing to wear."

"You look beautiful as always and very Boston Rebels in your gold dress and red boots, but if you feel the need to change into something else, we have many options you can choose from."

"Uh. Well, um, I appreciate the offer, but I don't think—"

"Everyone is so happy you're back home in Boston. And engaged to one of our Fritzes. We simply love you here. You have so many fans in the stadium, not to mention the large number of armed service members and children in attendance."

Goddamn him, he's good. A pussy he is not. All I wanted to do was unwind, have a few drinks, and possibly bitch to Wren and anyone else who would listen about the ring Stone gave me. Oh, and the condoms. I'd love to bitch about those too. Not sure I would have in the end because it's not a good look that I went through his house in search of them, but the option would have been nice.

"Do you need someone to sing the anthem? Can't the game start without it?"

"It's what's always done here in this stadium, and it would be unpatriotic if we didn't sing it."

I shift, my heart starting to beat faster. "What if you just drag out a few school-aged children onto the field to do it?"

"There are too many protocols to go through for that, especially when dealing with minors."

"Just play the music for it. You don't need an artist to sing it."

"It's how we do things in this stadium. Ownership is very firm on that. You truly are our only and best option. We need you, Miss Monroe."

I'm one hundred percent going to regret this. "Fine. Let's go," I grumble, not even caring if I sound begrudging about it because I am.

"Thank you. Thank you so much."

Immediately, he ushers me along, moving me back into the employee-only part of the stadium.

"If I squeak or crack or say the wrong damn word, I'll... well, I don't do diva or threats especially well, but I'll seriously be unhappy."

He smirks but quickly clears it. "Understood, miss. You just have to sing it. We have the music for you to listen to and practice with, and I have a sheet with the lyrics."

"You should tell your boss you deserve a raise, Albert. That was masterful manipulation and dealing. Now show me to the room where I can practice."

~

THE MOMENT I step onto the field, the natural grass crunching beneath my boots, and my name is announced through the stadium speakers, is when my nerves hit me in the chest. Before they had been chilling in my stomach, fluttering around, but mostly held at bay. Now they're in full force, making my hands shake and my knees wobble with panic attack quality anxiety.

The crowd cheers and whistles, and I force a smile on my face. I didn't let anyone know what I was doing. Loomis, Vander, Katy, Bennett, baby Willow, Sorel, Serena, Owen, Estlin, Rory, and others are up in the booth watching me walk out toward the center of the field, waving like I'm Mrs. America walking across the stage.

"Are you kidding me?!" I hear Mason's hoot from the sidelines, and I look over at him to find him laughing, with his hands on the top of his head, shaking in disbelief.

I give him a simple shrug and a wave because we're not only being watched but broadcast around the country. After that, I get myself mentally in the game—pun intended. I stand in the spot they tell me to, and when the instrumentals start through the earpiece in my ear and across the stadium, I close my eyes and picture the lyrics sheet in my head. My lips part and sound pushes past my lungs, and with it, my nerves dissipate as they always do when I get to this point, and I sing my heart out.

It isn't until I'm finished and walk off to hand the guy the microphone that I realize I was holding it with my left hand. The hand sporting the ring. The hand I held up by my mouth the entire time I sang.

God, what did I do?

As if echoing my thoughts, my phone starts going off like a series of grenades.

My manager calls me at the same time as Stone texts.

"Hey," I answer but quickly rush out, "Before you say anything, I know. But they cornered me, and the guy had a return strike for my every parry. Or however fencing metaphors go."

"Oh, I'm not going to yell at you," Carol says into the phone with a hearty chuckle. "You just put yourself out in the spotlight wearing your ring to sing the national anthem. Your album sales have already skyrocketed since your engagement was announced, but I bet my next paycheck they double after that move."

Ugh.

She continues talking, and I half listen as I check my message from Stone.

Stone: We have the game on in an empty patient room, and I just saw your impromptu performance. You were incredible.

Me: Thank you.

Stone: At least now I can tell people that my favorite attributes about my fiancée are her spontaneity and unpredictability instead of that she's a sexy pain in the ass. I'd say it has a better ring to it, don't you?

Fucking bastard.

"Carol, I'm sorry to cut you off, but can we catch up about this tomorrow?"

"Sure, doll. No worries. Go enjoy the rest of the game."

I disconnect the call, deciding that verbally eviscerating my fiancé is more important than sales and marketing strategies at the moment.

Me: I hate you. It's official. And I hate your ring too.

Stone: Glad you're wearing it, though. It looked beautiful on national television, future Mrs. Stone Fritz.

Me: I wish it would fit on my middle finger. Then you'd know how I feel about wearing it.

Stone: Nah, you obviously love it since you showed it off so much. The announcers loved it too. All the nurses and patients here as well. I told them my nickname for you and they all swooned.

Me: I'm sure it'll help you get laid.

Stone: My fiancée told me her legs were closed to me, so I doubt it unless she's willing to change that decree.

Me: I don't fuck players.

Stone: Good thing for me since you're at a football game surrounded by them. What's with the thorns, little rose? You're the one who went primetime with our engagement and the ring. Not me.

I sigh. He's right on that. We went from website photos to nationally televised.

Before I can respond, my parents call. I talk to them as I head upstairs, some of my anger about Stone waning. I have no right to it. He is free to fuck whomever he wants, just as I am. We're not in a relationship and never were.

Just before I enter the suite and the madness and uproar I'm about to face in there, I text him back.

Me: I'm sorry. I didn't think about the ring when I went out there. I shouldn't have done that.

Stone: I'm not mad, baby girl. I like my ring on my fiancée's hand where everyone can see it. I like everyone thinking you're mine. The only people who know it's fake are us. And I'm not planning to tell anyone.

24

STONE

Forest lost his absolute mind on me for about the hundredth time in a span of forty-eight hours. First with what our grandmother said about the engagement and his relationship with Tinsley, again when he learned about her stalker and that she's living with me, and the last time after she sang the National Anthem with my ring front and center.

"What's with the ring? Why the real fucking diamond, Stone?"

"Because I'm a Fritz and I can't have any fiancée of mine walking around with a cheap, fake diamond. It wouldn't pass, and right now, that's what she needs to stay safe."

It wasn't a total lie, even if it felt partially like one.

"Why are you even part of this? The only way you knew Tinsley was through me. None of this makes any sense, and I don't get it. It should be me she's living with, me as her fiancé. Not you."

I didn't know what to say to that because guilt sucks, so I said nothing, and it only angered him more until I told him point blank that the reason we were doing all this was for her safety. He couldn't argue with me after that, though he did try, and it did little to ebb his anger with me. I don't blame him for being upset. I'd kill me if I were him, and he's right to question me.

So I told him the truth. Tinsley isn't mine, and she doesn't want to be, and anything he's seeing is fake. I wanted to ask him why he's still holding on after all these years. Is he expecting her to come crawling back to him? Tinsley and I never talked much about Forest. He always felt like an out-of-bounds topic for both of us. But I have to wonder, does he still love her, or is his fixation with her something else?

My grandmother won't answer or return my calls. All I get when I text her, asking why she won't pick up the phone, is a smiley emoji. The woman is up to something. She never does anything off-the-cuff or without intention. This keeps up, I'm going to drive out to the compound and demand answers.

It was a media storm but containable until Tinsley went on national television with my ring on her hand front and center. Now it's a Category 5 cyclone. We have vans parked out front of the building and in the back too. Paparazzi littering the sidewalks. News outlets reaching out to us personally, as well as our "people" asking for statements and wedding dates and plans. There is a bump watch on Tinsley's fucking stomach, which inwardly makes me postal.

Watching a woman's body for physical changes is one of the most fucked-up things I can think of.

Add to that fun, Tinsley and I haven't seen much of each other in the few days since all this hit. She's avoided me for the most part, and I've worked long hours this week. She spends her days with Loomis and her security team on set, and I spend mine at the hospital. Our nights are spent on different ends of the apartment, with no middle ground between us. I cook dinner and make extra since I usually get home before her. Sometimes she eats it, sometimes she doesn't.

I may or may not get a thank you text for it since texts are our main form of communication, and even then, only when necessary.

I've gotten the impression she's mad about the ring I got her.

I had one of the family assistants take care of picking it up for her because there was no way I was going into a jewelry store to do it myself. That would have drawn too much attention. It should be fake. That's what Maria told me. But I couldn't do it. I shopped around online, and when I found the ring in a vintage jewelry store, I knew there was no other place for that ring than on her hand.

I didn't care about the cost. I would have paid anything for it. That was the ring.

I didn't want it to be fake or a lie like everything else between us is.

Tinsley is leaving in less than three months. It's a reminder that she will never be permanent in my life. This was my one shot to give her a piece of my heart, and it sure as fucking hell was going to be real. The only way I know she wears it is that she's photographed in it and obviously sang with it on.

It's only making the press more rabid for a photo of us together.

They're relentless, their coverage is over the top, and it's bleeding into every facet of my life. Like right now...

"You're Stone Fritz. I saw you on the news this morning."

Jesus. Not again. This makes the tenth patient or patient's parent today. I'm not even talking about yesterday or the day before or even while she sang the anthem, and they flashed the pictures of us together outside the hospital all over the screen.

"You're much better looking in person," she titters, shifting in closer to me, and I can't even with this. "Not that you're not gorgeous on camera, but in person, just wow." She fans her blushing face. "I feel like I'm watching a live-action soap opera or an episode of *Friends* where Joey is Dr. Drake Ramoray."

"Except I'm an actual doctor, you're in the emergency department of Boston Children's Hospital, and your daughter requires abdominal surgery for appendicitis."

"Mom, just get the picture," the daughter hisses under her breath, though there was no way I wasn't going to hear that. Despite being in pain, on morphine, and having been throwing up for the last two hours, she has been trying to get to her purse. Thankfully, it, along with her phone, are on the other side of the room. Her mother's, unfortunately, is right in her hand.

"Oh, yes!" The mother giggles and bats her eyelashes at me. "Can you say all that again? In that same gruff, sexy voice? I want to record it. My friend Cara is going to be so jealous that I met you. She's been obsessed with your family forever. Especially Oliver Fritz."

She holds up her phone, and I turn and walk out of the room before she can start recording.

Owen is standing outside the patient room, his lips bouncing in amusement. I called him down for a consult on this patient, and as far as I'm concerned, he can have her and her mother too. "You saw all that, didn't you?"

"You have some fans."

I roll my eyes, fold my arms, and sag against the wall. "How am I supposed to treat patients if they only see me as the future Mr. Tinsley Monroe?"

Owen snickers. "Actually, I believe the press have dubbed you Stoneley."

I groan. I didn't know that, and I wish I still didn't. "Remind me why I'm doing this again?"

"Because you're in love with a woman you shouldn't be who happens to be in danger and you're in a position to help keep her safe. Even if said woman is giving you the cold shoulder at the moment."

I grunt. For everything Owen just said and the fact that Tinsley is still in danger. The FBI took the envelope, but the only prints on it were Tinsley's from when she opened it. They didn't have much more than we did with the video from the warehouse and were able to confirm that Terrance Howard wasn't behind the letter. All things we already knew.

"Thanks for keeping it real."

"You mean because you're not."

"Ha! Funny. I think I liked you better when you were miserable and grumpy."

"Blame Estlin for making me happy and reminding me I have a sense of humor." He grins. "How's this? I'll take the super fan and her kid off your hands, and one day, hopefully, you'll either tell Tinsley how you feel or find someone to fall in love with?"

I smack his arm and push away from the wall, ignoring the second half of all that bullshit as I say, "They're all yours."

"Are you playing this weekend?"

By playing, Owen means in our hockey league that he, Vander, and I play in. I'm usually pretty regular when my schedule allows it, but over the last couple of weeks, I've missed our games.

"Hope so. Catch you later, man."

I meander back toward the nurses' station, grateful my shift is over. I sign out my patients and head out. For a few minutes, I sit in my car, debating if I should go home or figure something else out on this Friday night. The heat is blasting because it's unseasonably cold for the end of October. Halloween is next week, and the trees have all but shed their multicolored leaves. Fall is shifting into winter early this year, and I won't complain about it.

It's my favorite time of year in the city, but once January

hits, I'm going to want to take a trip somewhere south. Somewhere warm. Maybe on Benthesicyme because it's been too long. I wonder if I can talk Tinsley into—nope! Not even gonna think it.

By January, this will all be over, and she'll be gone.

Maybe I should just sell the boat. I don't see how I can ever go back on her when—

My phone rings through my sound system and Tinsley's name along with a picture of her singing the anthem with my ring on her hand pops up on the screen. It's as if my mind conjured her.

I smirk and answer, "First-time caller, long-time listener."

"Huh?" she replies, and I chuckle.

"Clearly, you're not a Boston's sports radio listener."

"Clearly," she deadpans.

"What brings you to my world, little rose? You haven't called me in… well, I don't think ever."

"Probably because I haven't, but this wasn't something I could easily text. Is now a bad time?"

"Not even a little. Now is perfect."

"Okay good." She blows out what sounds like a relieved breath, and I hate how uncertain and shaky her voice is with me. How cold and detached. We both said we'd keep our distance, and we have, but that distance is starting to get to me. She's right here, but she's also not. "We're on set, and I slipped, and, um, got hurt."

I shift, sitting upright as alarm flitters through me. "Hurt? Are you okay?"

"Uh, I think so."

"*You think so*? How did you get hurt? What's the injury? Do you need the emergency room? Are you bleeding? Where are you? Do you need me to come get you?"

"Stop with the fifty questions, Doctor."

"I'm worried."

"You are?" she asks incredulously.

I roll my eyes though she can't see it. "Of course I am. You called me. It has to be pretty bad for that once-in-a-lifetime phenomenon to happen."

"Sorry, I didn't mean to worry you. It's not that bad."

"Okay." I tap the steering wheel, anxious to go to her. "What's going on?"

"We were filming a baking scene, and I slipped in the flour and twisted my ankle. I tried to brush it off, but it hurts when I stand on it, and Loomis reminded me that my fiancé is a physician. The director asked if I'd call you to see if you could come and check me out. I told him you're a pediatric doctor, but he didn't care. We're behind schedule. Again."

I grin like a bastard. "You hate that you had to call me, don't you?"

She huffs. "I'd rather have taken a cheese grater to my skin."

I laugh. "That sounds painful."

"Now you're getting it. But will you come anyway?"

I smirk wryly, never one to miss an opportunity with her. "For you? I always come."

"I know you do because, much like with Doe, you're a sucker for a sweet pussy. But seriously, I'm sorry to ask, and I'm sure you're working or busy, but—"

"Stop. No need to explain. Text me the address, and I'll come take a look. As luck would have it, I'm done with my shift anyway." I would have gone regardless, but the timing couldn't be better.

"Thank you, Stone. That means a lot, and I'm very grateful."

I swallow down my flirty and sexy retort and say, "I'm glad you called. I'll see you soon."

I end the call, and a moment later Tinsley texts with an address, and I program my GPS and head that way. It's clear across town and over the bridge into Cambridge. I realize I have no clue what her movie is about other than she's filming it with Loomis, and I think it's holiday or Christmas-based.

As I approach the set, I follow the signs and park where it says visitor parking, and then I meander along, only for security to stop me.

"Sorry, sir, you can't go in there," the man wearing all black says to me without even sparing me a glance. I have no doubt he pushes tourists away all day.

"I'm Dr. Stone Fritz, Tinsley Monroe's fiancé. She fell and they called me to check her out."

Now I've got his attention, and his steady gaze drops to mine. I'm tall. Barefoot, I'm six-three, but he's got several inches on me. He eyes me, asks for my ID, and then speaks into a headset. A moment later, I'm allowed to pass through onto the set, and when I ask him where the hell I'm supposed to go, he says it'll be obvious.

It's not. There are three sets set up. Two outdoors that look like winter wonderlands, and one that's in a building where I assume they shoot the indoor scenes. I pull out my phone and text Tinsley, and after a few minutes, she hobbles out the door of the building, caked in flour with her hair piled on top of her head.

I snort out a laugh, and she flips me off.

"Don't make fun. I told you we're filming a baking scene. But here, look, you'll appreciate this." She twists to show me her ass, and she has two flour handprints, one on each cheek.

"I want to kill the person who got to put those on you."

She grins. "It was Loomis, but he went back to his trailer to call his mom since we're on break because of my ankle. Speaking of, can you check me out so we can finish up?"

She looks fucking adorable like this, wearing a red and white checkered apron with her hair twisted up into a messy bun and flour—whether real or movie fake—caked all over her.

"It's what I'm here for." However, that doesn't stop me from leaning in and kissing the corner of her lips. I'm her fiancé, and we're in public. Whether anyone here cares or not is a different story. "Just in case someone is watching," I tack on because she gives me a look. A look I hate. She's not amused that I kissed her.

I pull back and catch sight of her hand, but she's not wearing her ring not that I should be surprised. She's on set. I haven't seen the ring on her in person yet, and I can't help but be a little disappointed. With the way we've been avoiding each other, who knows when I'll get the chance.

I clear my throat. "Where do you want me to check your ankle?"

She gives me a wan smile and hobbles inside, wincing and bouncing, and what the fuck is this? Who let her walk around like that? I scoop her up in my arms, and she gives me yet another perturbed look, but she knows better than to fight me on it.

There are people everywhere in the background of the set, as well as a brightly lit stage-like area that resembles a large, high-end kitchen. "What's your movie about?"

"I'm a nanny, and Loomis is a billionaire single dad. It's an enemies-to-lovers rom-com."

I snicker. "Sort of like Estlin and Owen." She blinks at me, and I clarify. "Estlin was Owen's nanny, and he pretended he couldn't stand her for a while."

"Oh." She laughs. "I'm not sure I knew that. Wren never mentioned how they got together."

I follow the path she guides me, no longer fighting me carrying her now that we're inside the building. Having her this close, holding her in my arms, and feeling her tucked against me is the best thing I've felt all week. I'm an addict with her. Chasing small fixes wherever I can get them. Eventually, we reach the area where she points me to, and I set her down on a wooden bench, crouching by her feet.

She shifts to get comfortable, and I keep her injured ankle extended as she sits up and faces me.

"Hi," I say in a serious tone. "I'm Dr. Fritz. I understand you hurt your ankle?"

She rolls her eyes at me and points to her ankle. She's wearing a dress beneath her cute apron, and it slips up to her midthighs, but more than that, from this angle, I can see up it, and which draws my focus when it needs to be on her injury.

"Do you stare up the dresses of all your patients, Dr. Fritz?"

I beam at her. "Never. Not once. Wanna play doctor with me, though? Since I'm here to give you an exam."

She rolls her eyes yet again, but her lips twist into a smirk she's trying to hide. My girl likes to role-play. It's why she called me sir that night.

Her expression turns coquettish. "I slipped and hurt my ankle. Do you think you can help me, Doctor Fritz? It hurts *so* bad."

Fuck, do I love this woman.

"I'll do everything I can to help you. I'm going to put my hands on you now so I can examine you."

With that, my gaze drifts and snags on her swollen ankle. And it is swollen. To the point where it makes me frown, and all playfulness evaporates as I give her a thorough exam. I make her move it this way and that. Flex and extend. Wiggle her toes, rotate her ankle left and then right, and test her strength.

But after all that, once I've gleaned my diagnosis, I say, "I'm not sure I've gotten a full diagnostic picture yet. I might need you to spread your legs a little for me."

She blinks in that doe-eyed way of hers. "You think so, Doctor?"

"I do. I think you're going to need to relax your legs so I can make you feel better."

Her knees part slightly on the bench, while her eyes stay on mine. I can't help it. I sneak a peek and groan when I catch sight of her black satin panties. "Does everything look okay, Doctor?"

"Everything looks perfect."

"I was worried this injury would require surgery."

"No surgery is required." I lean in and kiss her ankle. Right where she's hurt. "I think you did sprain your ankle though, but I haven't seen anything to make me think it's broken. That's said, small fractures are easily missed on an exam, and we should order an X-ray."

"Do you play this game a lot, Doctor?"

I glance up at her and tilt my head. Her sudden bitter tone surprises me. "How do you mean?"

"You have so many women fawning over you. The gorgeous and sexy Dr. Stone Fritz. I'm sure you play doctor with them a lot."

I blink, slightly taken aback. "I haven't been that guy in a long time, and you're the first woman I've ever played doctor with."

She squints, disbelieving. "Maybe so, and maybe not." She closes her legs and pulls her ankle away from me, twisting to sit sideways on the bench. "Thank you for coming to check it out. I don't need an X-ray. I think I'm okay."

"Are you, though?"

Before she can answer, her director is in front of me, introducing himself as Johnny and insisting I stay to finish out the scene. So I do, much to Tinsley's chagrin. I stand by the side as Tinsley, some kid, and Loomis throw flour around a fake kitchen. She doesn't spare me another glance, and I wonder how much longer I can take this distance until I snap.

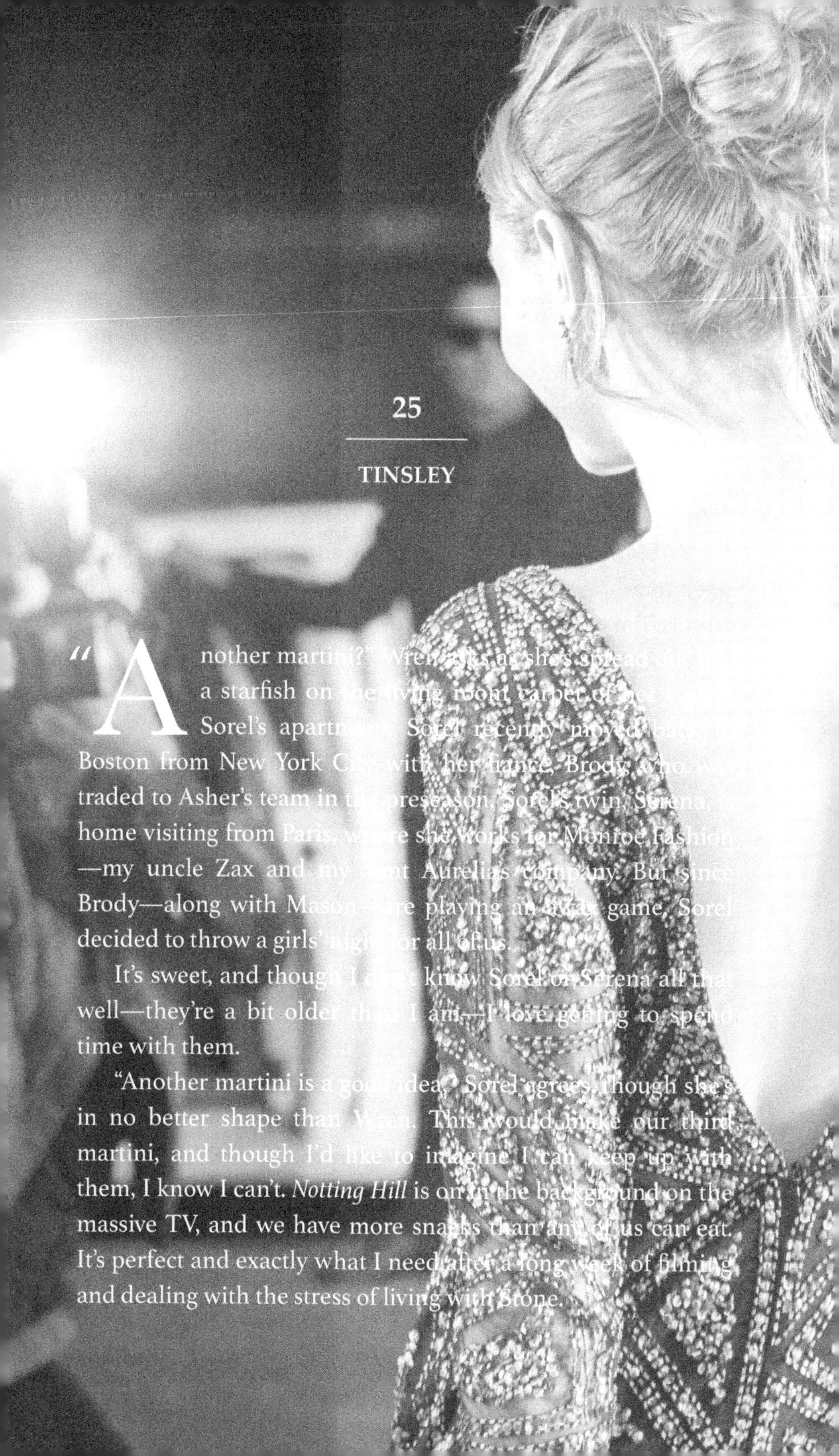

25

TINSLEY

"Another martini?" Wren asks as she's spread out like a starfish on the living room carpet of her sister Sorel's apartment. Sorel recently moved back to Boston from New York City with her fiancé, Brody, who was traded to Asher's team in the preseason. Sorel's twin, Serena, is home visiting from Paris, where she works for Monroe Fashion—my uncle Zax and my aunt Aurelia's company. But since Brody—along with Mason—are playing an away game, Sorel decided to throw a girls' night for all of us.

It's sweet, and though I don't know Sorel or Serena all that well—they're a bit older than I am—I love getting to spend time with them.

"Another martini is a good idea," Sorel agrees, though she's in no better shape than Wren. This would make our third martini, and though I'd like to imagine I can keep up with them, I know I can't. *Notting Hill* is on in the background on the massive TV, and we have more snacks than any of us can eat. It's perfect and exactly what I need after a long week of filming and dealing with the stress of living with Stone.

"I'm out," Katy announces with a hand stretched out like she's dropping the mic. "I have to leave soon and nurse Willow when she wakes up for her midnight feeding."

Serena half-sits to grab a pretzel from the bowl on the coffee table. She pops it in her mouth and crunches loudly as she talks. "I'm in, but only because I don't have to move tomorrow. Damn, do I love Sundays."

"Same," Sorel asserts, slouched back on the leather sectional. "And thankfully the guys are traveling for their game so I can simply be hungover and watch my man on TV instead of having to drag my sorry ass down to the stadium."

"I think I'm in for that," Kenna announces. "I don't have work tomorrow. Woohoo!" She holds up her glass and nearly dumps the tail end of her Cosmo on me. Thankfully she recovers at the last minute.

"We should all have a sleepover!" Keegan exclaims, going for the cheese and crackers.

"Yes!" Sorel and Serena shout together, and it's tempting. So very tempting. The idea of going back to Stone's isn't appealing. It's a Saturday night, and I happen to know he's out with Vander. He texted and asked if I wanted to have dinner out with him, like a public date to keep the fires of our engagement burning, and when I told him I had plans with the girls, he told me he was going to meet up with Vander for a couple of drinks but wouldn't be home late.

Whatever. I don't know what they're doing, where they went, or who they're meeting, and frankly, I don't want to know. He can use his twenty thousand condoms on whomever he wants because it won't be me. We never agreed as part of this fake engagement not to see other people, though obviously, I'm not. How could I?

He doesn't have the same issue I do. Not that he ever did.

Still, there was no way I was going to have dinner with him, in public or otherwise. Anytime I'm near him, I find myself slipping and doing things I know I shouldn't do. Hell, I freaking played doctor with him right there on set and spread my legs so he could look up my dress. All it took was one smile and a little flirting to get me there, and I was so mad at myself for it afterward. Once a player always a player.

I do much better when I don't see him, so I say, "I'm in for a sleepover. And another drink." Because why not? I'm only twenty-four. It's time I have some fun every once in a while.

"What about Stone?" Keegan questions, a coy look to her that I don't like.

"What about him?" I throw back at her.

"Won't he miss you tonight if you don't come home?"

I'm about to say I doubt it when Serena shoots Keegan a warning look. "Don't start. We said we weren't going to bring it up, so we're not."

Ugh. "What? Just ask." I get up and hobble over to the bar Sorel has set up for us. My ankle isn't perfect, but it's so much better than it was when Stone came and examined it.

"You're wearing the ring," Wren comments, still all starfished out. Wren isn't any better at holding her liquor than I am. We're usually wine or champagne girls, but when in Rome.

I glance down at my hand, at the pretty sparkly ring I can't seem to force myself to take off even when I don't have to wear it. "I'm afraid of losing it," I admit, which is partially true. I am. The other side of that coin that I don't allow myself to think about or admit to is that I *like* wearing it. Which sucks since it's not real. Well, at least not real in the way I'd like a ring like this to be.

"Is that the only reason?" Keegan presses.

I huff. "Yes." I take the enormous martini shaker Sorel has been using and start to add some ice to it from the ice bucket. "Why else would I?"

"Because you like it and the guy who gave it to you," Katy states simply, and as much as I love Katy, she's a little too honest and real sometimes. A bit too observant too.

"Nope to both of those." I give them my back so they don't see the lie on my face while I pour vodka, triple sec, lime, and cranberry juice into the shaker. This bad boy will mix up five good-sized martinis, so it's officially my new best friend.

"But if you marry him, you'll be my cousin," Wren whines. "Can't you just do that? Please? For me?"

"Wren, I love you, and I'd love to be your actual cousin, but there's no way I'm marrying Stone. I can hardly stand him."

Both she and Katy snort, but I start shaking the shaker vigorously, blocking them out with the loud clanking of ice against metal. I top off my glass and then hand the shaker to Keegan, who takes the honor of pouring the rest. The glass touches my lips, and I tip it back, slurping down two big gulps before I sink to the floor and lean against the cabinet because the couch is simply too far and I'm a little too drunk and unsteady on my bad ankle to attempt it.

The last thing I'd want is to spill my drink. That would be tragic.

"Am I the only one who noticed that Loomis sounds like Hugh Grant in this movie?" Keegan questions before tilting her head and squinting at the screen. "Or is that the other way around? No wait, that doesn't make sense. Whatever. He does, right?"

"He sure does," I tell her, bouncing my eyebrows suggestively. "He also thinks you're pretty. And funny. And smart."

She laughs and rolls her eyes at me. "That's because I am, but don't start with me." She points her finger at me. "I'm not going there."

"Oh," I remark as I take another sip of my pretty pink Cosmo. "But you can go there with me and Stone?"

"Definitely," they all shout at once before falling into a fit of drunken giggles.

"Wait, shut up!" Serena cries out, holding her hand up in the air and flipping her long, blonde hair over her shoulder. "This is my favorite part."

We all fall silent and watch as Julia Roberts tells Hugh Grant that she's just a girl, standing in front of a boy, asking him to love her. We all sigh. It's such a good line. Even better is when Hugh Grant finally gets his ass in gear and chases after her.

"Why can't movie love be real love?" Wren asks. "Only Katy and Sorel have found that."

"Yes, but I had to kiss an asshole of a frog before I found Bennett," Katy admits. "If movies or books, for that matter, were real life, no one would watch or read them. Who wants that when we can have the fairy tale? Or at least a hot guy to make us swoon and scream through orgasms."

"Personally, my toxic trait is that I read dark romance," Serena says. "Give me a dude with triggers and red flags, and I'm all over it. He can stalk my ass anywhere he wants." The moment the words leave her lips, she winces and looks apologetically over at me. "Shit, Tins. I didn't mean that. I'm so sorry."

I hold up my hand. "It's fine. I mean, the stalking thing isn't fine, but I'm not about to go into a panic over it. I haven't gotten another letter since the first one, and that was like two weeks ago. For all I know, it was a prank, and it's over. The sooner we can be sure about that, the sooner I can end this fake engagement and move out of Stone's."

"Here's to that!" Sorel declares, holding her glass up. "Cheers, bitches!"

"Fuck yeah! Cheers!" I hold up my glass and lean forward,and somehow we all manage to clink glasses, albeit messily, and then drink. After *Notting Hill*, we put on *Bridget Jones's Diary,* because evidently, we're having a Hugh Grant night, only to pass out sometime after two and be woken around eight when my phone rings.

I'm on the floor, my face mashed into the rug since my head slipped off the pillow I was sharing with Wren. My head is pounding, my mouth tastes like a desert of cotton and ass, and my stomach roils the moment I move to answer it.

Wren makes an annoyed noise, as do a few of the other ladies, and I drag myself up and off the floor, grab my phone, and go to the bathroom to answer it.

"Hello?"

"Where are you? You were supposed to meet me at my flat thirty minutes ago. Are you okay?" Loomis's urgent voice fills my ears, and I wince.

"Stop Hugh Granting so loudly in my ear."

"Pardon? Hugh Grant?"

I snicker and then groan in pain. "We had a Hugh Grant marathon last night along with a lot of drinks. I'm officially very hungover. Or possibly still a little drunk."

He sighs, his unease ebbing now that he knows I'm okay. "So I gather. Would you rather not meet?"

"No, I want to. I could use a greasy breakfast to absorb all the alcohol I put in my stomach last night. Hold on. I'm muting you." I put him on mute and pee because holy hell do I have to pee, and after I flush the toilet, I unmute him and put him on speaker so I can talk while I wash my hands. "Hi, I'm back."

"How much did you drink?"

"A lot. A lot," I repeat for no other reason than my brain is like a slushy right now. "Remind me not to do that again. I passed out on Sorel's carpet, and now my neck and back, along with the rest of me, are feeling the results of that."

He chuckles. "Do you want me to come pick you up? I'm not sure you should be driving right now."

"I agree. I don't think I should be driving either, but my car is here."

He grunts. "Text me the address and I'll come to you and drive for both our sakes."

He disconnects the call, and I text him the address of where I parked last night. I wince at my reflection that's a mass of bad hair, smeared makeup, and a carpet imprint on my cheek. *Hot!* After turning the faucet back on, I wash my face and use some of the mouthwash she has in here, which is nothing short of a miracle for my mouth. I don't feel any better, but at least it's something.

The bathroom door creaks behind me, and I sneak over to the front door, slip my shoes back on, and exiting the apartment without waking anyone else up. I take the elevator down, and as I do, I go through my phone, noticing missed texts from Stone that started around ten last night.

Stone: I'm home, are you here?

Stone: Where are you? Are you still at Sorel's?

Stone: Are you coming home tonight?

Stone: Can you please fucking answer me? No one is picking up their phones, and I'm getting worried.

Stone: Forget that. I just spoke to Katy, who was driving home. Glad you're spending the night and not driving. If you need me to come get you, I'm here. Hope you had a fun night with the girls.

I read each one twice, hating how every time I see his name on my screen a jolt of flutters hit me straight in the chest. This fake engagement needs to end, and I need to move out. Like now. The longer this goes on, the greater the risk to my heart is with him.

The cool early November air bitch smacks my hangover in the worst of ways. I reach my car, which is actually one of my parents' cars that I've been using while I'm here, and when I open the passenger door, I stop dead in my tracks. Sitting on the seat is a red envelope.

It's ironic, and I'm nearly tempted to laugh.

Did the motherfucker who put this here read my mind last night?

I glance around, but no one is nearby. I'm parked on a quiet side street in Beacon Hill and it's early for a Sunday. Which means he was watching me. Following me. Knowing exactly where I parked and where I was going. Something he must have been doing all along since he knew exactly where the cameras at the warehouse were located and precisely how to evade them. Only someone watching me too closely would have known any of this.

Another cold shiver takes hold, and I pick up the envelope as I get in the car and lock the doors. I dial 911 on my phone without hitting send, and leave it there, ready if I need it. For a moment, I simply hold the letter. Stare at it. Rage over it. And cry. I do that too. I haven't done much of that since this started, but I cry now.

Maybe it's the hangover or the fact that I was starting to think I was in the clear with this, but whatever it is, it has tears streaming down my face at an uncontrollable rate. Why is this happening again? I don't understand it. But worse, with no clue who is doing it or even where they are, I have no idea how we'll make it stop.

That last part takes hold of me in the worst of ways, and I reach over and press the ignition button to turn on the car. Loomis will be here soon, and I want a moment alone to read the letter. I open it up and pull out the thick cardstock handwritten poem.

Miles and moments, years between, time's bitter march leaving an ugly scene. No longer bound by patience's chain, my heart now speaks, unburdening my pain. With every dawn, I grow nearer, igniting my joy at your growing fear.

A sob hiccups out of my lungs, and my hands are trembling so badly I can hardly hold the paper. Christ, if that isn't a threat, I don't know what is. And he's letting me know that this is only the beginning. My face falls into my hands, and I cry and scream in frustration and anger. Fucking son of a bitch!

He's right about one thing. My fear is growing. But the question is, is it simply a celebrity obsession or is it personal?

26

STONE

Welcome to Boston in November. We're supposed to get hit with a nor'easter that could be a lot of rain and wind, or it could be a lot of snow and ice. A cold front is headed in from Canada along with this, and Boston is on the rain-snow line. Every few years we get one of these in the fall the way we are now, and it always leads to a crappy winter. Thankfully I don't have work for the next couple of days.

I slip out my phone as I walk to the garage, debating if I should text Tinsley. Today was a bastard of a shift, and I just want to hear her voice and know she's okay. That last letter from her stalker was a motherfucker, and it threw her—understandably so—into a bit of a tailspin. She's withdrawn further from me, and I don't know how to reach her or make her feel safe when that's all I want to do.

I have nothing to say. Not really. She's smart to keep her distance, and it would be wise if I followed suit. For the most part, I have. She hasn't given me a choice but to.

I haven't seen her since she sprained her ankle, and that was more than a week ago. Vander—not Tinsley—texted me about the letter she received over the weekend. I pressed her about it via text, since she's been evading me like it's her sport, but she pulled away even more, and I let it go, not knowing what else to do.

I'm miserable. There are signs of her all over my place, though she does try to keep mostly to her room. She uses the yoga mat I bought her in the gym, and I know she runs on the treadmill because the settings are left for her. Some of her food is in my fridge, and yesterday I found Doe playing with one of her hair ties.

She's here, but she's not.

It's driving me crazy.

I need this whole stalker thing to get figured out so she can go, and I can get my life back—one that hopefully includes meeting and falling in love with someone else. Only instinctively, I know that's a joke. It doesn't matter if she's right in front of me or three thousand miles away. It's her. It's always been her.

And frighteningly enough, it might always be her.

Karma never quite came back around in my favor where women are concerned, and now I'm being punished again. I'm engaged to the woman of my dreams, the woman I would want to be engaged to and marry for real, but it's not real and it never will be.

I put my phone back in my pocket and drive home. I'm in a shitty mood. Whether it's the change in barometric pressure, my crappy day at work, or that I'm in love with a woman who wants nothing to do with me, I don't know. Whatever it is, I'm fed up with everything.

When I get home, the apartment is quiet, and I don't bother knocking on her door to check if she's home. I never do. I make dinner the way I have been since she moved in and help myself to a few fingers of bourbon while bouncing texts back and forth with the guys as I settle in and put on Thursday Night Football since Mason is playing.

Poor bastard has a short week between games, but I have zero doubts he'll rise to the occasion. It's what he does.

Just as the game starts, the front door unexpectedly swings open, and there is Tinsley, all bundled up in a black winter coat and knee-high boots with leggings tucked into them. All of her gorgeous hair is piled on top of her head in a high ponytail, and her makeup is extra, which makes me think she came right from set. Her purple eyes meet mine, and she pauses, uncertainty flickering across her features.

She's not happy to find me here, and I know part of her is debating whether or not she should turn around and leave. I settle the debate for her as I stand and say, "Hey. It's getting cold out there."

Stupid and banal, but she likes her temperatures warm and balmy.

"Yeah. It's awful."

I chuckle and smile lightly, and immediately my gaze drops to her left hand. She's wearing the ring. It's the first time I've seen it on her in person, and knowing she must have put it on when she was done shooting for the day makes my heart give a heavy thud as if it's kicking me in the chest. She follows where my eyes are, and I clear my throat and look away.

I offer her a casual smile. "How was your day?"

"Good. Exhausting. You?"

"Same." I don't bother going into the bullshit of my day. It's the last thing I want to think or talk about. She's here, and it feels like I can finally take a breath. Even my salty mood feels lighter.

She removes her boots and takes off her coat, putting both in the front hall closet. "We had to do like a hundred takes on one scene because we couldn't get it right. It set us back a bit, but hopefully we can make up the time. However, I think the storm will push us even further behind schedule. Did you know we're supposed to get like two feet of snow and ice? What is that? It's barely November."

Oh, little rose. You're cute when I affect you and make you jumpy.

"The weather people keep going back and forth on snow versus rain. I guess we'll have to see when it starts later tonight." I pause because she won't advance. "That's too bad you're behind schedule."

It's really not. I'd love it if she were decades behind schedule. I'm also shocked that with the storm coming, she didn't intentionally try to hunker down somewhere else. Like with Loomis. Or maybe that's why she's so jumpy. My girl hates storms.

"Did you eat?"

"Eat?" Her eyes go a little round, and her eyebrows slant inward as if the word was foreign to her.

Fuck this. I cross the room until I'm beside her. "Yeah, you know, food."

"Oh. No. I didn't." Then she laughs. "I haven't had anything to eat since breakfast. Like I said, it was a crazy day."

"Go sit down. The game is on, and Mason is playing. I'll make you a plate."

Absently, she slides her ring back and forth on her hand with her thumb. "Um."

I roll my eyes, so done with this bullshit. "Go sit down, Tinsley. You can watch football with me, have a drink, and eat some food. Believe it or not, you're not so irresistible to me that I can't be around you without fucking you against the wall."

My dick twitches in my jeans, calling me a lying bastard, but I ignore it and go to the kitchen without another word or a backward glance. I made extra, and I know she likes this meal because she ordered it in a restaurant years ago for her twentieth birthday. I pour her a flute of her favorite sparkling wine from the wine fridge, make her a plate, and then carry it out to her, setting everything down on the coffee table because it's more casual and it's where she's sitting. If she gets food on my rug, so be it.

The tension simmering between us has a buzzing undercurrent. Something intoxicating and pounding. It's more than lust or the whisper of sex. But I don't push it or stoke it or even draw attention to it. The last thing I want right now, when she's actually sitting here, is to scare her off.

"Mason just ran for a first down," she informs me as I retake my seat on the couch, my drink once again in my hand.

"We've been working on his running game," I tell her. "I go to his place, or he comes to mine a few days a week to run sprints."

Her head swivels in my direction, eyes wide with shock. "For real?"

"He's great from the pocket, but his running game outside the pocket has always been his weakness. We've worked on making him faster and race each other on the treadmill. It's why I have two, or didn't you notice?"

"I was wondering but never asked. I like the one on the right the best."

"Same. That's the one I use, but Mason's is the one on the left. The loser has to buy drinks for everyone when we go out, but that's usually in the offseason."

"Wow," she exclaims, surprised, but there's a strange undertone to her voice. "That's a great bar story. It must get you both laid whenever you want."

I smirk. It forms like the wicked wind that's starting to whip outside the window. "Maybe for Mason, it does."

"Not you?"

I shrug and take a sip of my drink. I won't answer her. She's fishing, and I won't be her bait. My truth is a little more reality than either of us can bear. After she's done eating, I expect her to make an excuse and go, but she doesn't. She hangs around, her legs sprawled out toward me on the other side of the couch. After watching her roll and crack her ankles and flex and extend her toes for the tenth time, I scoot closer to her, lift her feet, and drop them in my lap.

"How's your ankle?" I press around the part that was swollen last week. She was walking fine when she came in, but it still might be tender.

"It's better, thank you." She tries to pull her feet back, but I hold them in my lap. "What are you doing?" she squawks, only for it to turn into a deep moan as I start to rub her feet, my thumbs digging into her insteps. "Oh god, whatever you're doing, don't stop."

"I love it when you say that to me."

She rolls her eyes. "Strange, since I've never said that to you. Ever."

"What? That you didn't want me to stop? Yes, baby girl, you have."

"Never. Not once."

I smirk. "Several times, actually. Screamed. Moaned. Whispered. Begged. You've said it to me all those ways."

"Ugh. I hate you." She jabs her foot at me, and I laugh and tickle the bottom of her feet until she squirms. "Shit, stop that. No more tickling. I like how you rub me, so keep doing that."

"That's what she said."

She laughs. "So lame. I was referring to my feet. Not anything else."

"Maybe, but it's still true."

"Is this how you woo all your hot dates? Make them dinner and a drink, and then rub their feet until they're putty in your hands and they beg you to rub them somewhere else? Or do you simply bring them home and fuck them on your entry table before they even take off their coat?"

"Huh?" I sit up a little straighter, my gaze snapping from the TV to her.

"Right. You have no clue what I'm talking about."

Her sharp tone and sardonic words give me pause, and I wait her out, even as I continue to rub her feet. And when she leaves it at that, I lose my patience. "Actually, I don't. Please enlighten me."

She makes a face, her lips twisted and pursed to the side. "It's nothing."

"Bullshit, it's not. Tell me." I squeeze her foot. "That's the second comment you've made tonight about me getting laid and using cheap tactics to make it happen, and last week you said something similar when I came to look at your ankle. Why? Where is this coming from?"

A huff passes her lips, her expression dismissive and annoyed that I'm pushing this, but tough shit.

"I found condoms," she bites out. "Everywhere. In the kitchen, in the freaking front entryway table, in your office. Even here in the side table drawer." She knocks on the table between the sofa and one of the chairs.

Oh. Interesting. "What were you doing searching through my drawers like that?"

"I was looking for paper."

Paper. Hmm. Okay. "I don't have a lot of paper around."

"I know. But you certainly have a lot of condoms instead."

I try not to laugh. "Does it bother you that I have condoms stashed all over my house and not paper?"

Those cute, pursed lips turn into a defensively infuriated scowl. "Why would I care about all the women you fuck or where you do it?"

"Because you brought it up. More than once. So clearly it bothers you."

She tries to jerk her feet back, but I hold on tight.

"Unh-uh. Tell me why you care. I'm sure you've fucked your share of guys over the years."

Color rises up her cheeks, and she looks away from me. I laugh. I can't help it. I'm jubilant.

"Let me go!" she snaps, working to free her feet. She thinks I'm mocking her when I'm anything but. I let them go, watching as she stands and storms off for the kitchen with her plate and empty glass.

Is she admitting she hasn't been with anyone else since me? No one else in these two years? Same as I haven't.

My chest inflates, and I rub at it, trying to settle the excited helium back down. It doesn't mean she didn't screw around because of me. Her life is as complicated as it gets, especially with men.

She heads for her bedroom, and I call out to her. "Did you happen to check any of the expiration dates on the boxes or condoms?"

She pauses but doesn't turn back to look at me, so I press on.

"They're old, little Rose. Honestly, I forgot about them. Yes, I used to bring women here, fuck them all over my house, and then make sure they were gone before first light. I didn't care about any of them, and they all knew the score before they signed up for it."

She tenses, her shoulders hiking up to her neck, and I stand, moving toward her but still maintaining several feet of distance between us.

"That was how I lived, and I was unapologetic about it until I spent ten days sailing around the Bahamas with a woman who changed it all for me. She sort of ruined me for anyone else, and after her, I couldn't bring myself to go back to how I used to be. It all felt empty and shallow because it was. I haven't touched a woman other than her in two years because I don't want any other woman but her."

There. I said it. It's out there.

Maybe that was stupid, but I'm so goddamn tired of holding it in. Of playing cat and mouse only to be left with a moldy slice of two-year-old cheese. I miss her, and I crave her, and I want her to be fucking mine. For two years, this has been sitting on my chest. With any luck, setting it free will give me freedom in return. A tip of the karmic scales.

I sure as fuck hope so.

I feel due when it comes to her.

I go to sit back down, pick up what's left of my drink, and swallow it in one gulp. My feet kick up on the coffee table, and I turn up the volume, letting her know I don't want to talk about this anymore. And without another word or a glance, she walks down the hall to her room and shuts the door behind her.

And for the first time with us, I don't chase after her.

27

TINSLEY

Blood red flashes before my eyes as an ice-cold hand drags down my spine making my insides freeze over, and a plume of vapor escape my lips. I feel him behind me, and I can't make my legs move. I'm paralyzed, and he knows it. He's practically gleeful with it. That hand starts to snake around me, going up and up, and just before it wraps around my throat, he whispers, "You thought I was gone, but I always see you, Tinsley."

"Tinsley." My name grows louder. More urgent. And I'm fighting it. Fighting *him*. "Open your eyes, little Rose. You're having a bad dream."

My eyes snap open, and I swallow the scream still trapped in the dream. Jerking upright, my head whips around until my eyes land on Stone's worried and cautious ones. My chest is heaving, my heart pounding, and I place my hand over it, hoping to slow it down.

"Hey," he says softly, his hand cupping my face. "It's okay. It was just a dream."

I nod, but it doesn't help. My emotions are too big right now

—a twisted, tangled ball so mashed together that I can't seem to separate one feeling from the other.

One hand slides under my thighs, the other around my back, and he lifts me, pulling me sideways onto his lap and tucking me in against his bare chest. I close my eyes but it's like I can still feel the remnants of the dream clinging to me. I shudder and he shifts, moving beneath my covers and wrapping my blankets around us. He leans back against the headboard and slides down so he's mostly supine, taking me with him.

"Your heart is racing," I mumble, almost absently.

"I heard you scream. Clear across the apartment, I heard you. I don't think I've ever run that fast or been that scared in my life."

I draw circles on his chest, chasing the patterns the ink makes. Anything to distract me from the curling end of the adrenaline and the fuzzy images sticking to the front of my mind. So far, no one has anything useful on who sent me the letters. It could all be nothing. Or it could be a lot of something. No one knows. It was likely just some asshole who thought he'd be funny and scare me.

But why? And the wording in the letters doesn't feel that way.

"It's been a long time since I've had a nightmare like that. It felt so real. Like he was here right behind me."

He holds me tighter, his lips pressing on my hairline against my forehead. "He'll never touch you. Not ever." He runs his hand down my hair and shifts us some more until he's completely on his back. His tenderness and ferocity tether me tighter to him as if I'm held by a string. "I promise, baby girl. It was a dream, and I'll never let it be anything more than that."

I gulp and nod. "Neither will I."

He kisses my head again. "Go back to sleep. I've got you."

"Stone, you don't have—"

"I'm not leaving you, so close your eyes and go back to sleep."

Ending the argument there, his arms completely encircle me, becoming a fortress surrounding me. It would be easy to lift my head a little and kiss his neck or aim a bit higher for his lips. I could even slip down his body and take his thick cock—something I can feel isn't oblivious to our position—in my mouth. That would chase the rest of this away.

He's good at mental diversions.

Instead, I stay put.

I have no idea how I'm going to fall back to sleep. Not only am I overloaded with the remaining adrenaline in my veins, but I'm lying in only a tank top and sleep shorts on top of Stone, who is only in boxer briefs. It doesn't take more than a half second before all that edgy adrenaline turns to heat and hunger, and I find my finger swirling along his ink once more like I did once upon a time. His ring on my finger glints in the burnished light, and that weird, nervous flutter I get every time I look at it hits me.

The only time I ever take it off is when I shower or I'm on set. I tell myself it's keeping up the fake engagement. Making it real for anyone who watches us. But I know that's not the full explanation for it, even if I don't allow myself to delve deeper into it.

He exhales slowly, thickly. Maybe he's thinking about the night when I asked him to take my mind off the storm and he did. Obviously, that's what *I'm* thinking about. My gaze casts over to the window, the shades and curtains closed, but I can just make out a sliver of glass, and with that, a hint of small white flakes bustling past.

"Is it snowing?"

"It started just before I went to bed."

If the weather people were right and this stays as snow and

ice, there's a chance I'll be stuck here in this apartment with him for at least a day or two.

"Did you mean it?" I ask, and my teeth sink into my bottom lip and my eyes snap closed. The question slipped out, and I immediately regret it.

"I meant it," he answers before I can retract it, and it's aggravating that he knew what I was asking him when there was no context to it. The condoms. The women. Or should I say the lack thereof.

I want to ask him what I'm supposed to do with that, but the words thankfully glue themselves to my tongue. I don't know what I want his answer to be, and it could only go two ways. It means nothing and we stay in this weird, in-between space we exist in. Or it means everything. It means rolling over on top of him and kissing him. It means doing this. For real. Me being his and him being mine.

It's a fantasy I've had on more than a hundred occasions over the last two years.

I don't fit as well with anyone as I do with him.

But our situation is unchanged.

I'm leaving in a couple of months, and I'm still his brother's ex and therefore, untouchable. Or at least undatable. I nearly laugh out loud. How could we date? That's such a ridiculous notion. We can't date. I'm his fake fiancée. His brother's ex. There is no dating with that. No taking it slow or seeing how it goes. No happily ever after or falling in love for real.

If something happened between us now, I'd fall in love with him.

That would be one hundred percent certain because I'm about ninety-three point six percent positive I was almost there the last time, and that was only ten days. These months, he'd not only own my heart but all of me, and I wouldn't be able to let him go. Not for Forest. Not for the world or my career. Not for anything.

It's why I've avoided him these weeks and had avoidance in every slot on my bingo card for this fake engagement.

Eventually, I'm lulled into sleep aided by the comfort of his slow, even breaths and strong body holding mine.

But right before I'm good and asleep, I hear him murmur so softly I'm not even positive I hear him right. "There is no one else for me but you."

I WAKE to blinding white and my alarm blaring, both so much more painful than sunlight on a hangover, and I groan in protest. Shutting off my alarm, I flop back over, but that sliver of open shades and curtains bleeds directly into my eyes, and I squint and roll over the other way, only to snap upright and look around the room. I didn't dream Stone coming in and holding me, right?

No. But I should still take the fact that Stone is gone as a gift.

I snatch my phone from my bedside table and see a myriad of texts. The first few are from the studio as well as the producers and directors confirming that they've shut down filming for the next two days due to the weather. Loomis is the next, telling me that he's obsessed with the snow and plans to stay inside, sit by the gas fireplace he has, and watch streaming television. He did say he'd be around if I needed an escape and wanted to go over.

Here's hoping I don't.

I drag myself out of bed, do my thing in the bathroom, and head out toward the kitchen in search of some much-needed coffee. Most of the lights are off, and the gunmetal gloom of the sky and the white of what should be the skyline and the park through the floor-to-ceiling windows make the apartment feel cozy and intimate. Small, icy-looking flakes fall fast and hard, and I can see there's already a good buildup of snow on the ground.

Stone has a couple of fireplaces. One wood, the other open gas, and I might take advantage of the day off with a book, a cup of something chocolatey—with alcohol—and silence.

Speaking of silence, I give a hearty listen, my ears searching as I hover between the great room, dining room, and kitchen. From this angle, I can't see into the kitchen and I'm afraid if I move left or right, if he's in there, I'll be caught. Am I being childish? You bet I am. Except immediately, I catch the scent of something yummy cooking and him moving around the kitchen.

Silently, like the coward I totally am, I lift my foot off the ground to take a step back when he calls out, "I'm making you an egg white omelet with spinach, mushrooms, tomatoes, and goat cheese. I also have turkey bacon."

Damn him.

"Now get your ass in this kitchen before I make you eat carbs."

I moan.

Whether it's from his bossy tone or the thought of carbs is anyone's guess.

"I might have dough hidden in the freezer I can make croissants with."

Double damn him. Croissants are my oysters. Aphrodisiacs that get me all hot and turned on, and he knows it. Especially when they come with—

"I also have raspberry preserves."

And that's it. I'm done for.

I've been good for like two weeks straight. I can eat a croissant or three.

"Talking dirty to me like that might make me sit on your face, but I can't promise you'll get any pleasure from it," I quip, playing on what he said to me that night on the boat when all this started between us. Why did I say that?

I slam my lips shut as I enter the kitchen and find his back to me and him wearing low-slung black joggers and a tight white T-shirt. The soft kind. The kind that makes you want to go up to him and pet or nuzzle him the way Doe is. However, I think Doe's nuzzling is based more on the cooked turkey bacon Stone is dropping for her and less on the texture and sexiness of his pants and shirt.

His head rolls over his shoulder and he grins at me. "Baby girl, anytime you want to sit on my face just tell me to lie down. But I think we both know there will be pleasure in it for both of us."

Fuck. I might have just come a little. It can't be helped. It's the bad boy tattoos, the sexy, sleep-mussed hair, the cocky smirk with devilish green eyes, and the man talking dirty as he cooks while feeding a cat.

"You always this sweet to your pussy?"

"She's the only pussy in this house who will let me pet her."

I shouldn't have gone there, and I shake my head, holding up my hand to let him know I don't want to keep this going. We do sexual banter like high school kids, and it's bad stuff.

Opening the freezer, he pulls out the pastry dough and sets it on the counter to thaw, and when he turns, my nipples harden.

"You're wearing an apron."

He hardly skips a beat, pouring a mug of coffee and sliding it over to me. I take a sip only to choke on it and burn my tongue when I read what his apron says.

"I like my butt rubbed and my pork pulled."

He winks at me and turns to pour the egg mixture into the sizzling pan. "I already know you do, little Rose, but let's eat breakfast first before I treat you to dessert."

I hover on the far end of the island, taking another sip

because I feel like I need a minute with this Stone. The one who's playful and too sexy for anyone's sanity as he cooks and flirts. Asshole, gruff, dominating Stone I can wrap my head around. This version kills me.

"I didn't take you for the funny apron guy."

"Mason gave it to me for my birthday last year," he explains, moving the eggs around in the pan. "I have another one that says *My meat is 100% going in your mouth.*"

"Oh god!" I laugh, only to choke on my coffee again, forcing myself to swallow it down so I don't spray it everywhere. "That wasn't fair or nice."

"I never said I'd be either with you." The way his voice drops makes my skin hum and blush. I hide it behind my mug, only to realize I've finished my coffee far too fast and need a refill. "How are you feeling this morning?" He holds up the carafe as if he knows my every freaking inner thought, and I come over to him, allowing him to refill my mug while he continues to make us breakfast.

I love that Stone cooks, but more so, I love how he doesn't do it to show off or impress. Yet another stupidly sexy thing about him. I hop up on the island counter on the other side from the gas range he's working at. If I straighten my legs, I could kick his ass—literally—but instead I settle for swinging them back and forth.

"Good. Better. Thank you for, well, everything."

He plates up the huge omelet and cuts it in half, giving me one half and taking the other. A couple of slices of turkey bacon are dropped on my plate, and he slides it to me. He joins me at the island, standing beside me while I sit, and we eat in silence for a moment.

I've been trying to remember what he said to me last night before I fell asleep. It's right there on the edge of my brain but just out of reach. He's doing all this and it's so much. The fake engagement and living here so he can keep me safe and the ring that's so beautiful I both love and hate it. Then there's the other stuff, like the cooking and making sure I've eaten and driving out to Cambridge after he's worked all day because I was hurt and the holding me all night after I had a nightmare.

I've been trying not to think about the stalker much, but clearly, it's weighing on my mind and coming out through my dreams. But right now, here, with him, with the snow falling outside in heavy droves, I feel safe. But it's more than that. So much more. And I don't know what to do about it.

I'm a mass of contradictions.

I pick up a piece of bacon and start munching on it. Stone checks something on his phone and it's all so normal.

"This is really good. Thank you."

He nods. That's it.

"I can make dinner tonight."

He grins wryly and looks up from his phone, his green eyes twin emeralds as they sparkle at me. "I was thinking we could go on a date tonight."

"What?" I sputter, my fork clanking on my plate. "Why on earth would we do that?"

"Because it's snowy out, which will hopefully keep the press at bay, but there will be enough people out to take pictures of us. A lot of the extra press on us has been because no one has seen us together since outside the hospital."

"Stone."

"Tinsley," he mocks my tone. "What's the big deal if we go out and have dinner together versus having it here?" He picks up my hand and starts playing with my ring.

"Because you called it a date and not dinner, and we'll need to touch and smile and look like we're in love."

It's what I've been avoiding. I feel like it'll look real because it might be. I want to touch him. I want to walk on his arm. I want to lean over and kiss his cheek or lips. I want to go on a date with him. And I want it to be real when it's not, and because of that, I don't want to do it.

"I think we can manage that," he says dryly, and he shifts until he's standing between my thighs, his hands on either side of me. He slides my plate away to give himself room to cage me in. His lips ghost over mine, close, but not touching. "We can say it's not real, that everything between us is fake, but we both know the truth."

That's when his words from last night hit me. *There is no one else for me but you.*

Before I can reply, his lips skim mine and float over to my ear. "I want to take my fiancée out for dinner tonight. Think about it."

With that, he walks out of the kitchen, leaving me reeling and rife with indecision.

28

TINSLEY

I haven't had a snow day since I was a kid. A little kid at that. I stopped going to high school when I was sixteen because that's when my first album hit it big, and I went on tour. I had tutors and got my GED a year later. My mother was adamant about that.

So today feels like a freebie. Like a gift.

I have nothing I have to do. It's an insane feeling as an adult because I feel like we always have something we have to do. We're always going and moving and taking on the world one minute at a time.

After Stone left me winded and out of sorts in the kitchen, I cleaned everything up and then climbed back into bed. I read for about an hour, took a bath, and then a shower after because I hate washing my hair in the bath.

By the time I get out of the shower and change into fleece-lined leggings and an oversized sweatshirt, I feel calmer and more relaxed than I have in ages. And ready to start writing some music. Only I'm not sure where I want to do that.

That is until I get a text from Stone.

Stone: Croissants and hot chocolate are in the library for you.

I didn't even have to say anything. How could he have known?

That's one of the rooms with a fireplace, and when I enter, he has that thing roaring. Doe is curled up on a little soft rug he has set up for her in front of it, contentedly napping. I sit down, set my guitar against the couch, and stare at the tray of warm croissants, butter, and raspberry jam along with a large mug of hot chocolate. My head swivels around, but it's just me in here. I lather up one of the croissants with butter and jam and take a bite, wash it down with my delicious hot chocolate, and wonder what the fuck.

Like for real. What. The. Fuck?!

Is he trying to make me fall in love with him? Is that his game? But to what end? Or is he simply trying to make me happy and feel at home in his home? But again, why do that when there's nothing in it for him? That's what I keep coming back to.

What's in it for him? My legs have been closed for weeks.

I snap a picture of everything and send it to Loomis. I need a little backup right now and as much as I love Wren, I need a male's opinion on this.

Loomis: Looks scrummy.

He sends me a picture of the Italian feast he's eating in front of his own fireplace with the television on something I can't make out.

Me: Stone did all of this for me. After he made me breakfast and held me all night when I had a nightmare.

Loomis: So why aren't you in his bed right now sucking him off under the covers?

Me: That's not helping.

Loomis: Fine. Because I know you, I know what you're

asking without asking, and the answer is simple. He loves you. A man wouldn't go to all that trouble otherwise.

Me: Not even for sex?

Loomis: Nope. Not even for that. He doesn't have to work that hard to win your panties, luv. But he does have to work impossibly hard to win your heart.

I shake my head and call him. I can't do this over text.

Loomis picks up with a chuckle. "Don't like my answer?"

"It doesn't make any sense. Why would he do that?"

"He might not be consciously trying to win your heart, but he loves you. That I'm sure of."

"But to what end?"

"I don't know. He's the one you should ask that question to. Not me. Now go enjoy your goodies. I'm watching an Alfred Hitchcock film and trying not to have my own nightmares."

We hang up, and I sit with what he said about Stone trying to win my heart for a very long minute.

Humans are inherently selfish creatures, but we're driven by love. Lust too, but love is what speaks to our hearts and souls. Lust doesn't make it past our brains and blood supply. So again, what is Stone doing with me?

I have more questions and no answers, and either way, it feels like I lose. I sit in front of the fire, drink my drink, and eat every crumb and morsel of pastry. It's impossible not to marvel at the fact that Stone is doing all of this with me. He gains nothing but a headache full of bullshit. But...

He's been doing one thing after another, and despite my cold behavior toward him, I'm not oblivious to it. It's messing me up.

Why do all this for me? Why try to make me fall in love if we can't have a future?

I lean forward, my hands covering my mouth as I stare into the dancing orange flames and then down at the ring on my hand. A ring I don't have to wear right now, but I am.

I think Stone may love me.

I think he might have fallen in love back on Benthesicyme and never stopped.

And I think it's time I stopped caring about what my ex might think. I can leave that up to Stone to decide. But for me, I no longer care. And the thought of moving back to LA without Stone doesn't hold much appeal. Boston is my home. It's always been my home. LA was a stopping point, a jumping-off point, and I don't see why I can't make music and film work from here.

But what if he doesn't want that in return? What if this is just his way of showing me this, knowing it'll never lead to more?

"You're killing my carb high! Argh!" I shoot off the couch and storm down the hall. I'm pissed off. At least I'm telling myself I am. I don't quite buy it. But who cares? I ride this wave until I stumble into his mostly closed door and push it open without invitation. Then I freeze like I just stepped outside naked.

Speaking of naked...

Stone just got out of the shower. The bathroom door is open, and a small amount of steam curls into the bedroom like a beckoning fog. Somehow, he didn't hear me burst in, and for a moment, all I can do is stare. His back is to me as he stands by his bed where his clothes are laid out, and I make note of his smooth skin and strong, toned muscles as he briskly rubs his towel over his hair to dry it. His perfect ass with the sexy dents above it. Those incredible tattoos. I categorize them all.

But the beautiful boat on his left shoulder blade that looks a hell of a lot like Benthesicyme with the entire mast snaked in ornate purple roses, surrounded by a compass is what finally makes me gasp and give up my voyeuristic enjoyment.

"Let me know when you're done ogling and I'll turn around so you can get the frontal view."

His teasing tone isn't all that teasing. It's tense, and I wonder if he knows what made me gasp. "Stone?"

He rolls his head over his shoulder, but he doesn't do anything. Not put on his briefs. His shirt. Nothing. His eyes linger on mine, and he knows precisely what I'm staring at.

"Can I help you, *little rose*?" The way he emphasizes my nickname. The way he follows that up with, "Your purple eyes seem a little lost. Or perhaps stuck on something."

I don't know what I'm doing, but I'm crossing the room. Finally, he pulls on his briefs and turns to face me. I point at his chest. "That's what Owen was talking about, isn't it?" It comes out as an accusation. "You're shirtless. I haven't seen your back shirtless since the boat. The same one that's tattooed on your back. With purple fucking roses on it."

His hands find my hips, holding me in place. "Ask me then."

I can't. Oh, hell, I can't. My heart thunders and my palms grow sweaty. I'm about to cross the Rubicon, and there will be no turning back.

"Go on, ask me," he cajoles when I still can't find my voice.

"You call me Little Rose."

"I do," he confirms.

"You have roses on the tattoo of your ship. A tattoo you didn't have the last time I saw your back."

"Correct. But none of those were the question you were supposed to ask. Those were a gimme. A layup. Simply stating facts." He leans in, pressing against me until his lips are right over mine, his eyes pinning me in place. "Ask me, little rose. Ask me if the tattoo on my back, the one with a vine of sweet, pretty, little purple roses, is about you."

Oh god. How do I ask that? Especially when I already know his answer.

I gulp and muster up my strength. My pissed-off resolve is faltering, practically nowhere to be found. "Is that tattoo about me?"

"Yes." No artifice. No embarrassment. Just honesty that cuts me to the quick and my knees give out from under me.

"Why?" I grit out.

"Because those ten days changed my life, and you were part of that."

Okay. I blow out a breath I didn't realize I was holding. That makes sense and I can live with that.

His hands slide up the sides of my body, up along my shoulders until they frame my face, and continue through my hair before he cups me, holding me steady, forcing me to see him. He moves in closer, and somehow, someway, he's all I can see, smell, feel, and taste. He's everywhere.

"Keep going."

"What do you mean keep going?"

He smirks and starts to trickle kisses along my jaw. "I know that's not your only question. Something brought you in here. Something had you storming down the hall." He continues with his kisses, pulling my oversized sweatshirt off my shoulder so he can kiss that spot between my neck and shoulder that he likes so much. I haven't stopped him. I *can't* stop him. "What had my girl so hot and bothered that she came to find me and didn't even stop to knock?"

"Why are you doing all of this?"

"All of what?"

"You know what." I shove him back, my anger ratcheting back up. "Why are you doing all of this?! Why am I in your house and wearing your ring? Why do you make extra food for me and goddamn croissants? Why did you hold me all night when you could have easily come back in here to sleep?"

"Because I fucking love you!" he yells, his hands flying about. "That's why. How do you not see that? You're my goddamn north. I have no direction without you. No path forward. Without you, I'm lost. I've *been* lost. Only the irony behind that is that you made me feel found and then took it all away."

I shake my head, and this infuriates him.

"Goddammit, Tinsley. You don't like my answer? Fine. Forget you fucking asked and forget I fucking answered. Just wear your ring and be mine for the small amount of time I can call you that. That's all I want with this." He puffs out a breath, his hands on his hips and his gaze on the small space between us. His voice simmers, his expression a contradiction of fury and despair, battling to see which wins. "I get it, okay? I get all of it. We're a mess, and I don't even know what I want or what I'm asking for from you. But fucking give me this. Give me this one piece of you I can call my own."

"You're so dumb."

He grunts. "How am I dumb?" He tugs at the long strands of my hair, trying to push me back and away from him, giving me one last out that I know I won't take.

"Because for the last two years, all I've been is yours."

With that declaration, I jump on him. He staggers back two steps and falls onto the bed with an oomph. My lips collide with his, and he groans, not skipping a beat as his hands dive up into my hair and he kisses me back like my mouth holds the only source of oxygen in the room. The heat of his lips and tongue light up a well inside me.

"I'm yours, Stone," I pant against his lips. "But I don't know how to truly be yours. I don't know how this works."

He flips us on the bed until he's above me, and I'm staring up at him in the waning winter light. "I love my brother. I love him with all my heart. I do. So it breaks me to say this, but I can't live my life for him. I've tried to be better. I've tried so hard to put the selfish bastard I was behind me. But if you're telling me I can have you—for real, have you—then I'll risk being selfish to make that happen. No matter the consequences."

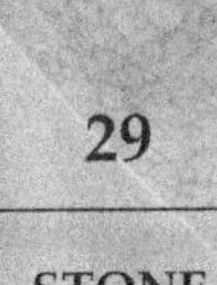

29

STONE

Her hands find the back of my head, and she forces my face to hers, our lips smashing together in a painful bam of teeth and misaligned lips. I can do this. I can take her mouth and her body and make them all mine. I can. And I wouldn't look back. I'd just keep moving forward, taking more of her. The selfish bastard in me who still likes to peek his head out every now and then would demand it.

The truth is, she can say whatever she wants, but I told her I love her. And she didn't say it back. Just that she's mine. But what does that actually mean? I know she likes me. I know she might even be infatuated with me. But is it enough? Is it enough to keep us together when everything about our worlds would seek to tear us apart?

I love her. But I'm afraid of loving her. Afraid of losing her. Afraid of losing myself in the process. I've worked so damn hard to get where I am. To be the man that I am. But she's a love I can't shake no matter how hard I try. She's burned into me. A tattoo on my skin—literally.

I kiss her back, and I lift her sweatshirt over her head so I can kiss my way along her perky breasts and tight nipples that are anxious for my mouth.

I don't know how to stop when I'm with her.

She's right here with me, anxious for more, and so beautiful she makes me ache. I want to demand a million things from her, but I won't. I've already given up. I'll take what she gives me and fight for the rest and hope I land somewhere on my feet with her by my side.

My hands fist deep in her hair as I lick and suck on her pretty nipples. Her head leans back, her eyes closing as she holds on tight. I press into her, letting her feel me. She tastes like chocolate and raspberries, and her skin gets so warm when it's touched. The best thing about fucking Tinsley Monroe is how I smell her like her after. For hours, I smell like her. To the point where I refuse to shower until the very last remnants of her are erased from my skin.

I tear down her leggings, toss them to the floor, and trail my hand back up to her wet heat barely hidden beneath tiny, thin satin. Satin. That's what she likes. Soft and silky and sweet. Just like her cunt.

I pull back and catch her face, hair wild on my bed, lips bruised and swollen red, eyes lavender and glowing. Fucking. Gorgeous. I've never been this raw or primal with anyone. I want to fuck her into tomorrow. I want to pound into her and come inside of her until she's sore and dripping me.

A wave of possessiveness boils within me, and I plunge my fingers inside her, pumping them furiously so she knows I will give up everything for her. And it'll be worth it. My regrets when I'm a hundred and thirty won't be that I didn't try, and they won't be that I didn't give her every piece of me.

I roll us once more until she's straddling over me. "Sit on my face, baby girl."

I pull her panties to the side, and she inches her knees up

my bed until her cunt is above my lips, her smell goddamn everywhere.

Her head falls back, and her hand grips the hair on the top of my head as she rolls her hips into my face. "God, yes."

She's so wet, already dripping into my mouth, and I lick it up, tasting her and groaning because, *fuck,* she tastes good. I've opened myself back up to this. My Pandora's box. I'll be done for and ruined when she leaves. And she will leave. I have no illusions about it.

I hate how much I need her.

My tongue dives up and in, circling around, and my nose presses on her sweet, tight clit. I wiggle my face back and forth, fucking her like this. It's not enough for her. I know it's not. But I can't help but want to punish her a little for making me so goddamn desperate.

"More." It comes out as a whisper. A sigh. A plea. "I know I can be such a bad girl, but please. I just need to feel you."

My balls tighten the moment she calls herself a bad girl and then nearly explode when she says she needs to feel me. I reach down and pull my boxer briefs off, kick them to the floor, and squeeze my cock so I don't come right now. I lift her a little and spread her thighs so she's completely exposed to me. My tongue strikes a path, ringing her asshole and playing with her opening, all the way up to her clit, where I suck her deep between my lips. Her hips buck, and her hand in my hair rips.

"Oh, god!" More grinding. "I want to come, Stone. I want to come so bad. All over you."

"Then do it, little Rose. Make me take it. Make me take all of you."

"Ah!" She falls forward, her hands hitting the bed above my head to hold herself up so she can watch me eat her out like a man starving. I devour her pussy. I hum and groan and lick and kiss and suck and even use my teeth. I never know with her. From one day to the next, I never know if I'll get this again, and

I never take it for granted. I like taking her so roughly that she'll be thinking about me tomorrow. That her pussy will clench with want and get wet from thoughts of this.

"Fucking bad girl, you're such a tease." I spank her ass. Hard. "Come on me. I need it too."

And she does. With those words she comes on my face, undulating her hips and pussy in my mouth as I take her over the edge.

Before her orgasm fully ends, I lift her hips, shift her again, and slam into her. "Fuck! Stone! Oh!"

Her pussy convulses around my cock, squeezing it with the aftershocks of her orgasm.

"Jesus." I throw my arm over my eyes. I was not prepared for that.

"You okay down there?"

I hold up a finger. "I need a minute."

"That's it? That's not exactly an enticing number to give a woman when you're inside of her."

I wheeze out a laugh, and my arm falls back. "You feel too good."

"That sounds like a you problem and not a me problem."

"Is that a challenge?"

I flip her over, making her yelp. My hands snatch her wrists, and I lock them above her head as I slide back into her when a thought strikes me. I pull out, much to her dismay, climb off the bed, and go to my closet.

"Oh my god! What are you doing?"

I laugh under my breath. "I just realized we're out of milk. I'm going to get dressed real quick and run out."

"What?!" she shrieks, and now there is no hiding my laugh.

"Relax. Be patient. Trust your sir."

"You're not my sir!" she yells. "If you're in there longer than two minutes, I'm going to make myself come, and I won't even let you watch me this time."

I shake my head as I open a drawer I have in here. A drawer I'm not sure I'll even be able to explain because it makes me come off as an obsessed psycho, but so be it. Maybe I am.

Pulling a few items out, I shut the drawer and return to my bad girl.

Her eyes widen and then narrow into slits when she sees what I'm holding, and she props herself up with her elbows. "Uh-uh. No."

I stop dead in my tracks. "What?" I never expected her to say no.

"I'm not letting you use that stuff on me." She looks like she's about to bolt out of here, fury dancing across her face, and I climb back on the bed and straddle her thighs before she can escape.

I set the items down and lean over her. "Tell me why."

She bites her lip and turns away from me, covering her tits from my view as if this all made her feel vulnerable. What the fuck is going on?

"Tinsley." I move her jaw back. "Tell me. If you don't want me to tie you up or use a toy on you, that's fine. But why do you look angry that I have these?"

"Because I don't want you to use something on me that you've used on countless other women!"

Oh. I smile because my chest feels like it's about to explode. My girl got jealous. I push her back down and kiss her lips even though she doesn't kiss me back. "I've never used them on anyone. I was in a sex shop with Vander—don't ask." I follow up quickly when she throws me a bemused look "I saw these things and thought of you. The rope. The toys. I bought them not knowing if I'd ever get to use them."

She gulps and takes them in with new eyes. "You bought these for me?" Her fingers run along the soft black rope, bottle of lube, butt plug with a purple jewel, and silver vibrating bullet.

I hold her face in my hand. "I don't want anyone else. Not ever again. I only want you. If you don't want to play—"

"I want to play." Her eyes meet mine. "I love you, and I trust you, and I want to play."

Holy shit. Holy fucking shit.

I kiss her senseless, with everything I have. "I love you. So much." I'll love her forever.

I move us up toward the headboard, my mouth never leaving hers. The rope slides through my hands, and I start to push her wrists up to the headboard when she goes to push me away.

I blink at her, a little stunned, but then I see it in her eyes. In the glimmer she has there. She wants me to force her a little. She wants to play.

"Little rose," I warn, my voice turning deep and deadly. "Are you going to be a good girl for me and put your hands up there?"

"No."

Fuck. My dick pulses.

I lean in and whisper as I pick up the bullet, "Bad girls get punished. Is that what you want me to do? Punish you for being bad?"

She squirms but refuses to answer me, and I bring the bullet up to her lips.

"Open and suck on it. I'm not giving you lube, so you better make it wet."

Her violet eyes spark defiantly at me, but she opens her lips, and I push it in. She starts to suck on it, and I take the butt plug in my other hand, dragging the cold metal over her belly and up to her nipples. She shivers, and goose bumps erupt along her skin.

"Is it wet enough?"

She hums against it, and I slip it from her lips and turn it on. The buzzing sound fills the room, and I don't waste time before I press it to her clit.

"Ah!" she cries out only to whimper when I immediately pull it away.

"Do you want it back there?"

"Yes."

"Arms up."

She hesitates, and I do it again, showing her how good the bullet feels and then immediately withdrawing it.

Finally, she raises her hands, her middle fingers a salute to me, because she always has to have a say even when she wants it as badly as she does. I make quick work of tying her wrists to the headboard and checking her circulation. Once she's good to go, I shove her thighs wider and shift back to take her in like this.

Jesus, she's fucking stunning. Earth shatteringly gorgeous. Never have I seen a more beautiful or erotic sight than this. I am one lucky bastard. With an incredulous shake of my head, I turn the bullet back on. Only I don't bring it to her clit. Instead, I leave it vibrating against her inner thigh.

"Christ, you're a sadist."

"I warned you. Bad girls get punished."

I pop the top on the lube and hold up the butt plug so she can see what I'm doing. I know she's never had any anal play, and I won't question or think deeper about that. I'll just take the gift I've been given and be eternally grateful for it.

Nervously, she worries her lip with her teeth.

"If you don't like it or it's too much, tell me, and it stops."

"I want to feel it. And if it feels as good as I think it will, I might want your cock in there sometime soon."

And I'm dead. Gone. Buried. There's no return from that. The sight of her like this and her telling me she wants my cock in her ass is officially the death of me. I pant and pinch my eyes shut, clenching my ass cheeks, because yeah, I'm about to come and I can't come yet.

Blowing out a breath, I open my eyes and adjust her body, bringing her knees up and running the toy and lube inside the crack of her ass.

"Ah! That's cold."

"I know. It'll warm up fast. Trust me."

I bring the bullet back to her clit, swirling it around and working her back up. Her skin flushes pink, and her nipples grow tight and impossibly hard. The tip of the plug finds her asshole, and I start to work it in slowly as I take her nipple in my mouth and use the toy on her clit. I want her as turned on and relaxed as she can be while I work the toy into her ass.

"Oh. Oh my hell."

"Shhh. Relax, baby girl. You can take it. It'll feel so good soon."

I twist the plug, and she moans, her pussy dripping onto the plug, helping me along. I pull it back out a little and then push it all the way in. Her back arches, and she tugs on the restraints. I continue to twist the plug, keeping the toy on her clit, and she thrashes wildly, the sensation overwhelming.

"After you come again for me, I'm going to fuck your tight cunt with the plug in your ass."

"Jesus. I..." She shakes her head. "It's so much. I don't know..."

"Too much?"

She swallows. "No. But... oh my fucking god!" She screams as her orgasm slams into her with such force the headboard creaks. Her body grinds down against the toy, pushing the plug deeper into her ass, and she moans and shakes, her beautiful face pinched up in ecstasy. The moment she starts to sag, I pull the toy away, lift her slack legs onto my shoulders, hike her hips and ass off the bed, and then slide back into her.

And *fuuuuuuck* is she tight like this. Even tighter than she normally is. I cannot wait to get into her ass, but I'll have to come about a dozen times before that, so I don't blow the second I get in there.

I give her a minute to settle and adjust before I start moving inside her. All she can do is hold on, her hands gripping the headboard as I slam into her. Each movement feels more intense than the last, and I can't help but look between us, watching as I move in and out of her. Sweat clings to my brow, and I plant my hands on the top of the headboard for leverage.

Moans and grunts and cries fill the air. We both watch as our bodies take from each other. The slapping heat and intensity of being inside her is a feeling I will never grow accustomed to or tired of.

Her eyes are closed, and her moans grow raspy as if her body is spent, but she still craves more. She's lost it. Totally at my mercy, and I take advantage. Holding her against me, I pound into her, thrusting up and up, making her feel my piercing as it slides in and out and drags along her front wall. And fuck does my girl feel good. Like nothing else.

"Next time, I'm going to blindfold you, little Rose," I growl. "When you feel my cock in your ass for the first time, I want that to be the only thing you know."

"It's so full like this, but god, it feels so good."

I bend down and take her lips. "You were meant for me and no one else."

My lips feast ravenously on hers, and I continue to fuck her, bending her in half. The plug in her ass fucks into her with every thrust of my cock. The moment her orgasm hits her, I can no longer hold off. I pump three more times as pleasure clenches my insides and shoots through me. With a roar, I come harder than I've ever come in my life, shaking and spasming, and filling her up with my cum.

I collapse against her, her body limp under mine, and I force myself to move so I can untie her. Her arms drop in a heap of dead weight, and I bring them into my hands, massaging them and checking them over to make sure no skin is broken and she's not too red.

"You okay?" I murmur against her, rolling her so she's on top of me and I can hold her.

"Mmm."

I grin and kiss her sweaty forehead. "Do you want me to remove the plug?"

"Not on your life," she mumbles, her lips half-planted in my chest. "That I'll do myself."

"I love you. Maybe that was a fucked-up way to show it considering what we just did, but I do."

I can feel her smile against me. "We wouldn't be us if we did things by the rules."

"Then I hope we continue to break them." And pray they don't break us in the process.

30

TINSLEY

"Do you ever miss the stars?" I ask lazily, staring out Stone's bedroom window. The gunmetal sky has morphed into a deep reddish-black as snow continues to fall.

"I'm looking at one right now."

"So cheesy." I snort and roll my eyes, but end up giggling as he nibbles on my neck and tickles my side.

"So true. Did you know because I'm engaged to one, I have over fifty thousand new followers on my Instagram? I'm super famous now. If I knew getting engaged to a hot celebrity was the key to fame, I would have done it a long time ago. It's been awesome so far."

"You're a butt face, and no one appreciates your sarcasm."

He rolls over me until I'm beneath him, his hands on the bed on either side of me as he planks above me. But that smile… holy shit, that smile might be the best thing ever. "A butt face?"

I shrug. "Just calling it as I see it, though lucky for you, your butt is pretty hot."

He laughs and drops down until he's smothering me with

his weight. I pretend I hate it and squirm to shuck him off, but it's a pathetic attempt at best.

"You like my face. You like what my mouth does to you." He licks my neck and nibbles on my chin, and yeah, I do like his face and mouth. But wait...

I smack his arm. "I was making a point, and now I forgot what it was."

"Stars," he murmurs into me, kissing down my neck to the tops of my breasts.

"Right. Stars. We don't get a lot of them in LA, and obviously I'm talking about the ones we see in space and not the ones you're teasing me about being. The street pollution and smog sort of kill them there. Boston doesn't get a ton either. I don't like it."

He shifts until he's snuggled into my side, his face in my neck, and his arm draped heavily around me, holding me close. Neither of us has the desire or drive to move from his bed. I did remove and clean the plug, and then he fucked me in the shower, and after that, we crawled back into his bed and have been here since.

"The night sky is one of the things I love most about sailing and being out on the water. It's endless."

"Have you been back on Benthesicyme since then?"

He sighs and holds me closer as if he's afraid I'll slip right through his fingers and disappear again. "No. I've thought about it. I have vacation time the hospital has been pushing me to use that I never do, and I thought about going back for a few days. I just haven't been able to make myself do it. You were a pretty powerful ghost."

That earns him a kiss because that breaks my heart for him. He loves to sail, and he loves that boat, and I'd hate to think he hasn't gone back because of me. I don't dwell on that. Hopefully, things have changed for him now.

"I think back to all those stars we saw out there, and it calms me when I'm feeling overwhelmed," I admit. "I remember feeling so small and insignificant."

He chuckles, the sound vibrating into my skin. "And that calms you?" He's incredulous.

"It gives me a bit more perspective. Perspective I need. It's easy to get wrapped up in the moment and emotion of a situation. I'm good at that. Call it my toxic trait, but it's mine, and I own it and I live it like it's my job. So whenever I get to that point, I think of us rocking on that ship and staring up at the night sky, and it calms me. It reminds me that my problems aren't always as big as I think they are, and there are so many out there who have it way worse than I do. That's for damn sure."

"It's one of the reasons I started my charity," he says, popping up and resting his head on his hand with his elbow digging into the pillow beside my head. We watch the snow fall, and it's so beautiful and peaceful, I never want to move again. "I have so much, and there are so many who have so little. So many who need more when I don't. Kids are the most vulnerable with this."

"Is that why you went into pediatrics?"

He nods. "One of the reasons, yeah."

"I donate a chunk of money to your charity every year."

A smile curls slowly up his lips, but he keeps his gaze trained on the window. "I know you do."

I gasp. "How? I do it anonymously."

His chin dips down to me, and he quirks an eyebrow. "Have you met Vander?"

I sigh, slightly peeved by that. "I should have known."

"Honestly, it's more for security reasons than anything else. I just like to make sure that large anonymous donations are on the up and up and not some asshole trying to hide or offload money for one reason or another. I don't want to be a tax shelter."

"It's a good charity."

"It's a great charity," he tosses back at me. "It's what I'm most proud of, and I follow the kids and the families it helps. My mom, who has been running the Abbott-Fritz charity for our family, has more or less taken this on with me, and she's big into fundraising galas. We have one next week." He pauses. Hesitates. "Do you want to be my date?"

His date. Why does him asking me to be his date make my heart pitter-patter and my chest squeeze?

"I'd love to be your date." Now it's my turn to pause. To hesitate. "Are we going to talk about this?"

"Which part?"

"I don't even know." I roll so I'm facing him in the muffled darkness, my hands tucked against my chin. "I don't know what happens next."

"Me either," he admits soberly, his finger tracing circles on my hip beneath the T-shirt he gave me to wear. It's all I have on and he's only in boxer briefs, and I'm doing my best not to get distracted by his touch or his body especially as I can see the guilt in his eyes. What we're doing and what this is, with all our love and uncertainty and complications, scares and worries him. It does the same to me too. It comes with heavy consequences and life-altering risks. Still, his expression turns resolved as he says, "All I know is that I want this, and I want you."

"I'm here for only another two months. After that, I'm not sure. But I want this, and I want you too."

He hitches a shoulder. "Then we'll figure it out as we go and see where we are then."

I chew on my lip, and he smirks, leaning forward to pull it from my teeth.

"Relax. It'll stay our secret for now. I have no intention of broadcasting what we're doing in here. The world already thinks we're engaged. No one needs to know the rest. At least not yet."

"Loomis will know. He'll take one look at me and know."

"My guys won't ask directly because I'm not sure they want to know. Forest, I don't think will ask either because he won't want to know and probably doesn't think his brother would betray him like that." He sighs. "Thankfully, he's in LA and not here and doesn't know his brother is actually a piece of shit."

"You're not a piece of shit. This is what's right. I was a child when I was with Forest, and we've been over for years. I know you feel guilty, and part of me still does too. I don't want to hurt him. But I don't want to stop living my life or give up on the things I want because his feelings will be hurt over it."

He nods, but I don't think he's fully sold.

"We'll keep it a secret." It's not a question. Right now, I think it's a necessity.

"Wouldn't be the first one we've kept."

True. "I'm good with—" My stomach gurgles so loudly it cuts me off.

"Hungry?" he deadpans, his lips twitching.

I laugh. "Evidently. All your sexing worked up an appetite."

He leans in and kisses me. "Then we should feed you because I plan to sex you up again when we get home."

"When we get home?" I parrot.

Another kiss, and then he rolls out of bed and goes for his closet. "Yup. We're going out on a date, remember? Go get dressed into something warm. I know where I want to take you."

"It won't be open. It's a blizzard outside."

"It'll be open. It's just some snow. Welcome to Boston. Now move your adorable ass."

I do as I'm told—for once—and drag my adorable ass down the hall because I am hungry and the idea of a snowy date with my guy sounds pretty great.

With both of us bundled up in large, dark coats, beanies on our heads, gloves on our hands, and boots on our feet, we venture out of the building. It must be too cold or too snowy for the press, as it seems they've given up and think we're too chicken to go out into the storm because the sidewalk is clear for the first time in weeks. As it is, Boston Common is mostly empty save for a few scattered people brave enough to walk through.

Stone takes my hand, and we cross Beacon Street to head into the park, immediately turning right and meandering toward the Public Garden. This is my favorite part of the city, especially in the spring when everything is in bloom, and you can't help but be in awe of its beauty.

It's funny, I grew up in this city, but when you grow up in a totally awesome place, it just becomes part of the fabric of your life and being. I haven't walked the Freedom Trail, or been to Paul Revere's house. I haven't done a Duck Boat tour or been to the science museum or aquarium since I was probably toddling about. I've been to countless sporting events, but that's just my family, and that's just Boston.

We make sports look good.

But I think when some of the madness dies down, I'm going to take Loomis, who has never been to Boston until now, and we'll take the city by storm, tourist style.

Stone and I race through the park, feeling like we're getting away with something, because for now, we did when I nearly trip over something that wrenches a screech from my lungs. I look down and then burst out laughing.

"Oh my god! I nearly killed Mama Duck!"

"What?" Stone turns back around, and a smile erupts across his lips. "Christmas isn't for another seven weeks."

I shrug, taking in the large mama duck, cast in bronze, with her trail of baby ducks waddling behind her, all of them wearing scarves and Santa hats. "But look how cute they are all in a row and all dressed up. I want one."

"A duck or a bronze statue?"

"Probably a statue. Ducks aren't the nicest animals. One beaked at my toe when I was a kid."

He laughs, his head thrown back and everything.

"Hey! It's not funny."

"A duck beaked at your toe? Yeah, that's funny. And the fact that you want a bronze one? Well, I guess that's what makes you you."

I raise an eyebrow. "If by that, you mean awesome, then yes."

"That's one word for you."

I flip him off, and he catches my hand and brings my gloved middle finger to his mouth so he can kiss the tip. He holds it between us along with my other hand.

"My favorite is when one of our teams is in the playoffs or wins a championship and they're dressed in jerseys," he remarks and then smirks. "I put Mason's jersey on Mama Duck last year with his signature on it. It lasted three days out here until someone realized and took it."

"I remember coming here once around Halloween and seeing them in costumes. Little witches and ghosts and spooky things. I didn't think to look at them last week, but I bet they were dressed up. I'm kind of bummed I missed it."

He closes the small gap between us, snow falling all around us, the city white and calm and beautiful with yellow street-lamps not too far in the distance. "They do a parade every spring where kids dress up and walk through the park like little ducklings."

My eyes bolt wide as my smile spreads. "Really? I didn't know that. I might have to see that for myself."

"It usually rains because that's Boston in April for you, but yeah. The kids are cute. Rory comes all dressed up, and Owen takes about ten thousand pictures of her."

"I want like ten kids. Not really, but that sounds fun and daunting and terrifying all at once." I don't even know where the sentiment comes from, but even in the dark, I can see the way his eyes blaze and are almost victorious. It makes my hands shake in his.

For a moment we're silent. Just staring at each other, the ducks between us. Then he whispers, "I would never turn down ten kids with you."

That's all he says, but already, this is the best date I've ever been on.

"You'd have to teach them to sail. I still don't know larboard from starboard and aft from—"

"I taught you aft tonight. You seemed to like it and take quickly to it."

I blush Red Sox red. "Only when my *sir* tells me to relax and that I can take it."

He grins. I grin back. Then he leans over the ducks and kisses my lips, his hands climbing to frame my face as snow falls all around us. "You're perfect, you know."

"I know."

He smirks. "And humble."

I smirk back. "Totally."

"Are you brave?"

"What?" I snort.

"Are you brave?"

"Sometimes."

"Come here. We're going to cause mayhem." He pulls back and points to the ground. He lies on his back on one side of the ducks, and I do the same on the other, ignoring how freaking cold and wet the snow is beneath me. His phone with the camera app opened is held over our faces, and he says, "Smile."

I smile, and the flash pings, momentarily blinding us.

He sits up. "That's one for our eight thousand grandchildren. Ready?"

"For what?"

He grins at me. "To show them all up. I have fifty thousand new superfans to feed."

He uploads the picture to his Instagram, writes a caption about how beautiful Boston in the snow is with his fiancée, and that's that. We're out there. On social media as a smiling couple for his new fifty thousand and the rest of the world to see.

"I can't believe you just did that," I snap, a little annoyed.

He chuckles. "I didn't. It's in my drafts. I'll post it tonight after we're safely in bed."

Okay. That I can live with. "You hate that you have fifty thousand new followers."

"Yep. But you're worth it. Now let's get some dinner."

He stands and takes my hand, and we race through the rest of the park, slipping and sliding on ice and snow until we're across a street and down another and on some snowy sidewalk that hasn't been shoveled or plowed and snow is up to our mid-shins.

He opens the door to a small restaurant and peeks his head inside. "Are you open?" he calls out, and immediately an older woman comes bustling out from the back.

"Ah, Mr. Stone. Come in. We're open." She snags on me and then him and smiles broadly. "But for you, we're now closed."

And that's how it goes.

Stone and I eat a Mediterranean feast only lit by candlelight. We share a bottle of red wine and are talked into a couple of shots of some alcohol with a crazy name I can't pronounce that tastes like licorice. It's insanely romantic, but more than that, it's us. It's the us back from the boat. The us with no one else watching as we hide from the world. Where we just talk and laugh, and it doesn't matter what we say because the other listens and understands and never judges. It's freedom and intimacy and feeling heard and seen.

I eat my weight in everything because the food is out of this world good, and when we leave, Stone pays as if the restaurant had been full of patrons this entire time. He doesn't flaunt his wealth despite his gorgeous apartment and lavish yacht. He never wears designer clothes or speaks to expensive tastes. He has a very nice car, but rarely drives it, though he has been since all this started.

He's so different from the man he used to be. The man he was before he got on his ship two years ago.He has changed. Or maybe matured is the better way to say it. The old Stone was the definition of a playboy. Women and extravagance.

He grew up, and I know he's worried about reverting back to his old ways or being that selfish man again, but I don't ever see that happening. Falling in love and wanting happiness for himself doesn't make him a bad or a selfish man. I understand his quandary and why he thinks that, and I don't have a lot of answers for how to fix it.

He thanks our hosts, and we leave the restaurant, heading back out into the dark, snowy night, hand in hand. And right now, the city is ours, empty and cold with our breaths a plume of white vapor. No one is around. Hardly anyone.

And for right now, it's just us, and us is perfect. Only perfect never lasts.

31

STONE

"You're going to make me late," Tinsley admonishes, swatting at me as I lean over her back and pepper her neck with kisses.

"Don't care. You look so fucking hot right now."

She does. She's wearing panties that cut up and across her ass and nothing else. Her body is bent over the sink so she can be closer to the mirror, which means her ass is sticking out and her tits are poking forward. Plus, she's making this adorable squinty face as she applies her makeup.

This is my version of happiness right here. Tinsley Monroe in my bathroom, practically naked, and putting on her makeup because this is now her bathroom too. It's something I never thought I'd get but definitely fantasized about. Speaking of...

I grind into her backside, trying not to smile triumphantly as she gasps and then emits a tiny moan.

"No! No nookie for you. That's your punishment," she chastises as she waves a mascara wand over her lashes.

I chuckle, kissing up and down her spine. "You're cute when you try to punish me."

It's my fault she's running late. She was playing and writing music for the better part of the day, and the moment she set her guitar down, I had one thing on my mind and one thing only, and that was putting my mouth between her thighs. It didn't matter to me that she set it down because it was time to get ready for the gala.

"Is that your way of saying I shouldn't do it again?"

She bumps her ass into my dick, making me oomph with the way it hits as if to say *you better do it again*.

"For real, we have to leave in half an hour, and there is no way I'll be ready for the gala tonight by then."

"Fine. But I get to fuck you later in your pretty dress. I want to ruin all this gorgeous hair and makeup with my hands and lips."

"I'll let you. Now bugger off."

I kiss her spine one more time and leave the bathroom. Truth be told, if I don't move my ass, I'll be late too, though it doesn't take me all that long to get dressed. I put on my tux, run my fingers through my hair, and I'm done. I've already showered and shaved. Women don't have it nearly as easy, though ninety percent of the time we prefer them without makeup and in their pajamas. There's something about a woman who doesn't think we're looking and is comfortable being casual that is the most beautiful.

This last week has been exactly as we designed it. The media went batshit crazy over the post of us in the snow by the ducks. Fans are obsessing. The media is in a tailspin. And much to Tinsley's dismay, she's been tailed and followed everywhere she goes.

She hates it, and I hate it for her, and I hate it for us, but it's a necessary evil. At least for now.

Vander and Lenox are at a dead end in figuring out who the copycat is, as is the FBI. It feels like we're sitting and waiting for something to happen while doing our best not to think about it. The first letter was spooky but not all that threatening, but that second letter talked about her fear, and how they're done being patient, and nothing scares me more.

Does that mean he's always following her? Always watching? It's a chilling thought.

For the most part, we do what we can to remove it from our thoughts without being stupid. She has her security, and she goes nowhere without them. So until something else happens or another letter comes along, we watch and wait.

Thirty minutes later, Tinsley steps out of the bathroom in her ice-blue gown with her dark hair swept over one shoulder in long, thick curls. My jaw hits the floor. The way the dress hugs her every curve, slinks to just beneath her collarbone, and floats down her arms in long, sheer sleeves, only to have her turn around to reveal a completely bare back is the sexiest tease I've ever seen.

"Wow." My throat dries, and for a moment, I'm rendered speechless. "My fiancée is a goddess." I blink and then have to blink again. "Seriously I've never seen anything more beautiful than you are right now."

"You're not so bad yourself there, Dr. Fritz. I'm very proud to be on your arm tonight, helping to celebrate and raise money for your charity."

I cross the room and place a soft kiss on my spot on her shoulder. I don't want to muss up her hair or smear her red lipstick. Not yet at least. That'll come later.

"Exquisite." I look up into her eyes. "You have no idea how much I love that I get to touch you and be with you in public as my girl tonight."

I stand and hold out my elbow to her. Her hand loops through it, cradling itself against my inner arm, and I lead her outside to the waiting limo, keeping our heads down as we're bombarded with cameras and questions.

Tonight is the annual gala event for my charity, and with that, my entire family, their friends, as well as the Central Square crew—minus Tinsley's parents—and their friends all come out for it. The hospital is here in full force with board members and department chiefs. Various society pages and sites are here taking pictures and interviewing random attendees.

Tinsley stayed on my arm while I glad-handed big supporters and introduced her as my fiancée.

To my parents, my family, and my friends, it's fake. To everyone else, it's real.

The lies burn my tongue, and there will be a reckoning for them. A lie this big doesn't fade into oblivion. It grows like a fire, unpredictable, destructive, and too hot to handle. With any luck, we'll be able to douse the flame when the time comes, but I have no idea how to do that now that Tinsley and I are secretly together.

There is no calling off a fake engagement and staying together if staying together is even an option for us. I'm doing my best to take it day by day, to not think about the future and what's next, or how things are already spinning out of control. And when it's just us in the apartment or we're going about our daily lives in different places, that's easier to do.

But being here tonight, the lie is even more flagrant, the secret is blurring lines, and it feels nearly impossible to keep up. I love that I can be out with her tonight, even if it's not real. She's in my bed, wearing my ring, but it's still not real.

I sip on my bourbon and watch Tinsley from across the room chatting with Wren, Katy, Keegan, Kenna, Sorel, and Serena. Sorel and Serena are my uncle Landon's twin girls, and it's great that Sorel recently moved back home to Boston. Serena works for Monroe Fashion and per Tinsley, she only wears Monroe gowns to events. I have no complaints given what she's wearing tonight.

I can't take my eyes off her.

As if reading my thoughts… "Your fiancée looks stunning tonight."

I turn and find my grandmother standing at the cocktail table behind me, a full martini resting on the table in front of her.

I give her a meaningful look. "You've been dodging me for weeks." I even drove out to the compound, but she wasn't home or had the staff tell me she wasn't. I join her at the table and kiss her cheek. "What's going on, Grandma? Why did you make that statement to the press?"

She places her hand over mine, and for a moment, she stares beyond me at the large ballroom. "This is an incredible thing you've done here, Stone. This charity you've built helps so many children."

"Thank you," I reply, trying not to let my impatience get the best of me. Not with my grandmother.

Her green eyes, the same color as mine, cast back at me, and she smiles. "You've grown so much in the last two years. You've matured and become the man I always knew you'd one day be. But it was hard won, wasn't it?"

I pause, studying her. I didn't tell everyone what I was doing when I went to Benthesicyme. I told my guys, and I told my parents, but that was about it. I didn't tell Forest and I certainly didn't tell the rest of my family including my grandparents. Most people think I was doing my billionaire bachelor playboy thing or just getting away for a bit on my sailboat. It wasn't the first time. I bought that boat when I was eighteen and spent time on her any chance I could.

So the fact that she knows has rendered me stunned.

"Yes. It was." It's about all I can muster.

She smiles knowingly. "You came for dinner at the compound the night you returned. Do you remember?"

I shake my head and then tilt it as the memory comes back. "It was Rory's birthday. You had a special dinner for her."

"Yes. And Forest was there."

I nod slowly, my eyes unblinking and my heart accelerating. How could she know? How could she possibly know?

"You couldn't look him in the eyes."

I swallow audibly, utterly frozen. "No. I couldn't."

"He was anxious to return to LA. Tinsley had returned home from her own trip a few days prior, and he was anxious to go and be with her."

"Grandma—"

"I've been around a long time, Stone. I watch the people I love very carefully. You were miserable that night. Heartsick. Your guilt was all over your face. You told everyone you were just exhausted from your trip. That being out on the boat for ten days alone was a lot. But you weren't there alone. Were you?"

I lick my suddenly dry lips and utter, "No. I wasn't."

No one knew that. Everyone, other than my guys, who knew about my mystery woman, thought I met her after that trip.

She smiles, but it's not smug or triumphant. It's a happy smile. A soft smile. "I thought not. When I saw those pictures of you and Tinsley outside the hospital, I was so pleased. Even if the headline was fake, the way you felt about her wasn't. If that didn't tell me everything, the ring you bought her does."

"That's why you invited her to your party. That's why you made a point to tell me she wasn't with Loomis and that she didn't belong to Forest anymore. You knew. All this time you knew how I secretly felt about her."

It's not a question. It's a bold statement, and it leaves me a little winded.

"As I said before, you've become quite the man and doctor, and I'm so very proud of you. Of everything that you are. But the one thing you've been missing since you came home is her. Love doesn't make excuses or allowances for other's feelings. When it's real, it cannot be denied. Nor should it be. Love is always worth the fight to win."

"And Forest?"

"Unrequited love breeds madness and obsession. He needs to stop living in the past and forcing something that will never be again. Sometimes that's a difficult habit to break until something makes us do it. Besides, I happen to know he dates regularly, whereas you do not."

I don't know how to respond, and I don't know what to say. Luckily, I'm interrupted by Tinsley, who comes over to greet my grandmother with hugs and kisses, and all conversation about Forest and love and my secret relationship with Tinsley immediately stops. The two of them chat about Tinsley's film, the album she's slowly been working on, and the Abbot-Fritz charity.

And when that's all done, my grandmother passes her back over to me with a mild, "Why don't you dance with your fiancée? She's too beautiful not to be shown off."

With that, my grandmother leaves us, and I do as I'm told, still a bit shell-shocked. I take my fiancée onto the dance floor, draw her close, and dance with her.

"Are you okay?" Tinsley whispers as we sway near other couples.

"My grandmother knows the truth about us. About how I feel about you. She's known it all this time."

Her violet eyes round. "She has?"

"I shouldn't be surprised. Octavia Abbot-Fritz seems to know everything at all times, but I didn't see that coming."

"Oh my god, that's wild." Tinsley laughs lightly, but all I can think about is how my grandmother told me to fight for Tinsley. To fight for something that can't be denied. I don't have to act yet. I have another couple of months to figure this out and see where Tinsley is. But my grandmother is right. And I plan to fight like hell for Tinsley when the time comes.

The rest of the night passes quickly. I make a speech, and we do our slideshow of kids who have benefited to let everyone know exactly where their money is going and how we spend it. There's a silent auction as well as a live one, and when the night is done, I can't wipe my smile, knowing we just raised a hell of a lot of money that's going to change the lives of kids who need it most.

Between that and my grandmother's words in my head, I feel light. Almost euphoric.

"Our pictures are everywhere," Tinsley muses, her head on my shoulder, her feet kicked up onto the seat across from us in the back of the limo.

"I'm not shocked."

There were photographers all over the event. The room was packed with local celebrities, Loomis came as well, which was very cool of him.

"It's a good one. See?" She turns her phone, and there we are, Tinsley on my arm, both of us looking at each other and smiling.

"It's a good one," I agree. "Yet another one for our future nine thousand grandchildren to see."

"Speaking of, everyone I met tonight wants to know if we've set a date. I didn't know what to say."

"January twelfth," rolls off my tongue without any thought. That's the day after her last Boston concert. By then, she's done filming. Usually, films don't take this long, but with the holidays thrown in there and the fact that they've fallen behind schedule, things are getting stretched. "Or maybe we should just fly to Vegas tonight and get married."

Her head swivels in my direction, and she stares at me while trying to read my expression to determine if I'm serious or not. My tone wasn't, but the thought is starting to brew a little despite how flippantly it first rolled off my tongue.

She snorts incredulously. "You want to fly to Vegas tonight and get married?"

I shrug and then tilt my head. "Bad idea?"

She laughs. "Um, yeah. I'd say it is."

"I take it a quickie Vegas wedding isn't on your bucket list."

"My father would cut off your balls."

"It's true. He would. Bad idea then. I'm very fond of my balls," I quip, my voice light as I continue to tease her a bit. "Besides, we'll need them for our ten kids if we want nine thousand grandkids."

She gives me a look. "Are you okay?"

"That's the second time tonight you've asked me."

"I think the question bears repeating."

I chuckle. "My grandmother threw me off tonight. She has a tendency to do that. I'm also living a life with you that's part fake and part something I never thought I'd get. I'm not sure I know how to do that so well. We'll tell people my kickass, superstar fiancée has a busy schedule, and we haven't figured out a date for our wedding yet."

She frowns, but before she can reply, we pull up in front of my building, and the driver opens the door for us. I take her hand and we race for the door, fighting the chill in the air and a couple of tabloid assholes still there. We climb into the elevator, and she wraps her arms around my neck as we shoot up sixteen floors.

"When I get married one day, I don't want it to be following a fake engagement."

"I know. Me either. I wasn't serious about Vegas." My hands meet her ass over her coat and dress. "What do you want?"

"You." The word comes out sweet and easy.

"You have me. Anytime you want me."

I dip and take her lips with mine in a demanding kiss. The

truth is, I've never felt such a tormenting mix of protectiveness, love, and blinding desire to make someone mine. It's making me rush things I don't want to rush. Things that should never be rushed.

Part of me can't seem to help myself. She's water slipping through my fingers.

32

TINSLEY

We cross into Stone's apartment, shutting and locking the door behind us. He helps me out of my coat and hangs it up in the closet before he does the same with his own. I can't believe Octavia knew all this time, and it makes me wonder who else knew or at the very least suspected.

Honestly, I don't want to know, and I sure as hell am not about to start asking.

I slip off my shoes, dropping down about six inches, the balls of my feet sighing in relief. The apartment is quiet and dark, and silently we enter Stone's bedroom, but in a flash, he has my hips and is swinging me over to the windows over-looking the park.

He presses me against it, forcing my hands to the glass to brace me, and then his lips are at my ear, his eyes glowing green in the reflection of the window. He's so gorgeous my pulse thrums through my body just looking at him.

With those eyes locked on mine, he takes the top half of my dress and wrenches it down, the sound of fabric tearing along with my loud inhale the only sound.

"I told you I was going to ruin this dress."

"And the window?"

"Do you trust me?"

He's asked me that before. When he took me in public at the Queen's Bath. And just like that day, my answer is immediate. "Yes."

His hands cup my breasts, and he starts massaging them, running his calloused palms over my stiffening nipples. "I want you naked and wet and getting fucked right here in front of this window. I want you to be so loud that the people walking their dogs or heading home from the bars know it's me who's doing that to you."

"Then you better make it good for me."

He smirks and nips at my neck but almost immediately the kisses turn tender and reverent, his touch following suit. "You're so beautiful you make my chest ache," he whispers against my skin. "All fucking mine, Tinsley Monroe. You're all fucking mine."

The dress ends up at my feet, and I kick it away as Stone takes a step back, his eyes molten as he rakes in my naked body.

"Rub your pussy, baby girl," he orders. "Get her nice and wet for me. Raise your left hand on the glass. I want to see my ring on your hand as you stand naked in my window."

My left hand slides higher up the glass, while my right slides down the front of my body and in between my legs. I dip my middle finger inside me and spread my wetness up to my clit. He licks his lips as if he can taste me, and I play with myself in front of a window high above Boston while I watch his reflection as he starts to undress. His bowtie gets undone first and hangs loosely around his neck as he works the buttons on his shirt before he pulls it over his broad shoulders revealing smooth skin, colorful ink, and stacked muscles.

"You're staring awfully hard, little Rose."

"I like what I see."

"I like what I see too. Does that feel good?"

"Your fingers feel better, sir." I smirk, and he follows suit.

I turn and press my ass and back into the cold glass as I continue to rub my clit in circles that make my skin tingle with electricity. I have no idea if anyone can see into these windows. We're sixteen stories up but knowing Stone and how protective and careful he is with me—not to mention the fact that he's a Fritz—I'd bet money they're tinted.

"I didn't give you permission to turn around."

"I want to see my tattoo. Please, sir."

The most breathtaking smile hits his lips. It's almost shy. Almost.

His pants slip to the floor, and he toes them off along with his socks and shoes. In only his briefs, he beckons me with a crook of his finger, and because I'm feeling naughty and in love and overwhelmed by absolutely everything and I know it will drive him crazy, I drop to my hands and knees and crawl toward him.

"Fuck," he hisses, his eyes going wide and unblinking. His hands rake back through his hair. "Jesus, Tinsley. You know how to make a man putty in your hands. Crawl right onto my lap, baby girl." Step by step, he moves backward toward his bed until his knees hit the mattress and he sits.

His hands are trembling, and I hold in my self-satisfied smirk. When I reach him, I climb up his thighs until I'm straddling him. Automatically, his hands meet my waist, and I stare into his eyes as I dip down and kiss him. Slowly I start to roll on him, grinding ever so softly along his hard cock, still hidden beneath his briefs.

He cups my face, pressing his lips harder to mine, and I force him back, going with him until we're chest to chest, lying horizontally on his bed.

"Roll over," I murmur against his lips.

"You want to be in charge tonight?"

I grin. "I definitely want to be in charge tonight."

Without another word or any protest, he rolls onto his stomach, and I shift so I can pull down his briefs. I want him as naked as I am. Then I'm back to straddling him, only now it's his firm ass that's between my thighs. Immediately I go for my tattoo. A hand plants into the bed to hold myself up, and I kiss his skin.

He grunts and then groans, "I can feel how wet you are. It's killing me that I can't turn over and thrust up into you."

I roll my hips on his ass, rubbing my clit on his right cheek. "Mmm. That feels good."

"My naughty little tease."

"Shhh. I'm exploring." My fingers and lips trickle along his skin, and I savor the way his breath hitches and his muscles quiver.

"Can you make yourself come like that?"

Good question. "Would you like me to try?"

"I can't see you like this. I want to see your pretty face when you come."

I glide my hips back and forth, rubbing my clit and my pussy on him. Kissing and smelling his skin as I get wetter and wetter. His hands fist the blanket, and I know he's struggling not to take charge. He's letting me have this, and it only makes me love him more.

"Little rose." His voice is shredded.

"Beg me," I whisper into his ear.

I catch the corner of his smile as he says, "Please let me turn over. Please let me watch you come."

"Good boy."

He chokes out a laugh. "But what if I want to be bad?"

"Tough choice. I'll think about it. Roll over and make me come."

He doesn't have to be told twice. I'm on my back with him above me, his knees on the mattress, and his forearm beside my head. His mouth captures mine as his free hand slides up between my thighs. Our foreheads press as he slips two fingers inside me and starts to pump with deliciously aching slowness. I close my eyes and get lost in the way he feels, in the way he touches me.

He steals kisses, his tongue a devouring force, only to pull back so he can watch me. My eyes are still closed, but I feel him all over me. His thumb works my clit, and I draw my knees up and out, opening myself up more for him.

He's quiet, breathing heavily as he increases his pace, finger fucking me in earnest, pushing me to come and come hard. I reach up and grab his shoulders, holding on, and getting close.

"Stone."

"I'm here, little Rose. You feel me? I'm here." His fingers slip away only to immediately replace them with his cock. He doesn't thrust inside me. Instead, he glides his cock up and down my pussy, making sure his barbell hits my clit with every upward motion.

My eyes snap open, and my chin drops.

"Does that feel good?" I ask, mesmerized by the sight of him against my pussy.

"So fucking good. Nothing has ever felt better than you."

His lips take mine, and he kisses me deeply, our tongues dancing and twirling as he swallows my gasps and moans. I try to hold off. I try to keep this going. It's impossible. My orgasm barrels into me, and I cry out, clutching him as I spasm and shake and grind myself against the head of his cock and that piece of metal that might be the best piece of metal ever.

With a simple move of his hips, and before I fully come down from my high, he slides inside of me with a low groan. His body drops down, and he covers me, kissing my neck, my jaw, my cheeks, my nose, my lips. His weight on me, the way he smells, and the sounds he makes, I'll never grow tired of him.

Nothing we do will ever feel conventional or boring.

"I love you," he rasps, his voice hoarse.

"I love you," I manage, holding onto his broad shoulders, my hand over my tattoo, feeling every muscle bunch and flex as he moves over and in me. He continues to kiss me as he takes me, making sure I feel every inch of him, savoring every inch of me.

He starts to speed up, both of us breathless with sweat sticking to our skin and making us slippery and tacky. We cling and breathe and kiss and pant and get lost in each other until there is no him or me, it's only us.

His face buries in my neck, and he starts to move faster, pounding up into me, and driving me to the point of insanity. He hikes my leg higher up his waist, pivoting his hip, driving in deeper, as deep as he can go, until I shatter around him, calling out his name, and going even higher when I feel his cock thicken inside me right before he starts to come.

His body stills and he squeezes me tighter as his low groans vibrate against my neck.

I hold him, cradling him against me. After a few minutes, we get up, shower, brush our teeth, and climb back into bed naked and wrapped around each other. And that's how we fall asleep. As one.

33

STONE

"Do you want to go out for brunch?" I ask Tinsley as I finish rinsing the shampoo out of my hair.

"Brunch?"

"Yeah, you know, breakfast and lunch combined make brunch."

"Thanks for that," she deadpans. "The word I was actually more focused on was *out*."

I bend down and suck her nipple into my mouth, dragging it out with my teeth. I have a problem. A serious problem. It's no joke. I have a real and living fear that I might never be able to get enough of her. I just fucked her not even five minutes ago, and I'm already getting hard again.

"I got a text from Vander. A bunch of people are meeting at my cousin Stella's restaurant in about an hour."

Her stomach grumbles, and I chuckle. "I'll take that as a yes?"

She smacks my shoulder. "Shut up. I can't help it if I have a very vocal stomach."

"Everything on you is very vocal, and I wouldn't have you any other way. But for real, do you want to go?"

"Can I bring Loomis?"

I work my way up her neck, and she pushes me away so she can condition her hair.

"Sure, but can I ask you something about him?"

She squints an eye open to me as she works the conditioner through her long, dark hair. "What?" she asks warily.

"He likes women, right?"

She laughs. "Yes, he likes women. Why do you ask?"

"You guys spend a ton of time together. I don't get it."

"Have you ever had any attraction toward Katy?"

My face curls up in disgust. "Fuck no. But I grew up with Katy as more or less my cousin. Her stepmom, Layla, is my uncle Oliver's stepdaughter. It's convoluted, but that's what she is to us."

She shrugs. "Loomis is like Katy to me, and I'm like Katy to him. We love each other and have insane chemistry on screen, but there is no sexual spark or desire between us. There never has been."

"You have no idea how jealous I was of him."

She wraps her arms around my neck. "You have no idea how jealous I was of all your miscellaneous women. It seems we both fooled the other because you didn't have any and I was never with Loomis."

I kiss her lips, brushing some of the wet strands from her face when her stomach growls again.

I laugh and kiss my spot on her shoulder. "Let's go feed you."

An hour later, we walk into Stella's. Kenna waves us over, and we greet everyone and take our seats. Stella pulled up three tables in the back room to accommodate all of us and also to give us privacy. After we order, I get up to go into the kitchen and say hi. I haven't seen Stella in a while since she's always here and I'm always at the hospital.

She and Layla used to babysit me a lot as a kid, which is

likely another reason I consider Katy my cousin. But Stella also catered the event last night, and not only was the food outstanding, but her staff did an incredible job, and I want to thank her since she donated all of that.

I swing open the kitchen door and pop my head in. It's all hustle and bustle back here since the restaurant is packed on this Sunday.

"Stella?" I call out, but shockingly enough, my parents intercept me.

"She had to run over to Bongay to deliver something," my mother informs me. "She should be back soon. What are you doing here?" Bongay is one of Stella's other restaurants, and it's just as popular as this one.

"A bunch of us are having brunch in the back room. What are you doing hanging out in the kitchen?"

"We just finished brunch but wanted to thank her again for last night."

I grin. "That's what I'm back here to do."

My mother takes my hand and leads me out of the kitchen, over to a quiet corner of the restaurant. "I'm glad I ran into you. Did you hear what the preliminary numbers are from last night?"

I shake my head. "No. Tell me."

She can't contain her smile, her brown eyes glittering. "Somewhere around one point eight million."

My eyes bulge. "Are you serious?" I look from her to my father and then back. "That's insane."

"People came out big last night for the event."

"Your grandparents donated a hefty chunk for it too," my father follows up.

I cover my mouth with my hand and shake my head incredulously. "That's gonna cost me." I laugh. I have this thing where I match whatever the total amount raised from the gala is. Last year, it was half that amount. "Wow. I'm floored. And so grateful." I lean in, kiss my mother's cheek, and hug her. "Thank you for all of your hard work on this."

"You did all the hard work, Stone," she says, pride all over her face. "I simply helped put together a gala. One that's being talked about everywhere, not just in Boston, so don't be surprised if you start getting more donations."

"I have no idea what you're talking about."

My dad rolls his eyes at me and folds his arms. "You know we're not stupid, right? You can talk to us about this. Even tell us the truth."

It feels like I just swallowed a bug. I've hated lying to my parents, but it seems, like my grandmother, they too know the truth. Which gives me worry. Everyone seems to be figuring out the truth, but that truth comes at a price. Especially with my parents.

"What do you want me to say?"

"I don't know," my mother admits honestly. She places her hand on my arm as pain flashes across her pretty features. "We haven't said anything. We've stayed out of it because ignorance didn't mean lying, and that meant we were able to tell Forest the truth so far as we knew it. But you look happy, Stone. You look so happy, and I saw it in your eyes last night."

"Did this all just happen between the two of you?"

I look at my father and shake my head. "No. She was with me on Benthesicyme," I concede woefully and explain the story to them.

"God, Stone. All this time." My mother's fingers press over her lips.

"Is she worth it?" my father asks, and I stare down at the tattoo he has on his forearm just visible beneath his pushed-up sleeves. A stone in the forest. My brother and I are named after my father's college best friend and my mom's stepbrother. It's how my parents knew each other long before they got together. His name was Forest Stone, and he died when my mom was only a teenager. But growing up, my father would always tell us that we were one unit. That brothers look out for and take care of each other.

And I haven't done that lately. If anything, I've done the opposite.

Still, I can't lie. "Yes, she's worth it. She's worth everything. I didn't steal her, and I tried to stay away. What started as an undeniable infatuation grew into a love neither of us can deny. I'd never want to hurt Forest. I'm just not sure what else to do or what other outcome there will be."

My mother's hand squeezes my arm. "Then I suppose you have to follow your heart and hope it all turns out as it should in the end." She leans in and kisses my cheek. "For what it's worth, we're very happy for you. We love Tinsley as you know and have always thought of her as part of our family."

"Let's hope she is one day, but for now, if you can, I'd like you to keep that to yourselves. I will have a conversation with Forest when the time is right, but I'm not sure where this all goes. Tinsley and I have a lot to work out. There is a lot of uncertainty. I hate lying and hiding this from him, but right now, I'm not sure what else there is to do."

By the time we make it back to our building, our stomachs are stuffed, and my head is full. It's been a wild, whirlwind weekend with far too many revelations and truth bombs. We duck inside, keeping our heads down. Something that has become a ritual, almost automatic now. I suppose being Mr. Tinsley Monroe comes with this. I've had press, and I've had photos taken of me that end up in various places on the internet, but this is a totally different league.

"Dr. Fritz, Miss Monroe." The doorman stops us before we can get on the elevator. "I'm so sorry to hold you up, but something was delivered overnight for you, and I wanted to make sure you got it."

He scurries behind his desk only to return a moment later.

"A man came by and delivered this." He holds up a red envelope. "He handed it to Isaac, who was on last night. He told him it was for Miss Monroe and asked us to make sure she got it this morning. He seemed pretty sketchy, and Isaac couldn't see his face because it was completely covered. He asked him to leave immediately."

Tinsley hisses out a curse and takes a step back toward the elevator, but the moment I reach out to take it, she shoots forward. "No. Don't touch it."

I look at her. "It's too late. There are already several sets of prints on it." I turn back to him and take the proffered envelope.

"Is everything all right, miss? Was I not supposed to—"

"No, we appreciate you passing this along. You said it was hand-delivered overnight?"

"Yes, sir," he replies, looking nervous and unsure, especially with Tinsley's reaction.

"Thank you. Can you do me a favor?"

"Of course, sir. Anything."

"Can you get me Isaac's personal cell phone? He's not in any trouble or anything. I'd just like to ask him a few questions about the person who dropped this off."

He nods. "Right away. I'll text it to you."

"Thank you." I pull out my wallet and hand him a hundred. "I appreciate you keeping this to yourself."

He pockets the cash and promises not to say anything, and I guide a shaking Tinsley onto the elevator. The moment the doors close, I wrap one arm protectively around her and start shooting off texts like grenades. We reach our floor, and Mason comes flying out of his door, his hair wet and all over the place, wearing nothing but a fluffy white bathrobe and slippers.

"The fuck you wearing, brother?"

He glances down at himself and then back up at me and shrugs. "I was taking a bath. It helps keep my muscles loose, and I have Monday Night Football tomorrow. You fucking judging?"

I shake my head. "Never. Can you do me a solid and stay with my girl while I go in and inspect my place?"

"No," he replies instantly. "Don't fucking move."

In a half-minute, he's back, still in his bathrobe and slippers with the biggest butcher knife I've ever seen.

Despite herself, Tinsley laughs. "This isn't *Scream*."

"Thank God for that." Mason shudders. "If anything, I'm the star like Drew Barrymore was, and I'd hate to be disemboweled. Let's go."

I snicker, but it falls flat. I have no humor at this moment, but thank God for Mason.

Tinsley is chewing on her lip, staring at Mason's thriller knife. "All *I* can say is thank God I'm not blonde. Those bitches always get it."

"Will both of you stop making me laugh?" I bark. "I want to get in there and make sure everything is okay so we can figure this all out."

Tinsley's expression sobers. "Right. Sorry."

"I'll go in first," Mason declares. "You stay out here with Tins, or better yet, go into my place."

"I don't think anyone is in my place because the doorman was downstairs and how would they even get up here? It's precautionary but you're extra backup."

"I'm definitely extra," he agrees. "But I'm also not going in there unarmed, and guns aren't my thing."

"You have your phone?" I ask her.

"Yes, but this is ridiculous. They dropped off the damn letter. That was all. Mason, you lead the charge with your slasher knife, but I'm not standing out here in the hallway, and I'm not cowering in Mason's apartment like a scared little girl."

I start to argue with her when she gives me a withering glare that would shrink a lesser man's balls. So naturally, I relent. "Fine. Just stay behind us."

With that, we walk into my apartment that's exactly how we left it. Within minutes we're calling the all-clear right as Vander comes in with his laptop bag on his shoulder. He spots Mason and starts cracking up, doubling over in laughter.

"Yeah, yeah, fuck you too," Mason gripes. "I'm going to get dressed."

"Don't change on my account," Vander wheezes, holding his side. "We love you just as you are, little rabbit. Can I pet you? Is that robe as soft as it looks?"

Mason flips him off. "I'll be back in a few, but I'm telling security not to let you into the game tomorrow night," he warns Vander.

"Uh-huh. And yet somehow, magically, I'll be back on the list."

Mason rolls his eyes, and then he's gone, the door shutting behind him only to immediately reopen with Wren and Loomis.

I have a feeling it's going to be like that again. A revolving door of people.

"All right," Vander states, setting up at my dining room table. "Let's see this letter."

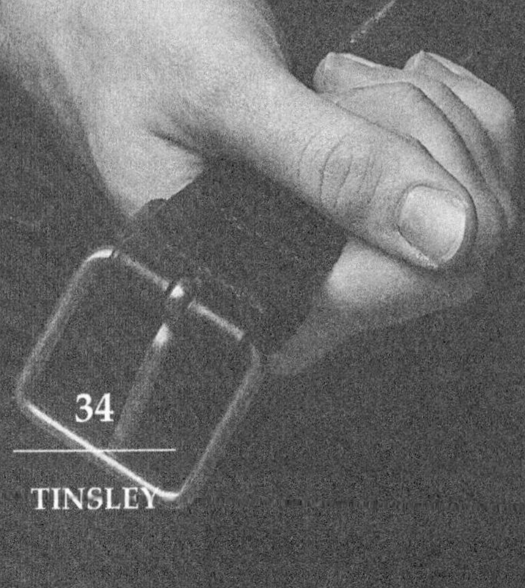

34

TINSLEY

"I watch you all day and night. No matter how hard you fight. You thought you could get rid of me. I'll ruin you, just wait and see." I finish reading, and for a few long seconds, I can't do anything other than take in the basic block script letter by letter.

"Not exactly Dickens, but at least the chap rhymes." Loomis sighs. "I think this calls for some champagne, don't you?"

I turn my head and narrow my eyes at him. "Champagne?"

"Never let him win, luv. He can send you cut-rate poetry, but he's not going to steal your fire or your spirit again. Fuck him."

Hard to argue with that. "Fuck him. Champagne it is."

"It's in the wine fridge," Stone tells him. Take any glasses you want, but the good ones are on the glass shelves in my bar."

Loomis excuses himself to tend to the champagne, and I take a step back, no longer wanting to see it. This isn't why I got into music or acting. I'm a bit over the psychos.

Vander is typing away on his laptop thing. I'm not even sure if that's what it is. It's weird-looking, but he seems to know what he's doing.

"I think I need a minute," I declare.

Stone's head snaps in my direction, and I place a kiss on his cheek, letting him know that I'm okay, but sometimes a girl just needs a minute.

"Do you want company?" Wren asks, and I shrug.

"Sure. But we're not talking about Joe Stalker. That's my rule."

In the great room, a loud *pop* sounds, and out of the corner of my eye, I catch Loomis pouring three large flutes.

"Hey." Stone grabs my hand and pulls me back to him, not caring in the slightest about our audience as his hand meets my waist and his forehead meets mine. "We'll figure this out, okay? We have cameras and doormen who stopped him, and he never got near our apartment."

"I know. I'm fine. Sort of. I think I just need to process this a bit."

His lips press to mine, and he gives me a kiss before he takes my hand and twirls me away as if he's spinning me on a dance floor.

"Grab the bottle," I tell Loomis as both Wren and I snag our glasses and head for my old bedroom. I don't want to take them into Stone's. That feels too intimate, and right now, I want to lie down.

The three of us plop down on my old bed, glasses in hand. I take a sip but before I can swallow, the door bursts open, and Vander is standing there.

"The poems aren't online," he announces.

"What?" I sit up a little straighter.

"You had said that many of the letters were leaked or used as evidence and were public information, but they're not. The threatening letters he sent you are. Those became evidence, but love letters sent to celebrities of a non-threatening nature are not considered criminal, and they weren't part of the case against Terrance Howard."

"Um. Okay. I'm not sure I'm understanding."

Vander steps into the room, grabs my glass from my hand, and gulps down all of my champagne. Before I can get a protest out, he refills it and hands it back to me. "Whoever wrote you these new letters knew that the fucker wrote you poems and that not all of the letters were threats. You said so yourself. That's how they started out and then became threatening later."

"Like this one is," Wren states. "But this one is still a poem."

"Yes. This one is threatening as was the last one, and technically, if needed, you could make an argument that the first one was as well, but I looked at the available letters online. None of them are like the ones we received last time or today. The ones online were more desperate as well as angry and violent, and they were not rhyming or poetic in any way."

"So whoever wrote these saw the first notes?" Loomis surmises.

"Seems that way," Vander concludes.

I stare up at him, my mind whirling, and my voice a soft, shaky whisper. "Not that many people saw the early letters."

"I'm going to go through all the video footage I can now, as well as any we have of you coming or going from the building and anything public. If this guy is watching you as he claims to be, we might get lucky and find the asshole. But this was a fuck up, Tinsley. A huge one. The pool of people who knew of these letters written in that format is limited. If you could think of each person and write them down, I can dig into them one by one. We'll find them. I promise."

He gives my shoulder a reassuring squeeze and leaves, shutting the door behind him.

I'm too flabbergasted to speak as I think through all the people who were around me at the time and who saw or knew of the letters. "I need to think. This is all too much. And Stone doesn't have freaking paper here." I learned that the hard way.

"I'll write them down on my phone," Loomis offers,

polishing off his glass of champagne and setting the empty down on the side table so he can pull out his phone.

"I'm sorry." Wren holds up her hand. "I won't lie and say he hasn't been at the top of my list, so I'm going to ask the hard question. The one we've all sort of had in the back of our minds but haven't asked yet."

I know what Wren's about to ask. And that alone makes my chest hurt and my body shake, because yes, I've thought of it too, and I hate myself for that.

"Could it be Forest?" she continues.

"He's in LA," I answer, only my voice isn't selling it. "No chance he can hand-deliver them."

"Okay," Loomis picks up. "And I'm not saying it's him, but couldn't he hire someone to do that bit for him?"

I gulp down my freshly refilled glass, set the empty on the bedside Loomis's, and flop back onto the bed. "Yes," I answer reluctantly. "It could be him. He was mad about the hickey he saw on my neck and how he thought I was lying to him about you"—I point at Loomis—"and hasn't been shy about how unhappy he is that we're no longer together. Last night Stone and I looked like a very happy couple in all those pictures, and I'm positive he saw them. He also knew about all the letters. All of them. He could easily pay someone to hand-deliver them to throw us off his trail."

My eyes close. I don't want to think it's Forest. He was there for me night and day when all of this was happening the first time. I loved him. He was my childhood sweetheart, and some of my best memories are memories that include him.

"There were other people too. Not just him. How do I accuse him? How do I write his name down? He's Stone's brother."

"You don't think Stone has thought of this?" Loomis says. "My bet is he has."

My cell phone rings in my pocket, and I slip it out, laughing mirthlessly. "Are his ears burning? Maybe I'll just ask him and see how he responds."

"We'll give you a few minutes." Loomis climbs off the bed and takes Wren with him.

My finger slides across the screen to answer. "Hey, Forest."

"Hey," he responds. "Where did I catch you?" He sounds agitated. Off.

"At Stone's."

"Oh. Is he with you?" His voice is sharp, and he's speaking fast. Almost like he has a point he wants to reach and can't stand the back and forth.

"No. He's in the other room. How are you?"

"I saw the pictures from last night, Tinsley. Can we not pretend I didn't? How do you think I am after seeing that?"

"You sound upset."

He laughs mirthlessly. "Yes, I'm fucking upset. He's my brother. You're living with him, looking happy and cozy on his arm, and wearing his motherfucking ring on your goddamn finger. How am I supposed to respond to that?"

"I got another letter today," I say instead of addressing any of that.

"You did? Shit, Tins, I'm sorry. What did it say?" His voice instantly goes from infuriated to alarmed.

"*I watch you all day and night. No matter how hard you fight. You thought you could get rid of me. I'll ruin you, just wait and see.*"

He's silent for a minute, and I hear him scream, "Fuck!" and what sounds like something shattering in the background.

"What was that?"

"I threw a glass. Jesus Christ. What the fuck does that mean that he'll ruin you and that he's watching you day and night?!"

"I don't know," I cry, getting upset. Tears begin to leak from my eyes, coasting down my temples and into my hair. I don't know if it's from the letter or his reaction to it. "Exactly what it sounds like, I assume. He's watching me and he wants to ruin me."

He blows out a torrent of air into the phone. "I'm sorry, baby. I didn't mean to get so upset and make you upset. How can they not find this asshole?" Another breath. "I hate you there. I hate you being in Boston when I'm in LA. I hate that you're with Stone and not with me. I hate that some psycho is stalking you and making threats. I can't stand this, Tinsley. Any of it. It's driving me crazy."

I can't ask him. I can't ask if it's him. I don't think he'd react this way if it were. Right? He wouldn't. This doesn't seem like an act, but—

The door bursts open. "We've got him." Loomis comes racing over to me and grabs my hand. "Vander's got him. Get off the phone. We need you."

"You've got him?" Forest barks.

I stare into Loomis's gray eyes as I say, "I'll call you back, Forest."

"Fine. Go. But please call me back."

He disconnects the call, and I follow after Loomis. "Tell me it's not Forest."

Loomis gives my hand a squeeze. "It's not Forest."

I hiccup out a sob and my face falls against Loomis's shoulder as I start to shake.

"Hey, no, none of that."

"I hate that I thought it was him."

"My darling, just because he's not outwardly stalking you with red paper and poetry doesn't mean he's not disrupting your life in a very toxic way."

I nod against him. "I know." I sniff and wipe my face. I blow out a calming breath and settle myself down. "I need to do something about that."

"Yes. You and Stone both because this concerns both of you. It's okay to care about him, but the way he cares about you isn't right. Your heart is big, and you never want to hurt anyone, and I love you for that, but his reach over you needs to come to an end."

"I agree. I need to be the thorns and not the petals. Sometimes we don't see how bad a situation is because we're on the inside and not on the outside of it. I've taken the passive route of distancing myself, hoping he'd naturally get over it, but I can't be passive anymore where he's concerned. Thinking it was him who was sending the letters really drove that home."

Loomis kisses my forehead.

"Who was it?" I press. "Tell me."

"Apollo. Your former manager. The one you said was a bit of a creep—you weren't wrong in that—and actually texted you right when you got the first letter. Because he had been watching you the entire time.

THERE IS no denying the video. The man who walks into the building at two in the morning to deliver the letter is wearing a hood, sunglasses, a face covering over his nose and mouth, and leather gloves. There should be no recognizing him. But he holds up his hands to the doorman who challenges him after taking the envelope, and when he does, his hoodie slips up his arms ever so slightly revealing a hint of yellow ink.

A sun.

Apollo Sun—he always loved his name, and I never knew if it was his real name or not—has a bright yellow sun on the inside of his wrist. But that's not how Vander knew it was him. Apollo had been true to his word and followed me. Vander was able to catch his face on more than one occasion. Especially outside of the warehouse, which is how he knew where the cameras were and how to evade them. He studied their angle and location. He kept his distance, and stayed far out of my sightline, but it's him, and Vander had met him once years ago after one of my concerts, so he recognized him.

The FBI came after everyone left, and Stone and I showed them the video footage from the building, which we had once again been given access to by the building manager. I told the FBI I recognized the tattoo and that he had reason to hate me because I fired him, and when I did that, he tried to blast my name, which didn't sit well with some of his other clients. People I'm friends with within the industry. They left him as well, and after that, his career took a sharp decline.

The FBI left, promising they'd find him and bring him in for questioning and that was that. They'll get him, and hopefully, this will be over.

Stone and I curl up on the sofa to watch football together, and when halftime of the four o'clock games hits, I turn to him and say, "We need to tell Forest that we're together."

He blinks at me and shifts so I'm completely on top of him, his arms banded around my back. "When would you like to do that?"

"I don't know. He's in LA, and we're here, it's not right, and I can't do this with him anymore. How do you feel about that?"

"I feel sad about it because it'll hurt him and likely ruin my relationship with him completely." He brushes some hair from my face so he can see me better. "But it's what needs to be done because I love you and I want you. Not just for now or the next couple of months, but for always. If that means I move out to LA, then—"

"I've been thinking about moving back here," I interject.

His eyes sparkle. "You have?"

"Boston is my home. I have Wren and the other girls and my parents. My dad made his music career work from here, so why can't I? Whenever I have a film, I'll have to travel for that, but that would be the case anyway whether I was living in LA or not."

"What about Loomis?"

"You'll have to get used to sharing me with him. He's my other half, and you're just the guy I'm sleeping with."

He bites my shoulder and I yelp. "Are you ever not a brat?"

"Nope. Never. For real, though, I'll go visit him a lot, and he'll visit me, and we'll talk on the phone way too much. It's what we do, and I'll miss the hell out of him. But he's not a reason to stay in LA, and you're a reason to be here."

His lips brush over mine. "You have no idea how happy that makes me."

I drop my head to his chest, listening to his heartbeat. "What about the engagement?"

His fingers twirl in my hair. "For now, we'll keep it going because undoing it isn't easy with us staying together."

"We'll keep it going, but eventually. We'll have to figure out how to end that. I don't like having something fake between us."

"Me either. I agree, we'll figure it out."

Only I don't know how to end a fake engagement when what's between us is real.

35

STONE

I have trouble sleeping. All night I toss and turn, thinking about everything that happened yesterday. Not just that we caught her stalker, but what we talked about on the couch after. She doesn't want something fake between us, and neither do I. But when she said we have to find a way to end the engagement, it was a sucker punch.

She's right, though. The engagement isn't real, and with that, it has to end.

Monday morning returns to normal after the hectic weekend. I have a shift, and Tinsley has a full day of filming. But as we descend in the elevator and both of us are quiet, I turn to her.

"I don't want to wait to tell Forest. It needs to be done, and it needs to be done in person."

That's what was bugging me all night. I've been lying to him. I've betrayed him. I can't fix any of what I've done, but I can change the lying part. I need to be the one to tell him.

"What are you suggesting then?"

"I'm suggesting I fly out to LA Friday night after my shift."

She studies me for a moment. "Do you not want me to come?"

I thought about that too. I know she needs to tell him as well, it's not just me. "That's up to you."

She takes my hand and rests her head on my shoulder. "I'd like to tell him with you, or at least talk to him about it myself. He needs to hear it from both of us, not just you."

"Okay. Let's do that."

The doors open, and we step out into the lobby. It's just us and the doorman, who studiously makes himself busy to give us a moment of privacy as he does every morning. My hand glides along her jaw, and I bring her lips to mine. I kiss the hell out of her, needing her to ground me. All too soon, I pull back, kiss her forehead, and take a step back.

"You good?"

She gives me a sassy look. "I'm badass."

I chuckle. "That I already knew, little Rose. If you need me for anything, just call or text. Have a good day. I love you, and I'll see you tonight. What time are you done shooting today?"

"Should be around five or so, but I promised Loomis we'd grab a drink after, so I'll likely be home around eight-ish. What about you? What time are you done?"

"Seven if all goes well, so I'll likely be home around the same time."

"Perfect." She leans in and gives me another kiss, and I watch as she exits the building, her security around her as they always are.

Only the moment she steps outside, she's swarmed. It's not the two or three guys who have been lingering either. It's at least a dozen press. What the hell? I move toward the door, listening as they yell questions at her about her former manager being arrested for stalking. How on earth did that hit so fast? Her security gets her into the back of the car, and she's whisked away.

I emit a mournful sigh. Will this madness ever end?

I shoot her a quick text.

Me: You okay?

Tinsley: Yes. Obviously the word got out about Apollo.

Me: Never a dull moment with you, is there?

Tinsley: Nope. Never. I hope you know what you're getting yourself into.

Me: Yes. You. In as many ways as I can.

Tinsley: *eye roll emoji* *heart emoji*

After her last concert on January eleventh, I'm taking her somewhere. Back on Benthesicyme or anywhere else she wants to go, as long as it's just us and no one else.

I leave the same way I always do, through the back, and when I make it to work, the hospital is its usual hustle and bustle. A trauma is there to greet me, and it doesn't stop. It's one thing after another, and by the time I look up, it's time to go. The drive home is quick and uneventful, which is exactly how I like it. I park in my spot and climb into the waiting elevator.

Sagging against the wall, more than a little tired, I check my phone for the first time all day. My eyebrows slant inward when I find it riddled with texts and missed calls.

Shit.

I open my text stream from the guys.

Mason: If you wanted to keep it a secret, you likely shouldn't have made out with her in the lobby.

Beneath it is a series of pictures taken this morning of Tinsley and me kissing inside the lobby. There are screenshots from Intertainment along with a headline: *Tinsley Monroe Taking a Private, Comforting Moment with Fiancé Stone Fritz Amid Ex-manager's Stalking Arrest*. It's clear we were having a private moment and had no clue we were being photographed, much like the first pictures of us outside the hospital. These aren't for show, and the paparazzi captured them all.

My heart picks up a couple of extra beats.

Vander: They're everywhere, along with the headlines about Tinsley's former manager. To most of the world, it's more confirmation you're together. To those who thought it was fake, it's confirmation that you're not.

And that's the problem. The lies Tinsley and I have been spreading to our family and friends. Only a select few knew we were together despite the engagement being fake. Well, them, along with my parents and grandmother. But to everyone else —including Forest—it was a ruse. A way to keep her safe. There is no explaining these away, and it's not how I wanted the truth to get out.

It's not how I wanted Forest to find out.

I search for messages or calls from him but don't find any. There are plenty from my parents and uncles and aunts, though.

I check my watch. It's almost eight, and Tinsley should be home soon. We have a lot to talk about now. More to figure out.

Christ. I drag a hand across my face and through my hair and stuff my phone back in my pocket. The elevator stops, and I step off, anxious for some food and Monday Night Football to take my mind off the latest round of crap that's being slung at us.

Opening the door to my apartment, I toss my keys, wallet, and phone on the table beside the door and stroll toward the kitchen, only to freeze when I catch someone out of the corner of my eye. Forest is sitting on my sofa, hunched forward with his elbows digging into his knees and his head in his hands. When he hears me, he looks up, and I practically gasp at the sight of him.

His hair is a mess, his eyes are more than a little bloodshot and ringed in purple bruises, and he's pale and gaunt and sickly-looking. But it's more than his eyes being a little bloodshot. They're wild and impossibly dark, his pupils blown out. Then I notice the mostly empty bottle of scotch sitting on my coffee table along with a glass. He picked the good stuff. I suppose I can't begrudge him that.

"Are you okay? What are you doing here?"

"Sort of a dumb fucking question, don't you think?" He lifts his glass and finishes it off before refilling it practically to the top, and if memory serves, that bottle had a hell of a lot more in it the last time I saw it. He's been here drinking for a while.

"Have you had anything to eat?"

He chuckles and wipes at his face. "You trying to take care of me, big brother? You think that will excuse the fact that you've been lying to me while fucking my ex-girlfriend behind my back?"

"How much have you had to drink?"

"Fuck you. That's how much. I love her, you asshole. I've loved her my entire life, and you knew that. She was mine. Not yours." He stands and sways, one fist balled up, the other still wrapped around the newly refilled glass that's now spilling scotch on the floor. "How could you do that to me?"

"I fell in love," I tell him simply because I don't have an excuse for what I did to him, and he has every right to his anger.

"You fell in love?!" he shouts and throws the glass. It hurdles through the air, splattering scotch everywhere before it smashes into the wall, spraying crystal shards like tiny diamonds across the floor. "She wasn't yours to fall in love with! How the fuck did this happen, Stone? And don't feed me bullshit." He points at me. "I want the fucking truth. When did this start?"

"Two years ago. A little more than that now. That time she disappeared and told everyone she was at a yoga retreat, she was actually hiding out on my boat. I came there and found her. It wasn't planned. Nothing between us was."

His arms fly behind his head, and he rips at the back of his shirt. "Two years?! You've been fucking her for two years?"

I shake my head. "No. We had a thing together on the boat, and then I didn't see her again until the night of Grandma's ball. We stayed away from each other."

I can see him working this out in his head. The timeline of it. "Because you knew it was wrong. How could you do that to me?"

"I'm sorry—"

"I said don't fucking lie to me!" he screams at the top of his lungs, making me wince. He charges me, and shoves me with all his might. I fall to the floor and immediately get up when he swings and smashes his fist into the side of my face. I stagger back a step, somehow managing to right myself even as my vision crackles and sways. My left eye feels like it's about to pop out of my face as white-hot heat pulses beneath my skin.

Fuck, that hurts.

I ignore the urge to touch my face and assess the damage. As it is, I can feel a trickle of blood running down my cheek and dripping onto my shirt. I try to calm myself down, but it's not easy. I'm breathing heavily, and my fists are balled up, but I won't hit him. I deserved that from him, but he only gets one.

He shuffles back a step, notes my face, and spins around as if he's trying to get control of himself but doesn't know how. He's swinging like a pendulum—blind rage one minute and crushing heartbreak the next. Forest was always over the top with his emotions, and this seems to have pushed him past his breaking point.

He starts to pace, his hands on top of his head, the hand he hit me with red and a little swollen already. It was a good hit, and I wouldn't be shocked if he fractured my orbital bone and his hand.

"You're not sorry," he seethes. "I saw those pictures outside the hospital. I saw those pictures of you two this morning. Why do you think I came? I needed to see it for myself. Hear what a lying piece of shit my big brother is from his own mouth." He stops and faces me, his expression pure agony. "You knew how I felt about her. You knew how much I loved her. All these years, you knew. How could you, Stone?"

I glance down at the floor, my hands going to my hips, hating myself for what I've done to him.

"Why her?" he presses. "Of all the fucking women on this planet, why her? You could have anyone, and you chose my girl."

I meet his eyes. "I fell in love with her, Forest. Same as you did. It wasn't intentional. I tried to stay away. I didn't *want* to love her."

"You didn't put up much of a fight either!"

If only he knew the fight I put up. Two years of it. Two years of wanting only one woman and not being able to have her because she belonged to him. He knows I wasn't with anyone else over those two years. He didn't know I was with a woman on the boat. He thought the mystery girl I had a fling with came after because that's what I let him believe.

He wipes his forehead, and I can see he's sweating. He's more than a little drunk if the slur of his words and the stagger of his gait are anything to go by. He's had a lot of alcohol. More than I could ever drink and still be standing. That in combination with his anger and heartache is making him volatile and unsafe.

I need to text Tinsley. I need to tell her not to come home, but my phone is by the front door, and—

The door opens, and Tinsley sings out, "Lucy, I'm home. It's been a nightmare day, Stone. We need to talk about those pictures."

Fuck. *Fuck!*

"Tinsley, don't come in here."

"Don't tell her not to come in here, you piece of shit," Forest barks.

Tinsley's boots tap along the hardwood, and I hear her

move in behind me. She gasps when she sees what's going on, likely noting the broken glass, the reeking scent of scotch, my bleeding and swollen face, and Forest looking like he was just pulled off the floor of a dive bar.

She searches my face, her chin trembling. "Are you okay?"

I give a slight nod, keeping my eyes on him, and Forest makes a pained noise in the back of his throat as he watches us.

"Forest," she whispers, her voice shaking. "What is going on?" She takes another step, and I reach out to push her behind me. She doesn't know how drunk and unhinged he is.

"I'm not going to hurt her," Forest says, his eyes locked on her. "I'd never hurt her." He crumples, and my chest quakes. I want to fix this for him. He's my little brother, and not only did I hurt him, but he also needs help.

Tinsley steps around me and I throw her a look that tells her not to. I haven't taken my eyes off Forest this entire time, but my instinct is to pick her up and get her the hell out of here. She doesn't need to see him like this, and though he says he won't hurt her, he's not thinking rationally and is unpredictable. She could get hurt whether he intends for her to or not.

"Was it the pictures?" she asks him softly, her steps gentle and cautious as if approaching a cornered animal. "Is that why you came?"

"I woke up to them. More Google alerts going off about you, and when I saw those pictures..." He trails off.

"I didn't want to tell you over the phone," she explains. "We were going to come this weekend to talk to you in person."

"We?" he asks, his expression hardening once more.

"Yes. We. Stone and I."

He shakes his head as if that doesn't make sense. "Are you just fucking him, or is it more?"

"It's more. For both of us. I love him. I don't want to hurt you, I never wanted that, but I love him, and we're together."

I'm afraid to move. Afraid to get closer. I don't want to escalate this with her right in front of him, but I don't know how this ends well. As if proving my point, he storms away from her, picks up the bottle, and chucks it the same way he did the glass. Tinsley screams, and I spring into action. Just as the bottle hits the wall, I've got my arm around her, and I'm pulling her away, turning my back, and hovering over her to shield her from it.

"Are you okay?" I whisper urgently against her face.

Tears track down her cheeks, and I wipe them away. "This isn't Forest."

"I know."

I twist around but keep her behind me. Forest is sitting on the sofa, his head in his hands, his body rocking back and forth.

"How much did you drink?" I ask, wanting to check his vitals.

"A lot," he responds vacantly. "I drank a lot." He looks up at me with those big brown eyes.

"Did you take anything with it?"

He shakes his head. "No." He blinks and then sighs, a tear on his cheek. "I started drinking more when we broke up, but I've been drinking a lot over the last few weeks."

Tinsley is shaking behind me, and I hear her suck in a sob. I have no doubt she's blaming herself for this.

He wipes his face and looks at her behind me, stricken by what he sees. "I'm sorry," he cries, tears falling down his face. "I didn't mean to scare you. I swear, Tinsley, I'd never hurt you. I don't know who I am anymore. I just wanted it to go away, to feel better, but it never did, and those pictures this morning..."

Threw him over the edge.

I walk over to him, keeping my hands by my sides and posture loose. I kneel on the floor beside him and take his wrist to check his pulse. Forest isn't a doctor, but he knows what I'm doing.

Fuck. How did I not know about his drinking? How did any

of us not know it was this bad? I knew he drank. I knew he was drunk at the ball and then again on the phone with me. I didn't think much of it. We were all drinking at the ball, and I didn't blame him for having a few drinks after seeing the pictures of Tinsley and me outside the hospital.

Still...

"I didn't know," Tinsley sobs as if voicing my thoughts. "How could I not have known?"

"Because I hid from everyone. I drank socially around people who were drinking, or I drank at home alone and didn't talk to anyone when I was drunk."

"I should have known," I state emphatically. "I'm a doctor and your brother. I should have seen the signs. I should have known you being drunk like that wasn't normal."

His forehead falls to his knees, but his pulse is a mess. Fast and thready, and he's sweating. I know what was in that bottle. He's had a lot of alcohol, and it's scaring me.

"You need help," I tell him. "I know you hate me, and I know you have every right to, but I still love you, and I want to help you."

"I was devastated when she broke up with me," he continues as if I didn't speak. "I started drinking to help with that. It wasn't this bad until she moved in here with you. Then I felt so fucking out of control. So goddamn angry and resentful and jealous, and I didn't know how to stop it or shut it off." He sits back, his eyes on me. "I hate feeling like this. I hate being this guy."

"Then let us help you," Tinsley begs. "Please, Forest. Please let us help you."

He looks at her and then back at me. "She was the reason you didn't date. She was your mystery girl you couldn't get over."

It's not a question, but I nod all the same.

He licks his lips, and another tear slips out. "I don't forgive you. Not right now, and I'm not sure I will. But if you hurt her, I will kill you."

"I won't," I promise him. "Like you, I'd never hurt her."

He swallows. "Your face looks like shit."

I choke out a laugh. "So does yours. You need the hospital. You need help."

"Yes," he agrees. "I think it's long past time I get my shit together."

36

TINSLEY

Stone calls Jack, Estlin's brother and Owen's best friend on the way to the emergency department. Jack is an emergency department attending at MGH, and we want this handled quietly for Forest's sake. He also calls his parents and lets them know what's going on and asks them to meet us at the hospital. I'm sitting in the backseat with Forest beside me. He's shaking and sweating as his head sits on my shoulder and my arm is around him.

"Do you hate me?" he asks quietly as the car moves through the city.

I turn away from the window and stare down toward the dark form of his head as he rests on me. "I could never hate you. Do you hate me?"

"I could never hate you," he parrots and then sighs, tilting his head back to meet my gaze. "I've held on too long."

"Yes," I agree.

"Are you going to marry him?"

I gnaw on my lip. "Maybe one day."

He taps the ring on my hand. "It might not come to that. Don't be offended."

"I won't be."

He searches my face. "I want you in my life, Tinsley. That's what I've always wanted. I know it hasn't been good for you, and that's my fault. I'm sorry. I really am."

"We'll get there. I want you in my life too."

"As your friend."

It's a statement and not a question, but I answer him anyway. "As my friend." The thought makes me sigh. "I wish you had told me."

"I didn't want you to know. You already had trouble being around me, and I didn't want to drive you away completely. I didn't want oversight. I didn't want people all over me."

"I'm glad you're going to get help."

He blows out a heavy breath. Like the weight of the world is being lifted from his shoulders with it. "Me too." He pauses for a beat. "I fucked up your boyfriend's face."

I roll my eyes, but snicker. "You did."

"It felt good."

"No more throwing punches or anything else. I already had to deal with one crazy Apollo, I don't need another in my life."

"Sounds like a plan, but I'd like to be Rocky, not Apollo. Rocky comes out on top and beats all the odds."

I take his hand. "You've got this, Rocky. You do."

We pull up in front of the hospital, and he climbs out with the help of Stone. Jack is out here to greet us, along with Stone and Forest's aunt Rina, who is an ICU nurse.

"I have a bed for you upstairs," she tells Forest, giving him a hug. "Once Jack checks you out, we're going to admit you for alcohol withdrawal. After that, we'll figure out the best place for you to go."

Forest nods, turns, and glances over his shoulder at me and then Stone. He extends his hand to Stone, who grabs it and hauls him in for a hug. I can't hear what he's saying to him, but in my heart, I know they'll be okay.

I hug Forest too, and then Forest lets Jack and Rina take him inside, but before we can get away, Katy comes flying out the door, her head swiveling left and right until she snags on us. "Oh, hells bells."

"You should see the other guy."

Katy rolls her eyes at Stone. "Not funny. Come inside. You need an X-ray and stitches."

"You're a trauma surgeon. I'm not letting you stitch my face. How'd you even know we were here?"

"As luck would have it, I just finished with a trauma and saw Forest. Now get your ass inside."

Stone takes my hand and begrudgingly follows Katy. She guides us to a small room at the back of the ER and closes the door behind her. She slams an ice pack on his face and gets him an X-ray without him having to leave the room.

A few minutes later, she's back declaring, "Good news. It's not fractured. If you don't want me to stitch you up, I'll get one of the interns."

"Ha," he drolls. "Fine. You can stitch me up, but make it good. I have a pretty face."

Katy leaves to get what she needs, and I hop up on the gurney beside him and yawn.

He kisses the top of my head. "Tired, baby girl?"

"Mm-hmm." My stomach gurgles loudly. "And hungry."

"Obviously," he deadpans, and I nudge him with my shoulder. "Are you okay?"

"I'm okay." I pull back and meet his eyes. "Honestly, I'm good. No more secrets."

"No more secrets," he parrots. "Are you okay with staying fake engaged to me for a bit longer until we can work all that out?"

I smirk at him. "Yes. I think I can manage that. Lucky for me, my guy bought me a gorgeous ring."

He kisses me just as Katy walks back in, her face scrunched up.

"Gross. Get a room, but not this room. No more tonsil hockey. I have to get home to my baby, so let's make this snappy."

I pull back with a giggle.

"No rushing, Katy. I mean it." He gives her a warning look.

"Fine, but only because you helped save my baby's life."

"What happened?" I ask because this is news to me.

"Baby Willow had an intestinal blockage about a month or so ago," he explains. "She came into the ER at Children's, and I triaged, stabilized, and got her upstairs where Owen came in and did the surgery."

"Wow. That's intense."

"Tell me about it," Katy asserts. "This will sting."

Katy numbs him up, stitches his face, and sends us on our way. Stone orders a pizza before we leave the hospital, and when we get home it's waiting for us courtesy of the doorman. The mess Forest made is also waiting for us, and Stone and I quickly clean it up and then catch the very end of the game with our pizza when my phone rings.

Stone gives me a questioning look, and I shake my head, not recognizing the number. For a moment, I'm tempted not to pick up but end up swiping my finger to answer.

"Hello?"

"Miss Monroe? My name is John List with the Boston district attorney's office. I'm the one working your case. I'm sorry for calling you so late."

"That's okay. What can I do for you, Mr. List?"

Stone sits up and motions for me to put it on speaker. I hit the button and place my phone between us.

"I wanted to let you know that the FBI ended up turning the case over to the Boston Police Department and my office, but that Apollo Sun has officially been arrested for stalking and harassment and will be arraigned by a judge tomorrow. I will be seeking remand with no bail since he has access to money and a passport and followed you from Los Angeles to Boston. You should know he confessed to everything, and I believe a plea deal will be worked out in lieu of a trial. Whether that will include jail time, I can't say at this point. He has no criminal record and was never physically violent."

"Okay." I'm not sure how I feel about that.

"Regardless of jail time or not, part of his deal will be that he's not allowed within a hundred yards of you and isn't allowed to make any personal contact."

I blow out a breath. "That's a relief."

"If you have any questions or would like one of your attorneys to speak with me, I can be reached at this number, or you can always call my office."

"Thank you," I say. "Have a good rest of your night."

"You too. I'll be in touch as further details arise."

He disconnects the call, and I throw myself at Stone. There's a lightness in my chest for the first time in a long time. No more stalker. No more Apollo Sun. Forest knows everything and is getting the help he needs.

"I think this calls for some anal."

"What?" Stone wheezes, but there is no mistaking the smoldering look in his gemstone eyes.

"Anal. You know, where you lube up my ass and stick your dick in it."

He falls apart with laughter. "Can we make it a bit sexier than that?"

"Most definitely. Come on."

I grab his hand and drag him across the apartment to his room. I'm not sure if he thinks I'm serious, but I am. We've done some exploring and we used that toy, but tonight, right now, I want the real thing.

We reach his bedroom, but he doesn't let me go for the bed.

Instead, he swoops me up and brings me into the bathroom, slamming me against the wall hard enough to make me *oomph*. His lips come down on mine in a hot, fervent kiss, his hands tearing at my blouse.

I get greedy too and rip his shirt up and over his head, my hands roving when he captures them and pins my wrist above my head. His hips swivel forward, pressing the hard ridge of his cock into me.

"In the shower," he growls. "I'm going to take your ass in the shower."

The dirty, delicious promise makes me shiver and moan.

"But first..."

In a flash, he wrenches me away from the wall and spins me, so my hands are on the counter and I'm facing my reflection in the mirror. With a reach around, he undoes my jeans and slips them down my legs, leaving my thong on. His hand grips the triangle just above my crack, and he pulls it up, tightening the fabric against my pussy and running the string along my asshole.

My hands grip the counter, and I bite my lip. I can feel how wet I am with the crotch of my panties cinched tight against me. His other hand starts rubbing my ass as he slides his covered cock up and down against my other cheek.

"You put yourself in danger tonight, little Rose."

"What?" My half-mast eyes blink wide.

"You didn't listen to me when I told you to stay away. I don't care that it was Forest and he promised not to hurt you. You scared me. I didn't know what was going to happen. Now I have to punish you for being a bad girl and disobeying me."

Oh.

I watch in the mirror, his eyes on mine, as his hand comes up. On my next heartbeat, it slices down, and I hear the sound before I feel the sting. *Oh*. My eyes close, and I try to stifle my moan. It's even more intense with the way my thong is pulling and rubbing against my pussy and asshole.

More, I want to beg, but keep my mouth shut. That's not the point of this, and that will change my punishment. His lips kiss along my spine and up to the back of my neck where he one-handedly removes my bra and tosses my long mane of hair over my shoulder.

"When I slip my cock in your ass," he says in a low, deep voice. "I want to see my handprint on it."

Christ, this man and his mouth. I rub into my underwear, desperate for friction when his hand strikes again. My underwear is torn from me, and he kicks my legs farther apart so he can plunge two fingers straight inside me.

My head falls forward and my body bows. "Are you going to behave?"

I shake my head. "No. Not ever."

I can feel his smile against my skin. "Then I guess I'll just have to keep punishing you."

"Yes, sir. I understand."

With his fingers inside me, he spanks me. Hard. Harder than he has before, and the burn coupled with the pleasure of his fingers rubbing my front wall is unlike anything I've ever experienced. I want to come. I want to come so badly. I want to come all over his fingers and then his cock and his mouth after all that for good measure.

"Please. More." It slips out, and just as I knew he would, he pulls his fingers from me. I whine in protest, only to arch up onto the balls of my feet when one finger goes right into my ass. Immediately, he pulls it out and then pushes his second finger in, still wet from my pussy.

He sucks on my ear. "Open your eyes."

I hadn't realized I closed them, but slowly I open them to find him behind me, the width and musculature of his broad shoulders make me look small and fragile by comparison. His fingers pump in and out of my ass, and his other hand comes around to play with my clit.

"You're not allowed to come."

"I'm sorry?"

He smirks as he fingers my asshole and rubs my clit. Is he kidding me with that?

"I don't want you to come. I'm serious. I want you as wet and turned on as possible so that when I slide in your ass, your body will crave it and take me easily."

"But..."

He uses his fingers on my clit to spank my ass, and I grind down into his fingers.

"I'm so close." I lean back against him, spreading my thighs wider as he returns to my clit.

"Then it's shower time."

With a kiss on my neck, he pulls his fingers from my ass and clit and races out of the bathroom. A moment later, he returns with the bottle of lube and finishes undressing as he goes into the shower to turn it on. My hand covertly trails down my body toward my pussy and—

"Don't even think about it."

"You can't tell I'm doing anything."

"I know you, my little rose. I know your propensity to play with that pretty pussy of yours. Hands back on the counter."

"Ugh. You're a tyrant. And a sadist. *Sir*."

"And you get hangry when you don't come."

I flip him off, and he turns to catch it. He laughs and crooks his middle finger at me.

And because I'm such a slut for him and his sadist ways, I walk into the shower with one hand on my breast and the other rubbing my clit.

He slams me up against the shower wall and once again has my hands pinned above my head. "Do you want me to edge you some more? I will. You know I will."

He bends to bite my nipple, and I whimper at the zing.

"I'll be good." Maybe.

He reads the maybe loud and clear even though I didn't speak it. He kisses me—a deep, hungry kiss that is more than lust and sex. It's love and devotion and possession. It's a kiss that says *we might play, but I'll take care of you, not just tonight, but always.*

"For your first time, I think it might be easier with you standing rather than sitting on me. But if you have a preference either way, I'm fine with that."

I shake my head.

"Good. Hands on the glass then, little rose. Press your tits into it too while you're at it."

He releases me, and I walk across the large shower and put my hands and tits against the cold glass. I shiver and shudder, anxious and more than a little excited. He picks up a bottle of lube and pours some into his palm.

"This view of you," he rasps, half-groaning. Heat skitters through my limbs as steam and water surround us, making the air hazy and my body pliant. Desperate.

Stone moves in behind me, his hand stroking his cock with the lube before he uses his wet finger in my ass, spreading it around and pushing it in so I'm as ready as I can be.

His mouth comes to my ear, and his finger slips away only to be replaced by the wide head of his cock.

"Try to relax. Remember to breathe. If you don't like it or it hurts too much, tell me. Okay?"

"Okay."

"I love you."

"I love you."

His cock starts to push in, and I bend my knees ever so slightly and close my eyes. I focus on my breathing. On the sound of the water hitting the marble. On the feel of him behind me. The warmth of his body and the rush of his breaths. He continues to move in and out and with every push in, he goes deeper than the last time.

It burns. There is no denying that.

My fingers rake against the glass, and I wince slightly.

His fingers find my clit, and he begins to whisper a myriad of sweet and filthy things into my ear. Instinctively, I reach back to spread my cheeks for him. To make more room, but something about that sets him off, and he growls out a slew of curses and drives himself all the way in.

"Shit," he hisses. "Fuck." The side of his fist rattles the glass. "Are you okay?"

He's still, not moving an inch.

I whimper, but manage a nod because, yes, I am okay. I'm more than okay. It's foreign and deep and strange, but so fucking good that I can hardly make sense of it.

He mistakes my whimper for pain and starts to pull out. "I'm sorry, baby girl. I got carried away." But I stop him by rising up onto the balls of my feet, pushing back against him, taking him in deeper. "Yeah?" he questions.

"Yeah. Definitely yeah."

And now that growl is a loud groan.

"You have no idea how hot and tight you are." He turns my face and kisses the side of my lips. "Are you ready?"

I nod against him as I kiss him, and he starts to fuck me. One hand on my hip, the other still on my jaw, and I press into the glass for support. He strokes in and out of me with smooth, even, slow fucks. Deep and languid, but with every push, I feel his piercing rub the walls inside me, pressing me in hidden, unknown places. His hand slips from my face to work my clit, stoking the fire of my denied orgasm.

All too soon, once he's sure I can take it, he speeds up, thrusting harder. He smacks my ass and bites into my shoulder, only to kiss me and suck on my skin. I meet his thrusts, marveling at how I'm about to come. It's more than just his fingers on my clit. It's him inside me too, along with the sounds he makes and the way he feels.

My hands crawl along the glass, leaving wet, streaky imprints. I wish I could see it. I wish I could watch his cock in my ass the way I know he's watching it. It's tight and I'm stretched full, but I want more. I want it all. Everything I've never thought to experience, I want to experience with him.

"Next time we do this, I want a toy in my pussy."

"Fuck!" he bellows and picks up his pace, his hips slapping against my ass at a pace that has my breath scrambling from my lungs. I reach back and split my cheeks again, and he goes wild. Fucking me so good and so hard, it tips me over the edge.

"Stone." Fuck. "I'm going to..." I can't even finish saying it because right at that moment, my orgasm plows through me. On a scream, I come to the point where I'm seeing stars. I clench around him, crying out as I hold him tighter in my ass. He presses me into the glass so I don't fall, and when I start to come down, he pulls out of me. With a couple of jerks of his cock, he comes all over my ass and back with a pounding roar.

I run my fingers through it, loving how messy he makes me.

He captures my mouth in a searing kiss, and before I know how I got here, he has me on the bench, sitting sideways on his lap, and cradled against his chest. His hands run down my hair, his body surrounding mine, and more words are being whispered into me.

I lie like this for a few minutes, dazed and shattered in the best of ways.

"Let's get you cleaned off and into bed."

I nod against him, exhausted.

He tilts my chin up and meets my eyes. "Thank you. Thank you for sharing that with me. Thank you for giving me that first. Thank you for being everything perfect and lovely that you are. Thank you for breathing life back into me and seeing the light in my darkest places. Thank you for believing in me. But most of all, thank you for loving me."

My arms wrap around his neck. "Thank you for giving me the courage to soar. For reminding me that I'm strong enough to be the thorns and soft enough to still be the petals. Thank you for being there when I needed someone. Thank you for seeing me, the real me, and for understanding and never judging her. Thank you for loving me."

"Those sound like wedding vows."

I smirk. "But they're not."

"Not yet. But one day they will be, Tinsley Monroe. There's nothing stopping me now."

EPILOGUE

TINSLEY

Shit. *Shit!* Where is it? *Where the fuck is it?* I wore it today. I'm pretty sure I did at least. I was rushing around this morning because I had to be on set early since we were wrapping up the final scene, and I woke up late because my alarm didn't go off. I stand here for a moment, staring at my nightstand, and trying to recall if I put it on my finger.

I haven't been wearing my engagement ring as much now that things have settled down. The press don't follow me around the way they used to, and no one lingers outside our building. Occasionally we'll get some fans taking pictures, but that's it, so my ring hasn't been all that crucial for me to wear. Stone and I haven't figured out a way to gracefully back away from the engagement, other than for me to stop wearing the ring.

But I could have sworn I slipped it off my finger and set it right here before I got in the shower. Maybe it fell? I drop to the floor and search around the rug, under the bed, and around the nightstand. Nothing.

"Shit!"

How could I lose my fake engagement ring?

Tonight is the wrap party for the film, and tomorrow Stone is taking me away for a week over New Year's before my Boston shows. I have to find this ring!

My hand slaps in frustration on the soft rug.

"Little Rose?" Stone calls out, and I jerk up and smack the back of my head on the edge of the nightstand.

Ow! That freaking hurts.

"I'm not trying to rush you, but we have to leave in about ten minutes to get to the party."

Double shit!

"I'm almost ready," I call back, rubbing the back of my smarting head. It's a lie. I'm not almost ready. I'm nowhere close to ready. I've spent the last twenty minutes since I got out of the shower searching for the goddamn ring. Did I leave it on set? That has to be it. Maybe someone found it. One of the crew or another cast member has it and they'll give it to me tonight at the party.

I race into the closet and scan through my clothes until I find a cute purple sweater that'll make the purple in my eyes stand out, a pair of fleece-lined leggings because those seem to be all I wear lately in this Boston winter, and cute black high-heeled booties. Then I race into the bathroom, brush out my hair, and do a quick blow-dry, followed by some simple makeup.

Twenty-five minutes later, I'm presentable and heading out of the bathroom and bedroom when I smash right into Stone.

"Sorry," he says, steadying me. "I was coming to check on you. Are you ready?"

"Yep." I smile. I hope it passes muster.

"You didn't get a chance to pack, did you?"

"Uh, no. I thought we had time in the morning." That's when I glance to my left and see his suitcase against the wall, all zipped up and likely already packed. Christ, I'm a hot mess today.

"We can fly out a bit later or even the next day if you need."

I shake my head and wrap my arms around his neck. "Nope. I'll be good to go. Promise."

He chuckles and takes my hand, intertwining our fingers, and when he feels I'm not wearing the ring, he stares down at my hand. The wrap party is going to have press there, and when there's press, I wear my ring. He frowns.

"You're missing something, baby girl." His thumb brushes over the base of my left ring finger where my ring should be.

"Um. So." Right. I don't know what to say. "I'm not going to wear it tonight." Not until I find it.

"Hmm." That's all he says and thankfully lets it drop.

We get to the party, and I peel myself away from Stone, who is thankfully sidetracked by the director, when I spot Loomis. I race across the room, grab him by the arm, and drag him to a dark corner.

"What in the bloody hell?"

"I lost my ring," I hiss, scanning around to make sure no one is close enough to hear that or see us.

"What do you mean you lost your ring?"

"I think that's pretty self-explanatory. Was I wearing it this morning when I came in?"

Loomis tilts his head, his eyes going foggy as he thinks about this. "Um. I honestly can't remember. Where was the last place you remember having it?"

"I don't know!" I cry, only to temper my voice and lower it to a whisper. "That's the problem. I thought I wore it today and took it off before my shower, but I couldn't find it, and I searched all over the goddamn bedroom."

Loomis snickers. "You're freaking out a bit."

"Um, that's putting it mildly. We're going away tomorrow."

"But it's just the two of you, yeah? You can say you didn't want to bring your ring and then search when you get home."

I sag. "I guess. I didn't want it to be fake, but I sure as hell didn't want to lose it."

"Accidents happen, luv. He'll forgive you."

My forehead meets the center of his chest. "I love that ring. That's my ring. Even if it isn't."

He kisses the top of my head. "I know. I'm sorry. It'll be okay."

After everything that's happened over the last two months, the last thing I ever wanted was to lose that ring. Forest made it out of withdrawal and is now in a ninety-day treatment program. He can't receive calls, but Stone and I went up for a visiting day, and he unleashed some stuff, and we did too, and it was good. So good. So necessary.

He's getting the help he needs, and I know he'll come out on top with this. Apollo Sun didn't receive jail time, but he's not allowed back in Boston for a decade, and he's not allowed to contact me, come anywhere near me again, or even mention my name publicly. If he does, that's a violation of his plea agreement and he'll serve ninety days in prison.

Stone and I have been great. Our families have been great. And tomorrow we leave for a much-needed vacation.

So losing my ring… it fucking sucks.

I pull myself together, and the rest of the party is a lot of fun. I thank everyone, so grateful for this opportunity and what I know this film will become. Stone and I get home and climb into bed, falling asleep fast and hard, but my mind is unsettled. To the point where I wake up before dawn to search some more for it, and when I come up empty, I pack a large suitcase instead, feeling nothing short of miserable.

"Hey," Stone says, squeezing my hand as we step off the plane. "Are you okay? You seem… a little down."

"I'm fine. Just tired." Yet another lie. "I think being on Benthesicyme will help."

Stone has us sailing around for a couple of days and then

straight for Cuba and other islands around the Caribbean after that. It's going to be romantic and fun and the escape we both need. That's what I have to focus on. Not anything else.

The ring will turn up. It's likely someplace I haven't thought to look for it yet.

It also feels good to be back here. Like it was a long time coming, but also full circle. I get why Stone feels at home in this boat on the sea. There is something so mind-quenching about it. And when we fall asleep with the waves rocking us gently good night, all feels perfect, and I forget about everything else but being with Stone.

For two days it's sailing, swimming, sex, food, drinks, and laughs. It's absolute heaven.

But when I wake up on the third morning at sea, nothing makes sense. For one, the ocean water is like pool water—turquoise and crystal clear. For another, the beach is about a hundred yards off the starboard bow and there is nothing there. Just an empty, secluded beach surrounded by grass, shrubs, trees, and a couple of buildings. No umbrellas or resorts or even people walking the island. Plus, the island is a hell of a lot smaller than what I imagine Cuba to be, though it still looks like a decent size. There isn't much to it other than one large house, a smaller house, and a large pool. That's seriously it.

"What in the hell?" I ask as I stare out at a strip of land that isn't a whole lot.

"Not what you were expecting?"

I laugh. "Um, no. This doesn't look like Cuba."

He comes in behind me, his chin on my shoulder as I take in the island. "Do you remember when you said you wanted your own island filled with champagne, charcuterie, vibrators, dirty romance books, and fucking peace?"

I snicker. "I said that?"

"You did. I remember it very clearly. You were yelling at me. But it got me thinking how that might not be a bad thing."

"A private island?" I'm incredulous. And a little excited, truth be told. There is nothing around. There are a few scattered islands in the distance, but that's it. I could walk around naked if I wanted to. "You rented this for us?"

"No, I bought it for us."

"You what?!" I shriek and spin around in his arms. My sunglasses slide up my face so I can see him better. "Are you kidding?"

"I can't tell if you're upset by this or not."

"I don't know what I am. People don't just buy islands."

He grins and nips my bottom lip. "Actually, they do. All of these islands around us are privately owned. We're between Nassau and Eleuthera, but closer toward the northwest point of Eleuthera."

I blink at him, unable to wrap my mind around this. I turn in his arms, finding the blinding white land. "This is ours?"

"Well, mostly. Vander went in on it with me. I didn't ask why, but I can assume to a certain degree. Anyway, he doesn't sail, but you can get a charter from Eleuthera, or he'll come with me. The big house is ours and the guest cottage is his."

"Stone." I'm a bit at a loss. "How big is the island?"

"About seven acres. The house has full plumbing and running water.

"How many bedrooms is it?"

"Six, so we can bring people. You see that rocky area?" He points past my shoulder to the space behind the house. "That's partly why I picked this island. That bluff will protect us against storms. I mean, it's far from foolproof, but that's the east side of the island where larger storms come in from, so it'll help keep the house and the rest of the island protected."

"You did that for me, didn't you?"

"Yes. My little Rose doesn't like storms." He kisses my neck, and hell, I didn't think it was possible to love someone as much as I love him.

"It needs a little work. I plan to build a dock for Benthesicyme, and Vander wants to do some stuff with the internet or other technology. I'll likely have the bathrooms and kitchen updated too."

I shake my head. "What's her name?"

He smiles against my neck. "Rose Cay."

I laugh, reaching behind me to cup the back of his head. "You did not."

"I didn't, actually. It was the name of the island before I bought it, but it made it seem like it was meant to be."

"I love it," I exclaim. "I don't think I've ever been more excited for anything. Can we go to it? Explore a bit?"

"It's ours. We can do anything we want."

I spin back around and pepper him with kisses. "I love you. This is the best surprise ever."

"I love you and I'm glad, but I'm hoping this will be a good one too."

"What?"

He drops down to one knee and pulls a box from his pocket. I gasp, my hands covering my mouth. His green eyes sparkle up at me, but I can see the nerves all over him. "I had a whole speech planned. All these things I wanted to tell you, but looking up at you right now, I can't remember a single one. All I know is that I love you and want to spend forever with you. Not just the rest of my life, but beyond that. That's what soulmates do with each other. So will you marry me?"

He opens the box revealing my ring. "How?"

"I stole it the other day when you were in the shower. You told me you didn't want anything fake between us, and now I'm asking you for something very real. Marry me, Tinsley Monroe. Please, marry me."

I drop to my knees and throw my arms around him, hauling him against me. "Yes. Of course, yes. A thousand times yes."

His lips crash down on mine, and for a few minutes, I get

lost in the feel of his mouth, the slide of his tongue, and the endlessness of how he loves me.

Then I smack his shoulder. "I can't believe you stole the ring. I was going out of my mind, thinking I lost it."

He smiles against my lips and chuckles lightly. "I know. But it was worth it." He slides the ring back onto my finger, and it feels right. It feels perfect. It feels like forever. Like us.

BONUS EPILOGUE

TINSLEY

Two years later

"It's a star-studded extravaganza where we come to you live from the Kodak Theater and the Academy Awards. Tonight is such a special night, filled with glitz, glam, and the biggest stars as they arrive on the red carpet. We want to know who they're wearing, who they're with, and who will win. Chief among those are superstars Tinsley Monroe-Fritz and Loomis Powell. Both stepped out of their usual rom-com roles and straight into the drama. It seems to have paid off for them as both these talented actors have been nominated for their fourth feature film together, Undeniably Infatuated. Oh! And look now. They're walking the red carpet, heading our way."

"Tinsley! Loomis!" a reporter for *E* calls out, waving frantically to get our attention.

"Ready?" Loomis whispers in my ear, and I cling tighter to his arm and smile up at him. That's what you do. You never nod or shake your head. You sure as hell don't frown. It's smiles and sunshine on the red carpet, but tonight I don't mind in the least.

Loomis guides over to the female reporter holding the large microphone in her hand. "It's fabulous to see you both together tonight and congratulations on your nominations for best actress and best original song for you Tinsley and best actor for you Loomis. You must both be thrilled."

She thrusts the microphone in my face. "Absolutely. It's an incredible night and I know I can speak for both of us when I say we couldn't be happier. Win or lose, we both feel incredibly blessed and honored to be nominated."

"Is it true that neither of you has attended an award show without the other since you met and starred in your first film together?"

Loomis chuckles, his hand on my back and a gleam in his gray eyes. "That's true. Other than my mum, there's no other woman I want on my arm at these events than my favorite costar and best friend. She lights up the night, wouldn't you say?"

"You both do in your stunning gown and tuxedo. Who are you wearing?"

The reporter steps back to allow the cameras to pan down our bodies and take in everything from our outfits to my jewelry and accessories. I keep my small clutch in front of me to help hide my lower belly. I'm not showing much yet, but there's no hiding this bloat no matter how hard I try. When I had Aurelia design the gown for me, I wasn't pregnant yet, and the last thing I wanted to do was announce it to the reporters on the red carpet.

"We're both in Monroe fashions, the gown a Lia Sage original."

"Absolutely gorgeous. Speaking of, Tinsley, where is your husband tonight?"

I keep my smile locked on my face. My cheeks are already

starting to hurt and so are my feet. It's going to be a long night. "He's waiting for me inside the theater." At least he better freaking be.

"Have a wonderful night and best of luck to both of you."

"Thank you," Loomis and I say with a smile and wave before we step away, ready to go to the next reporter in a long line of them.

"Bloody hell, can't we just get inside already?" Loomis murmurs through his smile. "I'm sweating my arse off out here in this tux with all these hot lights on us."

"I know," I say, leaning into him and turning so the cameras snapping can get my back because the back of this dress is what makes it. It's cut very low and lined with crystals. "Remind me next time we do this not to wear six-inch heels. My toes are numb and I'm almost positive I have a blister on my foot that's bleeding."

"Mrs. Monroe-Fritz, Mr. Powell, this way, please," the handler calls and waves us toward the entrance of the theater. Finally! We're escorted inside, the theater dark and cool, and we're led up toward the front. I frown when I see the empty seat beside where mine is.

"He'll make it," Loomis promises, giving my hand a reassuring squeeze before he turns and starts chatting with our director, who is also nominated. How I got that role, I have no clue, but it was the leap of a lifetime for me and Loomis. No longer are we George and Julia. we're Leo and Kate, and yes, I know there's a Jack and Rose joke in there.

There are cameras everywhere, that's how this event goes, and I hug and air kiss a couple of friends of mine. In addition to having to sit here all evening, I'm also performing the nominated song I wrote for the film.

It's going to be a crazy night for me, regardless of if I win or not, and Stone is late.

He flew out to LA a week before me to visit Forest, and the

two of them went camping together. Since Forest got out of rehab, he's changed his life. He's sober and stuck with it, and through the help of therapy and a lot of determination, he's refocused his energy into hiking and mountain climbing. It's been amazing to see him do so well, and his relationship with Stone has continued to improve. It's not perfect, but it's nearly there.

It helps that he's no longer in love with me. I think he realized that by holding on the way he was, he wasn't able to create a life for himself beyond what we had, and it turned into a toxic obsession in his head. Speaking of obsession, Apollo moved to India, and last I heard, he was working with clients as part of Hindi films there. I just hope it's going better for those clients than it did for me.

My husband still isn't here as the lights start to dim and the host does his shtick to start the show off. Corny and somewhat inappropriate jokes are slung our way and we laugh through them, even if they're not all that funny. Well, in fairness, they might be, but I'm having a hell of a time concentrating. I need to talk to Stone. I've been bursting to tell him something incredible—something life-changing—and I couldn't do that over the phone. Not that he had cell service in the freaking wilderness, but still.

I had planned to tell him at the start of the night, but he's not fucking here!

The show goes on, winners are announced, and finally, I'm called up to sing my song. The stage lights lower, and I walk out to the center as the background is made to look like tiny, dazzling stars in the sky. It reminds me of nights on the boat, on our island. Stone completely renovated the house and pool as well as built a dock. We spend as much time as we can there. Stone is an attending now, so that's not always the easiest thing, but we do the best we can with it.

This song is a ballad. When I read the script, the song just came to me. I wrote it in one day because I couldn't get the lyrics or notes out of my head. It's a love song filled with heartache and pain since it's about a couple who fall in love at the wrong time in their lives and split, only to reunite years later, but it's a hard-won love. It's titled after the film, and I sing my heart out to it.

For as much as I love acting, I love performing on stage a million times more.

After the song ends with a standing ovation, I'm ushered off to the side because they're about to announce the Best Original Song award, and I don't have enough time to make it back to my seat before the announcement.

They show each of our pictures on the large screen, and I do my best to smile and not move or fidget when in reality my heart is hammering, and I wish I were beside Loomis so he could hold my hand or whisper something ridiculous in my ear to calm me down.

"And the Oscar goes to..." They pause for dramatic effect, which only makes us want to strangle them more. "Tinsley Monroe for Undeniably Infatuated."

A gasp flees my lungs, and my hands cover my mouth as I blow out a torrent of air into them. Oh my God. Oh my freaking motherfucking God! I just won an Oscar. An Oscar! Holy shit, how on earth did this happen?! And why don't I get to hug Loomis for this?

As it is, I can hear him cheering.

While I'd love to win for best actress, this was the one I wanted to win the most.

On shaky legs, I walk back out onto the stage, thanking and hugging the announcer as she hands it to me. For a moment, all I can do is stare at the heavy gold statue in my trembling hand. Then I blink and squint out into the audience, anxious to find Loomis when I end up snagging on Stone instead.

A laugh flees my lungs. "You're late," I say, making the audience laugh. "Um."

I shake my head. I had a speech, but it's in my purse, which is down by my seat because I didn't realize they were announcing this category immediately after my performance. I start to thank everyone I can remember off the top of my head. The academy, the directors, producers, cast members, and even someone who I don't think worked on this particular film. Oops. Oh well. It's not my fault. I've never been this nervous in my life.

I lick my lips, blow out a breath, and find Loomis. "Thank you, Loomis. I love you endlessly. None of this would be possible without you as you drive me to be the best I can be. You are so much more than a best friend. You're my rock. But not my stone." I raise an eyebrow and look at my husband as if we're the only two people in the room. Adrenaline clouds my thoughts and words continue to spill without much thought. "You're lucky I love you. If you had come in a few minutes later, all bets would have been off." I shake my head, my mind frazzled and I'm not even sure what I'm saying. They start to play the music that tells me to get the fuck off stage, but before I do, I look him in the eyes and say, "I was supposed to tell you earlier that it's twins."

Gasps fill the audience, quickly followed by whistles and cheers, and I blanch. Shit! What did I just do? I let them lead me off stage. I can't believe I just told him that at the Oscars on national television. We weren't even going to announce the pregnancy for another couple of weeks, but here we are. I'm only ten weeks along. That wasn't smart. Too late now.

They guide me toward the green room in the back, but before I can reach it, I hear another round of gasps and turn to catch Stone racing up the steps to the stage. In a flash, he lifts me off the ground and kisses me in front of everyone, including the cameras, before he walks me off stage like this, his lips still melded to mine. My arms wrap around his neck, the heavy statue hanging against his back, and I hold on as he carries me.

"Twins?" he murmurs against my lips.

"Yes, you jerk! And I just announced it to everyone. At the Oscars." I kiss him deeper, feeling a strange combination of hunger and euphoria dance through me. "And next time you go into the wilderness, bring your goddamn satellite phone with you so I can reach you!"

"Yes, ma'am. Whatever you say." He kisses my neck. "Fuck, little rose, I'm so fucking proud of you. You absolutely amaze me. Even if our secret is out now."

I laugh as we reach the green room. "I know. I don't know what I was thinking. That's what happens when I'm forced to hold it in for the last five days. Blame the hormones and endorphins running through me."

He sets me down and locks the door behind us even though he's not supposed to do that. Then he has me pinned against it, his hands all over me before he drops to his knees. Reverently, he kisses my lower belly, holding my hips so he can press himself against me there before he looks up at me through his lashes.

"Twins and an Oscar. Pretty fucking great night, Mrs. Fritz. I love you. I love you so much. I'm seriously glowing with how fucking impressed I am by you."

I glare. "You nearly missed it."

"I know." He slips his hand under my gown and starts to run it up my thigh. "I'm sorry. There was horrific traffic and then I couldn't get close to the theater. The streets were blocked off for miles and they wouldn't let me through the blockade even with my ticket and ID. I had to find a parking spot, which was no easy feat, then run here, practically breaking through security. As it is, they held me for an additional twenty minutes while they radioed around to make sure I wasn't a scammer or a threat."

I huff. "Fine. You're forgiven. But just barely."

"How about I make it up to you." He lifts my dress and groans when he discovers I'm not wearing anything beneath it. "You're naked under this? Jesus hell, how am I supposed to sit next to you all night knowing you're naked under these pretty layers with my children growing inside of you and not fuck you?"

"You'll manage."

"I won't. I can't. I need to taste you."

He starts to play with my pussy, and I bite my lip and shake my head.

"You can't do that now. We don't have enough time."

He grins devilishly. "You've got two minutes to come."

I laugh and glare challengingly down at him. "Is that so?"

"Yes. But this time, you'll get my fingers and my mouth. And I promise we'll both enjoy it."

With that declaration, he puts my knee on his shoulder and covers my pussy with his mouth, giving it a wicked French kiss. The back of my head bangs into the door, only to have my chin drop so I can watch him. I shouldn't let him do this. Not here. We could so easily get caught. Commercial break or not, they'll be looking for me and there are likely attendants right outside the door.

But I can't stop him.

Not tonight. I just performed my song, won an Oscar for it, and announced to my husband and the world that I'm pregnant with twins.

He rings my clit with his tongue as he plunges two fingers inside me. Immediately, he sets a fast pace, finger fucking me as he works my clit with deep sucks and fast flicks. My fingers rake through his hair, and I push him deeper into me, needing more if I'm going to make the two-minute deadline. My other hand comes up and rubs my breast over my gown. My tits are sensitive, and if this is how being pregnant is on my body, I'm not complaining.

I swallow down moans and whimpers as he gets messier with me. He sucks my clit in between his lips and uses the tip of his tongue like a delicious weapon on it.

There's a knock on the door that bounces me forward.

"Mrs. Monroe-Fritz? Are you in there? We need you out in your seat, the show's about to come back from a commercial break."

My eyes bulge and flicker down to Stone, who looks nothing short of amused. "I'll be right out."

"You better come quickly," he whispers before increasing his pace.

Oh hell. Knowing Stone, he won't stop until I come regardless of whether the show is starting or not.

I close my eyes and focus on what he's doing to me. On his mouth and his fingers and the sweet, aching build heating my blood and flushing my skin. I want to come. I freaking need to come. And when he drives a third finger into my pussy and rubs my front wall, I lose it, coming so hard it's a wonder I'm still upright.

Panting out a breath, I put my hand over my racing heart, trying to calm myself down. Stone slips his fingers out of me, sucks them clean as he stands, then kisses me.

The knock at the door comes again, and I break out into a fit of giggles. "Where were you before the show? I could have used that to calm my nerves."

Stone grins against my lips. "Better late than never. I'm sorry I was late, but I never would have missed your big moment. Never. Not for anything. I love you so much. More than anything in this world."

"I Love you too. More than anything." I turn and open the door, dodging the attendant's eye since I can't help my blush.

Stone takes my hand, chuckling at my embarrassment. "Let's go see if you win two Oscars to go with our two babies."

Thank you lovely reader for taking the time to read Undeniably Infatuated. I hope you loved Stone and Tinsley's story as much as I do.

XO,

J. Saman

[illegible] babies.

[illegible] you lovely [illegible] for taking the time to read [illegible]

[illegible] hope you loved [illegible]

[illegible]

Made in the USA
Coppell, TX
13 February 2025

45870945R00215